"Tell me about this conv[ersation with] Jack Clancy on Monday," [                    ] "I understand you were u[         ] in for him at the Thomlins[          ]

"Yes, I was upset. I'm sure [         told] you why there was no love lost between me and Eulilly. Had she invited me herself, I'd have declined. Jack wheedling, then demanding that I go did not make my day."

"Why was it so important for you to be there?"

Hannah explained Clancy Construction and Development's connection to Bethune Enterprises and that Jack was afraid snubbing Eulilly Bethune Thomlinson might scotch the deal.

"This meeting in San Diego Clancy couldn't reschedule," Marlin said. "Who was it with, and where was it exactly?"

"I didn't ask and Jack didn't say."

"Okay," Andrick said. "Then whose idea was it to invite Sheriff Hendrickson along?"

"Jack's. It was a bribe, of sorts. Make a date out of it and maybe I wouldn't complain as much later," Hannah explained.

Silence. Five seconds, then eight. "It wasn't that big of a deal, Marlin. Not really. Jack said to eat Eulilly's food, drink her booze and it'd all be over by nine."

"Those were his exact words?" Andrick asked slowly. "'It'll all be over by nine'?"

Silence—a longer one this time.

# SUZANN LEDBETTER

## West of Bliss

MIRA®

ISBN 1-55166-925-0

WEST OF BLISS

Copyright © 2002 by Suzann Ledbetter.

All rights reserved. Except for use in any review, the reproduction or utilization of this work in whole or in part in any form by any electronic, mechanical or other means, now known or hereafter invented, including xerography, photocopying and recording, or in any information storage or retrieval system, is forbidden without the written permission of the publisher, MIRA Books, 225 Duncan Mill Road, Don Mills, Ontario, Canada M3B 3K9.

All characters in this book have no existence outside the imagination of the author and have no relation whatsoever to anyone bearing the same name or names. They are not even distantly inspired by any individual known or unknown to the author, and all incidents are pure invention.

MIRA and the Star Colophon are trademarks used under license and registered in Australia, New Zealand, Philippines, United States Patent and Trademark Office and in other countries.

Visit us at www.mirabooks.com

Printed in U.S.A.

For Mom,
who I'm sure is dancing with Daddy to
"Minnie the Moocher" and the "Missouri Waltz"
once again, and for Jim Sieger,
who just may be inclined to cut in.

Enormous gratitude to the experts and friends behind the scene of the crime: Gary Smith, Kansas City Crimes Unit Detective (ret.); Mike Downs, Drug Enforcement Agency (ret.); Ron Knisely, former Chief of Security, Bell Telephone Company; James A. Ledbetter, consultant; Ellen Wade, R.N.; Dr. Loren Gruber, Missouri Valley College, Marshal, MO; Al and Betty Livingston, terrific go-to sources of numerous law enforcement contacts; Judy Sieger, dear friend and pool maintenance consultant; Doug Naselroad, musical adviser for truly obscure factoids and, as always, but even more this time out, Martha Keenan, editor, MIRA Books and Robin Rue, Writers House, LLC.

# 1

"**W**ill you marry me?"

The flickering candles and strings of tiny twinkle lights illuminating the banquet room pinwheeled and seemed to retreat. Three other couples sharing the parquet dance floor and the hundred-some guests seated at tables vanished into a perceptual black hole.

Hannah Garvey forgot to breathe. Mesmerized by the sensuous sway of waltzing in the arms of the man she loved, she couldn't comprehend the shift from what had sounded like small talk to him asking her to be his wife.

David Hendrickson's six-foot-three-inch, broad-shouldered build was born to wear a sheriff's uniform and made for a jet-black, satin-lapelled tuxedo. Laugh lines fanned eyes aged well beyond his thirty-six years. Tonight the irises were a clear, off-duty blue, without a trace of gray.

A stunned, disbelieving Hannah gazed into them. She felt as though she were aboard a high-speed elevator, rocketing from parking-garage level to the penthouse suite. The music's last stanza faded *con amore.* "Marry you?" she said. "But we haven't even had sex yet."

David's head angled a fraction. Realizing that what she'd blurted and what he'd heard were one and the same, his mouth curved into a lazy grin. "Well, sugar. You can't say we haven't tried."

His tone implied a willingness to remedy numerous episodes of coitus interruptus right there and then, in front of God and everybody—namely, the guests attending Leo and Rosemary Schnur's wedding reception, the bride, the groom, their families, the minister, the catering staff, the four-piece combo providing musical entertainment and anyone else drawn to Valhalla Springs' community center by orgasmic moans on the wind.

The band swung into "Some Enchanted Evening." More dancers streamed onto the floor. David and Hannah stood motionless, vaguely aware of perfumes, after-shave lotions and the swish of spring-colored dresses and sports coats in orbit around them.

His lips brushed hers. "Do you love me?"

A montage scrolled through her mind. David's body, slick and glistening, the morning they'd almost made love in a steamy, hot shower. The grief and guilt that contorted his face the night he was forced to take another man's life or lose his own. His head thrown back, laughing at the sky as he swung her around in a wildflowered meadow. His palm raised to deliver the Special Junior Deputy oath of office to an awestruck, six-year-old boy.

The only response Hannah could muster was a wobbly nod.

"Tell me."

"I love you, David...."

The hand at her waist glided upward. Fingertips skimmed her velvet gown, the nape of her neck, then parted the waves in her hair. His kiss was slow and sweet. His tongue caressed hers, daring her to believe in forever.

"Tell me again," he said. "This time, without any *buts* tagging along behind it."

Another *I love you* wasn't enough. He wanted an unqualified *Yes, David. I'll marry you.*

Hannah glanced at the bride and groom. Leo, a retired insurance executive, and Rosemary, a grand-mother of six, bumped bellies as they danced. Their courtship had been whirlwind. Leo's proposal had been as swift and sure as Rosemary's acceptance.

At their engagement breakfast, she'd told Hannah how rare it was to find true, abiding love once in a lifetime, let alone twice. "When what you want is right in front of you, what's the sense in waiting to have it?"

If only it were that simple.

Few things had been since the afternoon Hannah rolled her Blazer to a halt outside Valhalla Springs' brick-and-wrought-iron gates. From the dashboard speakers, Janis Joplin defined freedom as nothing left to lose. Hannah had squinted through the bug-splattered windshield and wondered whether the song was a rallying cry or a requiem.

At the drop of an inter-office memo, she'd down-sized herself from a twenty-five-year career at Fried-lich & Friedlich, a prestigious Chicago advertising agency. A future ripe with possibilities but devoid of income was beginning to sound Marxist, when Jack Clancy offered her a job managing his central Missouri Ozarks retirement community.

Jack, a longtime client and dear friend, was desperate to fill the position. Hannah told him she knew more about nuclear fission than she did about property management, had no desire to learn and wasn't about to waste a perfectly good midlife crisis playing bingo with a bunch of geezers.

What she'd wasted was her breath. Jack had leveraged his Saint Louis–based construction company into a premier, resort-development firm. Any entrepreneur who could transform worthless desert acreage into a tropical paradise could sell the sultan of Brunei a used Buick.

She'd expected the transition from corporate fast track to the Ozarks' famed, laid-back lifestyle to be a little disorienting, but a second chance to leave her past behind and start fresh in a new place was exciting. Invigorating. Lusciously self-indulgent.

And it had been, for approximately forty-eight hours. Then a retired schoolteacher was brutally murdered, Hannah and David's mutual distrust escalated to mutual lust and Jack Clancy's mother got busted for distributing marijuana to her Every-Other-Tuesday Bridge Club.

The pace picked up a bit the second week.

Hell and high water. That's how David described their emotional roller-coaster ride. It was apt and not all negative, although homicide, felonious assaults and the willful destruction of private property had been as central to their relationship as resisting the urge to have one.

"I'm not an impulsive man," David said, bringing Hannah back to the present.

"No, you aren't."

"Leo and Rosemary's wedding was beautiful, but it didn't inspire anything."

Hannah smiled. "Bull."

David's eyebrows crooked into upside-down check marks. "Beg pardon?"

"I know a conspiracy when I'm in the middle of one." She struggled to look stern. "Me, Cinderella bridesmaid. You, the surprise Prince Charming groomsman in an ooh-baby-ooh tuxedo."

His grin reappeared at the compliment. "I can see where that might arouse your suspicions."

Everything David said or did aroused something. It was a gift. Hannah wrenched her train of thought from the depths of unrelieved horniness. "Then you escorted me to the only table for two in the place, twitched your nose and, *allakazam,* the band struck up 'Could I Have This Dance.'"

"I don't twitch, Miz Garvey."

"I don't believe in coincidence, Sheriff."

He chuckled low in his throat. "I may have taken advantage of an opportunity, but there were extenuating circumstances."

"Such as?"

"I reckoned this was as romantic a spot to propose

as anywhere in Kinderhook County, seeing as how the moon isn't out and the chiggers are.''

What woman could resist a man who could use *romantic, moon* and *chiggers* in the same sentence?

He added, ''Except I didn't think about everyone and his uncle Bob watching us like hawks.''

Light ricocheting off the gawkers' trifocals and bifocals did lend a slow-motion disco effect to the festivities. Tomorrow morning Dr. John Pennington, Valhalla Springs' resident physician, would be mystified by the epidemic of mild whiplash complaints.

''Too bad we can't leave,'' David said.

Hannah agreed, trying to think of a tactful segue from matrimony to the Cardinals' chances of winning the pennant this season.

''But we can make ourselves a tad scarcer.'' Grabbing her hand, David forged a meandering path to the stairway leading to the basement's fitness center.

Hannah gazed longingly at the adjacent elevator, then gathered up her gown with her free hand. If she snagged a heel and fell to a messy and premature death, it would serve him right.

The tang of chlorine and dehumidified air pervaded the community center's spacious, AstroTurfed lower level. Smoked plate-glass windows reflected the lap pool's aquamarine glow. Cloaked in shadow, a complement of exercise machines sneered, ''No pain, no gain.''

Beyond the glass exterior wall, the distant outline of Hannah's cottage was visible, nestled in the trees on the far side of the lake. To a casual observer, it was a one-story, brick and cedar-trimmed bungalow with a railed front porch and a detached garage. To her, it was home. The only real one she'd ever had.

She hadn't cohabited with anyone since the Reagan administration. Her ten-year love affair with Jarrod Amberley, a British antiques dealer, didn't count. Transatlantic phone calls and literally flying into each other's arms as often as their work schedules allowed was supposed to be *très chic*. In reality, it was the emotional equivalent of a full-service truck stop.

Question was, after living alone for most of her adult life, could she adapt to sharing everything from toothpaste to tax returns? Adjust from self-centered independence to all you and me, babe, all the time? Remember to scoop ice cream from the carton into a bowl before eating it?

Conflicts large and small—and ludicrous to anyone to whom they didn't apply—squawked like mental magpies. David was her best friend, her soul mate, and she loved him beyond reason, but she needed a neutral sounding board.

"Earth to Hannah." Two champagne flutes were forked between David's fingers. "I swiped these when we passed by the buffet table."

The wine was puckery dry, with a slight almond flavor. A school of tiny bubbles mimicked the goose bumps tripping up Hannah's arms.

"Hey, sugar." David hooked a knuckle under her chin and raised it. He kissed her long and tenderly, as though it were their first, or might be their last.

Hannah's pulse raced, as a wondrous, liquid weight-lessness suffused her body.

His lips parted from hers hours too soon. "I didn't bring you down here to pressure you," he said. "I just wanted some privacy to rebut the *buts* I heard a minute ago."

Eyes hooded, she looked up at him and nodded. Her inner fairy godmother whispered, *Dump the doubts, girl. The shoe fits. He's the smartest, sexiest man you've ever known, the world's best kisser and he makes you laugh. This is no time to be mature. Say yes, you'll marry him, then rip his clothes off.*

Before she could suggest they talk later and get naked now, David said, "I'll bet the *but* at the top of your hit parade is the ever-popular difference in our ages."

Frowning, Hannah added *relentless* to his character traits. "Well, I haven't gotten any younger, you know."

"The argument's getting old, though. Fact is, I'd have sworn I won it, fair and square, a while back."

If those of the male persuasion could ever distinguish a cease-fire from a victory, the resumption of hostilities a few days or decades later wouldn't come as such a shock.

David's nonwinning argument, also known as the "actuarial theory," was based on women outliving men by about eight years. To his way of thinking, her racking up forty-three birthdays to his thirty-six was a statistical bonus.

"Since we'll kick the bucket at about the same

time," he'd explained a few weeks ago, "we're as near-perfect, agewise, as a couple can be."

Like most theories, his had merit, if taken at face value. Hannah had even high-fived celebrities she'd seen on TV and in magazine articles who were involved in December-May romances.

All freakin' two of them.

"Seven years doesn't sound like a lot," she allowed.

"I hope to shout, it doesn't."

"Except—" She removed a piece of imaginary lint from his lapel. "If you gave three little boys a rope, what would they do with it?"

David's features slackened to the classic "Huh?" common to boxers on the receiving end of a haymaker.

"They'll tie each other up with it," she said. "Or pull something with it, or use it to climb something. Right?"

"I s'pose." An uptick at the end denoted somewhat less than a hundred-percent commitment.

"Now give the rope to three little girls and what's sure to happen?" Wine drizzled over the rim of Hannah's glass when she waved it. "Two will turn it, the other will jump it and they'll all chant, 'First comes love, then comes marriage, then comes Hannah with a baby carriage.'"

David studied her for a moment. "In a perfect world, no baby would come into it unwanted by its mama *and* its daddy. A woman shouldn't ignore a man's wishes hoping for an ex post facto change of heart any more than she's obliged to bear a child, regardless of what she wants.''

Anger flared, a defensive, irrational reaction to his CliffsNotes version of a Human Relations 101 lecture. ''I'm talking about us, David. The *me* half of us. Any maternal desires I had are pretty much history.''

Or were. They'd lain dormant for years, but falling in love had a nasty, primordial habit of rekindling baby-makes-three fantasies.

''Even if they weren't,'' she said, ''my biological clock is running out. I don't care how many women my age are waddling around big-bellied and blissful.'' Her voice caught and she shuddered. ''The very idea of having—raising—a child scares the hell out of me.''

''I know it does,'' David said. ''I also know why it does. Your mother did the best she could, but she wasn't what anyone would call a role model for parenting skills.''

The truth hurt, regardless of how gently imparted. Unwed, alcoholic trailer-trash barmaids seldom hit the talk-show circuit peddling child-care how-to books.

Hannah was eighteen when Caroline Garvey died of a cancer as tragic and painful as her life had been. What money she earned went for booze, cigarettes and party-hearty losers who sweet-talked their way into her bed, but Hannah never doubted Caroline's love for her, even when she hated her mother for what she'd let herself become.

''I love kids,'' David said. ''Sure, I've imagined

what it would be like to horse around in the yard with a daughter or son. Who hasn't?''

That image swam before Hannah's eyes. She blinked away tears. ''Then don't cheat yourself out of having it. Not for me. Not for anyone.''

He shook his head. ''If there's anything you should know by now, it's that I don't lie to myself, or to you. I didn't decide to sacrifice my shot at fatherhood to spend the rest of my life with you. When I said you're all I ever wanted, I meant it.''

Hannah's throat tightened, threatening to close. ''Yes, but what about a year from now? Five years from now? You can't predict how you'll feel later on.''

''Neither can—'' Muttering curses a darker shade of blue than Hannah's gown, David glared at Chief Deputy Jimmy Wayne McBride, who'd materialized out of nowhere.

Someone, or something, *always* did. Time clocks, weekends and holidays didn't apply to retirement-village operations managers and county mounties. Neither did the Law of Averages.

Jimmy Wayne's feet were planted. The curved brim of a brown felt Resistol tapped his thigh. ''Sorry to barge in.''

''Then why did you?'' David snapped.

''Two prisoners broke out of the Dallas County Jail about an hour ago. One was locked up on rape charges. The other is a suspect in a multiple homicide.''

The angry flush leeched from David's face. In a

split second, private citizen Hendrickson morphed into Sheriff Hendrickson.

"They shot the deputy guarding them," Jimmy Wayne said. "Helped themselves to the contents of a gun case, too."

"Accomplices?" David asked.

"We've got a witness description of a male and a female seen entering the building about that time. They ditched their getaway vehicle outside Tunas and carjacked a van. Last seen heading north toward the Kinderhook County line."

Hannah plucked the champagne flute from David's hand. "Go."

His kiss was apologetic and brief. "I'll call as soon as I can. Don't worry."

Oh, well, of course not. Why would four armed, dangerous criminals on the loose and David duty-bound to stop them be cause for alarm?

The men jogged away trading questions and information. David's trouser leg hiked up as he mounted the stairs at a three-at-once clip, exposing a sizable lump in his sock.

Hannah's mouth flattened to a hard line. *I'll be damned. He stood up for Leo at his wedding, waltzed with me, declared his love and proposed, all ankle-holstered and loaded for bear the entire time.*

Yeah, well, what did she think that bulge was behind McBride's departmental windbreaker? A sack lunch?

David was a law enforcement officer. Carrying a gun was part of the job. In uniform or out, on duty or not, he'd sworn an oath to protect everyone around him and himself—in that order. Bad guys don't honor time-outs so the good guys can fetch their service revolvers from their glove compartments.

She sighed and started for the elevator. Bad guys didn't keep banker's hours, either—the profession David's ex-wife had nagged him to enter, as though the one he'd chosen was a phase he'd eventually outgrow.

He seldom mentioned his first marriage to his college sweetheart shortly after he graduated from the Tulsa Police Academy. Opposites attract but don't necessarily complement. Cynthia Hendrickson's affair and their divorce had left David bitter and with a keen sense of failure, yet he didn't deny the truth in "A cop is my husband" as opposed to "My husband is a cop."

Cynthia and David's differences were legion and irreconcilable, but whether pinned to his uniform or laying atop the dresser, she resented his badge always being between them.

Hannah poked the elevator's Up button with her elbow. Will I come to resent it, too? Kinderhook County wasn't a hotbed of criminal activity, but David wasn't a glad-handing desk jockey for whom crime scenes were photo opportunities.

No, she decided. I might as well resent his blood type as his career. Being called away at inopportune moments was aggravating, but it went with the territory. The key was making the most of opportune moments.

Assuming they ever had any.

The elevator doors opened to a blast of light, laughter and Willard Johnson standing with his arms akimbo. "Good timing," he said. "I got elected to find you before Leo and Rosemary cut the cake."

Hannah grinned. "Since when does the physical fitness instructor take the elevator instead of the stairs?"

He canted sideward to knead the back of his thigh. "Since he pulled a hamstring when his mother volunteered him to help unload the catering truck."

Hannah deposited the champagne flutes on a waiter's tray. The last time she'd seen Willard, he was sprawled in a chair, wigged out of his mind after accidentally ingesting a dozen of IdaClare Clancy's marijuana-laced brownies. The muscle-bound, twenty-six-year-old, part-time science-fiction novelist might be wise to beware of older women bearing desserts.

"I didn't know your mother owned Petits Fours & More," Hannah said.

"She doesn't. She just bakes and decorates their special-event cakes." Willard strained to see over the crowd gathering around a table near the end of the room. "Come on. I'll introduce you while Rosemary and Leo are stuck talking to the Simmonses."

He was only an inch or so taller than Hannah's five foot seven, but cleared a gangway as well as David could. No introduction was needed to identify the petite, fiftyish woman with shot-silver hair pinned into a tight chignon as Willard's mother. He'd inherited

Benita Johnson's high, intelligent forehead, deep-set eyes and dark-toffee complexion.

"Willard has told me so much about you, Ms. Garvey." Benita's handshake was as warm as her smile. "It's such a pleasure to meet you."

"It's Hannah, and the pleasure is mine." She winked at Willard. "At the risk of giving your son the big head, hiring him was the smartest move I've made since I came here. Every program, aerobics to beginning tae kwon do, has a waiting list."

"My son has never met a stranger, that's for sure. I remember when he was just a tiny thing, he—"

"Oh no you don't," Willard said. "You tell her one 'when Willie was a boy' story and I'm outta here. For good."

Hannah laughed. "I do believe we should have lunch together real soon, Benita. Just the two of us."

A portable microphone's feedback drowned out Willard's groan. "If I can have your attention," rasped a familiar voice, amplified to the decibel range of a 747 preparing for takeoff.

Hands clapped over ears and all eyes whipped toward Delbert Bisbee, the best man. The retired postal supervisor and self-proclaimed Renaissance man stood on the seat of a folding chair like a tuxedoed town crier. "Can everybody hear me okay?" he shouted into the microphone.

Residents of Sanity, the county seat town twenty-two miles north of Valhalla Springs, had probably vaulted from their sofas in terror that Armageddon was upon them.

Hannah motioned "Excuse me" to the Johnsons and scooted around to the opposite side of the cake table. Temporarily deafened guests gave her "Can't you do something about him?" looks.

Her response was a visual "As if you don't know, nothing short of sudden death can pry a microphone from Delbert's fist."

He'd introduced himself to Hannah within minutes of her arrival at Valhalla Springs. Delbert possessed the energy of a ten-year-old, a misogynistic streak, a marshmallow heart, an irascible nature and a harem competing to become the sixth Mrs. Bisbee. All things considered, if the skinny old fart were any more adorable, Mattel would name a doll after him.

Hannah chuckled. Make that a seafoam green–haired doll, due to Delbert's close encounter with a bottle of food coloring during his most recent amateur-detective caper. A master of disguise Delbert wasn't, but he'd nabbed a killer nonetheless.

An unseen saint pulled the plug on the PA system. Delbert tapped on and blew into the microphone's mesh windscreen, scowled, then hollered his toast to the newlyweds' health, happiness and prosperity into it.

To resounding applause, the bride and groom clasped hands around the handle of a serrated server. Bald, bespectacled Leo was a dead ringer for Mr. Potato Head and Rosemary resembled a Raphael model with a pixie haircut, but joy transformed them into the handsomest couple since the Brad Pitt–Jennifer Aniston nuptials.

Cameras flashed as Rosemary crammed a wedge of cake into Leo's mouth. Tongue darting to reel in every crumb, he cooed, "Ach, the butter cream…and the chocolate."

Overcome with rapture, Leo grabbed Benita Johnson and planted a gooey kiss on her cheek. "Dear lady, how could you know it is my *favorite?*"

"Gee, I can't imagine," Rosemary said. "Who do you think ordered it, you ol' goof?"

Wrapping his arm around her, Leo said, "My wife, she is the most wonderful woman in the world, yes?"

Rosemary's head tipped back so she could smile up at him, whereby her beloved stuffed a piece of wedding cake into her mouth, up her nose, and smeared icing all over her chin.

An incoming cloud of lily-of-the-valley perfume should have warned Hannah of Eulilly Thomlinson's proximity. Unfortunately, one cannot laugh and inhale at the same time.

The reason behind the two women's mutual dislike was known only to them and Jack Clancy. Their unspoken truce in the interest of the greater good had also protected Eulilly's sweet-as-sugar facade—which galled Hannah no end.

"Well, I'll swan," Eulilly said, her palm to her cheek. "That was *you* I saw dancing with the sheriff a while ago, wasn't it. I swear, I didn't recognize you, fond as you are of blue jeans and T-shirts."

"Your dress is quite becoming, too, Eulilly. I've thought so every time I've seen you wear it."

The *zing* was almost audible. Hannah made a note

to feel ashamed of herself someday—like on her deathbed.

The Queen of Simper and her husband, Chet, were moving back to her native Mississippi on Friday. Hannah hadn't made Chet's acquaintance and wished the same was true of his wife. Oh, how the beer tabs would pop on the porch of the manager's cottage five days hence.

Eulilly was nothing if not resilient. "I do hope you understand there's nothing personal in our leaving you off the guest list for our bon voyage party. The banquet room at the Royal Dragon simply isn't large enough to invite everyone."

"I'm not the least bit wounded, I assure you." Hannah turned and reached for two dessert plates, offering one to her nemesis. "In case I don't see you again before you leave, here's to a safe trip back to where you came from."

Eulilly's catty green eyes slid from Willard to Benita Johnson, then slanted at Hannah. Pushing away the plate, she drawled, "Really now, Ms. Garvey. Of all people, you should know that chocolate doesn't agree with me."

# 2

"No one is being persecuted," Hannah said into the telephone receiver the next day, then thought, *except me.* "Feng shui isn't a religion."

"It is to Master Yablonski," argued Juaneema Kipps. "He and his wife make a pilgrimage to China every year."

Hannah rested her chin on her hand. Mondays should be against the law. "For whatever it's worth, if Master and Mrs. Yablonski ever decide to move to Valhalla Springs, I won't let them put a three-ton concrete fountain in their front yard, either."

Juaneema's feng shui obsession began last week after a seminar sponsored by the garden club. The compulsion to put one's house in order was a natural reaction to life's upheavals; in her case, forced retirement as a pharmaceutical company research chemist.

Hannah sympathized, but what Juaneema needed was a reason to get out of bed in the morning, not exterior decoration. A remedy was in the works, though. Even the most introverted new residents couldn't withstand constant bombardment by the activities committee forever.

"My fountain is a genuine work of art." Juaneema's sigh intimated a hand fluttering to her bosom. "The dancing cherubs look like real children—right down to their cute little tallywhackers."

How did it come to pass—so to speak—that public urination was considered artistic, as long as the whizzers were carved from marble, stone or molded in concrete? Whether live, or in statuary form, Hannah had never found anything terribly compelling about a guy taking a leak.

Well, not since she was eight and Randy Arbeitman whipped out his cute little tallywhacker to water a tree on their way home from school.

"Juaneema," she said in her best "let's be reasonable" tone, "as I've mentioned before, Section II of your lease agreement prohibits the addition of permanent fixtures and structures to the property."

"But it isn't permanent. The men from the landscaping place are delivering it on a truck."

"No fountain, Juaneema. Sorry."

The retired chemist's adenoidal wheedle turned snide. "What about IdaClare Clancy's greenhouse? It's a permanent structure."

Hannah said, "And it'll be torn down before the month is out."

Judge Cranston Messerschmidt had given Jack's mother thirty days to remove her climate-controlled marijuana factory from the premises. The judge further warned that IdaClare's five-year probation would be rescinded if she ever grew, harvested or distributed her "medicinal herbs" again.

"Rules are rules," Hannah said. "Have a nice day, Juaneema."

"But Master Yablonski said I can't focus my chi without a fountain," bleated from the earpiece as the receiver settled into the cradle.

Hannah reached for her chi, contained in a mug on her desk. Anyone who disputed black coffee as a vital life force never wakened after a restless night with a beast of a headache.

The top-of-the-hour broadcast on KSAN, the only radio station in Sanity, said the multi-agency manhunt for the escaped prisoners and their accomplices was continuing. That much Hannah had already guessed. David would have called if they'd been captured. Jimmy Wayne McBride would have, if—

She shook her head. "Don't even *think* it, Hannah Marie."

Like the rest of the search team, David was surely tick-infested, grubby and in no mood to be trifled with, but unharmed. Instinct would tell her otherwise, just as it had for David, the night a murderer with nothing to lose broke into Hannah's cottage and threatened her life.

The scent of wilting greenery and roses drifted from the beribboned nosegay on the corner of her desk. Last night, while Leo devoured his third hunk of wedding cake, Rosemary had herded all the single women to the dance floor for the traditional bouquet toss. Hannah's retreat to the back of the pack was halted by Marge Rosenbaum, a co-bridesmaid and amateur Auntie Mame.

Accompanied by a snare-drum roll, Rosemary faked a couple of alley-oop upswings, then spun around and hurled her bouquet overhand. The incoming floral fastball left Hannah with two choices—catch it or eat it.

A chorused "You're next, you're next" had rung out in soprano disharmony.

Not hardly, Hannah thought. It was nothing but a silly superstition. If snagging the bride's bouquet presaged wedding bells, she'd have been married seven or eight times by now. Until last night, she'd never heard "Will you marry me?" spoken aloud without benefit of a ticket stub, a tub of buttered popcorn and a soda.

The desk chair tilted back smoothly on its oiled gears. Holding her coffee mug in both hands, she pressed the rim to her lips. No fountain or Polish feng shui master was needed to know her house was in order.

So what if oak pollen dusted the walnut rail separating the office nook from the great room, and the area rug beneath the leather seating group in front of the fireplace could stand a vacuuming? A sense of belonging didn't come from aerosol cans and whirling beater brushes.

The furnishings had come with the cottage and didn't belong to any particular style or period. Wood and leather, antiques and country contemporary, and hewn ceiling beams supporting a brass-fitted paddle fan blended into a cozy sanctuary—an upscale Walden Pond with walls and a shake-shingle roof.

For a trailer-park rat from Effindale, Illinois—a dreary burg locals called the butt crack of America—Hannah's twenty-second-floor condo in Chicago had seemed like a castle in the air. She'd spent years and thousands of dollars trying to make it a home only to realize it was a midtown lighthouse and she was its keeper.

Her mind's eye imposed David kicked back on the sofa watching TV. Eating dinner at the pub table in the breakfast room. Shaving in front of the master bathroom mirror. Sliding in beside her in the sleigh bed, its frame shuddering with his weight. His big, hard—

She yelped when the phone rang. Scowling at it, she presumed Juaneema had gotten her second wind. The answering machine could play secretary, but it would only delay the inevitable.

"Valhalla Springs. Hannah Garvey speaking."

"Hey, I finally got something besides a busy signal."

"Dav—" Hannah's breath caught, then rushed out in a sigh. The caller was male, but surnamed Clancy. "Oh hi, Jack."

The line hummed a few seconds. "Sheez. The thrill is definitely gone."

Thinking of her fractured daydream, she said, "You can say that again."

"Well, thanks a heap. You sure know how to take the steam out of a guy's self-esteem."

Hannah rolled her eyes. "Can we do a take-two on this conversation?" She cleared her throat. "Jack! Is it really you? Just hearing your voice gives me something to live for.''

He chuckled, said, ''That's more like it,'' then paused to add, ''Seriously, is there trouble in paradise?''

She bit her lip. Wish for a sounding board and the one you've relied on for fifteen years, both personally and professionally, enters stage right, courtesy of Ma Bell.

Except Jack might have actual business to discuss. If the tenor stayed social, the advice-to-the-lovelorn segment would follow his ''Are you sure nothing's wrong?'' or an ''Okay, sweetpea. Spill it.''

''No, it's paradise as usual,'' she said, and told him about Juaneema Kipps and her water-making monstrosity.

Jack asked, ''Do you think this Yablonski character is a con artist?''

''Your mother arranged his garden club seminar.''

''My mother is on probation for felonious brownie baking.''

''Good point.'' Hannah grinned. ''Master Yablonski might push sincere to the edge of fervent, but he's harmless. He and his wife own a New Age shop in Sanity and do feng shui consultations on the side.''

Twining the telephone cord around her finger, she went on, ''I think I'll call him later. See if he'll agree to a compromise that will satisfy Juaneema and doesn't require a forklift.''

Skepticism leavened Jack's ''Uh-huh...''

"Maybe a waterfall for her deck. One of those small, nonpermanent, recirculating jobs."

"Okay by— Hang on a sec." Jack muffled the receiver with his hand, the sound similar to a conch shell held to Hannah's ear. Garbled monosyllables leaked through, then "All right, Wilma. I *know.* I'll be off here in five minutes."

Briefcase latches snapped. "Sorry, sweetpea. Where were we before my secretary forgot how to knock?"

Hannah waved, as though Jack were in her office, not his, overlooking the Saint Louis riverfront. "Do you want to call me back?"

"Can't. My flight to San Diego leaves in fifty-five minutes."

So much for the sounding board.

He said, "I hate to give you the bum's rush before I ask a favor, but I have to get to Lambert Airport on the double."

"No problem. Ask away."

"What are you doing tomorrow night?"

Hannah's mouth tucked at a corner. "Why?" was the smartest comeback, but it smacked of distrust. "Depends" did, too, but left a window of opportunity for a plausible excuse to renege. "Nothing" was a commitment before the fact, usually resulting in a remorseful smite to the forehead.

Jack Clancy was her oldest friend, her employer and was flying far, far away in less than an hour. "Why?" she asked.

"I need you to pinch-hit for me at Eulilly and Chet Thomlinson's bon voyage party."

Hannah's jaw fell.

"This San Diego meeting jumped up out of nowhere. My return flight tomorrow night doesn't get in until six-something. Eulilly told me you'd already declined, but one of us has to be there."

"You talked to *her,* before you called *me?*"

"To phone in my regrets, yes."

Anger didn't thaw the ice in Hannah's tone. "She lied, Jack. I wasn't invited, and I'll be damned if I know why you were, or why either of us has to go."

There was a lengthy pause. "When you two butted heads, I didn't make the connection between Eulilly Thomlinson and Bethune Enterprises. I've been in negotiations with them for months to build a resort-casino-theme park complex."

Hannah raked back her hair and clenched a fistful. *Butted heads?* Her first official duty as manager had entailed firing Zerelda Sue Connor, the fifty-nine-year-old physical fitness director. Hannah had found Connor nose to nose with an obese, sweat-drenched matron, bellowing insults at the woman because she wasn't stair-stepping fast enough to suit her tormentor.

Thinking heaven had sent Willard Johnson to be Connor's replacement, Hannah was stunned when an anonymous caller left messages about a "puh-tish-un" being circulated for Willard's ouster. "His kind don't belong here," the woman had drawled, *his kind,* being a euphemism for *black.*

The racist's identity was revealed when Eulilly Thomlinson and the cronies she'd manipulated into believing Connor was fired because of her age, descended on Hannah's office and presented another "puh-tish-un" to that effect.

"Might I remind you," Hannah said into the phone, "Eulilly threatened you, me and Valhalla Springs, Inc., with a bogus age-discrimination lawsuit, which she could very well have won. That she didn't give a rat's ass who the physical fitness instructor was, as long as he or she was the right color?"

"Will you simmer down?" Jack forced a laugh. "You know, the Irish have a saying about beware the wrath of red-haired women."

Through clenched teeth, she warned, "Don't patronize me."

"I'm not. You bluffed Eulilly into a corner. She and her committee dropped the lawsuit and she's skedaddling back to the plantation with her tail between her legs."

"That's not the—"

"Aw, for Christ's sweet sake. You *won,* okay? It's bygones time. Eulilly is on the board of Bethune Enterprises. Her brothers control the purse strings, but they're clannish. My firm isn't going to lose a multi-million-dollar project just so you can snub Big Sister at her stupid going-away party."

Hannah shot to her feet. The swivel chair waddled backward and thudded off the credenza. Her strangled silence must have transmitted long distance. The uncustomary harshness in Jack's voice was absent when he said, "You're thinking that if I'd known Eulilly was a Bethune from the beginning, I'd have caved and told you to give Willard his walking papers."

"How psychic of you."

"You're wrong, Hannah. A thousand percent wrong. I shouldn't have to say, 'You know me better than that,' but I will."

No, he shouldn't. He'd been on the receiving end of intolerance too often to be party to it—a stellar corporate profit-and-loss statement be damned. Yet as Hannah's anger dissipated, a feeling akin to melancholy weighted her shoulders. How naive she'd been to presume their relationship would glide from client-pal to boss-pal.

Turbulence had blindsided them once, during an impromptu meeting at IdaClare's cottage with Jack's personal attorney. Discussing how best to handle his mother's legal defense had exploded into a shouting match. Hannah blamed the stress she and Jack were both under at the time, but the argument had bruised their bond.

"C'mon, sweetpea," he said. "You made nice to a jillion obnoxious Friedlich & Friedlich clients over the years. Drag Hendrickson along to the party. Knowing Eulilly, having the sheriff attend will be a feather in her cap."

What Hannah would rather bestow on Eulilly Thomlinson wasn't a feather and wouldn't lodge anywhere near her cap.

"Eat the woman's food, drink her booze," Jack said breezily. "I guarantee it'll all be over by nine."

"All right, already. Can the sales pitch. I'll do it, but I refuse to RSVP."

"No need."

In other words, he'd obligated Hannah in advance when he'd tendered his regrets. "I hate you, Clancy."

"Not a chance." This time his laughter was genuine. "Gotta run. I'll have Wilma fax a copy of the invitation."

Hannah lobbed the scraps of her sandwich in the garbage can. It just didn't taste right.

Actually, it tasted exactly like bologna, mustard and potato chips smashed between two slices of wheat bread should. Comfort was the missing ingredient. Without it, she might as well have eaten something healthy.

Judging by how the day began, she'd expected it to continue as though she was the target and the rest of the world was lined up in firing-squad formation. Ducking one volley after another wouldn't have allowed time to worry about David, expand her list of derogatory synonyms for Jack Clancy or brood about David's proposal.

Naturally, and in keeping with the Garvey family motto, "Life sucks, then you die," not a single, distracting soul had darkened Hannah's door, called to complain or incited a riot.

She knew she was desperate when she considered phoning Delbert Bisbee to ask him to come fix something. Repairs of any kinds were the maintenance department's responsibility, but slap a screwdriver in

Delbert's hand and collateral rubble was sure to result.

From the corner of her eye, she spied her Giant Airedale-wildebeest's covert advance on the trash can—as though an eighty-five-pound dog as tall as a runt Shetland pony could sneak up on anything smaller than a mountain range.

Malcolm's tongue dripped in anticipation. His mustached muzzle bobbed with each lusty whiff of discarded people food.

"Nah-ah-ah," Hannah said. "Bologna gives you gas and I'm not in the mood for a toot-fest."

Malcolm looked at her as though astonished by her invisible dog-detecting ability. Reeling in his tongue, Malcolm slouched against the refrigerator, a dejected, boneless wretch in the final throes of starvation.

The sum of his parts was the canine version of a "Suicide," a carbonated beverage every generation of kids thinks it invented: squirts of Coke, 7Up, Dr Pepper, Orange Crush, root beer, NuGrape and strawberry soda, topped off with dollops of cherry, vanilla and chocolate syrup.

Malcolm's genetic recipe included a golden retriever's feathered tail and legs, a Dalmation-spotted rump, a Great Dane's anvil head, a collie-like ruff and an Airedale's curly coat and gray saddle. His black ear stayed upright, the tan one flopped and his liquid-brown eyes were as vacant as a bankrupt motel.

Kennels and pet stores were rife with purebred clones. Malcolm was unique, housebroken and believed that Hannah was a goddess, in spite of her stinginess with the table scraps.

She drummed her fingernails on the bar top dividing the kitchen from the breakfast room. Sunlight angled through the window above the sink, burnishing the oak cabinetry's hourglass graining. Appliances large and small gleamed in expectation of a reason for their existence.

As Hannah perused the tiny, inert things Malcolm had shed on the floor, she imagined Eulilly Thomlinson instructing the chef at the Royal Dragon restaurant to add Crow Cordon Bleu to tomorrow night's menu.

Pushing away from the counter, she said, "Up and at 'em, Malc. Let's go for a ride before I do something rash."

The Blazer's tires whined on Highway VV's traffic-scoured surface. The first few times she'd driven it, the curvy, roller-coaster county road had welded a ten- and two-o'clock grip on the steering wheel. Now Hannah cruised like a local—single-handed steering, an elbow resting on the window ledge and eyes surveying the scenery.

Livestock grazed in rolling fields, their tails swishing like metronomes. Houses and outbuildings varied in age and size, some lovingly enlarged and maintained, others falling to ruin.

Gravel tracks led to mobile homes on concrete-block foundations ringed by spavined swing sets, bicycles, barbecue grills and dry-docked vehicles. Along the weedy verge, rural mailboxes were affixed to antique plows, or harbored in brick and fieldrock carrions impervious to juveniles itching for a game of sledgehammer polo.

Malcolm fidgeted in his harness, smearing fresh slaver on the passenger glass. Sidelong glances begged Hannah to lower the window so he could feel the wind in his ears and strain bugs with his teeth.

"Be patient, big guy. We're almost there."

A half hour later she was leaning against the Blazer's grill, her hands jammed in her jeans pockets and legs crossed at the ankles. Breathing in the loamy smell of sun-warmed earth, she pondered how a jaunt to the post office substation in Valhalla Springs' commercial district had evolved into a twenty-nine-mile journey in the opposite direction.

Birds bickered in the trees that flanked one side of the meadow. Atop the opposite bluff stood an A-frame house under construction. Plastic tarps tacked to its unshingled, plywood sheathing flapped and rustled in the breeze.

At the valley's far end, a Dodge Ram pickup's candy-apple-red tailgate and chrome bumper jutted from the doorway of a tumbledown barn. Unknowing trespassers would presume the adjacent, three-room farmhouse was occupied. If they didn't, the rottweiler guarding the porch discouraged confirmation.

Hannah shaded her eyes and looked up at David's sweat-equity dream house. The A-frame was elegant in its simplicity. Rustic stone, cedar and expansive glass merged form with function. The design complemented the natural landscape rather than lorded over it.

David had sketched the blueprint in a spiral notebook before he'd graduated from high school. Like the proverbial childish things, he'd put it away but hadn't forgotten it. Two decades later he bought the ruggedly beautiful, isolated piece of land to build the house on, just as he'd envisioned for half his life.

Hannah bowed her head to stare at her boot toes. David's nearest neighbor lived more than a mile away. Slides of June Cleaver guest starring in *Little House on the Prairie* clicked through her mental View-Master. A cold sweat prickled her nape at memories of childhood monsters and night-frights she thought she'd outgrown.

At the rumble of an approaching vehicle, her heart seized, then rattled off her ribs. Malcolm galloped past *bur-rurfing* a welcome. Rambo the rottweiler's echoing bark sounded carnivorous. The dog's viciousness was an act, but it was an Emmy-caliber performance.

The car was an elderly Chrysler station wagon, not a white-and-blue Crown Victoria with a lightbar bolted to its roof. Brake pads squealed as Claudina Burkholtz, the sheriff department's chief dispatcher, negotiated the sloped bends in the dirt-packed lane.

Claudina was as wide as she was short, had a mop of dishwater-blond curls and an unflagging lemons-into-lemonade attitude. After her husband deserted her and their three children, Claudina took a second job waitressing at the Short Stack Café to make ends meet. David had become a sort of foster father to her kids, but she bridled when he crossed the line between generosity and what she considered charity.

Nine-year-old Polly, seven-year-old Jeremy and five-year-old Lana bailed from the car before their mother switched off the ignition.

"Mom's gotta bake cupcakes for school tomorrow 'cause it's the last day," Jeremy announced. "She bought sprinkles for 'em and she said I can lick the bowl."

Polly rolled her eyes in typical big-sister fashion. "I get pizza and soda pop in the library 'cause I read the most books in my whole class."

Lana screwed up her face a moment, then gave Hannah a snaggletoothed grin. "Well, *I'm* gonna be in first grade next year and then *I* get to do homework and everything."

The little girl's excitement evaporated when she saw the stiff, gauze mask in her mother's hand. "Aw, Mom, do I *have* to wear it?"

"You do if you want to help feed and water Rambo. That new asthma medicine is helping, but there's too much pollen blowing around to take chances."

"It's okay, Lana-dana," Jeremy said, back-skipping down the lane. "You can lick the batter bowl when we get home."

Polly tugged the sleeve of Lana's T-shirt. "Mom wants us to scram so she and Miss Hannah can talk."

"She does?" Lana glanced over her shoulder. "What're they gonna talk about?"

"Prob'ly sex." Polly shrugged. "That's what grown-ups always talk about when us kids aren't around."

"Ew, *yuck.*"

Malcolm trotted after them, deaf to his name. Hannah hollered louder, then whistled to no avail.

"Let him go," Claudina said. "Rambo doesn't like him, but he'd never hurt him."

She braced a hip against the Blazer's fender, her muumuu billowing in the breeze. "Valhalla Springs' grapevine must be a doozy. David just reported they'd captured the escapees a few minutes before I left the office."

Hannah started. "He's on his way home?"

"Not until they sort out the charges and jurisdictions, and finish the paperwork. It shouldn't take more'n a month."

Claudina's eyebrow arched. "So, what's up? As if I don't already know." She splayed her fingers to examine the bitten-down nails. "Although I suppose a tip that somebody's planning to knock off Ingersoll's Jewelry might be the reason David has been frequenting the premises."

Great. Small towns were nothing but fishbowls with parking meters. Sneeze on one corner of the square and the pharmacist will have an antihistamine ready when you get to the drugstore. By sundown, the word on the street is double pneumonia, and get-well tuna casseroles are in mass production.

Hannah said, "Jimmy Wayne interrupted us before I could give David an answer."

"Lucked out, huh?" Sympathy laced Claudina's chuckle. "And while he's been off chasing bad guys, you've been in a tizzy about all the reasons why you can't marry him."

Hannah nodded. "Some of them are dumb, others—" She gestured frustration. "Damn it, it just won't work. We can compromise and sacrifice out the wazoo, but eventually we'll be miserable and resentful and asking ourselves what in God's name we ever saw in one another."

"Uh-huh. That sounds like marriage, all right."

"Hey, Mom." Jeremy waved like a flood victim signaling a helicopter. "Can I get a drink out of the hose?"

"Yes."

"Can I?"

"Can I?"

"Yes, yes." Claudina turned toward Hannah, then snapped to attention. "If you rug rats get those brand-new tennis shoes wet, I'll skin you alive."

They hollered back, "We won't."

"Yes, they will," she muttered. "What they won't do is remember to turn off the hose after they accidentally-on-purpose spray each other with it."

To Hannah, she said, "Lay a dumb reason not to marry the county studmuffin on me. I could use a good laugh."

"First off, I don't know how to cook."

"That's why God made Hamburger Helper. Whip up a salad, nuke a can of veggies in the microwave, then lick his tonsils the minute he walks in the door. The last thing he'll care about is what's on his plate.''

A horny Betty Crocker. Hannah made a mental note. It could work.

She jerked a thumb at Rambo, standing in the yard like a four-legged member of the Gestapo. No fangs were bared or hackles furled, but Malcolm got the message. He slunk off to the barn where he'd lived after David rescued him from the humane society shelter and before Hannah adopted him.

''The only fair solution would be to get rid of them both and find one we can agree on.''

''There you go,'' Claudina said.

''Except David likes intelligent, surly-looking beef-cake dogs and I love huge, stupid, ugly mutts.''

''This is biology, not rocket science, girlfriend. Breed Malcolm to a female rottweiler and take the pick of the litter.''

Hannah shuddered. ''Malcolm's been neutered, but I don't think there'd *be* a pick of the litter.''

''Um.'' Claudina batted at a cloud of gnats. ''We'll come back to that one. What's dumb reason number three?''

''Hannah Hendrickson. Say it slowly and it sounds like projectile vomiting.''

''Oh, cry me a river. Try Claudina Faye Meltabarger Burkholtz. I was doomed at birth.''

Ouch. Hard to believe Burkholtz could be an improvement on anyone's maiden name.

''How about the fact that David is a Libra and I'm an Aries. I checked *Cosmo*'s Bedside Astrologer. *To-*

*tally incompatible, disastrous* and *run* were in all caps and bold type.''

The dispatcher's entire body jiggled when she laughed. ''Are you kidding me? A high-toned city slicker like you is into astrology?''

''I was a city slicker by default. I grew up in Effindale, Illinois, the epicenter of effin graffiti, not sophistication.'' She hitched a shoulder. ''I was desperate for good omens and those psychics on TV charge four bucks a minute.''

''Oh, but I love that Jamaican tarot card lady. You know, the way she calls everybody 'beh-bee.''' Claudina lowered her eyes, her expression wistful. ''Me and Bruce were a perfect match—cusps, planet alignments, the whole hoodoo enchilada. I guess you can't rely on a horoscope to tell you which Scorpios are gutless, deadbeat assholes.''

Bruce Burkholtz drifted from state to state and job to job a step ahead of garnishment for back child support, but his picture hung on a hallway wall so Polly, Jeremy and Lana wouldn't forget him, or what he looked like.

Claudina had to borrow her neighbor's car, if errands were too far-flung to walk, sang of mansions on the hill when she ironed, bought lottery tickets with spare change from her café tip jar and never let her kids see a utility bill reduce her to tears.

''Is that it for the dumb reasons?'' Claudina asked.

''Pretty much.''

''Only a couple were bona fide dumb.''

"David just proposed eighteen hours ago. Give me another day or two and I can think up some more."

"Nah. Save them for the night before the wedding. Or the morning after. It's more traditional."

"There isn't going to be a wedding, Claudina." Saying it aloud felt like a sucker punch to Hannah's midsection. "I found out a long time ago that love isn't enough and it damn sure doesn't conquer all."

The dispatcher, who was at least as relentless as her boss, cocked her head at her kids. "The flower girls and ring bearer are finished with KP duty. We'd better take a stab at the biggies before Polly homes in on us."

A rueful expression contradicted the maternal pride in her voice. "The sound went out on the TV when Polly was about four. In a week she was lip-reading everything the Muppets said on *Sesame Street*."

Hannah's eyes strayed to the A-frame on the bluff. It wasn't a mansion. David's dreams were simple and rooted in his childhood. Hearth and home, a few head of cattle to tend, horses to ride when the spirit moved him or needed replenishing and a wife—a partner—to share them with.

"He can't give this up to live with me in Valhalla Springs. I can't be the on-site operations manager and live here."

"Whew, boy," Claudina groaned. "That is a biggie."

"Be honest. Am I selfish to want it all? David, my cottage, my job...my *dog*."

"He wants you, his land, his job and Rambo. Same

tune, different lyrics.'' She paused, her chin buckled in thought. ''I got married right out of high school. Life is a helluva lot less complicated when you're too young and ignorant to have one yet.''

Hannah crushed a dandelion puffball with her heel. It was comforting to know Claudina didn't think she was a deranged, commitment-phobic control freak, but talking wasn't solving anything, either.

''So, what's the answer to can't live with him, can't live without him?'' She squinted up at the sky as though a solution would materialize in the mare's-tail clouds, like an astral Magic 8 Ball. It didn't, but she heard her great-uncle Mort say, *If you don't know what to do, don't do nothin'. A shut mouth gathers no feet.*

If there'd been any money in homespun philosophies, Mort Garvey would have been a millionaire. Since there wasn't, he and his wife, Lurleen, survived on disability checks and by gate-crashing church socials, wedding receptions, post-funeral dinners and grand openings serving up free hot dogs and soda pop.

''Time,'' Claudina said, as if she'd channeled Mort's netherworldly advice. ''Give it some.''

''It won't change the logistics.''

''Maybe not, but David won't push for an answer. He's too afraid of a no.''

''The man *proposed,* Claudina. I can't just leave him hanging.''

''You're not. Oh, it'll bug him a little, but guys hear a non-answer as a maybe, which is a half yes.

Take sex, for example. Unless a man is a total Neanderthal, no means no. Anything else translates as, if they play their cards right, getting laid is in the foreseeable future. That's why they're pissed when a non-answer turns into 'Not tonight, dear, I have a headache.'"

The wind carried Polly's snippy, "See, I told you they were gonna talk about sex," followed by Lana's gauze-muffled, "Ew, *yuck*."

"Besides," Claudina added, "do you have any better ideas? Other than screwing up an almost perfect relationship?"

"No."

"All right, then. Now that that's settled, do you want to hear my other idea?"

Hannah lowered her voice. "Boink David's brains out in the meantime to distract him?"

"That's a given, but please, keep the details to yourself. It's hard enough not to hate you as it is." Claudina grinned. "My second excellent idea is you treating all of us to hot-fudge sundaes at the Dairy Queen."

Lana and Jeremy "Yippeed!" and raced for the station wagon. Polly halted in front of her mother and knuckled her hips. "I thought you were on a diet."

"I am." Claudina smoothed her daughter's bangs, then kissed her forehead. "This is one of those 'You'll understand when you grow up' things."

Polly peered through her lashes, obviously questioning whether adulthood was worth the cost of admission. At the moment, Hannah wasn't so sure herself.

# 3

Not a second too soon, David's brain recognized the significance of the brick gate with Valhalla Springs spelled out in brushed brass lettering.

Nodding off at his desk that afternoon hadn't compensated for the twelve hours of sleep he'd lost since Sunday night. Knowing he'd been on autopilot since a Toyota had rabbited from the First National Bank of Sanity's parking lot in front of him gave David the willies.

"At least I kept it on my side of the yellow line and out of the ditches," he reasoned, knowing his concentration hadn't wandered as far as it seemed. He consulted the pickup's dashboard clock. "Made pretty good time, too."

Whether it was fate, Murphy's Law or the Almighty's sense of humor, leaving a skosh late for somewhere you want to go gridlocks traffic. But root canal appointments or a bigot's bon voyage party guarantee green lights and streets as empty as an RV campground in February.

Malcolm was snoozing on Hannah's front porch. His head raised at the powerful purr of the Ram's engine, then cocked in confusion when the pickup rolled past instead of turning into the driveway.

David wanted to hold her, to feel as though he were drowning in her dark brown eyes, but prompt was a safer time of arrival than early. Hannah had made it clear on the phone last night and again that afternoon how much and why she dreaded attending the Thomlinsons' farewell banquet. No doubt she'd delayed getting dressed until certain she couldn't witch up the chicken pox or flu symptoms.

Even clearer had been the nervous pitch in her voice and the awkward pauses in their conversation where neither had occurred before.

Claudina had spent her lunch break in David's office noshing carrot sticks and relaying Hannah's objections. The chief dispatcher was Cupid in a polka-dot muumuu and jelly shoes, not a female Judas eager to betray a friend.

He'd grinned at their star-crossed astrological signs, winced at Hannah's description of her married name and assured Claudina, when Rambo understood that Malcolm was Hannah's dog instead of a rival for David's affection, the rottweiler would stop treating him like one. Probably.

The "biggies" he'd thought of before he proposed. He had no solutions. Wouldn't have suggested any if he had. It wasn't very romantic to compare marriage to a criminal investigation, but preconceived notions and presumptions erected walls too thick to see through. Solutions came from minds that were open from the ears on in.

Hannah said love wasn't enough, didn't conquer all, and she didn't believe in forever. A couple of months ago, David would have hoisted a beer and vowed a heartfelt "Amen to that." He'd fought conversion as hard as she had, but from the day they'd met, they'd been like two atheists skydiving with defective parachutes.

"Somehow or another, we'll find a soft place to land," David said. The eyes framed in the pickup's rearview mirror looked a notch shy of convinced.

If he'd been driving his patrol unit, the threesome chatting on a tee-box would have followed its progress along Valhalla Springs Boulevard, as would the fishermen casting for smallmouth bass from the lake's shore. The sweatbanded, cardio-walkers marching the trails with single-file resolve might not have noticed, but to strollers out for fresh air and companionship, a blue-and-white with gold shield decals on the doors meant trouble, not a routine patrol.

David braked at the boulevard's intersection with Main Street for a visual check-the-well-being. He hadn't met Jack Clancy, but admired the developer's restraint with bulldozers and earthmovers. Whether Hannah divined the slogan "East of Peculiar and the closest thing to paradise, this side of Sanity" before construction began or afterward, Clancy had invested millions to not make a liar out of her.

The commercial district's two-story brick stores and boardwalks resembled a nineteenth-century village preserved by a local historical society. Resident cottages terraced up the bowl-shaped hillsides, their lawns manicured by the Grounds & Greens Department and shaded by trees the streets were named for, rather than in memory of.

Safe from hunters and most other human hazards, deer snacked on residents' vegetable gardens. Possums, squirrels, rabbits and chipmunks were as bold as...

David shifted in the seat as the analogy trailed off unfinished and a second thought floated by in its backwash. Valhalla Springs was a theme park with houses. Between the American nightmare Hannah'd grown up in and her never adapting to bright lights and the big city, no wonder she's—

A horn blared. The white-haired matron behind the wheel motioned "Move it, buster." It was seconded by the drivers of the four cars lined up behind her.

Face redder than his truck's paint job, David pulled around the corner and onto the shoulder. His gaze swept Main Street's striped awnings and globed street lamps, tiered rooflines, then the forested hills and hollers beyond.

Whatever intuition had whispered an instant before that car honked was gone. All that remained was its vague attachment to Hannah and a lingering sense of importance. Nothing dire, just a mental lightning bolt that might strike again...and might not.

David circled around and backtracked to her cottage. He got out of the truck and approached the front door. Having wasted energy on his former owner's first drive-by, Malcolm just yawned, thumped his tail and drifted back to dreamland.

David thumbed the bell, then glanced at his watch. Right on time.

The woman who answered the door had spearheaded marketing campaigns from coast to coast. From her lipstick-red suit's mandarin collar, geometric cut-out neckline and side-slit skirt right down to her ankle-strapped pumps, this new-to-him Hannah Garvey was every inch a cosmopolitan corporate executive. She pushed open the screen door. "Is something wrong?"

"I, uh—" David stammered a few more syllables, then said, "You look fantastic."

"Liar. I look like Boardroom Barbie." She laughed. "I kept some of the wardrobe, but lost my edge at the Chicago city limits."

She stepped back. Her grin faltered, a hint of vulnerability and defiance tightening the margins. David thought it was awkwardness brewing again, until she said, "I can't out-belle Eulilly, so I went for the captain-of-industry shtick."

The suit became her—classy, tailored, overtly sex-appealing. Everything he'd seen her in became her—including nothing but soft skin and shimmery sheets of water—yet the outfit seemed more like armor she'd removed from the back of the closet and wondered if it still fit, while hoping it didn't.

"Don't demote yourself, sugar. You're at least an admiral." David's lips brushed her temple. He inhaled the scent of mousse and hair spray, not citrus shampoo and pure Hannah. "I, uh, reckon we have to leave pretty soon…"

She sighed and nodded. If disappointment had ever cut like the legendary knife, he didn't remember it. Watching her walk to the couch for her purse, he imagined himself hooking her arm, taking her in his and kissing her. And when she kissed him back, his brain would liquefy, then tomorrow morning, Jack Clancy would waken them when he called to fire her for missing the party.

Preceding him out the door, she turned to ask, "Are you sure nothing's wrong?"

Hell, everything was wrong. The tension lines scored between her brows. The slow burn in his belly. He hadn't felt as foolish and fidgety since he and his next-younger brother dared each other to jump out of the barn loft, then balked at the edge, arguing, "You go first. No, you go first."

He loved her. She loved him. Given time alone to shed defenses and pretenses, they'd resolve their differences. He was sure of it.

David bent his head. His mouth grazed hers, then claimed it. He savored the taste of her, the wild, heady rush of sensations and emotion and desire boiling up inside him. Pulling back before the urge to devour was too strong to resist, he said, "Nothing's so wrong that we can't fix it, Hannah."

Eyelids fluttering, she wobbled on her heels. She swallowed hard, blew out a breath and said, "I wish you'd gotten here earlier. A *lot* earlier."

The effect his kisses had on her made him feel both invincible and weak in the knees. "How about if I stay late?"

She slipped her hand in his. "How about if you just stay?"

"Might could." Looking back at the door, he ran his tongue over his teeth. "And now would be a fine time to start the clock."

"Oh, yeah…" She hesitated, a blush rising up her slender neck. "Except if we're no-shows at the restaurant, IdaClare, Delbert, Marge, the Schnurs and who knows who else will stop by on their way home to find out why."

Knowing Delbert, he'd muster the geriatric gumshoe gang in the Royal Dragon's parking lot for a full-scale, missing persons' investigation, complete with a code name.

David gestured a reluctant "after you," adding, "We're skipping dessert, though." In some states, his lecherous chuckle would be probable cause for a misdemeanor civil code violation. "Until later."

Hannah squared her shoulders, but not quickly enough to hide a shiver of anticipation. As he helped her into the pickup, his opinion of the Thomlinsons' party cranked a three-hundred-and-sixty-degree bootlegger's turn. After a couple of hours' worth of fantasizing, smoldering sidelong looks and discreet touchy-feelies under the tablecloth, they'd be so hot they'd be lucky to make it back to Valhalla Springs before they tore each other's clothes off.

His house was only six miles east of Sanity. Eight minutes from the restaurant. Rambo wouldn't let IdaClare and Company within ten yards of the porch.

Hannah tapped his arm. "I seem to recall a ticket-happy jerkface pulling me over for speeding a few weeks ago, right about here.'' She pointed at the speedometer needle. ''And I wasn't going anywhere near seventy.''

Grinning, he eased up on the accelerator. ''Sixty-seven in a forty-five, ma'am. Mighty risky, especially for a flatlander.''

She laughed. ''Gee, Sheriff. Do you remember everything you say to crabby law-breakers?''

''Nope.'' He winked. ''Just the pretty ones. With great legs.''

''I was wearing slacks that day.''

Her skirt was riding midway up her silk-stockinged thighs. Damn shame the slit was on the other side. ''If you'd been wearing that outfit, I'd have let you off with a warning.''

''Hah.'' She tugged at the hem, as though a sixteenth of an inch made any difference.

David groaned inwardly, dredging up the names of Heisman trophy winners before the seat belt gelded him.

''Jimmy Wayne would have given me a warning,'' she said, ''but not you.''

''Uh-uh. McBride would have pulled you over for thirty-seven in a forty-five.''

''Oh, he's not half the horn-dog he wants everyone to think he is.''

Yeah, well, David thought, all of a sudden I'm twice the horn-dog I thought I was. He twisted the cassette player's knob. ''You like Garth Brooks? Before he got famous, he and his band used to hang out at this cowboy bar in Tulsa.''

A wicked gleam flashed in her eyes. ''Do you want music to drive by, or are you trying to change the subject?''

''Both.''

Relaxing against the leather upholstery, she folded her hands in her lap like a good little girl. Or a naughty one, hiking up her skirt while her mother's attention was on the preacher. ''Tell me how you tracked the escapees to that shack in the National Forest.''

''I already did,'' he said. ''Last night on the phone.''

''Okay then, did anything exciting happen today?''

''Yep. But you were there, too.''

She smirked. ''I thought you wanted to change the subject.''

What he really wanted to change was their destination. Barring that, he reiterated details of the capture, although truth be known, crashing through brambles in the dark or daylight was a mile wide of high drama. The odds of being pegged in a rifle's crosshairs at any moment never left a cop's mind, but most fleeing felon's escape plan stopped at the jailhouse door. He recalled a half-starved, frostbitten honorcamp escapee whose first words when they found him were, ''What took you guys so long?''

Hannah said, ''I was thinking along those lines when Claudina told me you'd caught the prisoners and their accomplices. Thank God the deputy they shot is going to be all right.''

Living was better than dying, David agreed, but, only three years out of the academy, that young man's law enforcement career was finished. If getting by on one kidney didn't disqualify him for duty, a shattered kneecap would.

He turned off First Street, Sanity's main drag, onto an asphalted lane. Tree trunks and utility poles were smothered in kudzu, and May apples bloomed in the shady, premature gloam.

Hannah leaned forward and peered out the windshield. ''Who would build a restaurant out here in the boondocks?''

The Royal Dragon missed being within the city limits by a hundred yards and the courthouse was a rock's-throw away, but David chose history over a geography lesson. ''A guy by the name of Mansfield Louderbeck. As the story goes, Manny had a fondness for whiskey, women and high-stakes poker. He wasn't about to let Prohibition kibosh his vices or livelihood, so he built a speakeasy on a parcel out of the sight and short arm of the law—and members of the Women's Christian Temperance Union.''

David chuffed. ''Whose husbands, of course, frequented Manny's establishment in droves, along with visiting Capone *caporegimes,* the Barker gang and Charles Arthur Floyd, alias Pretty Boy.''

''Spats, gats and the Mob in Kinderhook County?'' Hannah said. ''I am amazed.''

''Some say Bonnie and Clyde wet their whistles at

Manny's, too, before their shoot-out with the police down in Joplin.''

The lane dead-ended at a low, whitewashed cinder block building with a crimson and gold pagoda-style roof. Fire-breathing dragons faced off on the lacquered double-doored entrance, illuminated by outsize Chinese lanterns.

David said, ''The place changed ownership and went bust a hundred times before Mr. and Mrs. Chau moved here from Fort Chaffee, Arkansas, and made a go of it.''

He shifted the pickup into park. ''Chaffee was one of the largest camps that gave asylum to the Vietnamese boat people. The Lutheran church in Sanity sponsored the Chaus and baptized the six kids that came along later. Four of them went off to college and didn't come back, but the two youngest still work for Mom and Dad.''

''Good for them.''

''Good for business, too,'' David said. ''Mr. Chau speaks some English and I think his wife savvies more than she lets on, but Johnny and Jasmine do most of the talking for them.''

A wet-dry board clipped to an easel directed the Thomlinsons' guests to the banquet room's side entrance. Hand in hand, David and Hannah strolled through a serene Oriental garden. An eyebrow bridge spanned a shallow koi pond ringed with ferns and pussy willow. Music lilted from hidden speakers and wind chimes tinkled on the breeze.

Hannah sniffed the air. ''If the food tastes as good

as it smells, at least we'll get a decent meal out of Clancy's command performance.''

"No insult to the Chaus," David said, "but I'd take a steak and a baked potato over rice and a mess of stuff I don't recognize any day.''

"Steak, huh?" A two-beat pause. "Does this beef fixation extend to Hamburger Helper?''

"Well, it's a far cry from a porterhouse, but it ain't bad for a box supper.'' Her inscrutable expression begged a "Why?''

She shrugged. "Just curious.''

He squelched the impulse to tell her he wanted her for his wife not a live-in cook. A wise man doesn't trifle with a woman girding for battle, though. Even if it wasn't with him.

Eulilly Thomlinson pounced before the pneumatic hinge closed the door behind them. Her pastel yellow, lace-trimmed jacket dress maximized her petite femininity and hourglass figure. A family fortune, plastic surgery and good genes had shaved a decade off her age, but if she'd ever had a genuinely happy day in her life, it didn't show.

"Sheriff Hendrickson? My heavens, is it truly you?" Her moonlight-and-magnolias drawl was as pronounced as her signature perfume. "Chet, honey, look who just came through the door. Why, I couldn't be more flattered if the governor was payin' us a call.''

Grabbing David's hand in both of hers, Eulilly slanted her eyes at Hannah. Her steady gaze assured that the snub was intentional and thoroughly enjoyed.

"I swear, this is the nicest surprise we've had in a coon's age, isn't it, Chet?"

"Hannah tells me that Valhalla Springs won't be the same without you, Miz Thomlinson," David said. He was male and born and raised in Saint Joseph, Missouri, but summer visits with his Alabama cousins had provided a crash course in the art of double entendres. "Saying goodbye and Godspeed was the least I could do."

He mistook Eulilly's nod as *touché,* not *En garde.*

"How kind of you," she said, and swung his arm sideward. "Allow me to introduce you to my husband. I do believe y'all have a lot in common."

To his credit, Chet Thomlinson aimed a withering look at his wife and shook Hannah's hand before David's. "It's a pleasure to meet you, Ms. Garvey...Sheriff." No accent, Southern or otherwise, was evident in his voice. "Eulilly failed to mention you'd be joining us this evening, but it's an honor to have you as our guests."

He was as tall as David, but his gray suit coat bagged from the shoulders like an aging body-builder whose muscles were thawing from neglect. Chet's eyes missed meeting David's and perspiration filmed his ruddy complexion, but the venom Eulilly radiated would make granite break a sweat.

With a gasp and squeak, she clutched at his sleeve. "I just had the most *marvelous* idea. Since Delores hasn't arrived yet—sure as the world, she'll be late for *her* own funeral—let's give the sheriff her place at our table and seat Delores with the Caldwells. She and Hetta are as thick as thieves, don't you know. I'm sure Delores wouldn't mind the teensiest little bit.''

Hannah blanched. Chet looked as though his gall-bladder had ruptured. It was all David could do not to laugh at Eulilly's audacity. Instead, he leaned forward and murmured, ''Beg pardon in advance for my language, ma'am, but where I come from, folks would say you've got balls bigger'n church bells. Now, unless you'd like to explain to all these people why Hannah and I walked out a couple of minutes after we walked in, I'd advise you to start acting like the lady you profess to be.''

If she reacted at all, composure reasserted itself in a blink. Along with a splash of acid, her tone engendered the respect afforded a worthy adversary. ''I understand perfectly, Sheriff. If you promised IdaClare you'd join her group, it would be rude for you to sit elsewhere.''

To Hannah, she added, ''You and your beau are such a handsome couple,'' then angled her head, ''Don't you think so, Chet?''

Her husband was staring a hole through a group of new arrivals entering the banquet room. If he heard the question, he didn't answer it.

David said, ''If you'll excuse us'' and wrapped an arm around Hannah's waist to guide her to their table at the back of the room.

Garish horseshoe and life preserver–shaped floral arrangements on wire stands wished the Thomlinsons ''Good Luck'' and ''Bon Voyage.'' Champagne chilled in silver buckets beside the table. Ribbon rip-cords streamed from the corners of a mesh netting tacked to the ceiling tiles and stuffed with balloons and confetti.

Framed Oriental pen-and-ink drawings and muted watercolors hung on the textured plaster walls. The irony of the Chaus fleeing their homeland with nothing but the rags on their backs wasn't lost on David.

"When did you promise IdaClare that we'd sit with her?" Hannah asked.

"Just now, when I noticed two empty chairs at her table."

"Oh?" She grinned. "So Mr. Truth, Justice and the American Way fibbed to Miss Candied Yam 1944, did he?"

"Nope."

A fair impression of a beached walleye commenced. "Then what *did* you whisper to her?"

"Nothing I'm proud of, but nothing she didn't deserve." David sent a silent apology to his mother, who'd raised her four sons to be gentlemen.

"Think it's going to stay yours and Eulilly's little secret, huh?" Hannah said as she took the chair he pulled out for her. "Wait'll I get you alone, Hendrickson. You'll sing like a bird."

Not tonight, he wouldn't. Touching her, tasting her, taking her higher and higher, past the stars and over the moon while she moaned his name like a hosanna was more what he had in mind.

Which he'd best get out of it before the table started levitating. He ran a finger around the inside of his shirt collar, then reached for his water glass, since dumping the entire pitcher in his lap might be a tad obvious.

Ice cube bank shots off his molars gradually restored his sight. If everyone kept talking at once until the jungle drums in his ears stopped pounding, he might catch a word or six, by and by.

Leo and his tan polyester suit blended into the wall, with Scarlet O'Hannah seated on his right and Rosemary in a low-cut sequined overblouse on his left. IdaClare's ruffled, pink chiffon dress was the same shade as her hair, as was every stitch of clothing she owned. Delbert's crowning glory had reverted from pea green to its natural snow white, but he was clad in his usual, dressed-during-a-power-outage style—a chartreuse shirt, gold and black plaid sports coat and a neon orange tie with hula girls painted on it.

To prevent hurt feelings among his Valhalla Springs harem, Delbert had asked Sophonia Pugh, a septuagenarian pillar of the community and courtroom groupie, to be his date. Sophonia had never married, but tongues still wagged about her youthful, abrupt transformation from Sunday-school teacher to hellion. Her vintage beaded cocktail dress and feather boa may very well have tripped the light fantastic when the Royal Dragon was a roadhouse, before World War II siphoned off Manny Louderbeck's dwindling clientele.

"Did Hannah tell you she caught Rosemary's bridal bouquet?" asked Marge Rosenbaum, seated on David's right.

She hadn't, but the question behind Marge's question was as transparent as her bifocals. Rather than beat down Hannah's door and demand to know if David had proposed and what her answer had been, the gang had stayed mum for forty-eight hours—which was forty-seven longer than David would have bet they'd last.

"Hannah and I haven't had much time to talk since the wedding," he said.

Marge peeked around him at Hannah, who was talking to Leo and Rosemary, then lowered her head to finger-iron a wrinkle from her pantsuit's slacks. "It's too bad you had to leave the reception early. You'd have gotten a kick out of Hannah trampling us sweet old ladies to snatch that bouquet out of the air."

As those who can't prevaricate their way out of paper sacks are prone to do, she looked up, adding, "I can't imagine why she'd do that. Can you?"

Eulilly couldn't have improved on David's ambiguous "I'll ask her later, then let you know what she says."

Over Marge's delighted gasp, Delbert chimed in, "That manhunt you were on sounded about as lively as a cemetery dance. Me and Sophonia were listening in on our scanners and—"

Her elbow bayoneted him between the fourth and fifth ribs. "You old fool. If I wanted the sheriff to know I own a scanner, I'd tell him myself. Eavesdropping on police radio chatter is a presupposition of prejudice. Thanks to you, I'll never get picked for jury duty again."

Palpating the injured area for evidence of a fracture, Delbert said, "Presupposition, my sweet as—"

"Del-bert," IdaClare trilled. "Watch your language. This is a nice restaurant, not the men's locker room at the clubhouse."

"What the hell's wrong with saying 'my sweet aspidistra?'" He crossed his arms protectively over his torso. "Sit down between two bossy old broads and a man can't finish a ding-danged sentence and gets his ding-danged lung punctured to boot."

Sophonia said, "Put some meat on your bones and maybe you won't bruise so easy."

"What? You're skinnier and older than I am!"

IdaClare flapped a hand. "I don't believe for a second that you were going to say aspidistra, but I shouldn't have interrupted. I'm just out of sorts because the Thomlinsons are moving away."

"They will be missed," Rosemary said.

Marge agreed. "Especially Eulilly. She always has a smile and a kind word for everyone."

David and Hannah exchanged an "If they only knew" look.

"I've been giving Chet pointers on his golf swing," IdaClare said. "He's a shoo-in for winning the men's club championship. I don't know why Eulilly refuses to stay until after the tournament in September."

"Ach, it is the homesickness, she has," Leo said. "America I love, and lucky I am to have lived here since the war, but forever I will miss Germany."

Delbert harrumped. "Eulilly isn't pining for Mississippi as much as she is for being the big duck in a small puddle.''

''Well, I don't know her from Adam,'' Sophonia said, ''but who doesn't want to be a big duck?''

Marge graced her with an indulgent smile. ''Her husband, Chet, for one. He's as sweet as can be, but he'd be happy just being the puddle.''

Delbert said, ''That's because he's—''

Everyone started at the mellow toll of a brass gong. Nineteen-year-old Jasmine Chau led a procession of waiters bearing huge trays of steaming food. With a flair for the theatrical, the beautiful, reed-slender baby of the family assisted each staff member with situating the trays on Lazy Susans built into the dining tables.

David caught Jasmine's eye as she refilled a guest's wineglass. Grinning from ear to ear, she turned and deftly traded the wine bottle for the iced-tea pitcher her older brother was pouring from.

His expression puzzled, Johnny Chau glanced over his shoulder and spied David. A curt nod assured the county sheriff that Jasmine wouldn't dispense another drop of alcohol to a customer until she celebrated her twenty-first birthday.

David's priorities at the moment didn't involve busting a minor on a liquor violation. Jasmine worked six fourteen-hour days a week in her parents' restaurant and had never so much as jaywalked across the square. He would, however, offer a friendly reminder to Mr. Chau that underage servers invited suspension or revocation of his liquor license.

After helping himself to a plateful of rice from the basin-size bowl in the middle of the lazy Susan, David frowned at the tureens encircling it. Tented cards identified each dish, but he wished he knew the Vietnamese word for squid.

Hannah wagged her fork at a bowl with a fluted rim. "That's beef and broccoli. Onions, baby corn, bamboo sprouts, carrots…no weird stuff."

"Scout's honor?"

"I'd swear it on a S'more, if there were any handy."

The door to the banquet room burst open and slammed against the wall. A man in a ski mask, dark T-shirt and jeans rushed in. Pistol in his left hand. Assault rifle in his right.

"Down—down!" Muscle memory sent David's hand to his hip. "Get down!" He yanked up his trousers, clawing for his ankle-holstered .38.

The man braced the assault rifle against his hip. Muzzle flash spit from the pistol.

Glass exploded. Screams pierced the rifle's staccato roar. Balloons and confetti rained down.

David leapt to his feet. Whipped the .38 into firing position. Aimed…

Chet Thomlinson jumped up into David's line of sight. Leveled a pistol. Fired.

Just as David leapt sideward, the gunman staggered backward. Bullets chewed a canyon in the ceiling. Chet's handgun recoiled once. Twice.

The gunman jerked, slumped. Head lolling, he wailed in agony and collapsed on the carpet.

# 4

The silence was stark. Surreal. Counterfeit.

It multiplied the mental chorus of gunfire and the cotton-batting deafness of swollen eardrums. Adrenaline overload reduced the flight-or-fight instinct to a cowering, stone-blind paralysis. The sharp, muggy odor of a Fourth of July fireworks extravaganza saturated the air.

The sensory barricade splintered like the door to the restaurant's banquet room. Calls for help escalated to banshee cries, moans to violent retching. Roiling into the sulphuric haze was the reek of spilled food, evacuated bowels and bladders, blood and raw sweat.

Pain throbbing in her wrist broke Hannah's stupor. Leo's fingers, as tight as a tourniquet, dug into fabric, flesh and gouged the very bone beneath. His other arm hugged his new bride. Glasses askew and eyes shut, he chanted in German, praying for salvation, or retribution.

Hannah had no memory of him hurling her and Rosemary to the floor and under the table, then clutching them to him, as though he could shield them from a madman's killing spree.

"It's over, Leo." Hannah gently pried his fingers

from her arm. "We're all right, thanks to you. You saved our lives."

"The war." Tears glistened down his cheeks. His hand fell away, his body slumped. "So like the war, it is." He choked back a sob. "Never again did I think I would hear the guns, the screaming…"

From the front of the room David yelled into his cell phone, "This is not a drill. All available officers and emergency personnel to the Royal Dragon, Code 1. Two possible gunshot fatalities. Multiple injuries. I repeat, *this is not a drill.*"

Rosemary turned Leo's face to hers. She kissed him, then hugged him close. Her nod told Hannah to go on, to see to those with visible wounds.

She squeezed Rosemary's shoulder, then scuttled from under the table. Glass crunched as she stood, the carpeted floor slick beneath her shoes. The ceiling was riddled, the walls pocked. Confetti sparkled and balloons bounced like a hideous, macabre joke.

The room keeled left, then right. Puddled light from fixtures not destroyed by gunfire tunneled to bilious yellow swirls. Hannah gripped the table's edge, swallowing down the sick-sourness burning her throat.

Figures rose and moved in the gloom like specters. Voices collided in a high-pitched, frantic garble. David halted the onrush from the main dining room and kitchen, shouting for any doctors or nurses in attendance.

Guests fleeing the scene gasped and staggered back, hands clapping their mouths in horror. The shooter lay just inside the entry door, the surrounding wall spackled in blood.

Chet Thomlinson sat in a chair, his head cradled in his hands. Beside him, Eulilly was sprawled on the table. Her cheek rested in a dark halo spreading on the tablecloth.

Johnny Chau rocked on his knees. He held his sister's body to his chest, keening, "Jasmine, Jasmine" as though she were asleep and the sound of her name would waken her.

Hannah wiped icy sweat from her forehead with her sleeve. She started around the table, kicking aside upended chairs. A pair of scissored legs and a swathe of pink chiffon stopped her heart.

"Oh God, oh please God, no." She knelt beside IdaClare. The older woman was unconscious, her arm and the front of her dress bathed in blood. Her breathing was labored, her skin waxen and clammy. The pulse at her wrist felt rapid but strong.

*Stop the bleeding. Shock—if she goes into shock, she'll die. Keep her warm. Must keep her warm.*

Hannah snatched a cloth napkin off the floor and rolled it like a kerchief. IdaClare's eyelids fluttered when Hannah lifted her arm and tied the cloth around it.

"You're going to be fine," Hannah promised, just as she had promised her mother, as if love and strength of will ever foiled the angel of death.

Sirens howled and chirped in the near distance. Hannah stripped off her jacket and tucked it around IdaClare. The hem barely reached her waist.

Leaping to her feet, Hannah wadded the tablecloth in her fists. Wineglasses toppled. Silverware clanked. Her head snapped up at a yank from the opposite side.

Delbert's eyes were dull, uncomprehending. Blood splotched his shirt and trousers. Grief and rage distorted his features. He jerked on the cloth. "Turn loose, damn it. For God's sake, can't you see that woman's dying over there?"

Dishes crashed to the floor. Delbert snapped the fabric and let it settle over the lower half of Sophonia Pugh's prostrate form. Her face was the color of antique linen. A bluish tinge ringed her mouth. Marge sat on her heels beside her, blood oozing between her fingers with every compression of Sophonia's chest.

Hannah looked from her to IdaClare, then to the scores cut by flying glass and china and the others bruised and battered in their panicked dives for safety. To Jasmine. Eulilly. Finally, to the monster who'd turned a celebratory dinner into an act of senseless carnage.

Knuckling the table's bare wood surface, Hannah hunched over the shard of a broken serving bowl and vomited.

The usual array of tattered, outdated magazines mounded the side tables in Mercy Hospital's waiting room. A muted television bracketed below the ceiling flashed light on the faux corduroy–papered walls. The room was chilly, windowless, suffocatingly quiet. Intermittent pages droned from public address speakers, deepening the sense of isolation.

Hannah's insides itched for a cigarette. She hadn't smoked in years, but sitting, waiting, praying for the best, fearing the worst, working up, then stanching, resentment at being shuttled into a carpeted cell had triggered a craving for nicotine—a manic need to occupy empty hands, seven minutes of empty time, and defy the red and white-enameled No Smoking placards sneering from every wall.

Beside her, Delbert roused from a short nap. In contrast with his golfer's tan, the butterfly bandages on his neck and temple seemed to stand out an inch from his skin.

During their tablecloth tug-of-war, Hannah had been as shock-blind to the gashes on his head and under his ear as he'd been to the woman stripped down to a lace camisole and skirt trying to steal the cloth away from him.

He chafed his face with his hands, then sat up straighter. "No word yet, huh?"

"It's only been a couple of hours." An eternity, for waiting-room prisoners.

"Since we got here, yeah." Delbert pushed up his jacket sleeve with his thumb. "Closer to four, since the EMTs hauled Sophonia and IdaClare out of the restaurant."

Paramedics, a vanload of trauma nurses, county deputies in midnight-blue uniforms and brown and khaki–clad Sanity Police Department officers had stormed the banquet room en masse. On their heels was Chief of Detectives Marlin Andrik and investigators Cletus Orr and Josh Phelps.

David seemed to be everywhere at once—barking commands, helping load gurneys into ambulances. He'd comforted the frightened, directed medical assistance where needed and coordinated county, city and highway patrol assistance efforts with a borrowed handset radio at his ear.

Guests had again stampeded for the exit. Officers had waved them back, their voices kind but firm. There were injuries requiring treatment, a crime scene to secure, evidence to protect, witness statements to record. Other than the wounded, medical personnel and investigating officers, no one would be allowed in or out without the sheriff's permission.

Cameras wielded by Andrik and his men had strobed in a race to capture every triangulated inch of the scene on film before its integrity was destroyed. Dust and insulation fibers filtered from the bullet-gnawed ceiling. On the floor, spent shell casings shone like stubby brass ingots. Tripod-mounted halogen bulbs reduced the scattered furniture, splattered blood and huddled, whey-faced survivors to props in a B-grade horror movie.

Hannah had stared at the expended ammo littering the carpet. Each casing represented a bullet fired. It was a miracle any of them were alive.

Junior Duckworth, the three-term county coroner and third-generation owner of Duckworth's Funeral Home, had gone about the grisly task of declaring the victims' deaths. Eulilly, Jasmine and their murderer's remains wouldn't leave the room, either, until Detective Andrik released them to Duckworth for the long drive to the state medical examiner's office in Columbia.

Hannah had ached for David to hold her. To declare a moratorium from being Sheriff Hendrickson, the go-to officer in charge, and take her aside for a moment's peace and reassurance.

Later, as she and Delbert were about to duck under the yellow crime scene tape barricading the parking lot, David had grasped her arm. "I love you, sugar."

Woven within those three little words was a thanks be to God that she wasn't hurt, a promise that Ida-Clare and Sophonia would recover and remorse that he'd been powerless to stop the shooter in time.

"I love you, too, David."

He'd kissed her brow, said, "I'll meet you at the hospital as soon as I can," then jogged back into the restaurant.

In accordance with law enforcement hierarchy, David outranked Marlin Andrik, but Hannah knew the irritable detective had taken command of the investigation upon arrival. David held the unique position of witness, participant and first officer on the scene. She'd be surprised if he left the Royal Dragon before dawn.

The waiting room's door swung open. A young woman dressed in the housekeeping department's coral scrubs smiled an apology for the intrusion. Hannah's and Delbert's eyes followed her as she collected empty soda cans, foam cups and gum wrappers, relined the underused trash can, then hastened out again.

Delbert uncrossed and recrossed his legs. "We should have lied, you know."

Hannah glanced at the door in confusion. "Lied about what?"

"Being next of kin. That's why that nurse stuck us in here instead of the family waiting room down the hall." His palms tortured the chair arm's vinyl upholstery. "If I'd said I was Sophonia's brother and you'd said you were IdaClare's daughter, they wouldn't be so damn slow to tell us what's going on."

Hannah massaged his knobbed knuckles. In addition to the shooting victims pouring into the emergency room, a motorcyclist had t-boned a pickup, two patients were being monitored for possible heart attacks, a little girl had fallen from a jungle gym and broken her collarbone and a barbecue grill had torched a man's clothing.

"I guess this is when I'm supposed to remind you that no news is good news," she said.

"Hmmph."

"And that much as I hate why we're here, it'd be a hundred times worse without you to hang on to."

Delbert splayed his fingers and caught Hannah's between them. "Aw, don't fret, ladybug. IdaClare hasn't practiced bossing everyone around down here enough to start giving God an earful, and Sophonia's already picked her bench in the courtroom for a child neglect trial next week."

He squinted at the flickering TV screen as though seeking affirmation. Presently, he said, "Maybe we shouldn't have told Leo, Rosemary and Marge to head on home. The five of us could've gotten up a game of gin rummy, or spades, or something.''

The conversation lapsed, each of them lost in private thoughts. A few hours ago marriage was the center of Hannah's mental universe. She'd dithered between telling David the future began and ended with the first line of the rope-skipping chant and suggesting they live together at her cottage, knowing full well that trial cohabitation was an amateur production of ''I Do, I Do,'' not Broadway.

Life-altering decisions? By Hannah's definition they were, until a lone gunman kicked in the banquet room's door and put his own into action.

''It should have been me not them,'' Delbert said. He turned and looked at her. ''I was sitting between IdaClare and Sophonia. How come they got shot and I didn't? Why are Eulilly and that waitress zipped up in body bags and I'm sitting here fit as a fiddle?''

Impossible questions had platitudes for answers. Hannah refused to insult him or herself with them. Marlin Andrik's ballistics report would pinpoint the bullets' trajectory, but science couldn't explain that existential why.

''It shouldn't have been anyone'' was all she could offer in response. ''The awful corollary is, if David hadn't been there it might have been all of us.''

Delbert started. ''You didn't see what happened, did you?''

''What do you mean?''

His eyes strayed to an artificial dieffenbachia. ''It's

a good thing David was there, no doubt about that, but the hero of the hour is Chet Thomlinson. He whipped out a sidearm and killed that murderin' son of a bitch. David never got a shot at him.''

The door whooshed open. A nurse in a patterned scrub top and purple bottoms paused at the threshold. Tension flatlined her eyebrows and mouth. ''Are you Ms. Garvey?''

Nodding, Hannah bunched the hem of her jacket in her fist.

''Would you mind stepping out into the hall, please? I think it's best to speak with you privately about Mrs. Clancy.''

Marlin Andrik jerked a thumb at the door as he peeled off his latex gloves. ''Got a minute?''

''Sure,'' David said.

The air outside the restaurant was cooler and smelled of humus. Marlin lit the reason for their departure. He took a deep drag and exhaled smoke out his nostrils. ''I hear our perp put us on the map.''

Minutes after the shooting, 911 started ringing like a twenty-four-hour news hotline. Dispatch started fielding calls from media stringers sniffing after a story. Claudina had been called in to help answer the phones and act as the public information officer.

David envisioned Lana and Jeremy curled up on the floor of his office. Polly had probably faked sleep until they'd conked out and was now sitting cross-legged at his desk, his Stetson wobbling around her ears, pretending to be the queen of the county.

"Before my cell phone's charge crapped out," David said, "Claudina reported that our 'incident' didn't have enough casualties to interest the network-news vultures. One said the small-town, can't-happen-here angle had been done to death."

"Cute." Marlin made rude throat noises. "How'd they get wise to it in the first place?"

It was a rhetorical question, but David answered anyway. "Listening in on highway patrol radio chatter would be my guess. Or a tip from somebody who does."

"Ears are everywhere, but county, city and state cops have to relay through dispatchers to talk to each other." Marlin's mouth spasmed into what passed for a smile. "Not that we give a shit ninety percent of the time."

"A universal channel would be damn handy the other ten, though," David said.

A debatable opinion, judging by the detective's expression. Interagency pissing contests were as common to law enforcement as to the military. City cops looked down on county cops, county cops resented the highway patrol, the highway patrol detested the ATF and everybody hated the FBI.

The latter two were graven in stone, but all-hands emergencies like tonight's eclipsed jurisdictional metes and bounds.

Marlin said, "I suppose you already know that our shooter didn't have any ID on him. No driver's license, no credit cards. Zip."

Cigarette dangling from his lips, the detective

flipped back several pages in his notes. "The kitchen help say his name was D. K. Bogart. Came in about a month ago looking for a job. No such luck—Mr. Chau had just hired a new dishwasher. A day or so later the kid didn't show up for work. Johnny Chau went to Bogart's apartment to tell him the job was his if he wanted it."

"Bogart wasn't local," David said. "Any idea where he hailed from?"

"Negatory. The first three digits of the social security number he gave Mr. Chau are two-two-four—issued in Virginia. I'll run it for wants and warrants when I get to the office.

"Officer Cornelius of the Sanity P.D. remembers stopping Bogart a while back on First Street at about 2:00 a.m. No ID on him then, either. He mouthed off to Cornelius about rousting him for 'walking while black.'"

David rolled his eyes. The controversy surrounding racial profiling in conjunction with traffic stops, aka "driving while black" was a sore subject for law enforcement. By all rights, officers guilty of the practice should be stripped of their badges, but feeding statistics into a computer and passing statutes based on the result confused, rather than clarified, the issue.

When David was a patrol officer in north Tulsa, an almost exclusively black and Hispanic section of the city, a Caucasian cruising the street or hoofing it was an automatic suspicious person. Besides, all cops had to do to crunch the numbers was issue citations for whatever probable cause induced the stop. God save the already clogged court system, but letting too many folks off with verbal warnings also made the computers cry foul.

Marlin said, "It looks like Bogart drifted into town and went out with a bang. Except leaving horizontal in the back of Junior Duckworth's meat wagon wasn't part of his plan."

Anger surged through David. His hands closed to fists. "So help me, if somebody had prior knowledge, I want his or her ass in jail for conspiracy, accessory—every charge the county prosecutor can hang on 'em."

Marlin shook his head. "Bogart was a loner. Clocked in on time, did his job, clocked out, walked home. He shot the shit with the busboys about the Cubs and bitched at the waitstaff for not sharing their tips with those that did the dirty work, but he didn't talk himself."

Fatigue and the lethargy from a full-born adrenaline rush whined in David's head, too loudly to think straight, much less fast. "Quite a few workplace massacres have ended with the perp committing suicide, haven't they?"

"Whether they did or didn't, punching his own ticket definitely wasn't part of Bogart's plan," Marlin said. "Deputy Vaughn found a pair of sunglasses, a yellow ball cap and a red shirt on the hood of one of the employees' cars. A one-way bus ticket to Saint Louis was in the shirt pocket. It's pretty obvious, Bogart was going to chuck the weapons and ski mask in a Dumpster, button the red shirt over the black one and top it off with that yellow cap.''

"Smart," David admitted grudgingly. "Witness descriptions might have put his height and weight from five-six and a hundred and forty to six-five and two-ten, but even if they weren't sure whether his shirt was black or navy, they wouldn't have mistaken it for red.''

Marlin agreed. "He'd have had to run to catch his bus, but Bogart might have been watching barges chug up and down the Mississippi before we figured out where he went.''

David peered through the woods adjacent to the restaurant in the direction of the bus station. "Even if we'd thought to send officers to the depot, they'd have asked after a black man in a black shirt, not a black man in a red shirt and a yellow baseball cap."

"That's a big if, boss," Andrik said. "Conventional wisdom would have put us on the second fucking nature walk this week.''

He flicked the Marlboro's scorched filter to the pavement. "Beth is still picking ticks off me like it's a new kind of foreplay. Only there's few things that'll get a guy out of the mood faster than a tick on his dick.''

David tried to laugh, needed to. No doubt Andrik had cracked wise before he could feed himself, but irreverent, off-color remarks were a coping mechanism. David just couldn't pause the loop-tape of the shooting replaying in his head long enough to blow off steam.

"Any theories on how a minimum-wage dishwasher came into possession of a TEC–9 assault rifle and a 9 mm Beretta automatic?"

"Well, the tooth fairy didn't leave 'em under his pillow," Marlin said. "If we're lucky, the Beretta's serial number will lead somewhere. Congress banned Intertec 9's, 22's and the like ten years ago. Before and since, assault rifles have been the darlings of gunqueer cops, white supremacists and gangbangers."

"Then Bogart brought his with him."

"Maybe." Marlin shrugged. "We both know all three of the above call Kinderhook County home and none of them would file a stolen-property report if their toys came up missing."

Legal ownership of an assault rifle required federal registration and a permit. Marlin had just busted a reservist on multiple weapons violations, among other things.

Rookie detective Josh Phelps yelled, "Hey, Sarge. C'mere a sec. I think I found something."

Under his breath, Marlin muttered, "Columbo Junior finds ass with both hands. Details at eleven."

David started for the door, then halted when Marlin asked, "So, what are you going to do about Chet Thomlinson carrying concealed?"

Voters in Missouri's three largest cities—Saint Louis, Kansas City and Springfield—had defeated a bill allowing permits to carry concealed weapons.

With some exceptions, their rural counterparts favored the issue. Decisions split by geography guaranteed an eventual encore at the ballot box.

"I don't know what I'll do about Thomlinson," David said. "There's about eight thousand priorities ahead of him."

The answer didn't meet with Marlin's approval. "Want my advice?"

"No."

"Good. I'm better at come-to-Jesus meetings, anyway." Andrik shoved his hands in his pockets and rocked on the balls of his feet. "You're a by-the-book kind of guy and I respect that. Thomlinson leveling a SIG-Sauer for biblical revenge on the drone that murdered his wife sits fine morally. Ignoring it legally leaves a greasy taste in your mouth. Am I right?"

"Yep."

"It does in mine, too. Vigilante justice is vigilante justice regardless of cause. But—and there are several to consider—Thomlinson is a hero to everyone who signed the party's guest book. By morning, everyone in Valhalla Springs will heap laurels, casseroles and cakes on him. Next Tuesday, when the *Sanity Examiner* hits the street, the whole county will be buzzing about it."

"I know," David said. "And I know where you're going with this."

Over three hundred and fifty potential voters lived in Valhalla Springs. The hotly contested primary election for sheriff was a few weeks hence. David's opponent, Jessup Knox, was a certified idiot who fancied himself Elvis incarnate. Knox was also native to Kinderhook County, related to half its populace, owner of Fort Knox Security, president of Sanity's chamber of commerce and a master of political innuendo—otherwise known as lying and getting away with it.

It wasn't difficult to anticipate Jessup Knox's response to the shooting. The kindest thing he'd called David was trigger-happy when Stuart Quince, a deranged man armed with a loaded 9 mm Glock, had recently had no qualms about killing David to implement a planned suicide-by-cop.

Now Knox would insinuate that David had clutched in a crisis. Froze like a treed raccoon. Didn't fire a single shot, while a private citizen—a *senior* citizen, for God's sake—did the sheriff's job for him.

David's somewhat black-and-white interpretation of the law wasn't the reason behind the greasy, queasy taste Marlin described. Self-doubt had clawed at David's entrails long before the acrid smell of gunpowder dissipated.

*Did* he clutch? Had Stuart Quince's death, the accusations of killing him in cold blood and the hindsighted fear that he'd taken a life unnecessarily haunted him more than he realized?

Instinct said no.

When all hell broke loose in the banquet room, instinct had sent David's hand to his hip first, as it would any cop.

Instinct had pulled the muzzle sideward when Thomlinson jumped up in front of David.

Instinct had pulled the trigger the night Stuart Quince died.

Jessup Knox would have shit in his socks when D. K. Bogart kicked in the door, but remarks to that effect would hold as much water with voters as a sieve. As Lucas Sauers, David's friend, campaign manager and the attorney defending him against a million-dollar, wrongful-death lawsuit filed by Stuart Quince's widow, would say, "He who slings mud loses ground."

Luke would further advise that, even if Knox developed lockjaw overnight, the court of public opinion would crucify David for charging a heroic, grieving widower with carrying a concealed weapon.

If only the same court could explain the hinky feeling behind David's breastbone. If he ever got home, swigging a cold beer on the porch with nothing but crickets and coyotes to distract him might weave thready thoughts into a skein.

"Just take it slow," Marlin said. "We've confiscated Thomlinson's gun and he won't get it back."

"Yeah." David's palm grazed his sports coat's pocket where he'd safekept the pistol until turning it over to Marlin. "I just wouldn't mind knowing why he had one."

"He's a retired fed." The detective craned his neck and spat. His love for *federales* was pure-de-heartwarming.

"What branch?"

"Secret Service." Marlin sneered. "Don't ya know, it was a thrill a minute hauling the president's kids to school and birthday parties. Why, there's just no tellin' when Pin the Tail on the Donkey is gonna go bad."

# 5

"If you insist, dear," IdaClare said, her voice slurry from the painkiller-sedative cocktail injected in the IV. "But when an hour's up, you're taking me home so I can sleep in my own bed."

Hannah knew the drugs would work their magic before she had to make good on her promise. The matter the nurse had summoned her from the waiting room to discuss was IdaClare's loud and adamant refusal to be admitted overnight for observation.

In the minds of many senior citizens, hospitals were where people went to die. IdaClare's parents, siblings and her husband, Patrick, certainly hadn't survived their stays. She believed in a heavenly reunion with her family and the love of her life but wasn't in any hurry to take harp lessons.

"Never could rest in a strange bed," she said, the pauses lengthening between words. "Patrick teased me about it. Told me it was just as well we raised cattle. He couldn't drag me off the ranch with log chains for more'n a night or two."

Her drunkard's smile and droopy eyelids would have been comical under other circumstances. She was pale, and lavender shadows pooled beneath her eyes, but an iron will is impervious to sedation.

Hannah wondered if Jack knew, or would admit, how much he resembled his mother. The similarities went beyond cornflower-blue eyes, a pug nose and stocky build. Patrick Clancy's contribution to and influence over his only child had undoubtedly shaped the man Jack had become, but his personality and grit were IdaClare personified.

The gunshot wound in her arm had bled profusely, but wasn't as serious as it had looked. Although the bullet had nicked bone as it passed through, it had missed severing an artery by a fraction of an inch.

The nurse told Hannah that IdaClare would almost certainly lose some mobility. Bullets don't drill neat holes. Torn muscles, tendons and nerves do heal, but like moth-eaten fabric, rents can only be mended, not restored to their original condition.

"Poor Itsy and Bitsy," she mumbled. "My babies must be worried sick about me."

Translation: She was worried sick about them.

"They're fine," Hannah said. "Marge picked them up at your cottage and took them home with her."

Volunteering to dog-sit the Furwads should put Marge on the shortlist for sainthood. She'd also offered to check on Malcolm. Assuring the Airedale-wildebeest that he hadn't been abandoned was a snap compared to caretaking a pair of yappy, psycho poodles—with or without their daily dose of Prozac.

IdaClare smacked her lips. "My purse...zinna drawer...may-be the cloz-zit." She heaved a deep sigh, said, "Car keys," then her head sank into the pillow.

Three more supported the fuchsia, fiberglass cast immobilizing her elbow and wrist. Gauze and elastic bandages swaddled her upper arm. The swollen, bloodstained fingers protruding from the cast's lower end brought tears to Hannah's eyes.

Residual fear, gratitude for the living and hatred for the man who'd killed or maimed seventeen innocent people and traumatized dozens more batted at her solar plexus. The shooting shouldn't have happened, she thought. Count your blessings—it could have been worse. You bastard, even if there is a hell, you got off too easy.

She stared out the smoked-glass windows. City lights glimmered in all directions. Traffic flowed along First Street. Neon signs glowed Christmas-bright. A beacon flashed in lazy revolutions atop the water tower emblazoned with Home of the Sanity Tigers.

Well, life did go on.

She didn't believe fate, Providence, predestination or a lottery system time- and date-stamped names drawn from a cosmic fishbowl. If such things existed, babies wouldn't die and pedophiles would top the to-be-smited list.

As the ever-pragmatic Delbert had said en route to the hospital, "There's just one absolute fact of life, ladybug. Nobody gets out of it alive."

The chair's metal feet glided across the linoleum as Hannah scooted away from the bed. She pulled a tissue from the box on the nightstand, gently wiped the drool from the corner of IdaClare's mouth, then kissed her cheek.

Combing back wayward strands of cotton-candy hair, she said, "Tomorrow, when that Irish temper of yours lets me have it for calling Jack, I can truthfully say I told you I intended to before I did it, and you didn't argue."

Convincing him that his mother's condition was stable before he dropped the phone, hopped in his Jaguar and zoomed westbound on I-44 at a hundred-plus miles an hour would be tricky.

Make that impossible. Hannah let the door snick shut behind her. Newton's third law of motion, that every action has an equal and opposite reaction, also applied to conversations prefaced by "Don't panic, but—"

The corridor's overhead lighting had been tamped to a somber, almost reproving dimness. Patient rooms exhaled fetid air, snatches of sitcom laugh tracks, snores and mewls of pain. Hannah shortened her stride, then tiptoed, but couldn't allay the *tick-tick* of leather-soled pumps on the mirror-waxed floor.

Her gaze averted from the nurses and aides cov-eyed around their station as though avoiding eye contact fostered stealth, she turned into the elevators' alcove...stopped...reversed herself.

A silver-haired man in a tailored dark suit pushed away from the desk. Head down, his shoulders hunched as if steeled for a third-and-one at the end zone, he made no effort to stifle his footfalls.

Ignoring the elevator's chime, Hannah said, "What are you— How did you—" then simply walked into his arms.

He held her so tight, she could scarcely breathe. Woodsy cologne filled her nostrils and his hair slid thick and soft through her fingers.

"God, you feel good," he said. "For a second I didn't believe it was really you."

"I've missed you, too. I just wish—" Her vocal cords seized.

David stood on the elevator's threshold, his hands flat against the door pockets. His expression couldn't have been colder, more menacing, if cast in bronze.

He walked toward them, his jaw working from side to side, his blue eyes locked on her brown ones. "Evenin', Ms. Garvey," he drawled. "Or should I say Mornin' considering the lateness of the hour."

Hannah stepped back. Fragmented thoughts skittered at warp speed. Gesturing "it's not what you think," she stammered nonsense in her own defense.

The secondary object of David's fury extended a hand. "Jack Clancy." He glanced at Hannah. "I'd guess by her 'oh, shit' look that you're Sheriff Hendrickson."

David shook on it. "Right on both counts."

"Helluva night you've had."

"Yep." An astonishing amount of venom leavened that one-syllable reply. "In more ways than one, sport."

Uh-oh. In the peculiar sphere of male vernacular,

*son of a bitch* often skated by with no umbrage taken. *Sport* did not. Ever.

Irate bulls snorted and pawed the ground. Jack Clancy snorted and rubbed the nape of his neck.

Cutting in on the testosterone titans, Hannah said, "I was just going downstairs to call you, Jack. How did you find out about the shooting?"

"A message was on the machine when I got home from the airport. Mother had—"

"What time was that?" David asked.

"Nine-thirty. Maybe a quarter of ten. I didn't—"

"Who left it?"

Hannah said, "Would you please give the man a chance to finish a sentence?"

Saying someone was "fit to be tied" was one of Great-uncle Mort's favorite phrases. What it meant he'd never explained, but David's seismic agitation seemed to exemplify it.

Jack said, "Mother had gallbladder surgery a few years ago and tried to keep it on the qt. She doesn't know it, but the hospital flagged her file to contact me immediately in the event of an emergency or an admission."

"She swore me to secrecy earlier," Hannah said. "Which I agreed to with my fingers crossed behind my back."

David chuckled. If there was any humor in the sound, it wasn't audible to the human ear.

"You can take the heat for me being here, then," Jack said. "I don't want her to know about the flags." He turned toward her room. "Give it to me straight, sweetpea. The nurses told me she'd be fine, the old 'resting comfortably' medi-speak.''

"She is. I wouldn't have left her alone if she wasn't. She lost some blood and her arm is in a cast, but the doctors only admitted her for observation.''

Hannah waited to let that sink in, then said, "She's also sedated. Big time. I don't think the Chicago Symphony playing 'The Star-Spangled Banner' at her bedside would rouse her.''

Jack grimaced. "Is she in that much pain?''

"No… She, uh—well, she voiced some objections to staying overnight.'' Hannah cleared her throat. "She informed several members of the medical community that she'd taken care of herself for sixty-seven years and had a private, perfectly lovely bedroom in Valhalla Springs that didn't cost twelve hundred bucks a night to sleep in.''

Even David had to laugh. "Sounds just like her.''

"Yeah, it does,'' Jack said. "The G-rated version, anyway.'' He sucked his teeth. "I'd better go in and see for myself and leave you two to…'' The hesitation intimated a warning to David. "Whatever.''

Hannah said, "I'll be right here if you need me.''

What sizzled between her and David was as sexual as the handrails bolted to the walls. A passing nurse did a double take, then focused on the medicine tray she carried.

"Since I already know the answer to us getting a cup of coffee,'' David said, "would you mind scooting over yonder so we can talk?''

"I don't think talking is a very good idea. We both have too much on our minds at the moment."

"I told Andrik I wouldn't be gone long, but I'm not going back to the Royal Dragon until we do."

"Fine. Have it your way." Her tone suggested he always did. Taking a stand between the elevators' cabs, she crossed her arms, her chin tipped defiantly. "Before you apologize for jumping to the wrong conclusion, have you heard anything about Sophonia's condition?"

"I asked downstairs when I came in. She made it through surgery okay, then they transferred her to the Critical Care Unit. Delbert's with her."

Hannah nodded. "Except he must be pretty close to collapsing himself."

"He said the same about you."

"I'm all right." Her stomach was so empty it hurt, her temples throbbed and she'd pay a hundred dollars for a cup of vending machine coffee.

David's thumbs hooked his belt. "No, you aren't all right. Neither am I."

In the alcove's harsh fluorescent glare, the mutton-chop stubble on his face looked villainous and endearing. Stress and exhaustion had deepened the marionette lines above his mouth and the creases at his brow.

Ye gods. This wasn't a bad time for a talk. It was the worst possible time.

"I told you a while back that I'm not the jealous type," he said. "At least I wasn't until the elevator doors opened a minute ago."

. Her foot tapped the floor, waiting for him to get on with the apology and be done with it.

"As far as jumping to conclusions, maybe I did—"
*Maybe?*

"But I've never seen Jack Clancy before. I can't help wondering how you'd feel if you caught me in a clinch with another woman."

Hannah bit the inside of her cheek to make herself, for once in her life, think before speaking. He was in the middle of a multiple-homicide investigation. His first wife had been unfaithful and gloated about her new lover's prowess before she left David. And it was true he'd hadn't met Jack—although he should have figured out who he was by virtue of IdaClare's hospital room across the hall.

He *had.* Somewhere between the elevator and "Evenin', Ms. Garvey," David had realized the man hugging her was Valhalla Springs' wealthy, witty, charming owner of whom he'd heard more about than he cared to. That's why he was as angry, if not more so, after Jack introduced himself.

In twenty words or less, Hannah could relieve that jealousy forever, but David either trusted her or he didn't. She was not the ex–Mrs. Hendrickson. She may have been labeled "a no-account Garvey bastard" the day she was born, but she'd be damned if she'd be millstoned by a slutty former wife's sins.

"Caught me?" she said. "You didn't *catch me* doing anything but comforting my oldest friend, who, after flying in from California, had the pleasure of hearing an answering-machine tape inform him that his mother had been shot, then driving hell-bent from Saint Louis.''

David flinched. "I didn't know who he was."

"Besides telling me you weren't the jealous type, you also said you'd never lie to me." Hannah's eyes narrowed. "You just did."

"Assumption isn't fact."

"Oh, really? That seems to depend on which of us is making the assumption."

David's lips curled over his teeth. His chest expanded and contracted as though he'd sprinted the distance from the restaurant. "I'm sorry. I was wrong. How about we start this conversa—"

Jack halted at the entrance to the alcove. He glanced from Hannah to David. "Uh, there's another bank of elevators at the far end of the hallway. I'll just meet you in the lobby."

"No." Hannah pressed the down button. The car's doors slid open. She looked David squarely in the eye. "I think we're finished here, Jack. Would you mind giving me a ride home?"

# 6

The Flour Shoppe was busier than usual for an early Wednesday morning. A few of the seniors dawdling over coffee and pastry had attended the Thomlinsons' party. Those who hadn't were eager for every gory detail.

They hadn't given two hoots about being left off the guest list and now were thankful they had been, yet were akin to *Titanic* passengers who'd missed the boat. Being a secondhand Rose to a disaster inflicted a strange sort of envy. Hannah supposed that was one reason "mixed" preceded "blessing" as often as not.

She stole into and out of the bakery with her order before anyone cornered her for her slant on the killing spree. Just as she pulled her Blazer away from the boardwalk, a minivan with *Sanity Examiner* painted on its doors cruised up Main Street, scouting for a parking space.

Chase Wingate, the county weekly's owner-editor, had been barred from the Royal Dragon by a Sanity P.D. roadblock last night. Hannah guessed the woman riding passenger and the men crammed shoulder to shoulder on the van's bench seat were out-of-town reporters and media stringers.

The entourage had surely stopped by her cottage. The advantage of a rottweiler licking his chops on her porch versus an Airedale-wildebeest whimpering an invitation to play Frisbee breached Hannah's emotional vault. Before other thoughts slithered through the cracks, she slammed the door and spun the lock wheel.

Bottling up pain wasn't healthy. The edict had become a mantra overheard in restaurant conversations and subway cars, repeated in magazine articles and on talk shows. Experts agreed that holding in the hurt was a self-destructive, even cowardly thing to do, but as options went, it was awfully damn popular.

For Hannah, it was a cross between habit and reflex. Her inner vault had opened wider to David than anyone she'd ever known. Old scabs had first been picked for shock value—to see how fast he'd run if he saw who she really was right down to the roots.

He wasn't shocked. He hadn't run.

No matter. What was done was done. The break in their relationship wasn't clean, but as necessary as it was inevitable. If David hadn't realized it already, he would soon enough.

Hannah turned off Valhalla Springs Boulevard at its intersection with Locust Street. The story-and-a-half row house–style condominiums on a shady knoll overlooking the golf course's back nine were reserved for visiting family members, friends and prospective tenants who wanted a taste of retirement-community living before the contracts were signed.

Clancy Construction and Development maintained

a permanent lease on the unit at the far end. Jack stayed there during infrequent overnight visits and encouraged business associates and investors to use it for getaway weekends.

Hannah slid from her truck, balancing a cardboard tray, and bumped the door shut with her butt. The extra-large cups of coffee and sackful of oven-warm bacon, cheese and tomato minicroissants smelled like ten pounds per thigh and worth every ounce.

Jack was waiting at the door. His blue oxford shirt and navy Dockers were slightly wrinkled from the emergency garment bag he kept in his trunk. He was barefoot and unshaven, his hair combed but damp from a shower.

Grinning, he took the tray from her hands. "If you'd gotten here fifteen minutes ago, you could have served me breakfast in bed."

"In your dreams, Clancy." In hers, too, once upon a time.

The condo's living room–dining room was furnished with floral chintz upholstered pieces, robust honey-pine end tables and brass lamps. Alcove bookshelves framed the gas-log fireplace. On the walls were large, wood-framed prints of the view from the patio as it changed from season to season.

"You're lucky I let you sleep in a while," Hannah said, eyeing the half-empty bottle of Irish whiskey on the counter.

Because a so-called "bartender's law" held liquor purveyors as liable as imbibers for their actions, the condo was as dry as a Baptist Sunday social. Jack had obviously packed more than a change of clothes and underpants in his overnight bag.

At no expressions of undying gratitude for her thoughtfulness, she said, "IdaClare called me for a ride home at six-thirty this morning."

Jack continued arranging croissants on a platter from the kitchenette's cabinet. "Did you tell her I was here?"

She shook her head. "We forgot to decide on a lie last night."

Another cabinet yielded ceramic mugs stamped with the development's slogan. Hannah's arm wasn't long enough to read her immortal spiel, but it pleased her to sort of see it.

"After IdaClare hung up, I called the nurses' station. She can't be dismissed until ten or after, depending on when the admitting doctor makes his rounds."

"Whew, boy." Jack rolled his eyes. "I'll bet she was dressed and sitting on the edge of the bed when she phoned you."

"I don't think so." Hannah's teeth scraped her lower lip as she recapped the paper coffee containers. "The dress she wore last night is ruined. On the way to the Flour Shoppe, I picked up the bag Marge packed for her."

His hands slid backward on the counter, then clamped the edge. "Her clothes. Jesus. She was in a hospital gown last night. I never thought about what she was wearing when—"

He stared toward the living room. A nerve twitched

at his temple. "I should have stayed with her last night. Shouldn't have left her alone."

"She was sedated, Jack. I could have stayed, too. She wouldn't have known either of us were there."

"She isn't your mother."

The sting was unintentional, but Hannah winced. "No, she isn't. Except sometimes I think I know her better than you do."

"Oh, yeah?" Anger shimmered like an aura.

"IdaClare is enormously proud and a tiny bit vain. Besides simply wanting to go home, she doesn't want anyone—especially you—seeing her in that tacky gown with her dentures on the nightstand, no makeup and porcupine hair."

He looked at Hannah. "She told you that?"

"She didn't have to, Jack. It's a woman thing and you confirmed it last night."

"I— What?"

"When you said she tried to sneak into and out of the hospital for gallbladder surgery. Sure, she didn't want to worry you, but mostly she didn't want you to see her at her post-op worst."

Jack mulled that over for a long moment. "You may have something there, sweetpea. I've wondered why she's never given me hell for bunking here when I visit instead of at her cottage."

His tone remained semi-unconvinced when he asked, "How did Mother sound when you talked to her?"

"A little groggy and weak but almost normal."

"Twelve hours after taking a bullet in the arm. Right."

"She did. Honest." Hannah rested her chin on his shoulder. "A crash course in doing everything left-handed will be a bitch. When the cast comes off, she'll need physical therapy and it'll be painful. But we both know she'll slap on a happy face for everyone's benefit, including her own. The mental-placebo effect."

She smiled. "I happen to believe that attitude is a leading cause of miraculous recoveries."

Jack chuckled. "No wonder she thinks you're the greatest thing since...well, me. You're the queen and princess of cockamamy notions."

"Hey, whatever works." Or appears to, if no one looks too closely.

They took their breakfast out to the patio. Jack went back for a kitchen towel to wipe the dew from the wrought-iron dinette's cushions.

After a deep slug of coffee and an appreciative sigh, he said, "When we get to the hospital, I want to stop by the extended care office and arrange for a live-in nurse until Mother's back on her feet."

Hannah devoured a whole croissant and half of another before he said, "What's wrong with that?"

"Nothing. It's very sweet of you."

He scowled. "Very sweet, huh? Next thing you'll tint your hair pink and buy a pair of poodles to match."

She laughed. "Pink isn't my color and you bought IdaClare the Furwads."

"Don't remind me."

"Want to hear her argument about the nurse in advance?" Ignoring his "not particularly" gesture, Hannah said, "She isn't an invalid and home health care is ridiculously expensive. She doesn't want a stranger snooping around her house, and Itsy and Bitsy would be beside themselves. Marge will stay as long as she's needed. And Doc Pennington is as near as the intercom's panic button."

"Hide and watch," Jack muttered around a mouthful of food. "I'll get something right before the day's over."

"Right idea, wrong patient. It's Sophonia Pugh who may need extended care when she's discharged. All the clerk I spoke with this morning would tell me is that her condition is guarded and she's breathing on her own."

"Whatever Ms. Pugh needs she's got." He sat back in the chair and propped an ankle on his knee. A corner of his mouth tucked upward. "I can't believe we're even having this conversation."

Neither could she. Robins mined for worms in the dew-frosty grass. The air's nip was thickening to a sultry haze. It was a beautiful morning, but "the closest thing to paradise" suddenly seemed like a vicious parody.

"I forced you to go to that party," Jack said, his expression grim. "For appearance's sake."

"Coerced, maybe. I could have told you to go screw yourself." God knows she'd thought it enough times during and after Monday's call. "I could also have gone AWOL last night."

"Much as you disliked Eulilly and were furious with me for pressuring you, I thought you would skip out."

Hannah shrugged. "I'm a good soldier."

"I should have been there. If anything had happened to you—"

She traced the rim of the coffee mug with her fingertip. "First Delbert, now you. Survivor's guilt, I understand. I feel it, too, but nothing compared to what Chet Thomlinson and the Chau family—especially Johnny—must be feeling."

If he was listening, there was no outward indication of it.

"Hindsighted what-ifs are a waste of time, Jack. It won't change yesterday and has no effect on today, tomorrow or a week from now."

His eyes slid to meet hers and held them. "What's done is done, eh? Phase two of the Garvey family motto."

She looked away. Playing visual chicken with someone who knows you too well isn't wise. She set her cup at the center of her plate, then stacked it on the platter. "We'd better head for the hospital. I'll follow you in my truck. I want to sit with Sophonia for a while."

"You were hoping for an out and Hendrickson gave you one, didn't he?"

The patio door's screen yipped in its track. Hannah stalked to the kitchen and laid the dishes in the sink.

She'd bought breakfast. If Jack was so eager to clean up after her, he could start here.

She stiffened when he laid his hands on her shoulders. Resisted when he turned her around. He cradled her face, his thumbs caressing her cheekbones. "David Hendrickson is a good man, sweetpea. He's in love with you. He deserves to be told about us. About me. If you won't, I will."

"Damn it."

The telephone receiver hammered the cradle. David glowered at the nicotine-stained ceiling and cloudlike remnants of water leaks from the building's second floor.

There was no answer at Hannah's or at IdaClare's cottage. Jet-set Jack Clancy had hauled himself out of bed mighty early for a fella who'd been dead-dog tired less than eight hours ago.

David envisioned Hannah's understanding, dependable, true-blue good buddy's triumphant smirk at her letting the machine screen her calls. David trusted her, but operators didn't come any smoother than Clancy and he did love Hannah. It was as easy to see as her love for him.

So, why hadn't they acted on those feelings? Or had they and it hadn't worked out? Maybe he only wanted Hannah when she was involved with someone else. David knew the type. Challenge junkies. They played for ego strokes not for keeps.

Hannah had burned her bridges in Chicago without severing her ties to Clancy. He'd fortified that bond by giving her a job and a home. IdaClare was like a second mother to her, and the other gumshoes, a second family.

David jerked up the receiver. A forefinger stabbed the keypad.

"Will you chill out," Marlin said. "Christ on a chariot, man. Don't you know anything about women?"

David hadn't divulged any details of last night's argument, but Andrik had known the minute David walked into the Detective Division's headquarters that something besides a homicide investigation was chapping his disposition.

Personal problems aside, Marlin's office was enough to make Chuckles the Clown tetchy. Dubbed the Outhouse, the dank storefront space on the west side of the square had been leased by the county commission after a bond issue to finance a new sheriff's department and jail tanked by a wider margin than the preceding six.

Separating the investigative branch from the departmental offices, dispatch and jail on the courthouse's third floor was dangerous at worst and inconvenient at best, but the commissioners smiled pretty for Chase Wingate's camera at the ribbon-cutting ceremony. And they'd be grinning like rats in a cheese factory next summer at the new bond-approved, semi-pro baseball stadium's grand opening.

David hung up the phone, his death-ray glare leveled at the bridge of Andrik's crooked nose. "Since when are you an expert on women?"

"I'm not. Women aren't even experts on women, but with a wife, a teenage daughter and three sisters, I'm closer to one than you are, pard."

The detective cocked back in his chair and winged his elbows. "Instead of getting bent out of shape when a woman lays the silent treatment on you, enjoy it while you can, 'cause it won't last long. If Beth's torqued at me, I'm lucky to squeeze out a couple of hours of peace and quiet before she starts the slice 'n dice."

Cynthia Hendrickson's silences had extended just long enough to strop her tongue on her teeth. Over the years, David had said plenty of things he hadn't meant, but not Cynthia. Angry or otherwise, her every word was gospel.

He strode over to the Bunn-O-Matic rusted to a cast-off utility cart. When fresh, Marlin's coffee tasted like forty-weight Havoline, then gradually congealed to the consistency of axle grease.

David filled a foam cup, thinking he should have checked his temper at the elevator door last night. If he'd listened when Hannah told him it was a bad time to talk, she wouldn't have said, "I think we're finished here," and taken off with Clancy.

Finished? Not hardly. But whether she was ducking calls or away from her cottage, the telephone was a lousy mediator. They needed a face-to-face.

Coffee splashed out the lip of the carafe. Drops hissing on the burner plate sounded amused, mocking. *Go for it, Sheriff. Dump the investigation in Andrik's lap, track the lady down and patch things up between you. No sweat. Women dearly love that alpha-male shit, don't they?*

The legs of the molded plastic lawn chair on the visitor's side of the detective's desk toed out when David slumped into it. He raised the cup to his mouth and blew across it.

"Ready for the preliminaries?" Marlin asked.

"Whenever you are."

An accordion file at his elbow held copies of his, Cletus Orr's and Josh Phelp's field notes, incident reports and witness statements. Andrik didn't have a photographic memory, but wouldn't refer to the paperwork during the briefing. Anniversaries and grocery lists were forgotten as fast as the next man, but case particulars stuck in Marlin's mind like cockleburs.

He shook a cigarette from the pack on this desk and fumbled in his shirt pocket for a lighter. Smoking was prohibited by law in governmental offices. Flouting the regulation gave Marlin a bigger high than a nicotine hit ever would.

"Top of the heap is, our Mr. Bogart is getting more interesting all the time."

"How so?"

"Courtney Sorenson, the Royal Dragon's main hostess, says Bogart had the hots for Jasmine Chau. Kept asking her out and wouldn't take no for an answer. He started making passes, sneaking feels—Mr. Suave with da boner.

"Courtney advised her to tell Johnny about it, but Jasmine refused. Said she could handle Bogart, and

Johnny beating him up for hitting on her wouldn't solve anything.''

David nodded. Jasmine adored her brother, but Johnny's overprotectiveness drove her to distraction. All the Chau kids were as Americanized as Opie Taylor, but cultural double standards didn't disappear in a single generation.

''Jasmine thought Bogart had given up,'' Marlin went on, ''then Monday afternoon, he trapped her in a walk-in cooler and assaulted her. She kneed him in the nuts and went straight to Daddy. Bogart told Papa Chau she was lying, that Jasmine had come on to him.''

David said, ''Mr. Chau fired Bogart on the spot, right? Probably told him he'd have him arrested if he saw him within five miles of his daughter.''

''That was the gist of the English part.'' Marlin tapped the Marlboro on the edge of the terra-cotta plant saucer he used for an ashtray. ''I expect what Mr. Chau said in Vietnamese didn't need an interpreter, either.''

Speculation leapfrogged facts. David didn't like how the dots were connecting. ''Bogart didn't go quietly.''

''Oh no. The usual 'I'll get you for this.' Like he was the CEO of General Motors and Jasmine had snipped the strings to his golden parachute.''

David focused on a warped seam in the cheap walnut paneling. Last night, Jimmy Wayne McBride had surfed the Internet and printed out background information on workplace massacres. The episodes he'd culled made a frightening overview.

Florida, 1990: four wounded and eleven dead, including the shooter who'd turned his gun on himself.

Long Island, 1993: a passenger aboard a commuter train killed six and wounded nineteen.

Atlanta, 1999: the shooter bludgeoned his wife and two children to death, then killed nine and wounded twelve at a day-trading office before killing himself.

Illinois, 2001: the Navistar International plant in Quincy; four dead, four injured.

The profile Jimmy Wayne had highlighted said a perpetrator's objective was to punish those he held responsible for his failures. Revenge killers were loners, mid-thirties to early fifties, but a few profit-motivated multiple homicides had been committed by teenagers to cover for an armed robbery.

Although single-victim killers were evenly divided between blacks and whites, seventy percent of mass murderers were Caucasion.

Deke Bogart was a young African-American male. Thirty percent wasn't a minuscule slice of the demographic pie, but a buzzer sounded when perps tipped the left side of the scale, especially in a county with a far smaller minority population.

What bothered David was that massacres weren't as random as the public wanted to believe. Shooters didn't just snap. The acts weren't spontaneous. As a general rule, people didn't buy assault rifles and warehouse ammunition on a whim, then suddenly go postal.

"Do you think Jasmine was Bogart's primary target?" David asked. "And Eulilly was collateral?"

"That's how it looks. Shooters with specific targets are about equal to shooters that bust in and mow down everyone in sight."

"Any wants or warrants on Bogart?"

"Not on the name." The detective's pauses for dramatic effect normally didn't annoy David. An investigator of Andrik's caliber was allowed a few quirks—except on mornings when the sky wasn't blue enough to suit his superior officer.

David's tongue probed a molar. Marlin got the hint.

"The sosh number Bogart gave the Chaus was bogus," he said. "It's registered to a six-year-old female in Alexandria, Virginia."

"Any relation?"

"The kid's Pakistani. Her parents have applied for permanent residency status, but she and a younger sibling were born here."

"No match on Bogart's prints, either," David said, answering his own unspoken question. "He wasn't very old, though. Twenty, maybe twenty-two at the outside."

Marlin agreed. "If he had a juvenile record, it's sealed and he's managed not to get himself arrested in the meantime."

"Saw the light, huh?" David snorted. "Rehabilitated choirboys don't use fake social security numbers, probable aliases, and travel with TEC–9s and automatic pistols."

"It follows that Bogart was on the run for reasons

unknown," Marlin said, "but we don't know if he packed the weapons along or bought them locally. He could have spent the rest of Monday working up a hate-on for Jasmine and how he'd make his 'get even' fantasy come true."

David knew documented evidence of copycat shootings did exist. In less than a month during the fall of 1991, thirty-nine people died in five mass killings in five different states.

A year later, some moron published what he called a satire on workplace massacres. The book read like a how-to manual for the homicidally inclined.

He said, "How long will it take to trace the serial number on Bogart's Beretta?"

Marlin took a deep drag on his cigarette and stubbed it out. A chuckle spasmed into a dry hack. "It's in the system, boss." Cop-speak for "The check is in the mail."

David slam-dunked the coffee cup into the trash can and shoved up from the chair. "This is coming together like a modern version of an old, pulp-Western novel. A stranger rides into town on a bus. Maintains a low profile while he's here. He's either armed to the teeth from the start, or buys, possibly steals, an arsenal to wreak revenge on the woman who spurned him, then gets in a draw-down shoot-out with a civilian who's got more balls than brains. Justice is served. The end."

The phone interrupted Marlin's reply. He snarled "Yo, Andrik," then looked at David and mouthed "Cletus."

The department's number two investigator had been sent to the medical examiner's office in Columbia to witness the autopsies. Cletus Orr was a competent detective with four years' service ahead of him before he'd retire with a full pension and benefits, but he lacked Marlin's bloodhound mentality.

If Andrik ever figured out how to clone himself, he could attend postmortems and head up investigations simultaneously. David had offered his services, but the gruesome grunt jobs were almost always Cletus's domain.

Josh Phelps was searching Bogart's rented room above EZ Tax Service and Accounting on the backside of the square. He'd then interview Bogart's landlord, neighbors—anyone who might have come in contact with the shooter.

Contrary to shows on TV, fieldwork was as tedious and methodical as disassembling a spiderweb from the outside in. It was apt to be repeated as new evidence was confirmed and contradicted which puzzle pieces fit and which didn't.

The Outhouse's matted, avocado shag carpeting stuck to David's boot soles as he paced the room. State-of-the-art videocameras donated by Jessup Knox's security firm whirred on their brackets. Good ol' Elvis. He was as adept at lying as he was at disguising influence peddling as civic-mindedness.

A legal pad slapped Marlin's desk blotter. "Describe it," he said into the phone. "Uh-huh. Uh-huh." His pencil sketched across the paper. "I want digital photos of that and all other physicals e-mailed

ASAP. Scars, freckles on his butt—anything we can use to ID the dirtbag.''

David halted in midstep and looked at Marlin, then the tablet. He couldn't make out the doodle or the writing, but hovering over the detective's shoulder brought out his surly side. Instead, David turned on hid heel and retook his seat.

Marlin scribbled notes, punctuating the one-sided conversation with throat noises. ''Keep me posted and tell the Troll how grateful I'd be if he got off his ass and had some preliminary results before Thanksgiving.''

David rolled his eyes at Marlin's nickname for the state's assistant medical examiner. The detective had one for virtually everyone he encountered with any frequency. Hannah's aka was ''Toots,'' David's secretary, Heather was the ''Guppy,'' due to her round-eyed airheadedness, and Judge Cranston Messerschmidt was the ''Fuhrer.''

David's alias had been the ''Monk'' until Hannah's arrival inspired a revision. To what, Marlin wouldn't say and David had given up asking. There were some things a man was better off not knowing.

Andrik cradled the receiver and fired up another cigarette. As he exhaled smoke at the ceiling, his eyes jittered in their sockets as though the water stains were tea leaves.

''Interesting,'' he muttered, then picked up the legal pad and held it out to David. ''One of the Troll's flunkies found this tattoo on Bogart's chest when he prepped him.''

The sketch was a bastardized Star of David. A three-pronged pitchfork angled from the base of the upper point. Short lines like legs projected above the lower one. At the center of the star were the initials B.D.

"Unless they've changed their symbols since I left Tulsa," David said, "this is a Black Gangster Disciples' flag."

"The Troll will go over Bogart's corpse with a magnifying glass, but Cletus says the drone also has a scar from a gunshot wound on his thigh."

"Left or right?"

"Right."

David whistled backward through his teeth. Street gangs traditionally belonged to one of two alliances, the People and the Folks. The People and their subsets displayed identifiers on the left thigh. Folks members, of which the Black Gangster Disciples were affiliated, represented themselves with right-side tags.

Bogart's scar could be the result of a gang war, an altercation with the police, or the punk could have accidentally shot himself. A single shot to the right thigh, aka "catching a V" was also a punishment meted out by gang leaders to members who violated the code of conduct.

"The People and Folks were established in the 1980s inside the Illinois prison system." David pushed the tablet across the desk. "Hybrids, renegades and wannabes have spread everywhere like a cancer, but what the hell's a Black Gangster Disciple doing here—alone—in Kinderhook County?"

''A working vacation from the mean streets of where-the-fuck-ever?'' Marlin suggested. He flipped to the next page of notes but didn't consult them. ''Orr also said Hampton Bethune, Eulilly Thomlinson's brother, called the M.E.'s office a while ago. He wanted to know how soon his sister's body would be released for burial.''

''Did Cletus talk to him?''

''He was taking a leak when the call came in, but a clerk logged Bethune's number. Seems he's the top banana at Bethune Enterprises, the family's money tree. Alas, the corporate jet is down for maintenance, but a friend offered to send his plane to Columbia to fly Eulilly's body home.''

Something in Marlin's voice galvanized David's nerve endings. ''Who's the friend?''

Marlin's face was never more inscrutable than when unforeseen tangents cropped up in an investigation. He tossed up his pencil and snagged it in mid-air. ''None other than Toots's boss and IdaClare's bouncing baby boy. Jack Clancy.''

# 7

The nurse's aide behind the desk looked about twelve years old. Six studs pierced each ear and her lips formed a natural pout.

Jack asked, "Has Mrs. IdaClare Clancy been discharged yet?"

"We can't give that information to anybody except, like, immediate family members."

"Is her son, like, *immediate enough* for you?"

Hannah started. Jack's ability to charm the uncharmable was a point of pride. Itsy and Bitsy were the only exceptions she was aware of.

The aide said, "I should've known you were related," and knuckled a hip. "The doctor's with her and it'll be a while before he gets loose. Your mother has hit the call bell to complain about a hundred times since I came on shift."

"Why, you little—"

Hannah laid a restraining hand on Jack's arm and set IdaClare's overnight bag on the counter. "Complain?" she repeated. "About what?"

Assuming an ally had presented itself, the girl warbled, "Her room was too cold. Then it was too hot. She wanted coffee not tea. How could she butter toast with, like, one hand? She couldn't reach the phone. She wanted the door closed and the drapes open.'' Her eyes did a martyr's roll. ''Gawd, you'd think this was, like, a hotel or something.''

Hannah gave her a saccharine smile. ''Are you aware of why Mrs. Clancy was admitted last night?''

''She broke her arm,'' the aide answered as though responding to an oral pop quiz. ''Probably fell down somewhere.'' With a toss of her head, she added, ''Old folks are worse'n kids about falling over their own two feet.''

Jack was on the brink of a nuclear explosion. Hannah tightened her grip on his arm. Her voice low, distinct and sinister, she said, ''Mrs. Clancy was one of the people shot at the Royal Dragon last night, hence the cast on her arm.

''Neither she, her son, nor I expect special treatment, but I don't think showing her some respect, making her comfortable and helping her eat the first food she's had since lunch yesterday is beyond the call of duty.''

''No, it certainly is not.'' An R.N. with the bone structure of the Madonna and the demeanor of a convent's Mother Superior emerged from an anteroom behind the desk.

The aide whipped around and the back of her shagged, purplish-henna hairdo seemed to pale six shades lighter. ''Mrs. Levin—I— Oh gawd, I like didn't know you were in there.''

''I'm everywhere, Janey. All the time.''

The nurse balled a paper towel and lofted it toward

an unseen trash can—a symbolic gesture anyone with an IQ larger than her shoe size could comprehend. "After you apologize to Mr. and Mrs. Clancy, you and I will take our patient's bag to her room and help her dress to go home."

"Yes, Mrs. Levin." The aide turned and did as she was told. "There's a room down that way with chairs and a TV and stuff and I'll come and tell you when Mrs. Clancy is ready, so you can bring the car around to the front door, so she won't have to wait."

The speech didn't mollify Jack much. Hannah nodded a thank-you at the girl, then smiled at Nurse Levin. "One thing, though. I'm Hannah Garvey, a friend of the family, not Mrs. Clancy's daughter-in-law."

Her smile broadened to a grin. "IdaClare is expecting me, but doesn't know Jack is here. Springing him and a wife on her might cause a relapse." She arched an eyebrow at Janey. "We wouldn't want that to happen, now, would we?"

The aide said, "Oh no, ma'am. I won't tell her a thing, I promise."

Hannah tucked her arm in Jack's and led him down the corridor, ignoring expletives regarding the state of the nation's health care system—Mercy Hospital's specifically. She'd seen him in every mood imaginable, but his warp-speed ping-pong from one to another had begun with Monday's phone call.

Great-uncle Mort would tell her that Jack had more on his plate than he could say grace over, which was true. She wasn't the Mount Everest of emotional stability herself, but only another woman would understand the significance of a meticulous, *GQ* kind of guy forgetting he hadn't shaved, then forgetting to zip his fly before he exited the bathroom.

A delicate floral scent wafted from the waiting room before they entered it. On a side table was a chinoiserie vase bursting with two dozen blush-pink roses. Sunshine backlit a man seated in front of the window, reducing him to a featureless silhouette.

Jack stopped short. His elbow caught Hannah in the ribs.

Chet Thomlinson rose from a chair and extended a hand. His black silk shirt, black blazer and muted tweed slacks were fashionable and better fitting than the drab suit he'd worn to the banquet. His eyes were pouched and his shoulders sloped as if anvils rested on them, but his expression was tranquil.

Or tranquilized, Hannah thought. The Caldwells had driven Chet home from the restaurant. It was a good bet they'd summoned Doc Pennington to dispense something to help Chet sleep and a few extras to take as needed.

She'd felt guilty when she'd wakened refreshed after a dreamless night's rest. Mental and physical exhaustion induced insomnia more often than it did a comalike stupor.

"I had no idea that IdaClare would be discharged so soon," Chet said. He waved at the roses. "I thought flowers in her favorite color might cheer her up."

"That was very kind of you," Hannah said.

"She'll enjoy them even more at home." Stepping closer, she said, "I'm so sorry about Eulilly. If there's anything I can do, please let me know."

Chet bowed his head. "Thank you. I, uh, guess it hasn't hit me yet, that she's gone." He looked up, his gaze shifting from her to Jack. "You'd think it would, wouldn't you? The way it happened and all."

Jack found his voice. "Better if it never does. A little at a time, maybe, but not at once."

Chet nodded and sat down, motioning for them to join him. He braced his arms on his knees, a posture reminiscent of the last time Hannah had seen him.

To Jack, he said, "I appreciate you loaning your jet for Eulilly more than I can say. The thought of her being in a commercial flight's cargo bay— Well, I couldn't handle that. Can't handle it either way, to be honest with you."

His cheeks bellowed with a sigh. "Her brothers are taking care of the arrangements. It'll be trial enough flying down for her funeral by myself."

"If you don't mind driving to Saint Louis, you're welcome to go with me," Jack said. "The plane seats twelve, if you know of others who'd like to attend."

Hannah teetered between sympathy and surprise at the two men's acquaintanceship. Then again, death forged instant bonds between strangers. Grief was the one emotion with which almost everyone identified.

Chet scrutinized the loop-pile carpeting. The silence was as oppressive as the solar heat streaming through the windows and the flowers' perfume. He steepled his fingers, the diamond-shaped hub flexing to an oval. "Eulilly was the smartest, strongest woman I ever met. By all rights she should have been running Bethune Enterprises, not Hampton and Clay. Would have, too, if her mama had outlived her daddy.

"She changed when her brothers took over. Like she had a grudge against the world. Moving here was supposed to help. Put some distance between her and her brothers. It didn't. Homesickness piled on top of everything else."

He sat back. "This isn't the time or place to mention it, Clancy, but I'm so frazzled, I'd better while it's on my mind."

Jack aimed a sidelong look at Hannah. "I think I know what it concerns and you're right. This isn't the time or place."

"If you gentlemen will excuse me," she said, "I saw a water fountain down the hall."

Chet protested, "No, don't leave. I trust you'll keep this confidential, and I suspect Jack already knew Eulilly was soliciting proxies from Bethune's minority stockholders to swing the board's vote against his resort project."

"I heard rumors." Jack fidgeted in his chair. "Unconfirmed rumors."

"I can't say whether she'd have gone through with it," Chet said. "In my heart, I believe seeing Hampton, Clay and you sweat until the last minute would have been enough. I'm just giving confirmation—" he smiled at Hannah "—with a witness present, that, as her beneficiary, I'll vote her shares and the proxies in your favor."

Jack didn't move, didn't speak for a long moment. Then he rose to his feet, said, "We never had this conversation, Thomlinson," and stormed from the room.

After two hours, the beeps, clacks and wheezes from the machinery surrounding Sophonia Pugh's bed had faded to white noise. Pinch-pleated sheers diffused the light and the hospital's monolithic climate-control plant cycling a few yards outside the window.

What did patients occupying the Critical Care Unit need with trees and landscaping? Hannah mused as she chomped the end of a bendy straw. Perhaps graduation to a room with a view was an incentive for recovery. Kind of like schools that remanded special-ed classes to the basement.

The mattress angled Sophonia's bandaged torso upward. Glycerin swabs had left a gummy residue around her cracked lips. Tubes and wires coiled on the bedsheet and snaked below the hem. Her skin was paper-thin and weathered, yet so translucent that she resembled a thousand-year-old child.

She'd swum into consciousness several times since Hannah curled up in the cushioned chair beside the bed. The twinkle in Sophonia's eyes wasn't an illusion. Hannah believed she was more alert than she appeared and wise enough to conserve her strength.

Once she'd said, "Where's...Delbert? He promised he'd visit...today."

"He will. He insisted I drive him home in his Edsel

last night, so he didn't have to bum a ride back this morning.''

"Stubborn ol' coot.''

Hannah laughed, but Sophonia had dozed off again.

*Cautiously optimistic* was absent from the head nurse's vocabulary. Allen Fogelsong stressed that Sophonia's recovery depended on the type of complications that could arise. Secondary infections, pneumonia, renal failure, heart failure, stroke—the possibilities were as dire as they were extensive.

Fogelsong was amazed that Sophonia had celebrated eighty birthdays without a broken bone, surgery or an illness requiring hospitalization and still had most of the teeth she was born with. But her advanced age was "a negative wellness factor.''

Hard as it was to hear, Hannah appreciated the nurse's candor, especially now that she was old enough to recognize it. Oh, how she'd hated the doctors who said her mother's rallies didn't herald a cure. Hope had dwindled to angry desperation when Caroline's newfound strength evaporated.

"You were doing so much better,'' Hannah had told her. "Now you're not even *trying* to get well. Please, Mama. You've got to eat. C'mon, just a bite or two. For me?''

The memory was as fresh as yesterday and as distant as a past life. Misgivings about the hospital's smells, sounds and sights sucking her backward to Effindale's indigents ward were unfounded. She'd buried Caroline Angelina Garvey twenty-five years ago, but hadn't laid her to rest until last Saturday.

Rhythmic thumps and a gasp from the doorway intruded on her thoughts. Sophonia's eyelids twitched. A monitor's LED spiked electronic mountains and foothills.

Jefferson Davis Oglethorpe, the county's hereditary kingpin and perennially losing Democratic candidate for sheriff, stood in the doorway. One liver-spotted hand gripped a hickory cane. The other held a straw boater over his heart.

Oglethorpe's grandfather had led a wagon train from Tennessee to Missouri and founded Sanity in 1842. The span of a generation attached the family name to hundreds of acres of land, including the parcel where Valhalla Springs was now located.

The eccentric bachelor was the last of the line. Thinning white hair brushed his shoulders and his goatee was trimmed to a dagger tip. His suit contradicted the dictum that seersucker shouldn't be worn by anyone other than small-town Southern attorneys in active practice.

He scuffled closer to the bed, as though his ankles were shackled and chained. Rheumy eyes traveled the length of Sophonia's inert form, then searched her face. His voice failed when he whispered her name.

"Don't get your hopes up, Jedo," Sophonia said, her tongue sculpting the consonants. "I'm not dead yet. Don't plan to be anytime soon."

Oglethorpe recoiled as if he'd been slapped. Or bitten. His cheeks pinked with indignation. "Sources informed me that your demise was imminent. There are no words with which to express my utter desolation that the reports were in error.''

Hannah's gaze swung from one to the other. Mutual animosity arced between them like supercharged ions. What was going on? Not five seconds ago Oglethorpe had been so grief stricken he could barely speak. Then he tells Sophonia he's sorry she isn't dead yet?

''If it's the last thing...I do,'' Sophonia said, ''I'll dance on your grave.''

''Out of respect for Ms. Garvey, I'll not divulge what *I* shall do on *yours*. It isn't proper for a gentleman to mention such indelicacies in the presence of a lady.''

''Oh?'' Sophonia inhaled oxygen from the tube under her nose. ''Then what's stopping *you?*''

He raised his cane and shook it at her. ''Jezebel.''

''Pusilanimous...scalawag.''

Oglethorpe hissed through his teeth, then turned on his heel. His expression was rigid, his eyes misty. ''Good day, my dear,'' he said to Hannah. ''It's always a pleasure to see you.'' He exited the room with a spring in his step.

Allen Fogelsong hastened in, pulling a stethoscope from his lab coat's pocket. Monitor displays were checked along with Sophonia's pulse and respiration.

''Ms. Pugh?'' he said.

''Umm?''

''Are you in any pain?''

''No.'' A bony finger raised and quavered at the doorway. ''It went...thataway.''

Humor was not the nurse's strong suit. "We got elevated blood pressure and fibrillation readings at the desk," he explained to Hannah.

"Has she stabilized?"

"Not quite, but they readings are leveling off." He glanced toward the corridor, then took a double take. "Good grief. *Another* one?"

Delbert stopped short in the doorway. Dressed in a rainbow-striped shirt, bolo tie, madras slacks, ancient huaraches and golf socks, he was the room's undisputed bright spot. "Another what?"

"Only one visitor is allowed at a time." Fogelsong's tone promised a reduction to zero if Sophonia's vital signs tripped the alarms again.

Hannah discarded the mangled bendy straw. Retrieving her shoulder bag, she motioned for Delbert to join her in the hall.

"Is Sophonia getting worse, ladybug?"

"I wouldn't say that." Nor would she mention Oglethorpe's visit. The switch from anguish to gallant slander was as baffling as Sophonia's bared-fang flirtation. Delbert would not take it in stride.

"The monitor at the nurses' station recorded an irregular heartbeat," Hannah said. "I don't think it's anything serious."

Not the spike itself. Hannah would bet a million bucks that Jedo was fibrillating, too. Where was all this passion coming from? What had happened to these two? Ferreting out the cause was precisely the diversion Hannah needed. After all, when your own life is spinning out of control, you might as well muck around in someone else's.

"Before I forget—" Delbert took a sheet of notepaper from his shirt pocket. "IdaClare wants you to pick up this stuff on the way home. Jack is taking the poodles to their shampoo and pedicure appointment, but she says he doesn't know cold cream from silver cream."

The list was printed in block letters large enough to read without squinting. Three yards of pink sailcloth, piping and thread for slings, peanut clusters, the cold cream, Metamucil, Gummi Bears for the Furwads, whiskey-sour mix, a jar of maraschino cherries, a lap tray, left-handed scissors and a bottle of extra-strength Excedrin for Marge.

Hannah chuckled. IdaClare was on the mend. Jack hauling Itsy and Bitsy to the canine beauty parlor was splendid retribution for his rudeness to Chet Thomlinson but the reason behind it was another puzzle in need of a solution.

Delbert said, "And Detective Andrik is waiting for you in the lobby."

"He is?" Her pulse rate would have outpaced Sophonia's by a furlong. If David sent Marlin to negotiate a peace treaty, she'd— She'd— Well, hell. Retribution was hers and it wouldn't be pretty. "Did Marlin say why he wants to talk to me?"

Delbert stooped to retrieve the paper Hannah didn't realize she'd dropped. "I'm just the messenger, but I figure he wants to ask some more questions about the shooting."

There was that, but... "Did he ask you anything?"

Delbert shook his head. "I asked him a couple, but the son of a gun's as closemouthed as a turnip." One caterpillar eyebrow dipped and rumpled. "Is there something going on that I don't know about?"

An involuntary shudder ricked down her spine, a foreboding she felt she was central to and yet disconnected from. Like the blue chip in a kaleidoscope.

*Exactly* like it, in fact.

When she was in the fourth grade, her teacher announced a dollar gift exchange would be held the afternoon school dismissed for Christmas vacation. Girls were to bring presents for girls and the boys for boys.

Scrounging under furniture and the bottom of Caroline's purse had netted Hannah a quarter, three nickels, a dime and six pennies. She rationalized that the empty pop bottles she took from neighbors' back porches and the filling station's wire rack wasn't stealing, because she'd spend the deposit money on a gift, not on herself.

She meandered through S.S. Kresge's plank-floored aisles, a bunny-eared hankie bulging with coins in her coat pocket, teetering between Ebeneezer Scrooge and Santa Claus. Finding a present that looked expensive but didn't cost a whole dollar grappled with dreams of buying everything in the store.

She imagined doling out gifts from a big, bottomless sack to every classmate, her teacher and the cafeteria lady who never sent Hannah to the rest room to wash her hands a second time, and didn't use a butter knife to level scoops of mashed potatoes or pudding when Hannah's tray passed by.

Come Christmas morning, she'd give her mother, Granny Garvey, Great-aunt Lurleen and Great-uncle Mort five—no, ten—presents apiece, and they'd all hug her and tell her she was the best little girl in the world.

Then the kaleidoscope sitting on a reachable shelf caught Hannah's eye and her fancy. With each twist, its orange, red, yellow, green and purple bits orbited like bright stars around a sapphire-blue sun.

The price was right. Even prissy ol' Brenda Frake who had Mary Janes to match every dress would marvel at the magic disguised as a simple cardboard tube. Or would have, if Hannah hadn't hidden the kaleidoscope under the sofa cushions and faked a stomachache the day of the party.

That night, Caroline's latest fat slob of a boyfriend flopped on the couch to watch TV. The tortured kaleidoscope split, its jewel-like bits spilling from the seams. Hannah tried taping it together, but the magic had leaked out.

The sapphire-blue stone—the axis the others revolved around—was saved in a Roi Tan cigar box to remind Hannah that the Seventh and Ninth Commandments were laws not suggestions.

Hannah folded IdaClare's list and put it in her purse. How arrogant and silly it was to feel as if she were caught up in a multi-faceted kaleidoscope she couldn't quite bring into focus.

Taking a deep breath, she smiled at Delbert. "I

guess I'll go see what Andrik wants. Happy-go-lucky guys like him don't appreciate being kept waiting.''

Delbert watched Hannah stroll down the corridor to the elevators. By cracky, he knew a shuck-and-jive routine when he heard it, and being female, she wasn't worth a damn at it.

He peeked into Sophonia's room. The male nurse was hanging a fresh pouch of God-knew-what on the IV tree. A second look down the hall confirmed that Hannah was in no hurry to meet with Detective Andrik downstairs.

The phone at the nurses' station rang unattended. Winking red buttons beneath the keypad indicated three additional calls on hold. Delbert scurried around the counter, slipped a lab coat off the back of a swivel chair and folded it over his arm.

The staff elevators were situated diagonally across from the desk. He pushed the down button, sweated buckets until the indicator lit two floors above him, then whipped on the coat. Not a second too soon, he saw a photo ID clipped to the lapel. Jerking it loose, he crammed it in the pocket.

His heart was pounding so loud he didn't hear the elevator's *ding*. The doors rolled open. Two nurse's aides holding thermal lunch boxes gave him the once-over.

''Morning, ladies,'' he croaked.

The blonde said, ''Hi!'' and sidestepped to give him more room. The frowny one with scraggly, Martian-colored hair narrowed her eyes. ''If you're, like, you know, a doctor, how come I've never seen you before?"

Delbert cleared his pancreas from his throat and stepped into the car. "I'm a forensics expert. From Sheboygan. The sheriff called me in for consultation on the Royal Dragon case." He tapped a finger against his lips. "Very hush-hush."

The Martian harrumphed. The blonde asked, "Which floor do you need, Doctor?"

"Well, to be honest, I'm not sure. What's the quickest way to the visitors' lot on the south side?" He plastered on a grin. "That's where I parked my Mazeratti."

The blonde thumbed the basement button, which was already aglow. The car, and Delbert's stomach along with it, dropped at twice the speed of the visitors' elevators.

"You're in luck," Blondie said. "There's a maintenance exit on that side and it's on our way to the lunchroom. Isn't it, Janey?"

The Martian popped a gum bubble with her teeth. "No."

The doors opened onto a dirty-beige painted hallway. Delbert gestured "ladies first," then said, "I know you girls are on a break. Just point me at the exit and I'll take it from there."

He started at a walk, accelerating to a jog when the aides rounded a corner. He'd arrived late at the hospital after wakening so muscle-stiff and joint-sore, he could hardly move. A hot shower and a handful of aspirin he wasn't supposed to take had put him on his feet, but he'd pay in spades later for pushing himself.

Sunlight blinded him when he sidled out the one-way exit door. His turquoise Edsel at the back of the lot gave him his bearings. Marlin Andrik's unmarked Chevy sat three rows closer. Hannah's Blazer was nosed into the sidewalk's curb, a dozen cars to Delbert's right.

He glanced around as he shrugged off the lab coat. The shrubs squatting in a bed of landscape stones were too puny to hide a hankie behind. Wadding the coat under his arm, he hurried along the sidewalk as fast as his aching hips and knees allowed, casting about for a listening post.

The conversion van on the passenger side of Hannah's truck was locked. Delbert felt under the front and rear fender wells for a magnetic key safe. Finding none, he debated hunkering beside Hannah's tire, but he'd be too easy to spot by visitors crossing the lot or driving through.

A newer-model sedan on her driver's side was also locked, but the windows were half-down. Glimpsing Marlin Andrik holding the lobby door for Hannah, Delbert reached over the sedan's passenger glass and popped the lock.

Everything fit in the space between the dash and floorboard except his ding-danged head. He couldn't see out the windshield or side window, but anyone looking in could see him.

Delbert's mouth parched at the drum of footsteps approaching and Hannah's nervous laugh. Wrestling the lab coat from under his arm, Delbert draped it over his head and shoulders. If it didn't cover him, or if Andrik had grilled her in the lobby and was just walking her to her truck, he'd gone to a helluva lot of trouble for nothing. He wouldn't even let himself think about his hideout's driver showing up before the coast was clear.

"Tell me about this phone conversation you had with him on Monday," Marlin said. "I understand you were upset at being ordered to stand in for him at the Thomlinsons' party."

"I bet I know from whom that *understanding* derived, too."

Hannah's purse clunked on the Blazer's hood. "Yes, I was upset. I'm sure David also told you why there was no love lost between me and Eulilly. Had she invited me herself, I'd have declined. Jack wheedling then demanding that I go did not make my day."

"Why was it so important for you to be there?"

She explained Clancy Construction and Development's connection to Bethune Enterprises and that Jack was afraid snubbing Eulilly Bethune Thomlinson might scotch the deal.

"This meeting in San Diego Clancy couldn't reschedule," Marlin said. "Who was it with, and where was it exactly?"

"I didn't ask and Jack didn't say."

Cellophane crinkled. A lighter snapped. Delbert's eyes watered. The sedan reeked of pine-scented carpet cleaner. He pinched his nostrils to dam a sneeze.

"Okay," Andrik said. "then whose idea was it to invite Sheriff Hendrickson along?"

"Jack's. It was a bribe, of sorts. Make a date out of it and maybe I wouldn't bitch as much later."

Silence. Five seconds, then eight. "It wasn't that big of a deal, Marlin. Not really. Jack said to eat Eulilly's food, drink her booze and it'd all be over by nine."

"Those were his exact words? 'It'll all be over by nine?'"

Silence—a longer one, this time. "Oh, for— Give me a freakin' break. Are you insinuating that Jack Clancy had anything to do with the shooting? That's the craziest thing I've ever heard."

"I don't insinuate, Toots. You know that. I'm an archaeologist. Dig a little dirt, sift it, dig some more. Most of the time there's no dinosaur, but it doesn't hurt to look."

"The hell it doesn't. What about Chet? He's the spouse. Have you set the bulldozer loose on him? Or is it just Jack's reputation you're trying to plow under?"

"This isn't a witch-hunt. Clancy has motive and the means to buy opportunity. If he didn't, I wouldn't be here."

The misery of being balled up and shrouded in a hot car diminished as Delbert recalled Chase Wingate's early-morning request for an eyewitness interview.

Delbert didn't divulge anything the newspaper owner didn't already know, but found out D. K. Bogart was an alias and that his personal effects, such as they were, included a bus ticket to Saint Louis.

Jack Clancy had lived in Saint Louis for years. He had millions of his own money and a chunk of his mother's invested in Valhalla Springs. To hear IdaClare prattle, the development was in the black. Maybe it was on paper, but Delbert had his doubts.

Andrik asked, "What did Mrs. Thomlinson say when you told her you and David would be at the party?"

Pause. "I didn't."

"The two of you just walked in and said, 'Surprise!'"

No answer.

"You're not doing Clancy any favors by playing mouse to my cat. He's your employer and a friend, but I've got two dead women, a bunch of injured and traumatized senior citizens and a dead drone on my hands."

Hannah's voice was flat and strained. "Jack called Eulilly to say he couldn't attend, but I would in his place. I don't know if he mentioned David, but Chet acted as though he wasn't aware either of us were coming."

A noise, like a shoe sole eviscerating a cigarette, grated outside. "Last question—for now. How well did Clancy know the Thomlinsons? Did he meet them before they moved to Valhalla Springs?"

"That's two questions."

"Sue me."

"Why are you asking me? Jack could—"

"You're here and Clancy isn't. Neither is Thomlinson, and his wife can't corroborate."

Keys jingled. Delbert stretched his neck and peeped out a wrinkle in the lab coat. Hannah's back was turned, but anger rose from her like heat shimmers. "All right. Yes, Jack and Chet were acquainted. I didn't know it until this morning and I don't know how well."

She started to open the Blazer's door. Andrik's fingers splayed on the window glass, holding it shut. She glared at him, her lips drawn back. "Damn you, Marlin."

"I've heard worse. From you, as a matter of fact."

"Did David sic you on me? Is that what this is all about?"

"Why would he do that?"

"Because he's jealous of Jack. Pea-green, stupid-assed jealous. We argued about it last night and *abracadabra,* his chief of detectives corners me in the hospital's lobby, bubbling over with questions about David's supposed rival for my affections."

"He doesn't operate like that," Andrik said. "I don't either."

"Yeah, well, I hate this. You have no idea how much."

"Then let's get it over with."

The steel melted from Hannah's face and backbone. "Chet was in the waiting room on IdaClare's floor when Jack and I got there. When they didn't introduce themselves, I presumed they knew each other."

"And..."

"Chet rambled on about Eulilly a while. How she should be running Bethune Enterprises instead of her brothers."

Her eyes lowered to stare at the pavement. "Chet said he was glad I was there as a witness, then promised to vote his and the proxies Eulilly collected in favor of Jack's project. Jack was stunned, then furious. He told Chet they'd never had that conversation and walked out."

Andrik's palm squealed down the window glass. "Thanks, Toots. You've given me a couple of things to go on."

"You mean *after,* don't you?"

The Blazer's door slammed. The ignition whirred. The truck's oversize tires spat gravel as it backed from the parking space.

"God, I love my job," Andrik muttered, then strode away.

Delbert tugged the lab coat off his head and dabbed the sweat from his face and neck. His legs were numb and he couldn't feel his feet.

He'd give Andrik time to drive off, then hobble on up to Sophonia's room. Keeping her company while he did some heavy-duty thinking was what Rosemary Schnur would call a two-fer.

# 8

The difference between personal shopping and surrogate shopping is an intrinsic need to buy something nonessential. Merchandise already rejected as frivolous, or too expensive, can be rationalized as a thank-me gift for being a good Samaritan.

That's from whence the retro-thirties oscillating fan on the dresser had come. When Hannah ogled it several days earlier, practicality had won out over covetousness. The heat and humidity were climbing, but her cottage had central air.

Then between checking whiskey-sour mix off IdaClare's list and heading for the store's fabric department, the heavy, nickel-finished fan that would have looked at home in Marlene Dietrich's boudoir mutated into a justifiable accessory for Hannah's.

Malcolm sat in front of it, his head pivoting along with each sweep. So fascinated was he by the amazing wind machine, if it had sprouted four legs and a tail, he'd have eloped with it.

Hannah lay stretched out on the bed like a snow angel in shrunk-to-fit men's drawstring pajama bottoms and a cut-off Cubs T-shirt. A hot shower had relaxed her body but not her mind.

The room was dark, but for the ambient light threading through the open windows' miniblinds. One ear was tuned to phantom rustles and skitters in the bushes and branches. A barn owl's wheezy cry. Toads calling, crickets chirping and a whippoorwill's eponymous song.

The scanner Delbert had given her crackled and droned in her other ear. Kinderhook County only appeared to roll in the streets at sundown. A bull blocking traffic on both sides of a low-water bridge had challenged deputies and citizen volunteers to a roadside rodeo. A fight at Mother Trucker's pool hall had sent one brawler to the emergency room and three more to the drunk tank. The man who'd reported his car stolen with his baby daughter inside was arrested after admitting he'd lied about the kidnapping so deputies would find his vehicle faster.

Adam 1–01, aka Sheriff David Hendrickson, hadn't initiated or received transmissions for a while. The second shift was an officer short, but David's earlier request to go 10–7—the code for out of service—must have been granted.

He'd left two messages on Hannah's machine, one that morning and another later in the afternoon. If he assumed she was screening calls, he was wrong about that, too.

She'd been so shaken by Marlin Andrik's questions, she was less than a mile from Valhalla Springs when she remembered IdaClare's shopping list. Taking Malcolm along for company on the return trip to town, Hannah had seriously contemplated pointing her Blazer west until the lights of Malibu Beach glimmered on the horizon.

Andrik examined a crime scene from three angles: what's there, what's there and shouldn't be and what isn't there but should be. It might be nothing more than a guess, but Marlin's radar screen had picked up a blip with Jack's name on it.

Hannah had supplied more information than he'd asked for. Keeping her own counsel served no purpose. He'd just keep pecking away. Besides, protecting Jack implied a need for protection.

The molecule of doubt Marlin had planted would have shriveled and died if Jack hadn't sidestepped her question about the meeting in San Diego.

They'd arrived at IdaClare's within minutes of each other to find an early potluck supper in progress. Leo was stirring a kettle of homemade chicken soup on the stove. "The cure it is, for what ails you, too," he told Delbert, who smelled like an ambulatory tube of Icy Hot.

Delbert said, "Ponce de León, you ain't, Schnur."

"Tomorrow, you will say different, I think."

Egg salad sandwiches and two lemon meringue pies were Rosemary's contributions. Marge had spread garlic butter on slices of bread and baked them crispy-brown to cut into croutons. When she saw Jack and Hannah sneaking samples, Marge ordered them to finish setting the table.

"You were right about not hiring a nurse," Jack said. "Money can't buy this kind of TLC."

Hannah's lips curved into a knowing smile. "What time are you leaving for Saint Louis in the morning?"

"Early thirty." He dealt dinner plates like a Vegas cardsharp. "I'll be out of the shower and ready for croissants and coffee about five. Unless you want to go for the breakfast-in-bed thing, around four-thirty."

This the man said with a straight face. Hers was a picture of the verb-pronoun combination that predicates *and the horse you rode in on.*

"I'd stay later or longer if Mother needed me," he went on, "but other than a couple of hours on Monday, I haven't been in the office since last Wednesday."

Hannah couldn't have asked for a better gambit to inquire about his trip to California. Eyes riveted on the napkin he was folding, he shot back, "It's too soon to tell what may come of it."

What the—? Who *was* this masked man? An edgy chuckle burst from Hannah's lips. "Yeah, well. The hawk flies at midnight."

As expected, Jack caught the attempt at spy-speak. "Not funny, sweetpea. Not one damn bit." He slapped the last two napkins in place and stalked off.

IdaClare kept her promise to stay in bed until supper was ready. The pink in her cheeks was brushed on and she didn't refuse Jack's help into the dining room, but despite the sling on her arm, she looked regal in her bat wing–sleeved robe and satin mules.

The doorbell rang as he was seating her. Hannah's surprise at seeing Chet Thomlinson standing on the other side of the screen door must have shown. "Am I too early?" he asked. "Or too late?"

Jack's "What the hell is he doing here?" carried to the foyer and, likely, the porch.

"No, you...you're right on time," Hannah stammered, and motioned him inside.

Chet greeted the Clancys as though they were equally enthused by his presence. Chet brought IdaClare's hand to his lips and kissed it, said she was as lovely as she was brave, then presented the two bottles of white wine held in the crook of his arm.

"This one is nonalcoholic. I know how much you enjoy wine with dinner, but was afraid alcohol might not agree with your medication."

IdaClare's appreciation for his thoughtfulness was effusive and echoed by Leo, Rosemary and Marge.

Jack muttered, "I've never seen her drink wine with dinner in my life."

Delbert grunted. "Me, neither."

The look they exchanged spoke volumes, but the meaning was lost on Hannah.

Other than compliments to the chefs, neither said another word during the meal. Rosemary kicked Leo under the table when he mentioned their planned honeymoon cruise. Apparently weddings and honeymoons weren't appropriate topics with a recent widower present.

The upcoming club golf championship seemed like a safe subject until Marge realized the reigning lady's division champion might never swing a club again.

Itsy's and Bitsy's panhandling, the weather and

Leo's recipe for authentic Jewish penicillin carried them through the coffee and dessert course.

IdaClare's flagging energy gave Jack reason to excuse himself and take her back to bed. He didn't rejoin the party, such as it was. Delbert said he had a date with the community center's hot tub and skedaddled. Chet insisted on helping Leo, Rosemary and Marge with the dishes.

Weighted down with leftovers and veiled misgivings, Hannah fetched Malcolm from IdaClare's backyard and went home.

Marlin Andrik squinted as a double set of round headlamps swept his county piece-of-shit-mobile. Forty years ago, British cops patroled in Jaguars because they outran everything else on the road, except other Jags.

He speared a cigarette butt out the window and reached for the Chevy's door handle. Two jerks and a yank was its magic open sesame. The hinges shrieked and groaned like a wounded water buffalo. Christ. Maybe declaring independence from England hadn't been such a hot idea, after all.

"Evening, Mr. Clancy," Marlin said, then identified himself. "Sorry to bother you so late, but I need to ask you a few questions."

Clancy looked around, then motioned toward the condo. "Let's go inside."

Marlin followed him into the kitchen. The condo's furnishings were several cuts above Sid's Factory Furniture Universe, but functional not fancy. He'd bet

Clancy's shirt was custom tailored, though, and his loafers hand-cobbled in the old country by Geppetto's great-grandson.

"How's your mom doing?" he asked, seating himself on a bar stool. "I was surprised they discharged her from the hospital so soon…much less that she was up to having company for dinner."

The shot glasses Clancy removed from a cabinet hit the countertop a fraction too hard. "I'd have voted against both if it would have done any good." He proffered a half-empty bottle of whiskey. "Care for a drink?"

Marlin eyed the label. Imported. Expensive. One snort and Old Crow would never taste the same again. "Sure. Why not?"

Clancy smiled as he poured the Irish equivalent of liquid gold. "I thought cops weren't supposed to drink on duty."

"I won't tell if you don't." He fished out a pack of Marlboros and a lighter from his sport's coat pocket. "Mind if I smoke?"

Clancy hesitated, frowned, then took a cereal bowl from the cabinet for use as an ashtray. Like the Good Book says, "If thine enemy hunger, feed him; if he thirst, give him drink."

His host knocked back his shot and smacked his lips. "I needed that. I love my mother dearly, and thank God she wasn't hurt any worse than she was, but it's been one helluva long day."

"I hear ya." Marlin blew smoke over his shoulder. "That's some house she's got. All that gingerbread and trimwork puts me in mind of a pink-and-white wedding cake.''

"Have you ever seen the inside?"

Marlin lied and said he hadn't. Reminding sonny boy that his mama had been busted for weed might spoil the camaraderie.

"She calls her decorating scheme country French. I call it a blind madam's whorehouse." He laughed. "Mother doesn't play piano, but she just had to have a pink baby grand for the living room."

"My old lady has a thing for primitives. If the food was better, you'd swear you were trapped in a goddamn cracker-barrel."

Marlin flipped an ash worm into the bowl. "Inviting Chet Thomlinson to join you for dinner was a nice thing to do. If anybody needed a reason to hold a grudge, y'all had a dandy."

"That was Mother's idea not mine."

"I take it you don't like him much."

"I don't know the man well enough to like or dislike him."

"Hmm." Marlin beetled his brow, as though confused. "My information must be wrong. I thought your company and Mrs. Thomlinson's family's business were involved in some kind of a…deal."

Clancy stiffened at the inflection. "Eulilly was more or less a silent partner in Bethune Enterprises. Her husband has no interest in the business whatsoever."

"He does, as of about eight o'clock last night."

The fingernails of Clancy's drinking hand bleached white.

"Just for curiosity's sake, where were you at the time of the shooting, Jack?"

"On a direct flight from San Diego approaching Lambert Airport." His eyes slanted to the whiskey bottle. He made a loose fist and nudged it away. "Either that, or on my way home from Lambert. I don't know exactly what time the shooting happened."

Marlin waved a dismissal. "You were on a commercial flight? Round trip?"

"Yes."

"Why?"

Clancy shifted his weight, then chuckled. "Because I left my wings in another pair of pants?"

Cute. Everyone's a comedian. "Why fly commercial when your company owns a private jet?"

"My pilot's wife was due to have their fourth child, any minute." Anticipating Marlin's next question, he said, "I could have hired a substitute, but Jerry's been with me for a number of years. I preferred taking a commercial flight over the hassle of finding a replacement."

"What'd she have?"

"Excuse me?"

"Mrs. Pilot. A boy or a girl?"

Wincing, Clancy ran his fingers through his hair. "Damn. I don't know if Lisa's given birth yet or not. I must have spoken with my secretary fifteen times today. Never thought to ask."

Marlin canted the cigarette inside the bowl, then

thumbed through his notebook for a blank page. "I'll need your pilot's name and a phone number." The flyboy wouldn't be worth a plug nickel as a collaborator. Employees with cushy jobs seldom ratted out the boss, but a genuine detective has to go through the motions. If for no other reason than civilians exposed to a steady diet of TV cop shows expected it.

While he copied the particulars, Clancy took out his wallet and laid a business card facedown on the counter. He wrote two telephone numbers on the back. "I'm leaving for Saint Louis early in the morning. If you need to reach me, my office number is on the front. Home and cell phone on the back." He slid it across the counter. A "see you around, pal," wouldn't have been more implicit if he'd said it aloud.

Marlin kept his head lowered, made a minor production out of flipping notebook pages back and forth. "You've never been married, have you?"

"No."

"Haven't found the right girl?"

Most questions were meant to solicit answers. Some weren't.

Andrik said, "You were in San Diego on business?"

"Yes."

"Who with?"

"I'm not at liberty to say."

Marlin gawked at him. "You're shittin' me." He crushed out the smoldering Marlboro, fanning away the smoke with his hand. "I've been a cop for twenty-two years. A detective for thirteen. Not once in my entire career has anyone actually told me, 'I'm not at liberty to say.'"

Clancy folded his arms. "Glad I could be the first. Now, if you'll excuse me—"

"Where'd you stay in San Diego?"

"I don't see what any of this has to do with—"

"Questions don't come much simpler, Clancy. You say you flew from Saint Louis to San Diego on Monday and flew home Tuesday evening. So where'd you stay Monday night?"

The wheeler-dealer CEO's bright blue eyes flashed *Fuck you, Andrik.*

"We both know I can check airline records and see if your name is on the passenger list, but what's that prove? Buying a ticket doesn't mean you're the one that used it. You won't tell me who you met with. You won't tell me where you spent the night. That leaves me wondering if you ever went to San Diego, and if you didn't, why you skipped out on the Thomlinsons' party."

Clancy rounded the corner of the bar, strode through the living room and opened the front door. "Good night, Detective."

Marlin packed up his smokes and his notebook. He slid off the bar stool, took a step, then turned. A teaspoon of whiskey ambered the bottom of the shot glass.

He drained it. No sense wasting good booze.

During the short drive to 1903 Larkspur Lane, an Altoid fumigated his breath and seared his sinuses like peppermint napalm. Clancy was no fool, but stonewalling a going-through-the-motions interview was a dick-tease, in investigative parlance. A dare to dig deeper for answers to no-brainer questions.

He'd flown to San Diego on business. In his line of work, confidentiality was a given, but who gave a rat's ass where he stayed while he was there?

The Thomlinson cottage could have been a cover shot for one of the decorating magazines his wife, Beth, ogled like his son did *Playboy*. White clapboard siding, a tile roof, a wraparound veranda with hanging ferns, a porch swing and wicker chairs and a love seat.

No curtains or shades obstructed the living room's picture window. Boxes were stacked like cairns and the furniture was in disarray. Marlin rang the bell while framing a tactful way to ask if the moving van had been canceled.

A needle-thin woman with frizzy blond hair and a lethal tan opened the door a crack. Recognition glinted in her eyes. "This isn't a good time, Detective. Chet is picking out Eulilly's burial clothes."

Ms. Manners had been a guest at the party. Scanning his memory for her name, Marlin swung open the screen, his hand stopping the door before it closed. "Sorry for the intrusion, Mrs. Cantwell, but I need to speak with Mr. Thomlinson."

"Caldwell," she sniffed. "Hetta Caldwell."

Whatever. "I'd appreciate it if you'd tell Mr. Thomlinson I'm here."

She stalked off.

Marlin plopped into an overstuffed, flounced armchair. Condolence flowers and houseplants banked the fireplace mantel and hearth. Ghosts of pictures, bric-a-brac and furniture appliquéd the pale green walls. Even stripped of its personality, it was a woman's room, a woman's house. Less flamboyant than IdaClare Clancy's, but undeniably feminine.

Beth would love it. Two weeks in Tinker Bell–ville and Marlin would be on industrial-strength Viagra.

He squinted at a prescription bottle beside a water glass on the other armchair's side table. Ear attuned to the low voices filtering down the hallway, he pried off the lid. Nine blue tabs, each with a heart impression at the center. Valium by the scoring and color. Ten milligrams each—the maximum dosage. A call to Doc Pennington would determine the original number of tablets prescribed.

The cushion wheezed under Marlin's butt just as Mrs. Caldwell and Thomlinson entered the room. Her eyes flicked to the open door, then to the audacious public servant who'd barged in and made himself at home.

"I told him you were in no condition for company, Chet," she said.

"I'm all right, Hetta." Thomlinson massaged his forehead. "Just a little woozy from that pill. Should have laid off the wine at dinner, too, I suppose."

Great. Under the influence of tranquilizers, the man could confess to capping Jimmy Hoffa and it wouldn't be admissible in court.

Marlin rose from the chair. "I apologize for disturbing you, sir, but I do have a few more questions."

The bony guard waved toward a banjo-shaped silhouette on the wall. "That can't wait until morning?" She started, realizing her melodramatic gesture suffered for lack of a clock.

Mr. Caldwell, a masculine doppelgänger of his wife, appeared behind them. He laid a supportive hand on Thomlinson's shoulder. "You'd be well within your rights to refuse an interview. I'd advise you to do precisely that."

Thomlinson shook him off. "He's just doing his job." His gait was steady as he wove through the obstacle course that was once his living room, but groaned as he seated himself in the other plump armchair. Bloodshot hazel eyes met Marlin's. "Do you have any objection to my friends sitting in on our talk? They're helping me with some things—with arrangements for Eulilly's service."

"I'd rather speak to you in private."

Caldwell said, "I am Chet's attorney."

As if Marlin hadn't already guessed. He shrugged. "Suit yourself." An implicit "Why bring a gun to a knife fight?" leavened his tone.

Thomlinson had the demeanor of a man stuck between the devil and the deep blue sea. The Caldwells must have insisted on staying when the three of them powwowed in the bedroom. Chet couldn't gracefully hustle them out the door. Marlin couldn't legally tell the attorney not to let it bang him in the ass on the way out.

They were at a stalemate, whether by accident or design. Plus, the subject was medicinally impaired. Shit on a stick, Marlin thought. Follow-up interviews didn't get any more worthless than this.

He limited his questions to background information. The Thomlinsons had been married for six years—her fourth, his third. The marriage was reasonably happy, but far from perfect—an admission ninety-nine percent of homicidal spouses wouldn't dare make. "I loved her/him more than life itself" was the top tune on that hit parade.

Thomlinson had signed a prenuptial agreement, but was the beneficiary of a half-million-dollar life insurance policy, as was Eulilly, if he croaked first. Her seat on Bethune Enterprise's board of directors and her stockholder's dividends were also bequeathed to him, but only for six months.

Eulilly's will prohibited the sale of Bethune stock, or pledging it as collateral for a loan. When the term expired, the stock would be split fifty-fifty between Hampton and Clay Bethune. Thomlinson would be on his own.

If they divorced, he received a hundred grand in cash, his personal possessions, including a coin collection and Civil War memorabilia. Period.

Dead or alive, Eulilly had hubby by the short curlies. Her will lined his pockets a tad deeper, but any drone, particularly a retired fed, knew a wife who died of unnatural causes leveled suspicion at the spouse.

"What about this project between Jack Clancy and Bethune Enterprises," Marlin said. "Was your wife opposed to it?"

"Not the project. She was opposed to accepting the bid from Clancy Construction and Development."

"Why?"

Thomlinson hesitated. His eyebrows raised a fraction. "I don't know."

Oh yes he did. He just preferred not to mention specifics in the Caldwells' presence.

"Well, *I* do," Hetta said. "The very idea of the owner of a retirement village firing an employee because of her age infuriated Eulilly. She did everything she could to help Zerelda Sue Connor, but Mr. Clancy wouldn't budge."

Marlin was aware of the particulars and the real reason behind Eulilly's outrage. "If she disliked Clancy so much, why was he invited to the party?"

"As a courtesy to his mother," Thomlinson said, at the same time Hetta sniped, "He most assuredly was *not* invited."

Marlin looked from one to the other. Thomlinson evil-eyed Hetta. "Yes he was, and he'd accepted, then had to leave town unexpectedly on business."

Her kisser puckered and unpuckered as though her fillings were electrified. "Well, I'm…*shocked.*"

Marlin bit the inside of his cheek to keep from laughing.

"I helped Eulilly address the invitations, Chet. If Jack Clancy's name was on the list, *I* didn't see it." Hetta's upper torso shimmied with disgust. "Of course, I didn't see Hannah Garvey's name on it, either."

"You're voting for Clancy's bid?" Caldwell said after Marlin's question to that effect.

Hetta was horrified. "Against Eulilly's wishes? How could you?"

"There's no rush, Chet," the attorney said. "If Clancy or the Bethunes are pressuring you, ignore them. This is the worst possible time to make that type of decision."

"I've already told Jack and Eulilly's brothers how I'll vote at the next board meeting."

Caldwell rolled his eyes. "Well, I'll untell them for you. First thing tomorrow morning."

"No, you won't," Chet said. "A deal is a deal."

Hetta's argument didn't advance past "But—" before Marlin broke in, "A deal with whom? Clancy? The Bethunes? Or someone else?"

"Don't answer that," Caldwell warned. "Not until we have a chance to speak privately."

"I have nothing to hide."

In Marlin's experience, the polar opposite was true. The phrase had less credibility than "Trust me."

"I never said you did, Chet, but I must caution you about how such a statement could be interpreted." Caldwell's sidelong glance at Marlin was as subtle as a baseball bat.

"That's enough. Please." Thomlinson leaned forward, his forearms on his thighs, his hands dangling between them. "As long as my wife was a Bethune board member, she had the power and voting bloc to force her brothers to find another developer, or scrap the project.

"My term as her proxy will expire in December. I could delay approval of Jack's contract for six months, alienate my brothers-in-law and cost both companies a considerable amount of money. I choose not to do so."

"Sounds kosher to me," said Marlin, the lapsed Catholic.

He left a quarter-hour later. Unlike Clancy, Thomlinson hadn't been evasive or hostile. No need, with Caldwell and his mummified wife champing to object, debate and contradict his answers.

Marlin's to-do list had lengthened. Nothing had been crossed off. He had enough loose ends to fringe a serape. More where they came from, when he reviewed Cletus Orr's and Josh Phelps's reports at the office.

The manager's cottage came into view. No sheriff's cruiser in the driveway. No lights. Hannah must have hit the rack early. Or wasn't home.

Damn. He could have used a cup of coffee. As torqued as she was in the hospital parking lot, he might have wound up wearing it, though.

Toots was scared spitless by the way Clancy had been acting. She was smart and had better than average instincts, but Marlin would love to get her in a poker game sometime.

His sixth sense told him she already was and didn't know it.

Brooding and hours of staring at the bedroom ceiling hadn't resolved anything, or bored Hannah to sleep. The longer she lay there, the more she felt like an acupuncture student's practice dummy. Rolling over on her side, she looked from the alarm clock to the sequential lights chasing across the scanner's face.

Did I put the garage door down? Of course I did. Probably. And what about the utility room door? Locked it behind me when I came in. Turned off the coffeepot after I gobbled a bedtime slice of pie, too. No doubt about it.

"Sheesh." She swung her legs to the floor, sat up and switched off the scanner. Raking back her hair, she wadded it at the back of her head, then yawned wide enough to crack her jaw.

Malcolm, the nimrod, was still watching the fan oscillate. The insomniac and the doofus dog. The two of them definitely deserved each other.

She slogged to the bathroom to rid herself of the coffee she shouldn't have drunk, then commenced to check up on herself. The French doors to the deck were locked. Ditto, the utility room. A peek out the miniblinds confirmed the garage door was down, but a small orange light was aglow on the coffeemaker. Oops.

Malcolm joined her midway through the great room. The front door was locked, too, until he flattened his nose against the crack and *moomphed*.

"Okay, but make it quick, big guy," she said as though she had anything better to do than sit on the porch steps while he wandered from this bush to that tree in search of an appropriate species to pee on.

Goose bumps stippled her arms. The air was clammy but cool. The creatures of the night had quieted. No stars shone through the spun-cotton layer of clouds. Peace and tranquillity out the wazoo. Another minute of it and she'd go stark, screaming nuts.

The screen door banged behind her like a rifle shot. She flipped the toggle to the recessed lights above the fireplace and opened the cabinet housing the stereo system. Head parallel to her shoulder, she ticked a fingernail across the spines of jewel-cased compact discs.

Creedence Clearwater Revival? No. Janis Joplin? Not tonight. Jim Croce? Thanks, but she didn't need a sound track for her photographs and memories. *The Eagles/Their Greatest Hits?* Right band, wrong album.

*Their Greatest Hits Volume 2* didn't include "Desperado." It was her theme song, but she couldn't abide Glenn Frey telling her to let somebody love her before it was too late.

It already was.

The mandolinlike intro to "Hotel California" blared from the speakers. Her cottage's separation from the residential area had its advantages. Swaying and lip-synching the lyrics, she boogie-shuffled to the kitchen.

Wine, woman and song. If only that trifecta had occurred to her sooner, she'd have fallen asleep hours ago.

The cork *thwoomped* from the wine bottle, its neck exhaling white vapor and a luscious aroma. A connoisseur she was not. The label's pastel watercolor landscape had caught her fancy. Recalling billboards advertising Saint James' Winery along I–44, she'd decided to sample Missouri's contribution to the vintners' art.

She filled a stemmed goblet to the brim. The wine's ruby redness matched its lush aroma. She closed her eyes and sipped. Icy-cold, slightly sweet Lake Country Velvet Red slid down her throat as smoothly as its name.

She turned to lean against the counter. Her heart faltered then banged in her chest. The glass slipped in her hand. "Since when do you just walk into my house?"

"IdaClare and Company do it all the time." David took a folded sheet of paper from the pocket of his chambray shirt. "And seeing as how I'm the sheriff, I'm here on official business."

Hannah set the glass on the counter. The bold header at the top of the sheet read *General Affidavit* in Old English type. *State of Missouri; County of Kinderhook.*

"You're serving me with a fugitive warrant?"

"The middle part supports probable cause," he said.

"I can't read the fine print." Her mouth pursed to stifle a grin. She wadded the paper in a ball and threw it at him. "But I can read Judge Wapner's signature at the bottom."

David snagged it and drilled a two-pointer into the trash can. "If you'd been asleep, I was going to throw rocks at your window until you woke up."

"That desperate, huh?"

"Damn right."

"I've missed you, too."

"How much?"

She arched an eyebrow. "More than I'd let myself admit."

His eyes homed in on her T-shirt. Specifically, the geographic center of her T-shirt. She pulled out the hem and looked down. "What?"

David shook his head. "Nothing."

"Oh, yeah? Well, number one, a smart man doesn't stare at a woman's chest, then when she asks what he's looking at, say 'Nothing.' Number two, I've seen all the significant glances and heard all the 'Nothings' I care to for one day."

He signaled surrender. "The logo reminded me that Deke Bogart was a Cubs fan, too. That's all."

Gee, what a vast improvement over "Nothing."

"His bus ticket was a one-way to Saint Louis, though," David said, as if thinking aloud.

Home of the Cardinals, the Gateway Arch and Jack Clancy. Hannah took a healthy swig of wine and returned the glass to the counter. A sharp edge tinged her voice when she said, "Chicago. Saint Louis. The bastard murdered two people. What difference does it make where he came from."

"At the moment, none." David pulled her into his arms.

She resisted. "Meaning, it doesn't matter right here, at the moment, or it doesn't matter to Marlin, at the moment?"

"Right here, at the moment, is all I care about."

Lord, she was so tired of fighting. With David, with Jack, with herself. David's embrace was a haven, an anchor. It always had been.

He fingercombed the hair from her face. "No excuses, sugar. I overreacted last night. Made a fool of myself in front of you and Jack."

"So did I."

"Maybe so, but I do trust you. If you ever found someone else, I'd be the first to know, not the last."

"But—"

"Let me finish. Please." The corner of his mouth crinkled into a smile. "I've been practicing this all day."

Hannah laughed. "You are such a dork."

"I reckon that's another thing we have in common, Miz Garvey." He paused, either regathering his thoughts or the courage to speak them. "This may push your mad button again, but I *don't* trust Clancy.

Not the way he looks at you, and, well, not the way you look at him. It isn't the same way you look at me, but near enough to hurt."

Hannah stepped back and took his hands in hers. Massaging the knuckles with her thumbs, she said, "The love Jack and I have for each other is very special. We tried to make it more once. Physically. We couldn't, but if anything, our friendship was stronger afterward."

She swallowed the knot tightening her throat. "What I'm about to say was beside the point when I thought you didn't trust me. Telling you last night would have gotten me off the hook, except that I didn't deserve to be on it."

"No, you didn't."

Hannah squeezed his hands to silence him. "Jack Clancy is gay. He's fought it, hated himself for it, tried desperately to change himself into something he isn't. His partner for the past several years has been a pediatrician named Stephen Riverton. Until they met, I don't think Jack had a contented day in his life and had given up hoping he ever would."

David gazed up at the soffit for a long moment, then let out a sigh. "I'd be lying if I said I wasn't a little bit relieved."

She hugged his waist. "There's another reason I didn't tell you about Jack when we argued. As he mentioned this morning at breakfast, I was looking for an out. Your distrust and jealousy gave me two."

His eyes searched hers. "Do you want out?"

"No. Yes. Sometimes." She laughed again, this time at herself. "How's that for decisiveness?"

"I know the feelings. Life was simpler before you moved in on me. Dull as dirt, but simpler."

"Moved in on *you?*"

"My county. My head. My heart. Every second of my every day."

The sexy, soulful bass guitar lead to "I Can't Tell You Why" thrummed from the living room. David pulled her closer. "I don't want to talk anymore."

"Neither do I."

His lips met hers ever so gently. The taste of his tongue sent heat coursing through her. His hands cupped her bottom, pressing her to him, promising all of him was hers for the taking.

*Every time I try to walk away...*

The kiss deepened, David's feet gliding backward on the tile. Her body moved in concert with his, their hips mimicking the dance of love to the music's slow, sensual beat.

*You don't have to worry, just hold on tight...*

She grasped the placket of his shirt, ripped open the snaps. Her palms skimmed taut muscle, silky hair, silky skin.

Their lips parted just long enough for David to lift the T-shirt over her head. Dancing, floating into the bedroom, her knees trembled at the erotic, indescribable sensation of her breasts against his bare, hot skin.

He toed off his boots. Kicked them away. She unbuckled his belt, unzipped his jeans. Fingers slipping inside the waistband, she eased them down, carefully, tenderly, as she lowered to a kneel in front of him.

*'Cause I love you...*

Teasing, licking, plying the furrow at his thigh, then the other, her fingers caressed their backs with feathery strokes, then his calves, then up again. On the next descent, she captured him with her lips. Satin and steel. A glorious, arousing, musky scent.

The shiver of pleasure given and taken swelled within her at David's gasp, his hoarse groans, his whispered "Oh, darlin'. I can't take much more of that." The fan's breeze brushed across her as he raised her to her feet. "Your turn."

He finished undressing her and she him, then they fell on the bed. Touching, exploring, hungry to become one, they fought the impulse, hungrier still to make it last.

David's mouth left hers to kiss her neck, the channel between her breasts. His tongue flicked each nipple, then sucked them full and taut. Butterfly kisses flitted down her belly, her hips, her thighs. A wave of self-consciousness rushed in behind her desire seconds before he claimed her as no man ever had.

Back arched, head tossing on the pillow, she felt as though she were flying and falling, her body at once rigid and liquefied. Climbing, climbing, then...the world exploded, shattered in torrents of white fire and light.

"You," she panted. "Give me you. All of you. Now."

He moved over her, easing inside her, letting her open to him, devour him. Thrusting harder, faster, the length, the thickness of him sent her up again, higher, higher. Climbing with her, his body slick with sweat, they rocked together...almost there, almost...

She pulled him deep inside her, his climax intensifying hers. Stars streaked past. She cried out his name, then hurtled over the moon.

# 9

The morning sky was a dingy white harbinger of rain. Wind gusted through tree branches, then retreated, the sound mimicking the roll and ebb of ocean waves.

Hannah's cheek nuzzled the pillow. She savored the feel of David's body cuddling hers like a larger, solid shadow of herself. His left knee crooked in the hollow of hers, their right legs parallel. At the swell of her hip, her arm rested on his, their hands loosely entwined.

They'd purposely delayed making love as often as past attempts had been interrupted. The first time only happened once. They knew they'd cheat themselves, and each other, if they rushed that indefinable, absolutely *right* moment.

She smiled, recalling her daydreamed and night-scaped Hollywood-meets-Victoria's-Secret fantasies where she glided into his arms wearing a clingy negligee that transformed a decent pair of middle-aged 34Bs into creamy, uplifted 36Ds with cleavage of suffocating proportions.

So much for Hollywood, Victoria and imaginary breast implants. The secret to incredible, monumental, mind - blowing, never - better - for - anyone - in - the - history - of - the - planet lovemaking was combining first-time sex with make-up sex.

No, the first time couldn't be repeated. Actually, the second couldn't either. In the future, all they had to do was be a lot more immature, overreact at every opportunity, get seriously pissed at each other, go twenty-four hours without speaking, then jump in bed and set the sheets on fire.

Good plan. Excellent plan.

Her eyes widened along with her smile. Hmm. Something was coming between them again, so to speak. Nerve endings she hadn't known she possessed tingled at the prospect. Yes-sirree-Bob. The sleeping giant was awakening.

David's lips grazed her shoulder, then traveled to that tender, sweet spot at her nape. His hand left hers, his magic fingers seeking the other sweet spot—the one that melted at his slightest touch.

"Once you get started, Hendrickson," she said, "you're insatiable."

"Think so?" His tongue traced the shell of her ear. "It wasn't me that put a move on you in the middle of the night."

"Bull-oney. It took a minute for the rest of you to catch up, but the idea presented itself to me in no uncertain terms."

The erection pressed against her was rock-hard, tantalizing, irresistible. "Kind of like this?"

She moaned. "Exactly like that." Her hand closed around him. Knee lifting from the mattress, she guided him to her. "Whoever said size doesn't matter was wrong."

"Not necessarily." He chuckled and held himself back from the targeted area. "Like my daddy always said, the size of a man's toolbox has nothing to with his mechanical ability."

"Oh, for—" Hannah craned her neck to give him the full effect of her glare. "Will you please shut up and make love to me?"

"I am, sugar." Those magic fingers delved deeper, quickened. "The best I know how."

That hot, liquefying sensation built within her, swelling, aching for release.

Voice low and husky in her ear, his words matched the rhythm of his touch. "Making love is all about you. Only you. Every second, every minute, every hour. Arousing you...giving you... whatever you want...anything, everything...you need... first. Now...always oh yeah, darlin'...you first, then..."

He slid inside her at the peak of her climax. Fists clenching the pillow, she rocked against him, doubling and prolonging the shudders coursing through her.

Waiting, somehow knowing the instant the jagged edge of hypersensitivity diminished, he moved within her, filling her, sending her up that glorious summit again and this time meeting her at its crest.

She must have fallen asleep, for when she opened her eyes, David was dressed and sitting on the edge of the bed. Over his arm was the mangy chenille robe that hung on the back of the bathroom door. Ancient mustard stains, ink spots and chocolate drizzles marked it as her favorite, except the transformation from naked and sated to Edith Bunker's younger sister seemed too large of a leap.

"I don't want to leave," David said. "I never have, but—"

"We can't stay in bed all day." She reached for the robe.

"We can," he said, helping her into it, "and we will. A thousand, maybe two thousand times, before the new begins to wear off a mite." A slipknot secured the sash. "Just not today."

Arms entwined, they ambled from the bedroom, through the breakfast room and into the living room. "I started a pot of coffee for you," he said.

She sighed and rested her head on his shoulder. World's best kisser, world's best lover and Juan Valdez rolled into one. What more could a woman want?

Spotlights still illuminated the fireplace wall. The stereo's speakers hissed. David must have shut and locked the front door before he served his bogus fugitive warrant. Her belly fluttered at the memory.

"I love you, Hannah."

"I love you, too." Stretching to kiss him goodbye, she chuckled. "Now for the god-awful awkward part."

His eyebrows arched. "Yep."

"As an exit line, 'I'll call you, later,' doesn't parse after a night of screaming, incredible, first-time, make-up, multi-orgasmic sex."

"Nope."

"It's better than 'Let's do lunch sometime,'" she allowed, "but not by much."

He blew out a raspberry. "I've never said that to anyone in my whole, entire life."

Hannah deepened her voice. "'I'm going to be pretty busy with this investigation for a while, but as soon as I can shake loose, we'll start over from where we left off,' is the truth, but a little tacky."

"You do enjoy torturing me, don't you, Miz Garvey?"

"So, why don't you just kiss me like you always have and leave it at that?"

His answer curled under her toes and left her shivering.

Malcolm cracked open an eyelid and swished his tail when David stepped out on the porch.

"Oh, no." Hannah winced. "I completely forgot about Malcolm. The poor baby had to sleep outside all night."

David rubbed a hand across his mouth. It didn't quite hide the grin behind it.

"You locked him out on purpose, didn't you?"

"Yes, ma'am." Boot heels thudded on the plank steps. "Treated him like a dog, I did. Shameful behavior. Pure-de-shameful."

He waved as he rounded the Crown Vic's front bumper. "I'll call you later." Unlocking the driver's-side door, he said, "Let's do it for lunch sometime," then slid into the seat.

It was late morning before David caught up with Marlin Andrik. Chasing after leads, be they gut-born or evidential, was hopscotch not geometry. Andrik was also a devout agnostic at keeping dispatch informed of his whereabouts, but ripped into Orr and Phelps when they failed to report theirs.

He stood in the Royal Dragon's ravaged banquet room with his hands clasped behind his back. Returning to the scene of a crime wasn't exclusive to perpetrators. Mental reenactments seldom inspired *voilà* solutions much less otherworldly assists. They were simply part of the process.

The stench of death and devastation wasn't as strong as it was forty-eight hours ago, but had ripened into a sickly sweetness. Flies swarmed and buzzed— a horde of scavenger janitors on cleanup detail.

"Hey, boss." Marlin did a slow up-and-down, snickered, then whistled the opening bars of "What A Difference A Day Makes."

David ignored him and the warmth spreading above his shirt collar. He'd like to believe last night had changed everything, demolished the obstacles between him and Hannah spending the rest of their lives together.

It hadn't. The possibility of not spending the rest of their lives together was simply less comprehensible than ever. They'd known making love was dangerous. If they had done so at the beginning, it would have only been physical—acting on an attraction, an infatuation, not something...*spiritual* was the word that came to mind, but language was too one-dimensional.

He had to keep believing there were no walls so

high, thick or solid that they couldn't be climbed over, tunneled under, blasted through or gone around.

"Did you just come down here to stare more holes in the ceiling?" Marlin said.

*Time to pin on your shield, Hendrickson. Put on the game face.* "That's what you're doing, isn't it?"

The detective angled his head, a muscle working in his temple. "The ones up there are real. What I can't decide is if others I see are or not."

His fingernails rasped a permanent five o'clock shadow. "I've got an almost hog-tight, gooseproof workplace massacre case. Deke figures the boys 'n the 'hood aren't worth prison or dying for and bails out. The alias and fake social security number gets him a grunt job with no paper trail for the brothers to follow."

Contrary to popular belief, gang activity wasn't limited to drug peddling, hanging out on street corners and turf wars. Like the Mob, gang subsets had branched out into computerized-identity theft, credit card scams, electronic money laundering, stock swindles and other high-tech, low-risk, lucrative white collar–type crimes.

"Gangbangers are paranoid as hell," Marlin went on. "A handgun and an assault rifle for security blankets were nice to have, but Bogart couldn't slouch around like Rambo disguised as Clark Kent.

"Officer Cornelius didn't pat him down for a weapon the night he stopped him. No probable cause, and in this burg a farmer is more apt to carry concealed than a kid moseying home from work at 2:00 a.m.

"If Bogart did have a pistol in his pants that night—and twenty bucks says he did—he'd have left it under his pillow from then on."

"I'm with you a hundred percent," David said, "but why'd he pick Sanity?"

Marlin shrugged. "It's a scheduled bus stop. Could be, Bogart liked what he saw out the window. Sooner or later he'd have been made in a bigger city. He'd walked the walk and talked the talk too long. He was on the run from the Disciples and a target for any rival gang. Wander into anybody's turf and he was dead meat—or believed in his bones he was. A small, boring town with a handful of wannabes was safer than a city."

A guttural noise that might have been a chuckle rattled out. "Gang indoctrination would be funny if it wasn't so pathetic. Fear is a recruitment tool. Once you're in, fear makes you toe the line."

"Bogart might have shaken the gang life," David said, "but he couldn't shake the mentality."

Marlin nodded. "Flying solo wasn't as free as he thought it would be. Kind of like a paroled lifer who can't adjust to the outside. Bogart had no friends, no turf, no status. The boss's daughter wouldn't give him the time of day. It'd be the same tune wherever he went."

"No place to go, nothing to go back to besides a bullet for dropping his flag," David said, caught up in the of-one-mind accord they'd reached during previous brainstorming sessions. "What would he tell the homies? That he'd been on vacation? Visiting a sick relative?

"It had to eat on him, day in, day out. Bogart wanted to go home worse than he'd wanted to leave. Desperation met rage and opportunity when Jasmine insulted his machismo."

Marlin gestured supplication. "By God, he'd teach her and the rest of us rubes a lesson in respect, make some headlines, come up with a horseshit story to explain why he left the 'hood, then step off the bus in a blaze of glory."

David's gaze swept the room. The scenario was nearer a hit than a classic workplace massacre, but the logic was solid. Bogart's scarred right thigh indicated punishment for a serious code of conduct violation. There was no such thing as a born-again gangsta. To break away and try to re-up was suicide, unless he convinced them a score had been settled. Even then, Bogart would have been lucky to keep breathing for long.

"Motive, means and opportunity," he said. "Bogart knew Jasmine was the hostess for the Thomlinsons' party. The main dining room and banquet room schedules were posted a week in advance."

Marlin chimed in, "The dirtbag worked weekdays. Had all weekend to premeditate. He bought his bus ticket Sunday afternoon. Monday, he sexually assaults Jasmine and gets himself fired."

"He could have quit," David said, "or not shown up for work Monday, or Tuesday, but where's the grudge angle? Anyone who's seen newscasts of prior massacres knows revenge is almost always the motive.''

Marlin agreed. ''Mr. Chau wanted to press charges. Jasmine talked him out of it. Told him if he did, everyone in town would know what happened.''

''And draw their own conclusions.''

''With some saying she asked for it.''

Swallowing didn't alleviate the nasty taste in David's mouth. Jasmine Chau was one of the finest young ladies he'd ever had the pleasure to meet, but character was a tissue defense against that kind of ignorance.

He shifted his weight and thoughts to something within his control. ''What Bogart couldn't have known in advance was that I'd be at the party, or *was* there, because I drove my personal vehicle that night. He also couldn't have anticipated Thomlinson being a retired fed with a SIG-Sauer holstered under his suit coat.''

Marlin twirled an unlit cigarette between his lips. ''Blaze of glory to John Doe in a body bag in three easy shots.'' He looked up. ''Not open-and-shut, but a no-muss, no-fuss package we can live with.''

His tone prompted a ''Who's we?'' from David.

''Cletus likes it. Phelps likes it. Theron Pike at the highway patrol likes it.'' Marlin's head ticktocked. ''You're about half-smart for an elected official. If you like it, we'll wind 'er up, have a couple of beers, then you and Toots can go back to humping each other's brains out.''

Realizing David didn't appreciate his choice of words, Marlin said, "Make that, so you and Toots can go back to doing whatever it was that slapped the big, stupid-ass smile you had on your face when you got here."

The detective was a master of subtle distinctions—so subtle, they barely existed. According to Hannah, it was one of his charms. That he had any was somewhat of a minority opinion. "When did I say I liked the scenario? More to the point, why don't you?"

Another gravelly throat spasm preceded, "Lieutenant Pike says I was a hemorrhoid in a former life. Once a pain in the ass, always a pain in the ass."

The soggy Marlboro rejoined four unmasticated ones in the pack. A loop-handled sucker materialized from Andrik's jacket pocket. He removed the cellophane and inserted the lime-flavored binky in his mouth. "Bogart stood about here. Beretta in his left hand, TEC–9 in his right."

David moved behind him, relating the stance to his position at the table Tuesday night. "Okay."

"It's a toss-up whether the watch on his right wrist was a gang tag, or he was wearing it because he was left-handed. I'm guessing southpaw."

"So would I," David said. "Pistols have to be aimed. A trained seal could rack off an assault rifle's magazine with its flipper."

David's eyes averted to the wall splattered with Jasmine Chau's blood, then the stained carpet where Eulilly Thomlinson had been seated. "Jasmine was to Bogart's left. Eulilly was nearer the center of the room, but not far enough right to cross himself up.''

Leveling his gaze at the table where IdaClare and Sophonia were shot set off an internal alarm. ''What's the result of the firearms examination?''

''The slugs the M.E. recovered from Jasmine and Mrs. Thomlinson matched the Beretta. The bullet removed from Miss Pugh was from the TEC–9. We can't be sure about Mrs. Clancy, unless we type every slug with blood on it and there's a sackful of them. Her wound was consistent with Pugh's, though. The trajectories indicate both were ricochets.''

David pondered the order in which the shots were fired. He'd focused on Bogart, but peripheral vision had captured Jasmine falling to the floor—more accurately, her white blouse falling from sight.

''I couldn't swear to this in court, but I'm as positive as I can be that Jasmine was shot before Miz Thomlinson.''

''Which fits with Bogart firing the Beretta left to right.''

''And makes Jasmine the primary target and Miz Thomlinson a wrong-place, wrong-time victim.''

Andrik snorted. ''Liking it better all the time, aren'tcha', boss?''

''I repeat, Kojak. Why don't you?''

''The straight chapter and verse would influence your judgment.'' Marlin delved into his pocket and offered David a purple lollipop. ''Chew on this while I do it my way.''

Noting that he always did things his way was futile.

Particularly when he was right. David wasn't impartial, but closer to it than anyone else involved. And he was half-smart, for an elected official.

"Eight people were seated between Jasmine and Mrs. Thomlinson," Marlin said. "Johnny Chau was standing behind the table. None of those nine were hit. Chet Thomlinson sat about a foot away from his wife's right, his back to the door. He wasn't even grazed."

Thomlinson's back *was* to the door. If the vacant seats at IdaClare's table had faced the wall, David would have apologized, then insisted on a round of musical chairs. Any law enforcement officer would. Even Hannah was no longer comfortable with that type of exposure.

"When did Thomlinson stand up in front of you," Marlin asked. "Before or after his wife was shot?"

Seconds extended to a half minute. "I don't know. Like I said, I was focused on the shooter."

"A Saint Louis metro gang specialist says Bogart is gang slang for a con."

Still mentally diagramming the incident, David said, "Before that, it was slang for taking extra hits off a joint instead of passing it on."

"Those were the days, my friend."

David tried picturing Andrik as a hippie-freak, age-of-Aquarius stoner, flipping the peace sign at his friends and half of it at the cops. Strangely enough, he could.

"The same source tells me D.K. is shorthand for Disciples Killer."

"Possibly his real initials," David countered. "Probably an inside joke. I busted a fence in Tulsa operating under the alias Jed I. Knight. Dispatch cracked up when I radioed in that I'd arrested him for possession of stolen property."

"Okay, so what's your explanation for the Beretta's serial number tracing to a burglary in Chicago six months ago?"

Hannah's Cubs T-shirt swam into view. David blinked it away before he envisioned her without it. Saint Louis was the Cardinals' home field, but no gangs he'd heard of represented themselves with their colors or logo.

Except, "Stolen guns rack up more mileage than over-the-road truckers. That pistol could have turned up in Boondock City, Utah, as easily as in Saint Louis, or here."

David waved his lollipop for emphasis. "The scenario still jibes, regardless of Bogart's jumping-off point. Maybe the bus ticket was to throw everyone off. He could have bought a second one-way to Chicago from there. The men's rest room at the Saint Louis terminal has more traffic in a day than Sanity's depot does all month. Unless Bogart called attention to himself, nobody would remember him."

"I'd be inclined to go along, except for a trip-up or two."

Verbal encouragement wasn't necessary. Anomalies and paradoxes were the tenderloin of a homicide investigation. Because the meaty part often contradicted evidence and couldn't be proven, detectives referred to cases as cleared rather than closed or solved.

"Both vics died of gunshots from the Beretta," Marlin said. "The TEC–9 inflicted wounds but didn't raise the body count. That stinks worse than this room."

The scratchy sensation at David's breastbone when he'd lined up behind Marlin unsheathed its claws.

"Bogart had enough cash when he blew into town for a month's rent on a furnished room, utility deposits and rent on a microwave oven, a big-screen TV, cable service and the installation fee."

David motioned *So what?*

"Not two months. Not six weeks. Thirty days."

"Could be that's all the money he had, or cared to spend."

"Could be that's all the time he needed."

David lobbed the sucker from one cheek to the other. Was Andrik shoehorning facts to fit a hunch or did the facts muddy the scenario? The only person who knew had a John Doe tag wired to his big toe.

"Bogart leased a home and all the comforts," Marlin continued, "other than a phone—landline or wireless."

Hannah thought she was the lone exception to the wireless communication rule. She'd snapped the electronic leash when she leapt off the career ladder, and hadn't missed either one iota.

A gangbanger without a cell phone was like a rabbit without ears. Deke Bogart was in hiding, but wouldn't he call his mother, a girlfriend, *somebody?*

Not to tell them where he was but to assure them he was all right?

"Then there's the dishwasher the Chaus hired before Bogart." Marlin's fingernail tapped a notebook page. "Wesley Noland, twenty-four, born with Down's syndrome, lives with his mother and stepfather next door to Deputy Tom Cahill.

"The evening Wesley got the job, he was riding his bicycle to his grandma's when he was attacked and beaten. Fractured skull, multiple contusions and a broken wrist."

"Any description of the assailant?" David asked.

"Noland hasn't spoken a word since it happened." Disgust leavened Marlin's voice. "The Sanity P.D. investigated but couldn't find a witness. When Cahill heard the Royal Dragon shooter was a dishwasher, he told Mrs. Parker, Wesley's mother, to call me."

David's molars pulverized the sucker. He twirled its handle between his thumb and forefinger. "I'm fresh out of patience. If you have an answer for how Bogart knew Noland had the job, much less glommed on to his home address, let's hear it."

"Johnny Chau thinks Wesley's paperwork was on the desk the day Bogart came in to apply. Chau told him the job was taken, but Bogart insisted on filling out an application. Again, Johnny isn't certain, but thinks he may have stepped out to sign for a delivery while Bogart was still there."

David shook his head. Why hadn't he said, "Congratulations" and gone back to the office when Andrik told him he had an *almost* hog-tight, gooseproof workplace massacre case?

The peculiarities stuck in Marlin's craw were circumstantial, conjecture, and all of them dead ends, unless they identified Bogart and worked backward. Even if they did, there was no guarantee they wouldn't be chasing their tails a month from now.

"Bogart didn't have a car," he said. "I doubt if he moseyed around town much. Go ahead and subpoena a Call Detail Record for the past thirty days for every pay phone within a six-block radius of his apartment and between it and the Royal Dragon."

"That's a NASA-size long shot," Marlin warned. "If the drone used prepaid phone cards instead of dropping coins or calling collect, there won't be any records."

"I realize that, but checking all calls to the Saint Louis and Chicago area may give us a lead on his ID."

A tortured, lime-scented sigh gusted from the detective's lips. "The wrap-up, brewskis and smile-along-with-Hannah option is still open."

"'Fraid not." As he turned toward the door, David said, "Fax copies of the scene photos of Bogart's face to all Chicago and Saint Louis P.D. units, too."

"I'm ahead of you on that one, but Thomlinson's SIG-Sauer put some major ugly to his kisser."

*Intentionally?* telegraphed between them.

"What's Thomlinson's excuse for the illegal carry?" David asked.

"He says when they moved here, he applied for a

commission from Sheriff Beauford, but it was refused.''

Law enforcement officers not actively involved with a federal, state, county or municipal agency apply to the sheriff's department for a commission, rather than a permit, to carry a weapon.

If granted, and most are, the holder is technically a commissioned officer attached to the issuing county's department and given a wallet-size photo and fingerprint ID similar to an active deputy's.

David's predecessor, the late and now-martyred Larry Beaumont, had a reputation for puckering whenever a constituent bent over. Beaumont was a magna cum laude graduate of the Good Ol' Boy School of politics, not a cop. The distinction had earned him three consecutive terms of office, but all the glad-handing and ass-kissing in the world couldn't save him from a fatal stroke.

''Did Thomlinson say why Beaumont turned him down?''

''No reason was given,'' Marlin said. ''Knowing Larry, it was to clip Thomlinson's wings in the event he got a hankering to be sheriff.''

''Or just because he could.''

''Uh-huh. An official mine's-bigger-than-yours G-man.'' Marlin added, ''Phelps wasted an hour on the phone this morning trying to verify Chester Arthur Thomlinson's attachment to the Secret Service. No confirmation, no denial.''

David rolled his eyes. ''Which is a confirmation. If

Thomlinson was impersonating an agent, the feds would have been real interested real fast.''

"Amen, brother. We'd have blue-suited, No Necks with mike cords pigtailing out their ears on the premises, as we speak.''

Points had to be given for consistency. Marlin's admiration for all branches of the Justice Department was equal opportunity slander.

David said, "I worked with a Secret Service agent on a counterfeiting ring back in Tulsa. He's been transferred several times since, but we still swap Christmas cards. I'll see if I can track him down.''

"Christ on crutches.'' Marlin jammed a cigarette in his mouth and lit it without removing the lollipop. "Got any more wild-hare, ain't-gonna-happen ideas?''

"A few.'' David grinned. "I'll let you know if they pan out.''

# 10

"Jack left last night, dear," IdaClare said. "Do you mean to say he didn't tell you goodbye after supper?"

She was seated at one end of her living room's l-shaped sectional, its arm the perfect height for elevating hers. Itsy and Bitsy roosted on her lap, their beady black eyes somehow managing to look up at Hannah and down on her simultaneously.

"No, he didn't." Hannah wasn't sure whether to be hurt or angry, then decided on both. "When we were setting the table, he said he wasn't leaving until this morning."

"That's odd. He came back last night after the news was over. He said he needed to be at the office first thing in the morning and was stopping by your cottage on the way out."

IdaClare clucked her tongue. "I can't imagine what's gotten into that boy. He had ants in his britches the entire time he was here."

Hannah feigned a forgiving smile. "To be fair, I haven't been operating on all cylinders for the past couple of days, myself."

"Oh, piffle. Concerned about me, I understand—

although he wouldn't have been if someone had done as she was told and not spilled the beans.''

IdaClare's good hand sliced the air and, metaphorically, any argument Hannah might attempt. Jack's hospital hot line remained his little secret, but in light of his horse's-ass behavior of late, it irked Hannah to cover for him.

Especially when he was hiding something, doing a wretched job of it, knew he was, and couldn't care less.

No, she thought, the last is my inner child stamping her foot and pouting. Jack cared. Enough to choose avoiding her, leave her twisting in the wind with Marlin Andrik's questions echoing in her head rather than lie to her.

Betraying her by not betraying her. Did comforts come any smaller than that?

IdaClare went on, ''Chet Thomlinson lost his wife, for heaven's sake, and he's not snappish and flibbertigibbety.'' She sighed. ''Of course, Jack always was excitable. Born with an electric gooser in his pocket was what my mama called it. Just like his father, God rest him.''

An electric gooser? Hannah filed away that gem for future reference. ''I'm sure his trip to San Diego was part of it. Worry on top of jet lag would make anyone moody.''

''He's making plenty enough excuses for himself without you stoking the coals,'' IdaClare said. ''Between you and me, I think it's menopause. Men have it, too, you know, though they wouldn't admit it to a mirror.

"One day, they're fine and the next—" IdaClare twiddled a button on her robe. "Well, the tra-lah-lah's still there, but they can't count on the boom-de-yah."

Hannah struggled to breathe and squelch the motorboat noises in her throat.

"Besides him being such a sweet man," IdaClare said, "I'm sure the sheriff being younger is why your sleeping with him got a majority vote at breakfast. It would have been unanimous, except Delbert abstained, the old hypocrite, but only because he's so fond of you. Not that the rest of us—"

"You *voted?* About David and me?"

"After Leo heard at Wiley's Newsstand that your cottage was dark and the sheriff's car was in the driveway all night?" IdaClare laughed, as though not casting ballots pertaining to David and Hannah's sex life would violate the Geneva Convention. "Rosemary and Leo thought y'all were boinking last week at the sheriff's house the morning of their engagement party, then Marge said you didn't have 'the look' when you got home."

*Boinking? The look?*

"I swan, you're glowing like a sun-kissed Georgia peach today, though. Anyone with half an eye can see that."

Ye gods. Calls into Valhalla Springs must be receiving a robotic, *We're sorry, all circuits are busy at this time. Please try again later.*

IdaClare's satiny palm caressed the back of Hannah's hand. Time had pocked her wedding band and distended the ring finger it encircled. "Listen to me, dear."

"Really, IdaClare. I think I've heard enough."

"Mind your elders, young lady. Marge will be out of the shower any minute and there's something I want to say to you in private."

Hannah sat back on the sofa, bracing herself for the traditional why - buy - the - cow - when - you - can - get - the - milk - for - free lecture. She startled when IdaClare said, "I could have died on the floor of that restaurant."

"Wha—? Oh, Lord, don't even *think* that."

"Why not? Being reminded that life is precious and can be gone in an instant is a gift." She smiled. "I'll tell you true, it'll be a while before I start the day complaining about sags and bags, chin whiskers and stove-up joints."

A schoolgirl bashfulness washed over her face. "Now, I'm not your mother and I'll never be your mother-in-law, happy as it would make me, but that doesn't mean I can't talk to you like one or the other.

"I haven't, in all my born days, seen two people as much in love as you and your sheriff. Best of all, you like each other. If you don't marry him, I can't promise you'll regret it, but I can promise you'll be emptier when you could have been full."

IdaClare paused, staring at memories as vivid as the peonies blooming in the wallpaper. "When Patrick passed away, I was lost and lonely but not empty. Some think a marriage license is just a piece of paper. Well, so's a deed, a diploma and the title to a car. If that's all it was, nobody'd bat an eyelash at getting one.''

"I know it's more than a piece of paper," Hannah said. "So does David. If we didn't, there's no chance we'd wave our arms and shout, 'I do, I do. Lemme go first.' When the minister asked if anyone had reasons we shouldn't be joined in holy matrimony.''

IdaClare didn't appreciate the sarcasm, but her look said she understood and sympathized. "Remember our talk in the kitchen after Leo and Rosemary's engagement party? My objections to them tearing hell-bent for election to the altar?''

IdaClare resented the inevitable demotion to third wheel, empathized with Rosemary's and Leo's children's horror at the surprise, long-distance telephone announcement, and was fearful of the financial entanglements involved in two single senior citizens becoming a couple.

"Some of them were silly," IdaClare allowed, "but most were commonsense reasons to hold their horses.''

Hannah agreed.

"What if they'd decided I was right? What if they'd postponed the wedding until all their problems were solved and everything was perfect?''

"Nothing is ever perfect," Hannah blurted, then realized her response was a shrewd form of ventriloquism.

"But what if they had, dear? What if Leo Schnur and Rosemary Marchetti had gone to the Thomlinsons' party and one of them had been killed?''

The Irish were renowned for their fatalism. The Garveys' gene pool was a cultural goulash, but the philosophies were similar. As cued, she substituted her name and David's for Leo's and Rosemary's. Like Clarence the unwinged angel had turned back the calendar for Jimmy Stewart in *It's A Wonderful Life,* Hannah's reversed to Sunday evening.

The image of sharing a bowl of popcorn with Malcolm, parked on the sofa watching *The Simpsons* reruns superseded those of Leo and Rosemary's lakeside wedding, the reception and David's proposal. The shooting was predestined, but if the outcome had been different…

The chill Hannah felt was not hypothetical. A 10–39 was cop-talk for "message delivered," but no revelations trod its heels. Her great-uncle Mort had jollified many suppertime conversations with "We're all born dyin', ya know. Could go tomorrow. Might hang on a hundred years and then some. There's just no tellin'."

These pronouncements were met with Great-aunt Lurleen's offer to alleviate the guesswork by sticking a meat fork in Mort's neck.

"What happened to 'Marry in haste, repent in leisure'?" Hannah said. "As I recall, you told Leo and Rosemary that about ninety-four times before the ceremony."

IdaClare laid her head back on the couch. Her eyelids closed as though their springs had broken. "That's all I have to say, dear. Go on now, and let me rest."

The Furwads bounded off her lap to nip Hannah's ankles on her way out. IdaClare assured her again that neither she nor Marge needed anything from town, "but you might ask Dixie Jo if she has an opening tomorrow for a shampoo and set."

Hannah cringed, and not from the dual sets of incisors gnawing her anatomy like cobbed corn. She should have known mentioning a haircut among her errands in Sanity would lead IdaClare to assume an appointment had been made at the Curl Up and Dye—which is what Hannah would sooner do than let Dixie Jo Gage within ten miles of her hair.

The shop's regular clientele thrived on toxic levels of Aqua Net, Dippity-Do, perm solution and gossip. All of them sported one of three hairstyles: earlobe short and back-combed extra large, a chignon with a pouffy berm at the crown or Florence Henderson's *Brady Bunch* shag. The latter looked cute on Rosemary Schnur. Hannah would wind up a dead ringer for Michael Nesmith of The Monkees.

"Don't you think tomorrow is too soon to—"

"No. I don't. We Clancys don't fiddle-fart around. You've got to get off your keister to stand on your own two feet."

Wherever Great-uncle Mort was spending eternity, Hannah hoped he heard that one.

IdaClare raised her head and shook it. "Never mind Dixie Jo, or me, either. It's aggravating enough having a wing clipped without being so mad at Jack I could just spit. There's no call for him leaving the way he did. None whatsoever."

"He'll regret it," Hannah said, her tone too casual and grin too stiff to fool his mother, or herself.

Additional evidence that she should have stayed in bed, with or without David, was leaning against his car in the driveway to her cottage. An unpaved maintenance road was an alternative exit from the development, but Chet Thomlinson had already spotted the Blazer. To wave back at him as she floored the accelerator might be misconstrued.

She should be ashamed. And was. His wife had been murdered before his eyes. Hannah's uneasiness around him was her fault not his. There were no right things to say at a time like this. Avoiding him to avoid saying the wrong thing was egotism disguised as kindness.

Still, her "Good morning" sounded mocking, although he returned it with a smile. "Nice dog," he said, petting Malcolm as people feel obliged to do when a dog nudges a hand atop its head, as if trying on a new hat.

Perceiving Hannah's pronunciation of his name as synonymous with "Scram," Malcolm trotted off to the porch.

"I'd say we're in for rain." Chet's shoulders squared as he took a deep breath. "It's near enough, you can smell it."

"Would you like to come in for a cup of coffee?"

"Thanks, but I can't stay." He checked his watch. "I have to pick up Dolores Trimble and the Caldwells in a few minutes to make our flight from Kansas City International.''

Question marks must have riven her expression. He explained, ''The funeral is tomorrow morning. I completely forgot that Eulilly had booked seats to fly us home Saturday, after the movers left. The travel agent rescheduled for today and reserved two more tickets for the Caldwells.''

Hannah nodded. ''Whether you'd flown down with Jack, or your friends, it's good you aren't going alone.''

''If you won't tell, I'll let you in on a secret.'' The mischievous glint in his eyes vanished so fast it could have been imaginary. ''I'd love a few hours alone. Everyone has been wonderfully supportive, but the bosom of friendship can be a little suffocating.''

Hannah contained a reflexive *Then why did you accept IdaClare's dinner invitation last night?*

''The reason I came by was to ask if an extension can be arranged on my cottage's lease. Vince Caldwell renewed the one on my car and canceled the movers, but—''

Chet frowned and looked again at his watch—a Cellini-edition Rolex identical to Jack Clancy's. ''If we can't work something out, I'll be homeless by midnight tomorrow night.''

Hannah didn't understand her hesitation. Chet hadn't signed Eulilly's petition. As far as Hannah knew, he hadn't been party to her threatened lawsuit. His signature was absent on the notice to vacate that

Eulilly had couriered to Hannah's office after the suit was dropped.

The lease agreement was in both their names. Only one appearing on the notice rendered it unenforceable by the Thomlinsons, or Valhalla Springs, Inc., but who was Hannah to quibble? At the time, it was all she could do to resist sending Eulilly a thank-you gift in the form of packing flats wrapped in ribbons and bows.

"What about Belle Rive the lakehouse Eulilly told everyone about?" Hannah waved the remark away. "None of my business. Pretend I didn't ask."

"It's all right. I know you aren't prying. Eulilly didn't lie, but wasn't entirely truthful about our new home. Belle Rive is the Bethune family estate."

Granny Garvey would describe Chet's shudder as someone walking across his grave—an analogy Hannah wished she hadn't thought of.

"It's a monstrosity of a house. We lived there for a year after we married. It has enough rooms for Eulilly's brothers, wives, visiting children, the two of us and half the county."

"It sounds lovely."

"Historically and architecturally, yes." His chuckle was humorless. "The constant infighting and tantrums are not. Eulilly promised it was temporary, but the estate is a King of the Hill game to her and her brothers, and may the best Bethune win."

Chet made a sour face and stepped closer. "Forgive me. I've told you more than you cared to hear and insulted my wife's memory in one breath."

"No, you didn't. With all that's happened, it's a wonder you haven't collapsed under the strain."

"Well, you have to get off your keister to stand on your own two feet."

A chill clattered down Hannah's spine.

"That saying isn't original with me." His wistful smile wasn't intended for her. It and the thoughts softening his features were directed toward a cottage trimmed with fuchsia millwork at 2404 Sumac Drive. "IdaClare Clancy is a remarkable woman. And, in my opinion, woefully underappreciated."

"Oh?" Hannah crooked an eyebrow. "How so?"

Chet laughed. "What woman isn't?" He reached to pat her arm. Her recoil was reflexive. His hand reversed trajectory and raised to smooth his hair.

Hannah inflicted a mental kick in the butt. What in the hell was *wrong* with her? "Of course I can extend your lease. Thirty days, sixty, whatever you need, including until October 31, the original renewal date."

His relief and obvious gratitude sent a second virtual boot to her behind. "Sixty would be a perfect deadline—with an option to renew, if it's amenable to you. Enough time to put my affairs in order, but not enough to procrastinate for weeks on end."

"Sixty it is, then. You will have to sign a new contract, though, to dismiss the notice to vacate."

"We're flying back from Mississippi tomorrow evening, but may not drive home from Kansas City until the next morning. Will that be soon enough?"

"Whenever you feel up to it is soon enough."

"Oh, Hannah, I can't—" Chet slid his hands into

his trouser pockets and looked down. A wing tip's heel ground the driveway's asphalt.

When he looked up again, tears rimmed his eyes. "After the trouble Eulilly caused you and Willard Johnson, saying thank-you is less than inadequate. Almost as inadequate as I was for doing nothing to stop her."

He smacked his lips. "I hoped—make that, I convinced myself that spiriting her away from the Bethune clan, their social circle and their prejudices would...well, temper her attitude somewhat."

A leopard in its natural habitat has the same spots as one in a zoo, Hannah thought. If I went back to Effindale tomorrow, I'd still be just another trashy Garvey. I didn't change my spots. I simply went to a place where no one recognized them.

"I was wrong," Chet said. "I vowed 'for better or for worse,' then set about to change the things about her I didn't approve of."

"Isn't that what everyone does?" Hannah lifted her shoulders. "Find the perfect someone to love, honor and cherish, then start buffing the blemishes the minute you get home from the honeymoon?"

"A little cynical, but yes, I suppose that's true." He smiled as he opened the car door. "If you and Eulilly had met before her, uh, crusade, I think you'd have liked each other a great deal."

He thanked Hannah again, then turned from the driveway and headed toward the residential area.

A dedicated operations manager would take the opportunity to check her messages before continuing to town. Hannah climbed into her truck, mulling over Chet's parting remark.

"I'm sorry Eulilly's dead, but no, I wouldn't have liked her, regardless of when we met." Glancing in the side mirror, she had the strangest feeling that Chet's comment was a form of doublespeak, and not the first instance of it.

He's a retired federal agent, she reminded herself. David, Marlin, Jimmy Wayne McBride—they all spoke in code, too. Observing them in action had undoubtedly fine-tuned her hearing—and transformed an average amount of latent paranoia into the chronic variety.

The seat belt's tongue clicked in its clasp. Kinderhook County's finest cop-talked among themselves, though. Other than inside jokes, cryptic remarks weren't insinuated into everyday conversations.

Then again, maybe Chet had been in law enforcement so long, he'd forgotten how to be a civilian. The Blazer's eight cylinders roared to life. Or maybe, as Delbert would say, Hannah was nuttier than a fruitcake factory.

David reviewed his notes on the legal pad and expanded on them while the morning's second telephone conversation was fresh in his mind.

The first call to the Bethunes' home county had gone pretty much as he'd expected. Sheriff Filo W. Imes expressed shock and sorrow at Eulilly's untimely death. She, her brothers and every Bethune begatted since Noah nailed the last board on the Ark had been pillars of the community, champions of the common man and leapt tall buildings in a single bound.

The second call connected David with the doyenne of the daily newspaper's gardening, food, home and society pages. Thalia Honeycutte had started writing a Bethune roman à clef in 1963 and was within fifty pages of the finale. To cover her derriere, as she put it, she related information about her subjects in the manner of a novel synopsis.

Hampton Bethune was portrayed as a puff adder, the reptilian equivalent of a harmless blowhard with delusions of being a cobra. Clay, the baby of the family, was a walking cliché—the dashing, handsome boozehound who couldn't keep his pants zipped and had never done a lick of work in his life.

"Eulilly is—was, God rest her—as cunning and ruthless as her daddy and his daddy before him," she told him, "but suffered the egregious misfortune of being the firstborn and female. She might have salvaged some usefulness to her father had the endometriosis she suffered as a young woman not left her barren."

The newspaperwoman's monologue itemized the sins of the father and sons for several minutes, then she drawled, "I thought it peculiar when Eulilly decamped to Missouri with her latest husband. Belles aren't given to wandering afield of their roots and setting them down elsewhere. It's a second cousin to treason in these parts."

"Do you have any idea why she did?" David

asked, as though Miss Honeycutte needed prompting. "Sheriff Imes was vague on the cause."

Laughter cackled from the earpiece. "Filo's vague on pert-near everything, 'cept which side of his bread is buttered and who owns the churn." After a pause, she said, "Ever hear of giving a man enough rope to hang himself?"

David smiled. "Yes, ma'am."

"Well, long story as short as I can tell it, Eulilly told Hampton, Clay and everyone in creation that Mr. Thomlinson was the love of her life and how right her daddy was about a woman's place being in the home not behind a silly old desk.

"After a few years of out-of-sight, out-of-mind up north in your part of the world, Eulilly began a whisper campaign among select board members and people of influence. Her being a Southern lady and slicker than goose grease on a doorknob, none of the innuendos slandering Hampton's management decisions and personal peccadilloes circulated with her name attached.

"Eulilly was opposed to what she called 'Hampton's Mississippi Disneyland,' due to the size of Bethune's investment," Thalia continued, "only she must have had an ax to grind with that Saint Louis contracting outfit besides. No matter. Her scheme-within-a-scheme was securing the proxies necessary to kibosh the project, which also put Hampton on notice that her voting majority would next be used to oust him as Bethune's chairman and chief executive officer."

Thalia laughed again, a note of admiration and sheer delight in it this time. "There's more than one way to skin a cat, Sheriff Hendrickson. Leave it to one with abiding patience, cunning and intestinal fortitude to divine the perfect comeuppance for her littermates."

By her sigh, David imagined the woman sagging from head to toe. "Alas, it wasn't meant to be. I'd outlined the last chapter of my book as a triumph. The prodigal daughter's victorious return to her rightful place as head of the family and its fortune.

"Life truly is stranger than fiction, Sheriff. Ending with a funeral will tug heartstrings, but it simply *ruins* any hope of a sequel."

David said, "I really appreciate your taking the time to—"

"Unless—" Thalia's thoughtful drawl added an extra syllable and an uptick. "What if Eulilly faked her own death for some plausible reason? Then Hampton could be disabled by a heart attack—no, a stroke! Why, I can picture him, helpless as a newborn babe..."

Click. Dial tone. David had cradled the receiver, chuckling to himself. Thalia Honeycutte's information was a far cry from gospel, but he couldn't remember when he'd enjoyed listening to hearsay as much.

Rereading his notes wiped the smile from his face. He wondered how long it would take Miss Honeycutte to parlay Eulilly's "untimely death" into a motive for Hampton Bethune to rid himself of the only threat to his cushy kingdom.

Can't scratch Jack Clancy off the list, either, David thought. Eulilly might have been the foxiest of the three Bethune sibs, but Hampton could have leveraged the resort bid into incentive for Clancy to arrange Eulilly's demise.

Money talks, listens, silences and blinds. It had since the dawn of time when he who had the most shells made the rules. Eulilly was worth more dead than alive to too many people for too many different reasons.

A flash of color in the doorway to his office caught David's eye. Claudina's bird-of-paradise print dress was smudged at the bustline and belly, as was the tip of her nose.

"No commission applications in the name of Chester A. Thomlinson," she said. "Not many in the files during Beauford the benevolent despot's reign, period."

David motioned for her to come in and shut the door behind her. "I distinctly remember asking Heather to do the records search. Who handled dispatch while you did her job for her?"

She flapped a hand. "Lose the Andrick impersonation, boss. He looked just like you, only shorter, until he scowled once too often and it stuck."

"Funny."

Claudina wedged herself into a barrel-backed visitor's chair. "Heather just had a manicure, she's allergic to dust spores and she can't answer phones and work the front desk from the basement. I knew more or less which corner of the dungeon the records were in, Jimmy Wayne took over E–911 for me and a good time was had by all.''

"Yeah, I'll bet.'' David doodled a three-dimensional cube on the desk blotter. "How many refused applications were in the files?''

"That would be none. If you ask me, which you didn't, Larry lit his cigars with the rejects. Ashes to ashes was his favorite method of recycling.''

David had guessed as much by the skimpy, selective records he'd inherited. Scuttlebutt said the emergency room doctor hadn't pulled the sheet over Beaumont's head before his buddies converged for an office cleaning party.

"Want another opinion you didn't ask for?'' Claudina said.

"Do I have a choice?''

"The majority of us peons think you and Marlin are barking up the wrong tree.'' She gestured like a traffic cop. "Actually, the consensus is you don't have a tree to bark up.''

David's pencil tinked on the side of his coffee cup. The thought had occurred to him a time, or twenty.

"You've worked three, mind-bending homicide investigations back to back,'' Claudina said. "A workplace massacre in the capital of 'It Can't Happen Here' has everyone scrambling for answers to why it *did* happen here. The saving grace is that the shooter was an out-of-towner, but—''

"An out-of-towner murdering two locals and in-

juring fifteen is scarier than the devils you know,"
David finished. "Folks can't shake their heads and
say, 'I knew that boy was trouble when he was knee-
high to a grasshopper.'"

He sat back in his chair. "That blue folder on the
corner of the desk? It's full of news clips and printouts on every mass shooting in the past five years.
What they have in common is that the shooter's plan
was cut, dried and simple. No tangents, coincidences
or question as to who the killer was."

Claudina eyed the folder, her expression pensive.
"Aren't there always tangents and coincidences, even
after a conviction?"

"Is that private citizen Burkholtz talking or deputy
candidate-to-be Burkholtz?"

Sitting straighter, she splayed her arms as though
preparing to take a bow. "Notice anything?"

An uh-oh tolled in David's mind. In addition to
"Does this outfit make me look fat?" and "What are
you thinking about?" those two words siezed a man's
heart faster than a congressional declaration of war.
Frantic to get the answer right for once in his life, he
checked items off the standard list.

Claudina's dress wasn't new. Her hair was the
same color and style. Makeup the same. That left
weight loss—the diciest guess of all. Tell a female
she looks like she's lost some and she'll either kiss
you, ask if you're insinuating she needs to or say
she's gained ten pounds, which proves that as far as
you're concerned, she's the Invisible Woman.

Courage mustered and service revolver holstered

on his hip, he said, "You've lost a little weight, haven't you?"

"A *little?*"

Oops.

Claudina huffed, "I'll have you know I've dropped three pounds, not counting the ten I sweated off taking the stairs to the basement instead of the elevator."

He made a mental note to strike "a little" from any future responses. "Numbers on the scale are just scorekeeping. Setting goals and sticking with them. That's what's important."

She crossed her arms as her lips pulled back in a close-but-no-cigars wince. "The Andrik impersonation isn't bad, but your Yoda needs work."

Whoever knocked on his office door didn't wait for an answer before opening it. Heather Gray's head craned inside as though less than a full-body commitment didn't constitute an interruption. "A Mr. Webster Phillips is on line two. He says he's returning your call."

Phillip Webber aka Webster Phillips of the Secret Service. A tad cloak-and-dagger, but David understood Phil's cautiousness. Whatever the background information he'd collected on Chester A. Thomlinson, if anyone traced the leak back to him, he'd be transferred to Point Barrow, Alaska, until eligible for retirement.

"Thanks, Heather." David's finger hovered above the blinking hold button. "And thank *you*, Miz Burkholtz."

"You're welcome, Sheriff Tall, Dark and Tactful."

Claudina heaved herself from the chair. "May the force be with you."

The downpour had discouraged most foot traffic around Sanity's square. A few store owners and passersby stood with their feet slewed and arms akimbo under droopy awnings, as though the canvas promontories could deflect lightning.

The Blazer's windshield wipers *whumped* in time to Hannah's a cappella "I Love A Rainy Night." It was only half-past ten, but as dark as dusk, and the lyrics suited the crackling light show and rolling thunder.

Circling from the square's west side to the east, she saw that the space reserved for Marlin's Coupe de Cruddy sedan was empty, as was the adjacent slot Orr and Phelps had to share. Outside the courthouse's south entrance, David's cruiser was between another patrol unit and a Saint Louis TV-news van.

Nothing ominous or unusual about that, Hannah lied to herself. Farther-flung broadcast and print-media crews often covered trials moved to Kinderhook County on changes of venue. Its central location also generated backyard-travel features targeting city-dwelling canoeists, anglers, campers and hikers.

For the time being—however the hell long *that* was—there were three distractions she couldn't allow. One was the continuing dirgelike bad vibe with Jack's name on it, its possible cause too hideous to contemplate.

David's pending proposal was another. The harder

everyone pushed, the deeper her heels dug in. A genuine devil's advocate would be grand, but she couldn't remember David's ex-wife's second husband's full name.

Last of all, letting her thoughts wander to last night's lovemaking, their middle-of-the night lovemaking, their early-morning lovemaking and images of future lovemaking was dangerous. Explaining the accidental demolition of a half block of parked cars, utility poles and Keep Sanity Beautiful trash receptacles to her insurance agent would be a bitch, and could have a negative effect on her premiums.

Condensation fogged the plate-glass window of Eli Cree's barbershop. A brick that might have toppled from the building's crenelated facade held open the original wood-framed, beveled insert door. Beside it, the traditional and virtually extinct red, white and blue-striped pole turned stuttery revolutions inside its yellowed glass fixture.

The proprietor was as much a museum piece as the ornate, mirrored backbar and filigreed nickel-and-oxblood leather chair he was napping in. His starched white shirt was as immaculate as the apron worn over it. Even with his chin nodding along with his snores, the bow tie clipped to his collar stayed ruler straight.

Fearful of startling the old gent, Hannah dropped her shoulder bag on the seat of one of the painted metal and black duct tape–upholstered chairs. The timid *thump* was lost in a glass-rattling peal of thunder. Similar to the *Titanic*'s band, the barber slept on.

She was about to join her purse and wait for Cree

to finish his forty winks when a crusty voice announced, "I already give to the Red Cross, the 4-H and the cancer society. I found Jesus afore you was a twinkle in your mama's eye, can't afford no free samples, and from where I sit, lifetime guarantees ain't worth the paper they're writ on."

KSAN's midday farm-to-market report droned from the Philco cathedral radio on the backbar. Cree hadn't moved a muscle. The snoring recommenced as though it were God who had spoken.

Hannah knuckled her hips. "How long have you been awake?"

He grinned like a wizened leprechaun. "Oh, since about five this morning." Scooting forward in the chair, he planted his six-eyelet spectators on the terrazzo-tile floor, as if assuring himself his legs would go the distance before committing himself.

"Beg pardon for funnin' with you. miss. T'ain't often I get the chance to jokify a pretty lady." He wiped off the seat he'd vacated with the corner of his apron. "What can I do you for? Or did you just venture in out of the storm?"

Hannah ruffled her hair. "Do you trim women's hair, Mr. Cree?"

"Been known to have. Scalped dogs and docked horses' tails, too, if it's of interest to you." From wire-rimmed spectacles thumbed higher on his nose, he scrutinized her coiffure, then motioned for her to turn around.

"There's a fair acre of threshin' needing done,

miss. 'Fraid I can't wade into it for less'n ten dollars.''

She'd tipped Henri of Chicago twice that, but be still her heart at Eli's choice of words. A haircut wasn't the prime objective. Neither was spending the summer with a bag over her head. By trade and age, the barber was a font of local history—and she wanted some.

"A trim." Her fingers clamped a section, sliding down to within a millimeter of its split ends. "Just a trim."

He shrugged. "How's about I shape it real nice for nine-fifty and throw in a sodie pop?"

"Deal." For which she'd give him a twenty, then argue him into keeping fifteen.

Eli swathed her from neck to knees in a cotton bib as large as a bedsheet, then moved to a soft-drink machine that advertised "The pause that refreshes" for five cents. A slug tied to a piece of twine jiggered the coin slot. With a rattle and a clunk, a chubby, hourglass-shaped bottle flumed down the chute. A recessed opener peeled off the cap.

"I didn't know they still made sodas this size," Hannah said. "Or in glass bottles."

"S'pect that means you're a foreigner." A wide-toothed comb gently unsnarled her hair. "In these parts, everyone knows a soda has ice cream in it."

"They did where I grew up, too. After I moved to Chicago, it took a couple of years to learn to call a soft drink a soda."

Eli spun the chair away from the mirror and

pumped the foot pedal to elevate it a few inches. "Back when I was coming up, often as not, jobs paid in milk bottles instead of cash money. Sometimes 'twas two, three days afore the grocer had enough coin in the till to pony up the fifteen-cent deposit."

"You've lived here all your life, then," Hannah said, as if she didn't already know.

Twice a month, Eli gave David a trim and told him about his and his beloved wife's courtship. David's hair didn't need cutting that often and he could relate the story as well as Eli, but said he never tired of listening to it.

"Yes'm." The comb coasted down her hair; scissor blades snipped in two-beat syncopation. "Never lived farther than five miles from the cabin I was born in, 'cept for that expense-paid European vacation I went on, courtesy of FDR."

Dry cuts must be Eli's forte. Okay, so real men don't eat quiche and real barbers don't spritz. Her fingers gripped the soft-drink bottle like a rabbit's foot. Mind over matter. No guts, no glory—crowning or otherwise.

"Is Eli short for Elijah?"

He laughed. The scissors snippety-snipped. *Yikes.*

"Elias. The granny woman that slapped the squall out of me told Ma that Elias Millhaus Cree was a whopping handle for man or boy, but it got writ in the family bible irregardless."

Hannah repeated it aloud. "I think it's a wonderful name. Friendly and dignified. And not nearly as whopping as Jefferson Davis Oglethorpe."

Her attempted tongue-clucks had an unfortunate sucking-concrete-through-a-straw quality. "Isn't it sad that Jedo never married and had children?"

"Jedo?" Amusement and leeriness undertoned his voice. "That's a new one on me, and I've been lowering his ears since Heck was a pup."

The rain had stopped. KSAN's update on current feeder pig prices and soybean futures outroed to the MFA store's dealer spot. Range cubes and salt mix priced to m-o-ove segued to a song entitled "She Thinks My Tractor's Sexy."

Dots were dancing behind Hannah's eyes before Eli said, "A broken heart won't kill a man, but it don't always mend," and she could expel the anxious breath she'd held for what seemed like an hour.

"The girl that ripped out Jefferson's heart tromped it flatter'n a flitter. Being rich and not bad to look at, young ladies shoaled him as thick as flies to honeybutter. He dallianced with plenty, but was ruint afore his peach fuzz sprouted to chin whiskers."

Eli sidled into her peripheral vision. Hannah slanted a look at him. "Uh-huh. Sure." Her lips twitched into a smile. "This girl who broke Oglethorpe's heart. Did she die in a fire, drown in a flood, get thrown from a horse?"

"Come again?"

"Isn't that the way legendary love-gone-wrong stories always end? Whichever one does the heartbreaking dies a tragic death, leaving the other to grieve his life away, but—" She winked, then whispered, "To this day, on moonless nights, the lover's ghost haunts the place where she died, crying for a love that could never be.''

Just as she'd hoped, Eli threw back his head and laughed. ''Them kind of yarns is for spoofin' tourists and scarin' the britches off little kids.''

Sectioning the side of her hair, he flopped it over the top of her head. ''Hold that up yonder whilst I prune the scrub.''

''A trim,'' she reminded. ''Just a trim.''

''The girl that ruint Jefferson is a haint of sorts, only it's 'cause she's still kickin', not 'cause she's dead. Nobody knows for certain-sure what happened betwixt 'em, but they were doomed from the start. Her people and his people was close as kinfolk when they whoaed their wagons alongside Jinks Creek.''

Eli grunted and ratcheted up the chair several notches. ''Some say they fell out over money, others say 'twas politics, but t'weren't long afore they was feuding like wildcats in a tow sack.

''Forbidden fruit being the sweetest, the only surprise is that it took a couple of generations for a romance to spark and catch fire. Knowin' if their parents found out, there'd be worse than hell to pay, they conjured a way to leave messages, like the Indians did. A flower in the crotch of a tree meant one thing, rocks, lumps of coal, somethin' else, and so on.''

Hannah said, ''But somebody got wise—''

''I ain't liable for slicing ears off yakkety-yakkers.''

*All rightie, then. Tick a freakin' lock.*

''Figurin' they'd best light out for an Arkansas justice of the peace *before* their folks, or a busybody, caught 'em spooning, they set two different days and times, in the event one of 'em couldn't sneak out the first try.

"Jefferson was disappointed when she didn't show, but tickled they'd had the smarts to plan ahead. He was squirreling a bent twig or some such into the meeting tree's knothole when he found a note. It said she'd never loved him, and had beguiled him into falling for her to revenge him and his family for being lyin', cheatin', egg-suckin' spawns of Satan that weren't and never would be fit to wipe dung off her people's boots."

"Ouch." Hannah winced, inwardly and outwardly. "I have to admit, though, it sounds just like her."

The scissors hoo-*whacked* so near her earlobe, she felt a breeze off the blades.

Eli leaned around and looked at her as though she were picking his pocket with one hand and stealing his watch with the other. "Not nary once—*yet*—did I say the girl's name. First, middle or Christian."

Guilt at trouncing his punch line failed to burst her elated bubble. "I *knew* I was right. The pusillanimous scalawag and the Jezebel have been in love their entire lives."

Eli's head retracted like turtle's. "The who?"

"That's only half the story, too. *His* half." She guzzled the rest of her soda and held out the bottle. "I don't mean to rush you, but I have a sick friend I need to visit."

He wagged a finger at her. "You listen here, Miss

Hannah Garvey. You'd best tend to your own knitting with the sheriff and let them two sleeping dogs lie.''

Her mouth fell open.

"Think I didn't know who you were, where you come from, where you live and how long you and Sheriff Hendrickson's been courtin' a full month afore you sashayed in here, personal?'' His chin bobbed. "That's why I'm cautioning you like a father, pa'tickally seeing as how I am one, and you didn't have a daddy to call your own.

"Small-town folks don't cotton to strangers telling them how to fix what ails 'em. Now, Jefferson Davis Oglethorpe may have eight toes in the grave, but he still swings a big mallet in this county. Trifle with him, and David Hendrickson won't have a prayer of beating Jessup Knox in the August primary.''

# 11

"I didn't expect to hear from you again till next week," David said into the phone. "What did you do? Skip the morning latte and biscotti break?"

Phil Webster made an obscene suggestion. "When are you going to get out of Hooterville and run with us big dogs? Another year or two and you'll be too old to apply, man."

Consistency was the Secret Service agent's middle name. Every phone call, every Christmas card, was a recruitment tool. Back in his Young Turk days, not long removed from the Tulsa academy, David had seriously considered it, along with the ATF, DEA and U.S. Marshals Service. Playing cops 'n robbers on a grand scale sounded exciting as all get out for a pharmacist's son from Saint Joseph, Missouri.

Cynthia was gung-ho, too, until Phil's wife disavowed her of the notion that White House dinners and D.C. society cocktail parties were part of the package.

"I'm overworked, underpaid and the department's way understaffed," David said, "but I'm happy right where I am."

"Uh-huh." The telephone line hummed a few seconds. "So, what's her name?"

David grinned. "Hannah."

"Hmm. I see attractive but not drop-dead gorgeous. Street-smart. Smart-ass sense of humor. Stubborn, but not as bullheaded as you are, and what she has, Mumsy and Daddy didn't give her. She worked for it."

David pulled the receiver from his ear and stared at it a moment. "You got all that from her *name?*"

"No, I took what I remember about Cynthia and flopped it on its back." Phil laughed. "Opposites attract, but I hope you're thinking with the brain above your neck this time."

David bridled a little. Cynthia had her faults and he'd devoted more time and effort to saving the world than his marriage. But she was his first love, he'd spent a third of his life with her and Pin the Tail On the Ex-wife had never been his game.

Yeah, well. With the divorce rate nudging fifty percent, trashing former spouses was America's favorite pastime. He washed down an imaginary chill pill with a sip of lukewarm coffee.

"Did you just call back to draft me and discuss my love life?" he said. "Or is this your way of saying you don't have squat on the individual in question?"

"Oh ye of little faith." Paper rustled in the background. "It so happens, a friend of a friend of an acquaintance and our subject were on third squad detail at the end of Bob Dole's presidential campaign, aka the ninety-six-hour marathon.'"

Secret Service duties are split among four squads: Counterfeit Currency, Fraud, Protective Intelligence and another operating as a catchall for special investigations. Agents rotated into and out of squad assignments and were subject to transfer from one field office to another every three to four years.

The duty rotation had appealed to David, but even Phil admitted the long hours and relocation were hard on agents and doubly hard on their families.

"According to unnamed sources," Phil continued, "our man was a good guy who did his job. Dependable, professional, but didn't bust his hump."

"A few commendations and no black marks in his jacket."

"Affirmative. Which is commendable in itself, considering the hits on his personal life."

The hairs on David's forearms rose in anticipation. He hadn't disclosed the reason for background information on Chet Thomlinson. It was a given he wouldn't ask without sufficient cause.

"Shortly after he finished training," Phil said, "his college sweetheart disappeared. The body was never found. Evidence points to her being one of Ted Bundy's victims. Bundy was convicted of three serial killings and confessed to twenty-eight, but the death toll may have been quadruple that.

"Nine years later," Phil went on, "our individual's wife, six-year-old son and mother-in-law were killed in an automobile accident. It was raining, the wife lost control of the vehicle, crossed the median and went head-on into a semi. Four additional fatalities in the pileup, including the truck driver.''

''Mechanical failure? DUI?'' David asked.

''Toxicology reported no alcohol or drugs present in the driver's bloodstream. There wasn't much left of the vehicle, and no skid marks.''

''So the determination was, she was traveling too fast for conditions and-or oversteered, or fell asleep at the wheel.''

''Best-guess scenarios,'' Phil said.

''The husband told my chief of detectives he'd been married three times.''

More paper shuffling accompanied a lengthy pause. ''No notes here about a third wife, but the second died of postsurgical complications. Her gallbladder burst during the procedure. Sepsis set in. She seemed to be responding to treatment, then an embolism floated into her lung and killed her.''

''It happens,'' David said, ''but I smell fish.''

A throaty chuckle rattled from the receiver. ''You were smelling it before you called me, bud.''

''This source of yours. Any wink and a nudge implied?''

''I got this part fourth hand,'' Phil said, ''but you know how that goes. If suspicion was attached to either death, the farther our trout swam, the riper it would have become.''

David gazed out the window overlooking the square three floors below. Forget bringing Marlin in on a conference call. Sun-dried pavement surrounded the puddle where his sedan would be parked, if he were at his desk in the Outhouse.

IdaClare had been the interim manager at Valhalla Springs before Hannah took over. In passing, she'd complained about Jack frequenting Chicago on business an average of twice a month, but heaven forbid he make time to visit his mother half as often, or take over on weekends, so IdaClare could rest, relax and maybe play a little bridge.

David asked, "Did the individual do a tour in the Chicago or Saint Louis field offices?"

"Can't say about Saint Louis," Phil said, "but the friend of a friend of an acquaintance worked out of Chicago at the time of the Dole campaign."

Knowing duties overlapped in such instances, David said, "Which squad?"

"Counterfeit Currency."

Damn. The Fraud Squad investigated computerized larceny, which might have plugged Thomlinson into the gangsta network. Then again, counterfeit cash and drugs were symbiotic. Dealers selling kilos of cocaine in parking lots at 4:00 a.m. didn't black-light the cash received in exchange. A goodly percentage of the funny money that filtered into John Q. Public's billfold came from drug buys.

"If you're interested in footnotes," Phil said, "the primary source and our fish were amateur numismatists. Specialized in American coins beginning with first ones minted in seventeen…whenever. Ninety-two, I think."

"Expensive hobby."

"Tell that to my supervisor. He crapped two cows and a mule when he saw the charges for moving my wood shop from Baltimore to Denver."

The tale of Phil's latest relocation dwindled to white noise while David weighed and sifted the pieces of Thomlinson's bio. Dissect anyone's life and, like barnacles, a slew of dubious connotations cling just below the surface. Slip them under a microscope's lens and *seek and ye shall find* depends on the bias of the examiner.

"Anything else you can tell me?" he asked.

A shrug was audible in the agent's tone. "The guy was unlucky in love, but retired without a speck of tarnish on his shield."

"Well, he didn't retire his SIG-Sauer. Didn't have a commission to carry concealed, either."

"Aw c'mon, David. You busted him for that? Christ, nobody does this gig for twenty years without making heavy-duty enemies. Wear a sidearm your entire life and you feel naked without it."

"That's no excuse for breaking the law. We're accused of acting like we're above it too friggin' often as it is."

"Whose side are you on, man? Every cop hears the Get Even Choir, but eyeballing crowds for crazies rubs off after a while. Everybody from Aunt Gussy to the mailman looks two clicks left of normal and normal looks like Timothy McVeigh.

"Then there's the quarterlies, making the rounds of prisons and psych wards interviewing every squirrel that threatens the president. Five minutes with those freaks and you're thinking an electric fence and a couple of howitzers on your roof shouldn't affect the property value too much."

Parents gave misbehaving children a three-count to get their acts together. David mouthed a slow ten. "The individual's gun is a factor but not my main concern."

"Goes without saying." Most of the friendly returned to Phil's voice. "I hope keeping me in the loop on this one does, too."

Phil would quietly add to a back-of-the-briefcase dossier on Thomlinson, but feds gather information; they don't share. The info he'd provided was essentially public record. He'd just saved David the hassle of getting it piecemeal.

"Sure thing, ol' buddy," David said with a grin. "The same loop you'll keep me in."

Hours of research at the county library didn't yield Hannah much beyond eyestrain and sneezing fits from the local history room's moldy archives.

Money and influence were amazing editors. The Oglethorpes' financial support of the Kinderhook County Historical Society since its inception in 1880 had reduced the Pugh family's existence to *other pioneers* and *other settlers*. Much to the puckery consternation of the librarian, Hannah laughed aloud at a turn-of-the-century chronicler's reference to the *emigré agrarian sect* who cofounded Sanity.

From thumbing through copies of hardbound county histories compiled by Oglthorpe groupies,

Hannah hand-cranked reels of newspaper copy preserved on reverse-negative microfilm. Between laps of swimmy-headed motion sickness, she skimmed headlines, subheads and obituaries, bargaining with the newsprint gods to give her something worthwhile in exchange for leaving the boxes of wide, black film to rot in peace.

As Great-uncle Mort would say, the Oglethorpes didn't visit the privy lest someone took note, whereas the Pughs adhered to the custom that birth, marriage and death were all news befitting of the typesetter's art.

Sophonia's father, King Hiram Pugh, preceded his wife, Amaryllis, in death by three months. Six children were born of their union. Two sons and three daughters "went to the Lord" before their elders succumbed. There was no mention of their ages and causes of death.

By the listed clubs and activities, the Redeemer Baptist Church was Amaryllis's second home. King Hiram was a deacon, a lay minister, and held offices in the Grange, the county cattleman's society and the Fraternal Order of Masons.

Hannah drove home with a sheaf of photocopies as thin as the theory simmering in her mind. Generally speaking, the day's scorecard was neither blank nor bleak. Eli Cree had given her the best and cheapest haircut she'd ever received. And the doctor had said Sophonia was holding her own, as though he meant it, not preempting a future malpractice suit.

She *umm*ed softly, thinking of the box of micro-

waveable macaroni and cheese in the freezer and cold
Velvet Red in the fridge. What could be better than
a pasta pigout while obsessing about Sophonia and
Jedo?

Well, treating David with a call fraught with dirty
talk, heavy breathing and flaming-dessert ideas would
be *better,* but—

Internal heat lightning flash-danced from her belly
to the uncharted worlds he'd discovered, claimed and
conquered. Hannah's eyes slanted to the rearview
mirror. "Cool your jets, Ms. Nympho. His job has to
come first."

Her wicked grin flattened faster than Valhalla
Springs Boulevard's gradation. Malcolm, Itsy and
Bitsy were romping on her lawn, the Furwads' collars
trailing rhinestone leashes. Parked in the driveway
was a panel van, a flatbed truck loaded with rolls of
sod, a clay-crusted Jeep Wrangler, a white subcom-
pact and a PT Cruiser with Michigan license plates.
Roosting like pigeons on the steps and porch railing
were Willard Johnson, Bob Davies, the Maintenance
Department's head honcho, Henry Don Tucker from
Grounds & Greens, Rick LoBrutto, the new addition's
building contractor, an older couple in matching
denim jumpsuits, and Rosemary Schnur, gesturing
like Leonard Bernstein on speed.

Rosemary's head tipped skyward and she made the
sign of the cross. The Cruiser's owners' expressions
were common to those visited by the Prize Patrol.
Bob, Henry Don, Rick and Willard looked as though
they'd been taxidermied.

Damned if life doesn't always happen when you've made other plans.

Hannah was folding the photocopies into her shoulder bag's side pouch when Rosemary jerked open the Blazer's door. "Where have you been? Does it take all day to get a haircut? We've been worried sick about you. With the storm and all, we thought you'd slid off into a ditch somewhere."

Beside her, Malcolm *bur-rurfed* a yeah, what she said.

Hannah bumped the door shut with her butt. "In town. It didn't. You shouldn't have. I didn't."

Rosemary frowned as she connected the multiple answers to her multiple questions and comments.

"What's with the welcoming committee on the porch?" Hannah asked.

"I was walking Itsy and Bitsy down here when the Priestleys stopped and asked about touring the development. They're from Grand Rapids and I knew they were live ones, so I hopped in the car with them."

Rosemary had pinch-hit for Hannah on tour-guiding before and loved selling strangers on the perks of retirement-community living.

Rosemary added, "They're nice people. Two peas in a pod and they're gaga about Valhalla Springs." An earnest money check was produced from the depths of her cleavage. "They can't wait to sign a lease."

"On which cottage?"

"That *darling* Tudor on Blackberry Street. The carpenter installing the kitchen cabinets said it should be finished by the Fourth of July.''

June 20 was the contracted completion date for the new block of cottages. Just that morning, when Hannah dropped by the construction site, Rick LoBrutto had told her they'd be finished a week or two ahead of schedule.

Rosemary glanced over her shoulder. "Give me your keys. I'll start the Priestleys on the paperwork while you talk to the men."

"Oh, I couldn't ask you to—"

"You didn't. I'm volunteering." Rosemary extricated the key ring from Hannah's fingers. "Don't spoil my fun. I'm too fat for tennis, I don't like golf, there's nothing on TV but game shows and cartoons, and it's too muddy to weed the garden."

"Are you trying to hijack my job, Mrs. Schnur?"

Her mouth curving into a feline smile, Rosemary started for the porch. "I'll take the poodles inside with me so you won't have to watch them."

Something was afoot besides her five foot two in sneakers. Individually and collectively, something usually was with IdaClare and Company. Hannah had trouble enough to loan, but refused to borrow any.

She introduced herself to Sid and Phyllis Priestley, a retired orthodontist and a dentist, respectively. Their daughter was a veterinarian in Topeka and their son a postgraduate engineering student at the University of Missouri-Rolla.

Sid said Hannah's mild overbite could be corrected with invisible orthodontic appliances. Phyllis recommended a peroxide gel to whiten her teeth. Rosemary ushered them into the office before they whipped out bibs and stainless-steel picks and told Hannah to open wide.

Once the door closed behind them, Hannah turned to the quartet standing hip-shot, their arms akimbo. "Okay, so do I have four problems or one problem to the fourth power?"

Bob Davies, a blond Paul Bunyan in Levi's and a polo shirt, said, "One problem and it's a big 'un."

Henry Don Tucker looked uncomfortable, but no less angry. "That accountant fella called us all, bright and early Tuesday morning. Said to hold off paying for supply deliveries till we heard back from him. It seems the bank made an error and he oughtta have it straightened out by the next day."

Hannah set her shoulder bag on the porch, stalling for time to think. Tripp Irving, the CPA that oversaw the development's accounts, hadn't informed her of any errors or delayed payments. The operations manager should have been the first to know and the one to contact the department heads.

"Clancy insists I buy all my lumber, brick, plumbing, electrical—you name it—locally from independent suppliers," Rick said. "It costs a little more, but it's good business. Nearly everything's ordered in advance, then trucked out here C.O.D. The little guys can't afford to carry a five- or six-digit balance on their books."

The other three nodded.

"In all honesty," Rick went on, "most of them

could, but thinking what would happen if Valhalla Springs went bankrupt scares them silly. After all this time, asking for credit will really make them suspicious.''

"That's ridiculous," Hannah said. "How many hundreds of thousands of dollars in materials do we have to buy before they trust us? The millions Jack has invested in Valhalla Springs has been a gold mine for them."

Henry Don shook his head. "The slickers that dozed two hundred acres of prime grazing land called their theme park a gold mine, right before they skipped town. Same goes for the dam and lake the Corps of Engineers has been caucussing since long about 1951."

"Cash-and-carry is a dumb way of doing things," Willard allowed, "but it isn't the problem. The indoor pool has a bum filtration pump, a broken ladder and I'm almost out of chemicals. I can maybe slide by tomorrow, but then I'll have to close it."

"Rainey Oil won't refill the underground tank to my pump station on credit," Henry Don said. "No gas, no Grounds & Greens Department. I can't pay my crew to sit on their butts in the shed and play dominoes."

Bob offered Hannah a wan smile. "My straits aren't as dire as theirs—yet. We can't do interior and exterior painting without paint, but I think I can cobble together enough shingles to fix that leaky roof on Redbud Lane…"

"But any maintenance jobs requiring parts or supplies are S.O.L.," Hannah finished for him.

Henry Don grunted. "Shit outta luck—beg pardon—is what *we've* been, trying to get ahold of that weasel-bait accountant, Jack Clancy and, well, you, too, if you want the straight of it."

Malcolm growled. The ruff at his withers stiffened like a war bonnet.

"Take it easy," Willard said to Henry Don as well as the dog. "Can't you see she's as much in the dark as we are?"

"If that's supposed to make me feel better, it don't. No insult to you, ma'am, but you're the boss. You *not* knowing nary whichaway the wind's blowing makes my craw itch something fierce."

Whether for effect or from the power of suggestion, he scratched at the gray-tufted vee of his work shirt. "It was tickling 'bout midnight when I passed Clancy's fancy car on the highway after I got a call that the sprinklers were flooding the sixth and eleventh sand traps.

"This morning, sure enough, the housekeeper was cleaning his condo. I said to myself, now Henry Don, I said, why would a man whose poor ol' widowed mama was shot up a couple days ago tear out hellbent for election the night she got home from the hospital?"

Four pairs of eyes locked on Hannah's. She had no answer. No logical explanation. No excuses. A cold sweaty chasm spidered up her breastbone.

Tripp Irving amortized loans, disbursed allocations

to subaccounts and deposited developmental income. Each department head operated on a quarterly budget to cover expenditures, other than payroll. Expenses above that amount required an itemized voucher approved by Hannah and the CPA. Capping moneys available encouraged thrift and kept the supervisory staff aware of how many cookies remained in their jars at all times.

Hannah comptrolled the payroll, utilities, insurance and incidentals not charged to individual departments. No outgo was due until next Tuesday. Borrowing from Peter to pay Willard, Bob, Henry Don and Rick would befoul everybody's bottom line, but Tripp and Jack going AWOL left no wiggle room.

She glanced at her watch. Ten till five. Marvelous. "Look, fellas, I'll find out what the screwup is by noon tomorrow, even if I have to lock Mr. Irving in his office and threaten the family jewels."

The men laughed. "You can take him," Bob said. "I'd like to be there to see it, though."

"In the meantime, how much—and I mean the absolute lowball—do each of you need to limp along until, say, Monday?"

Rather than pull numbers from the air, they dug out scraps of paper and gimme pens. Tongue tips peeked between clamped lips. Nubs scratched out figures, jotted down others, added and carried over columns like schoolboys at a math bee.

The totals staggered her. The contractor's tab alone exceeded twenty-five thousand dollars. Hannah strafed her fingers through her hair, then laced them behind her neck.

"Okay. I can advance the cost of the gasoline, the pool repairs and chemicals, and most of yours, Bob." She turned to Rick LoBrutto.

"I know. I'm expensive and expendable."

"Delayable," she corrected. "None of the tenants will complain if the new cottages aren't ready for occupancy on schedule."

"True, and I'm not arguing, but I need an assurance, in writing, that Clancy won't initiate the deadline clause in my contract if I run over a few days."

"Consider it done," Hannah said.

He held up a hand. "I also have to pay my workmen, whether they're holding their hard hats or their nail guns. I squeezed every dollar out of the construction bid as it is."

"If they're idled for lack of supplies, charge the man-hours to Tripp Irving," Hannah said. "Not against the construction budget."

Henry Don coughed, then sawed a finger under his nose. "Much as I admire you taking the bull by the horns, aren't you biting off more'n you can chew?"

The mixed metaphor made a certain kind of sense. Drawling a jaunty, David-style "Might could," she swung up her purse and swallowed an *oomph* when it thwacked her between the shoulder blades. "Now, if you gentlemen don't mind waiting out here, I'll bring you your checks."

Rosemary, bless her, had escorted the Priestleys onto the deck. Hannah dialed the bank's twenty-four-hour account information line. Cursing the numeric menu, the electronic robot finally droned out her balance.

Dark dots on a red field obscured her vision. By her reckoning, the account was short twenty-some thousand dollars. Knuckles grinding the desktop, she inhaled and exhaled through gritted teeth.

Calling the CPA or Jack wasn't an option. They'd stonewall her, as they had the department heads. Three choices availed themselves.

Tell the men outside there wasn't enough money in her subaccount to float their expenses.

Alert IdaClare to the shortfall and beg a loan until her gutless wonder of a son, or his bean-counting lackey, could be reached.

Riskier, but imminently face-saving, was depositing the Priestleys' check in the operations account, kiting the departmental checks and praying to God the deficit was covered before the bank's computers screamed *insufficient funds* tomorrow afternoon.

Hannah unlocked a drawer in the credenza. The ringed binder she lifted out felt as if it weighed a hundred pounds.

# 12

"**I** don't like lying to Hannah," Marge said, tying a black scarf around her head. "Or to IdaClare."

Delbert chuffed. "You think I do?" Especially to Hannah, he thought.

Two fingers excavated a glob of Crisco from the can on the bathroom counter. "Can't be helped," he said, spreading the shortening on his face. "If they knew what we were up to, they'd stop Code Name Delta before it started."

Rosemary crowded in beside him in front of the half bath's mirror. She eyed the shortening and the adjacent tin of black shoe polish and wrinkled her nose. "The six of us are a team. You, me, Leo and Marge sneaking around having meetings behind Hannah's and IdaClare's backs makes me feel like a traitor."

"We voted this afternoon," Delbert reminded. "The ayes had it, unanimously."

He hadn't told them he'd hidden in the shrubs outside Jack's condo throughout Andrik's interview last night. He hadn't heard any of their conversation but dallied outside afterward until Jack packed up his Jag, tossed a bag of trash in the Dumpster and peeled out.

Picking the door lock was a snap. The condo's sink was full of dirty dishes, Marge answered at IdaClare's when Delbert punched the phone's redial and the bed looked like the chief's offensive line had scrimmaged on it—none of which was of any particular interest.

Neither was the garbage bag's contents at first. Wadded paper towels, tissues, take-out trash from the Flour Shoppe, an empty bottle of whiskey, notepad sheets with numbers and what appeared to be phone messages written on them. Then, at the bottom, were hundreds of shredded bits of paper, a majority of them scorched at the edges.

Delbert had hunkered over his kitchen table for hours reassembling the shards with tweezers and studying them with infrared binoculars to enhance legibility, as per the instructions in his *Trade Secrets from the Masters of Criminal Investigation* manual.

Dawn was breaking when he sat back in the chair and wished to Christ he'd fallen asleep in his recliner in front of the TV instead of skulking in the bushes. Culled from the fragile scraps were portions of the Royal Dragon's floor plan.

Detective Andrik would approve of preserving the evidence in a bread sack blown up like a balloon. Not telling him about it, until Delbert was good and ready, was obstructing justice. Absently, he'd wondered how many times he could plead ignorance before Andrik treated him to a night in the county jail.

He'd known when the gunsmoke cleared Tuesday night that the body count was too low. The shooter carried enough firepower to slaughter everyone in the room. Missing all but Jasmine Chau and Eulilly Thomlinson took more skill than pulling the triggers helter-skelter.

Jack Clancy had uninvited himself the day before the party and not only strong-armed Hannah into going, but into bringing the sheriff along. Was it insanity, brilliance or coincidence that Hendrickson was on the scene? Who'd believe a man would coconspire with another and gamble his mother's and oldest friend's lives to deflect suspicion from themselves?

However suspicions fell after tonight's caper, the courts and the Constitution hamstrung the cops' creativity. The rules didn't apply to four senior citizens out for an evening stroll.

Unless they got caught.

Rosemary sneered, "I suppose it doesn't bother *you* to fib to anyone, does it? Much less to Hannah and IdaClare."

"I already said it did, damn it." Delbert shot her a dirty look, then continued his facial lube job. "Besides, you care to explain the difference between you pussyfooting a way for Hannah to have her job and David, too, and keeping our investigation on the qt?"

Her mouth opened in protest, then clamped shut. It wouldn't last long, but it was a pretty sight nonetheless.

"The greater good, it is for," Leo said from the hallway. "We find nothing? No harm, it has done. We find something…" His voice trailed away, the sentence finishing itself in each gumshoe's mind.

Rosemary sniffed. "Well, I don't understand what we're looking for."

Delbert ignored her. *You'll know when you see it* was the best answer he had, but it would get him laughed right out of the bathroom.

Marge leaned sideward into the mirror, a bead of shortening poised on the tip of her finger. "Are you sure this gunk will wash off with soap and water?"

Delbert nodded, plastering his woolly eyebrows with shoe polish. He'd scrubbed his skin raw after a prior dark-of-night operation's attempt at camouflage. How he'd missed the tips on covert disguises in the manual was beyond him, but live and learn.

"A Crisco undercoat is the trick," he said. "Same as slapping petroleum jelly on your hands and arms before you paint a room. The greasy skid stuff keeps the shoe polish from absorbing in your pores."

"Eyew." Rosemary scooped out enough shortening to baste an emu.

Marge glanced at her, then redipped a four-finger measure.

Leo reached between his bride and Delbert for a handful. Clip-on shades awninged his thick, horn-rimmed spectacles. A backward Detroit Tigers cap would conceal his chrome dome, but a second pot of shoe polish might be needed to black out his round, Moon Over Miami phiz.

A quarter-hour later, Delbert lined up his operatives in the living room for inspection and final instructions. Dark clothing? Check—although he scowled at Leo's unheeled vinyl house shoes. Stealthier than his usual wingtips, but criminitly, hadn't the man ever heard of crepe-soled oxfords?

Sweating buckets beneath his sock hat, Delbert scratched around the rim, careful not to wipe away his face paint. Lucky Rosemary. Her jet-black, purplish-streaked dye job gave her a by on the head covering.

"Gloves?" he asked. "Flashlights?"

Check. Marge's gloves had cutesy little snowflakes embroidered on them, but Delbert reserved comment. She'd flimflammed Hannah into staying with Ida-Clare, saying she needed a break from being Nancy Nurse and that nobody else was available to baby-sit. One wrong word and Ms. Heart-on-her-sleeve Rosenbaum would run straight to Hannah and IdaClare and tattle.

"All right, then," he said. "From the time we leave the house until we've safely breached our objective, there's to be no talking, no coughing, sneezing, belching, not a ding-danged sound out of any of you. *Capiche?*"

The troops nodded in unison.

Whirling an about-face, he reviewed the hand signals they'd use for silent communication. "Any questions?"

"Uh-huh," Rosemary said. Her gaze flicked from her husband to Marge to Delbert. "If anyone sees us, how are we going to explain having lard and shoe polish smeared all over our faces?"

Leo's brow furrowed. "Ah. Is a good question, I think."

"Which I'd already thought of," Delbert said. He unzipped his duffel bag and removed a sheet of gold foil star stickers he'd bought at the educational supply store that afternoon after visiting Sophonia. "If anybody gets nosy, just say we're testing the Neighborhood Watch program. We'll give 'em one of these to show they passed with flying colors."

The operatives exchanged glances. "I hate like the very devil to admit this," Marge said, "but now and then, when he isn't dreaming up conspiracy theories, he hatches a genuinely good idea."

"Hmmph." Delbert returned the stickers to the fanny pack. The grandfather clock read 8:43. Heavy clouds were a godsend, as long as God didn't send rain along with them.

Gesturing forward march, he said, "Head 'em up. Move 'em out."

Five steps onto the deck, Leo banged full tilt into the patio table. Wrought-iron legs grating on wooden planks set every dog in a block radius barking an alarm.

Delbert whispered, "For the love of Mike, Schnur. Watch where the hell you're going."

His hands fumbling in the air, Leo said, "Too dark, it is out here. With the sunglasses on, I can see nothing."

Rosemary smirked. "I was afraid of that." Lifting her cotton-knit tunic, she uncoiled a length of rope wrapped in electrical tape knotted around her waist. She gave the end to Leo. "Our fearless leader isn't the only genius in the bunch."

Leo started to smooch her greasy cheek, then drew back and blew one instead. "My darling Rosemary, I would follow you anywhere."

Squelching a remark about her having him on a leash since day one, Delbert signaled for Marge and Rosemary to fall in behind him and Leo to take the drag position.

Hannah glowered at the letter tiles propped in the wooden holder. Tasting salt didn't preclude gnawing the stubby hangnail at the side of her thumb.

Itsy and Bitsy's tick-ticky toenails were an audible version of Chinese water torture. Jim Reeves crooning "Four Walls" on the stereo was as diabolical as the alleged back-masked, satanic messages imbedded in the Beatles' *Abbey Road* album.

What was taking Marge so long? She deserved a respite from caretaking duties, but she'd scuttled out— Hannah glanced at the clock affixed to Ida-Clare's kitchen soffit. It couldn't be right. Marge must have been gone more than a half hour.

The Scrabble timer dinged. Hannah's knee clobbered the jointure underneath the dinette table. Tiles crosshatched on the gameboard jumped an inch and clattered down again. The Furwads ran in yapping, manic circles.

IdaClare lifted her arm off the table and onto the pillow on her lap. "What on earth is wrong with everyone? Marge was as nervous as a whore in church all afternoon, and now you are. It's catching, I kid you not."

"I'm sorry." Hannah realigned the tiles to avoid eye contact. "It's the wrong time of the month."

No lie, if the excuse was as applicable to workplace shootings, Jack's assholiness and total abandonment, the siphoned developmental accounts, eighteen hours to set it right or be guilty of bank fraud, a balled-up stomach and a headache, as it was to its more common reference.

"I thought you said Jack promised to call tonight."

"He did." IdaClare sipped the toddy Hannah had made from Marge's recipe. "If he doesn't by ten, he'll wait until morning, though. He thinks I go to bed with the chickens."

Hannah had tried his office number, home, cell phone and pager. No Jack, no Stephen, no anybody.

Yelling at Tripp Irving's receptionist had gained the accountant's unlisted home number, but no answer there, either. Fear that he had young, impressionable children was all that stopped Hannah from recording a blistering, X-rated message.

She hesitated, then laid d-i-c-k on the board, connecting with IdaClare's paltry, eight-point *head*. The *k* hit on a double-letter square and the compound word's score doubled, too.

IdaClare jutted her chin. "That doesn't count."

"Is that an official challenge, because I'm positive *dickhead* is in the dictionary," Hannah said, thinking, as well as in your immediate family tree.

"I'm sure it is. But it's my turn to play, not yours."

"I haven't made a word since you put down *zebra*."

IdaClare reset the timer. "I know."

Oh, so cutthroat, down-and-dirty Scrabble is the name of *this* game, eh?

"I beg your pardon." Hannah plucked her tiles from the board. My kingdom for a seven-letter word. Or the *q* and a *u* to go with it on the next draw.

"That's all right, dear." IdaClare craned her neck. "Just don't forget to cross off the points you scored."

Carving a pencil line through d-i-c-k-h-e-a-d's tally, Hannah's eyes narrowed as her picky opponent capitalized on the *t* in *thyme* to stretch q-u-i-t-t-e-r to reach a red, triple-word point square.

Well, hell.

Just as Delbert lent an ear to the lock's stubborn tumblers, Marge whispered in the other, "What if they have an alarm system?"

"They— He doesn't. Now, hush."

Delbert slowed his breathing, hoping his heart would stop thumping ninety to nothing. Neighboring cottage walls and windows leaked laugh tracks, baseball commentaries and talking head–speak from televisions tuned to different stations.

Having unscrewed the porch light's bulb, he couldn't see diddly, especially with his operatives on his back like baby bats taking flight instructions from their mother. No problemo. Sound, not sight, was the key to successful lock-picking.

Key. Lock-picking. Get it, he thought, his grin widening at the snick of metal surrendering to his machinations. Headlights swung around the corner from Hawthorne Street onto Larkspur Lane.

He yanked the lock-pick gun from the doorknob. "Down. Everybody down. Faces to the door."

The car crept past, slowing...slowing. Fingernails clawed his shirt, raking skin, chiseling welts deep enough for bragging rights tomorrow in the clubhouse locker room. Or the next, if there was a problem making bail.

Brakes squealed. Gravel crunched under wheeling tires. The garage door diagonally across the street hummed open. "Steady...steady as she goes," he murmured, and blew out a sigh.

A second car cruised by from the opposite direction. Its horn tapped hello to the first, then accelerated.

Jehosaphat. Old folks ought to have sense enough to be home in bed at this hour of the night, not gallivanting around like teenagers, Delbert thought.

Once the coast cleared, the dead bolt relented in a matter of seconds. Hustling the troops inside, Delbert closed the door behind him and was relocking it when flashlight beams strafed the interior like kliegs at a Hollywood movie debut.

"Turn 'em off. *Off!*" His voice thundered through the half-empty living room. "There's no curtains on the goddamn windows."

Their heads hanging, Leo, Marge and Rosemary stood silhouetted in the gloom. Amateurs. God save him from them. Yet he was partly at fault for forgetting that women aren't good at following orders and that Leo was still bumbling around with his sun-glasses on.

"What did we bring flashlights for if we can't use them?" Rosemary said.

Marge chimed in, "And how are we supposed to see what we're doing without them?"

Leo motioned at the packing cartons scattered about the carpet like cardboard stalagmites. "So dark it is, we could trip and break the legs, or worse, and then what would we do? Tell the ambulance to come hush-hush, because it's the burgling we're doing and, *mein Gott,* don't wake the neighbors."

Quite the windy speech for a man not given to making them. Delbert put his duffel on a wing chair to stow the lock-pick gun and take out his night-vision binoculars.

*"Numero uno,"* he said, "you'll be able to see better if you take off your shades."

"Oh." Leo flipped up the clip-ons and gandered around. "A little better. Not much. Not good."

"As for *dos*, stuffing Rosemary's leash down your pants ought to be one less thing to trip over, too."

"It's a tether," she snapped. "Not a leash."

Slipping the binocular's strap over his head, he said, *"Tres* through siesta are, use your hands to stifle the flashlight beam and only at floor level or inside boxes when you're sifting evidence. In the garage or rooms without windows, shut the interior door, then have at it, Billy Ned." He handed each of them a box knife and roll of strapping tape from the bag. "Reseal any cartons plundered as near to the way they were as possible, and keep your gloves on, so as not to leave prints."

Delbert straightened his shoulders. "Code Name Delta hinges on speed, thoroughness and stealth. The longer we're here, the greater the risk. Questions?"

In a quavery voice, Marge asked, "What if somebody comes to the door?"

"Freeze. They can't see you and everyone with a key flew down to Mississippi with Chet this afternoon."

"Are you sure about that?" Rosemary said.

No. He wasn't. "Positive." Delbert signaled them to move out. "Now deploy as instructed."

Leo lumbered to the office nook in the kitchen to pilfer the computer and any paperwork. Setting the monitor on the floor angled away from the windows and darkening the screen should subdue the telltale glow.

Rosemary's assignment was to search and rifle boxes labeled in Chet's handwriting, or unlabeled ones, as would Marge, while scouring the garage.

Delbert worked cleanup detail. From sliding a hand inside zippered furniture cushions and pillows, he scrutinized vents, the furnace closet, cold-air return grates, and kicked baseboards that might have a hollow niche behind them.

After rooting through the vacuum cleaner's canister, he dragged a kitchen stepladder from the utility room to examine every interior door's top rail for a removeable cap-board. Private Spy Supply was temporarily out of telescopic rods, but rabbit ears cadged from an old TV in his garage plied the slits under the washer and dryer, block-footed dressers and the entertainment center just as well.

His head almost crashed through the underside of a bureau drawer when Rosemary whispered, "I found his coin collection in a box marked Americana. Cases and cases of them."

Massaging the goose egg sure to volcano from his skull any second, he growled, "Well, zippety-do-dah."

"Isn't that one of the things you told us to be on the look out for?"

Delbert admitted it was. "Any of them missing?"

"Leo found an inventory on the computer. There's a lot of them, but best we can tell, they're all there."

Or Chet was a stickler for keeping his inventory up to date.

The high-octane rush Delbert felt when the mission began was fading, along with his energy. If he was thirty years younger... Hell, if they *all* were, the floor wouldn't be so far down and up wouldn't racket knees and ankle joints like milk on Rice Krispies.

Atten-hut, Bisbee. Give the can a toss, then backtrack to Dogwood Lane for a cold beer. Or three.

The vanity table in the master bathroom resembled a department store's cosmetics counter. A lily-of-the-valley scent cloyed the air, a sickening-sweet ghost of the woman who'd sat at the mirror primping for a party three nights ago.

Delbert masked his personal feelings with a tight-jawed command to be professional. He'd chosen his search sites, knowing Marge and Rosemary would get all sniffly and weepy-eyed, if not actually refuse to invade Eulilly's posthumous privacy.

The sharp smell of chlorine wafted up when he removed the toilet tank's lid. No strings were tied to the tub or to the His and Hers washbasins' stoppers. The deck under the cabinet's bottom drawer was solid, stained plywood.

Same with the guest-bath, off the hallway, except the water in its commode was grotto blue—to match the frilly towels and shell-shaped soaps everyone knew better than to use, he supposed.

He closed the last of the cabinet drawers and was pulling himself up by the lip of the marble surround when he hesitated, then lowered again to a kneel. Tipping the drawer forward on its ball-bearing track, he directed the flashlight at a seam in the plywood base. Funny, there weren't any staples, screws or nails holding it down.

His heart nearly exploded when someone knocked on the bathroom door. "A police car. It is parked at the curb."

"Keep your shorts on, Leo." Cursing, Delbert slid the drawer back in place, then yanked open the door. "Where's Rosie?"

Leo pointed at a form squatted behind a carton rampart dividing the living and dining rooms.

"Marge?"

"Right here." She peeked out from behind Leo.

"Okay, now—"

A spotlight's blinding beam pierced the windows.

Swooping left to right and back again, its brilliance seared Delbert's eyes.

Mistake number one—he should have brought his scanner along.

They had two minutes, at most, before John Law exited the car to circle the house on foot.

"Down on all fours. Stay low. Crawl to the patio doors and unlock them. Don't move from there until I say so."

"But—"

"Shut up, Marge, and do as you're told."

First chance would be soon enough to apologize. Flattening himself against the hallway's wall at its junction with the living room, Delbert panted, waiting for the spotlight's arc to stray to the far ends of the cottage.

Mistake number two—he should have carried his duffel along with him.

Crab-walking to the wing chair, he grabbed the bag and backpedaled. A cardboard tower keeled over and crashed to the floor.

"Delbert!"

"Shh." The high beam spanked the front windows like a miniature sun. Boosting himself upward with the rail of the sofa, Delbert squinted through his infrared binoculars. A uniformed officer was emerging from the patrol unit.

He was too short to be David Hendrickson. Delbert wouldn't relish explaining a B and E to the sheriff, but the odds of talking him out of filing several misdemeanors, and a possible felony charge, would have been greater. Maybe.

Rejoining his partners in crime, he said, "When I say 'go,' run like hell straight for the groundskeepers' shed behind the fourth green."

If the Almighty was on their side, nobody would holler, "Stop, or I'll shoot," while they were doing it.

"Wasn't it sweet of Chet to call all the way from Mississippi to ask how I was feeling?" IdaClare said.

"Umm-hmm." Taking a sleeveless nightgown from the drawer, Hannah thought, Oh, yeah. Just wonderful of him to tie up the phone line so Jack couldn't get through. If he'd even tried.

There weren't any messages from him when she checked the office answering machine by remote. No mollifying words from Tripp Irving, either. Juaneema Kipps was thrilled with her mini-fountains, Rick LoBrutto would pay for supplies out of his own pocket until Monday and she and David were in the seventh inning of a telephone tag shutout.

IdaClare said, "When I told Chet I was surprised he wasn't too distraught to give a care about me—or anyone else for that matter—he said life is for the living. That's almost like poetry, isn't it, dear?"

Hannah battled the compulsion to crank her eyes backward in their sockets. Chet's koan was as poetic as the lyrics written by Cody Wyrick, her long-ago, live-in urban cowboy, who was neither and sang like a beagle with the croup.

"Poor man. I don't believe Eulilly's family is much comfort to him. If they were, wouldn't he at least stay the weekend instead of flying right home after the funeral?"

The question wasn't the type to beg a response, which was good, since Hannah didn't have one. Unlike Great-uncle Mort and Aunt Lurleen, funerals weren't social occasions to her, but a spouse's whirlwind attendance seemed callous, disrespectful and certainly wouldn't endear Chet to the Bethune brothers.

IdaClare grimaced in pain as she raised her cast, allowing the gown to slip over her head and arms. She'd pushed herself too hard all day. It showed on her face, in her voice and in her trembling hands.

"You aren't doing yourself any favors by skipping the pain medication," Hannah said. "I realize the pills make you woozy, but you'll heal more slowly if you're hurting than you will if you're not."

"Chet said the same thing."

The name-dropping was prickling Hannah's nerves. In seventy-two hours, the man had gone from Eulilly's faceless husband to a liturgy.

"Years before he and Eulilly met," IdaClare said, "Chet was shot—twice—during an assassination attempt on some visiting dignitary. The pills the doctors prescribed knocked him out cold, so Chet flushed them down the toilet.

"The doctors guessed what he'd done when his wounds didn't mend as quickly as they should have. He said that should be a lesson to me."

"Is it?" Hannah asked.

"I guess." IdaClare rump-scooted until her back rested against the pillows stacked against the headboard. Lying down wasn't comfortable, even with the cast elevated by cushions appropriated from the kitchen chairs. "Returning his kindness and consideration by fibbing to him about something as silly as a few pills wouldn't be right."

She told Hannah which medications to retrieve from the basket in the kitchen and to mark the time taken on the clipboard. After swallowing the rainbow assortment, she said, "But I am getting my hair fixed tomorrow, come what may."

Oops.

IdaClare laughed. "Think I couldn't see all those gears spinning in your head when you left this morning? That's why Alexander Graham Bell invented the telephone. Marge called Dixie Jo and she's squeezing me in at one-fifteen."

She relaxed into her pillow mountain, then her head jerked toward the door. "Where is Marge, anyway? Shouldn't she be back by now?"

# 13

"Ms. Garvey," said the secretary-receptionist, "as I told you earlier on the telephone, Mr. Irving has been out of town since noon yesterday. He won't be in until tomorrow morning."

"Tomorrow is Saturday."

The woman gave her an "and your point would be?" look.

"Saturdays aren't business days, Ms.—" Hannah's memory blanked. She glanced at the walnut deskplate. The surname was an end-of-the-alphabet string of consonants with precious few vowels.

"Mrs. Pyrtlbarszczak," the secretary supplied.

Lacking the phlegm to pronounce it properly, Hannah said, "As I told you earlier on the telephone, Valhalla Springs has major cash-flow problems. There isn't enough money in the departmental accounts, et al, to buy you and me a Happy Meal for lunch."

Her fingernail tapped tomorrow's date square on the calendar blotter. "Banks do record transactions made on Saturdays." Her finger zipped diagonally to the start of the next row. "But they don't institute them until *Monday*." She traced the perimeter of the neighboring box. "And the development's payroll must be met on Tuesday."

"Um...well, I see what you're saying, Ms. Garvey."

Thank God.

"I'm sure Mr. Irving will be happy to provide whatever help is needed to calculate the payables, first thing in the morning." Lips compressed into a rictus smile, she folded her hands on the blotter. "It's very conscientious of you to consider disbursements so far in advance, but Tuesday *is* four days away."

Was the woman a couple of pear halves short of a full can? Or had Tripp told her to act obtuse when clients demanded to know why their accounts were zeroed out?

"I don't need help calculating anything. I want answers to why there are no balances to deduct any payables from. I deposited a new tenant's earnest money on the way here, but I don't know whether the checks I wrote yesterday to keep the departments afloat will sink or swim by this afternoon."

Mrs. Pyrtlbarszczak clutched the chain to her locket. She croaked out, "You deposited an earnest money check?" as one would, "You tear the wings off flies?"

"I most assuredly did." Hannah struck an imperious pose. "And I'll continue to commingle funds, if that's what it takes to get Mr. Irving's, Jack Clancy's or the IRS's attention."

Bingo. Commingle and IRS are to accountants and their employees what pro bono and contempt of court are to attorneys. The desk chair shot backward, the castors *zwinging* on the ribbed carpet protector. Mrs. Pyrtlbarszczak screeched to a halt in front of a wall of vertical file cabinets, yanked a lapful of folders from the U-V-W drawer, did a bat turn and rolled to a computer workstation.

As she plied a keyboard at the speed of light, her nose hovered so near the VDT, the reflection mottled her face in flickering blue, green, amber and red.

Hannah's eyes lowered to the appointment book lying open beside the telephone. The left-hand page listed the day's schedule. A majority of the names and notations were x-ed out.

Chin resting on the heel of one hand, she surveyed the office's framed diplomas, plaques and motel-quality paintings. Her other hand slithered over the edge of the elevated counter as though it were prone to wander if not closely monitored.

A casual drag of her thumb brought the previous page into view. From noon on, Thursday's appointments had been crossed off, as well. A circled, *J/C—St.L.—counsel.* was written in the space above 12:00 p.m.

Hannah's hand retracted, her forearm scraping the counter's Formica lip. She mouthed the abbreviations. Even upside down, their meaning was clear. Yesterday, Tripp Irving had made an unexpected trip to Saint Louis to counsel Jack Clancy.

For all Hannah knew, they'd caught a flight to the Grand Caymans—or any tropical paradise without an extradition agreement with the United States. Fragmented thoughts whirred in her mind.

Jack saying, *My company isn't going to lose a multi-million-dollar project just so you can snub Baby Sister.* Confirming prior knowledge of Eulilly's proxy-gathering and planned vote against the project. *It'll all be over by nine.* Gunshots. Screams. Chet's promise to vote Eulilly's shares and proxies in Jack's favor. Him booking a commercial flight to Eulilly's funeral after accepting Jack's offer of the company jet.

Had Chet double-crossed Jack? Was Clancy Construction and Development bordering on bankruptcy, too? It must be, for Jack to bail out on Valhalla Springs. On his mother. On Hannah.

Had Mrs. Pyrtlbarszczak looked up when she trundled back to the desk, she'd have ushered Hannah to a chair and given her a paper sack to breathe into. Instead, she lifted the telephone receiver and punched a button adjacent to the keypad.

"Cathy? Susan Pyrtlbarszczak. Fine, and you? Yes, I'm tired of the rain, too, but we'll wish we'd had more come August.

"Listen, could you check some balances for me real quick?" Pencil at the ready, she recited the Valhalla Springs account numbers from a steno pad. "Uh-huh. Uh-huh. Uh—was that sixty-three cents? Uh-huh. Right. Thanks so much, and you have a nice weekend."

Reversing to the computer screen, she consulted it and the steno pad, then whipped a tissue from the box and dabbed her forehead. "Is this your idea of a joke?"

Hannah just stood there, head wagging in confusion.

"There's no shortage in any of the Valhalla Springs accounts, Ms. Garvey. Tripp's balances-on-hand and the bank's tally to the penny." Her glare should have set off the ceiling jets. "Except for the five-thousand-dollar overage in the operations account, thanks to your unauthorized deposit."

"I don't understand…" Hannah fumbled in her shoulder bag for a folded sheet of notepaper. "That isn't right. It can't be." Ironing the creases from the paper with her palms, she said, "I accessed the bank's electronic account information line last night. The largest balance was in mine, and it was only a few hundred dollars."

Mrs. Pyrtlbarszczak rose from her chair. The steno pad slapped down on Hannah's notes. The telephone banged the counter beside it. "Call First National if you don't believe me." She scrawled the bank's main number on the steno pad. "Ask for Cathy Nash. or ask for the *president,* if her word isn't good enough for you."

The organist's melancholy rendition of "Unto the Hills I Lift Mine Eyes" drifted out the open double doors of the Lutheran church. The drizzle falling like mist seemed at once appropriate to the occasion and a mockery of the young woman whose smile could light up a room.

In the parking lot, umbrellas snapped open and bobbed like upside-down hibiscus blooms. Mourners walked with their heads bowed, acknowledging each other with solemn nods. A freckle-faced boy paid for waving at one of his friends with a pinch delivered from his mother.

David took a folded pamphlet from the usher, then paused in the vestibule to shake hands with Junior Duckworth. The funeral director's skin was cold to the touch. A nerve twitched at the corner of his mouth.

"Sometimes I wish I'd chosen another profession," he said. "Or that another one had chosen me."

"Yeah." A rose-blanketed casket rested below the chancel rail. Wide, trailing ribbons read *Beloved Daughter* and *Beloved Sister*. David sighed and patted the mortician's arm. "So do I, Junior. So do I."

At a back pew, the Sanity P.D. officers who'd escort the funeral procession to the cemetery scooted over to make room for David. Cursory nods served as greetings. The younger of the two returned his gaze to the picture inside the brochure's flyleaf, as though if he stared at it long enough, his mind might reconcile its meaning.

David didn't set much store in the notion that the size of the crowd at a funeral was proportional to the popularity of the deceased. Still, it was comforting to see so many people had interrupted their lives long enough to pay their respects to Jasmine Chau and her family.

Tiered flowers of every kind, color and scent filled

the pulpit behind the lectern. Arranged in a triptych were enlarged, gilt-framed photographs of Jasmine. On the left, a chubby, sloe-eyed little girl with a cap of black hair hugged a Raggedy Ann doll as big as she was. In the second, she was wearing a mortar-board and gown, balancing a serving tray on her palm. Head thrown back, she laughed and mugged for the camera.

The last one hit David squarely in the gut. Jasmine's parents sat cross-legged on the lawn. Mr. Chau was planting a duck-billed kiss on his wife's cheek, her expression both delighted and appalled. In the background, their six children formed a catawampussed, cheerleading pyramid, Jasmine and three of her siblings' arms spelling out C-H-A-U. Backward.

The organist decrescendoed the hymn's final chord as Reverend Hoskins took his place behind the lectern. He expressed condolences to the family huddled on the front pew and the congregation at large, then launched into a diatribe centering on salvation for the living rather than a eulogy for the departed.

If it was sinful to tune the man out and hope the Chaus stiffed him on his fee, so be it. Jasmine deserved better than a reconstituted Sunday sermon.

Staring off at the stained-glass windows, David chafed his hands on his trouser legs. The last time he'd worn this suit was to an interview with the state's assistant attorney general. He'd been suspended from duty—accused of, but yet to be charged with, second-degree manslaughter in the death of Stuart Quince.

Then, as now, he wished Hannah was beside him. Last night their answering machines had gotten a workout, but they hadn't managed to speak to one another. If they had, he'd have mentioned the funeral, leaving the door open for her offer to come with him.

Childish and selfish, he supposed, and a reminder that he was his father's son. The stoic routine probably fooled Hannah about as well as Dad's did Mom, too.

He bit back a smile remembering the message Hannah had left on the machine. *No, I won't call you on your cell phone unless it's an emergency, and boredom after hanging around at IdaClare's until Marge dragged in isn't an emergency. Yes, I miss you, too. A lot. But don't let it go to your head.* Her naughty chuckle had sent it elsewhere.

*Oh, and please do continue feeling like pond scum for not talking to me, or seeing me since you crawled out of my bed yesterday morning. I can't imagine how you'll ever make it up to me, although I do have a few ideas, if you're interested.*

The minister's thundering exhortations to the flock jarred David back to the present. Louder than the doxology was the ongoing realization that Deke Bogart could have taken Hannah's life as easily as he had Jasmine's and Eulilly Thomlinson's.

Standing for the closing prayer, David's amen was spoken later than the congregation's, having added a few words of his own, for Jasmine, as well as for Hannah.

A soloist replaced Reverend Hoskins at the podium

to sing "The Old Rugged Cross." David's vision blurred at the wrenching music, the pallbearers carrying Jasmine's casket up the aisle and the grief-stricken Chau family walking behind it.

At the rear of the sanctuary, the procession turned and exited into a vestry for a private moment preceding the cortege to the cemetery. The pews emptied front to back, the attendants shunning the center aisle for those alongside the walls.

Women pressed crumpled tissues to their eyes and lips, while the men blinked and sniffed, stuffing handkerchiefs in their pockets as if their neighbors would think less of them for needing one.

Outside, the drizzle hadn't lifted, but it was human nature for spirits to rebound a bit after an emotional ordeal. David couldn't put names to everyone who shook his hand and said, "Good of you to come today, Sheriff." Much as he appreciated the gestures, the similarity to electioneering was too close for comfort.

A hard slap to the shoulder staggered him, then a voice boomed, "Lovely service for Miss Chau, now, wasn't it, Dave?" Even if he hadn't recognized the twang, no one had ever called him Dave, except Jessup Knox.

The burglar-alarm salesman and political rival wore a black, Western-cut suit tailored to hide his potbelly. The rain had flattened his pompadour and clung like dew to a new and scraggly set of muttonchops.

"Terrible thing to have happen to such a pretty, young girl," Knox said. "Jes' tragic."

David nodded.

"Mind if I ask how the investigation's going?" The man practically shouted the question.

"It's going the same as most," David said. "Slowly but surely."

"It'd be clipping along faster if you'd let the boys from the Multicounty Task Force in on it. I hear they offered their help and you turned them down."

"You heard wrong." David hiked his own volume up a notch. "The task force becomes involved if and when a sheriff requests assistance, not the other way around."

"Then why didn't you?" Knox's mouth curved into a sneering half smile. "You're forever grousin' about not having enough manpower for this, that and the other. With help so close at hand, I'd think you'd have fallen over yourself to dial the phone."

Murmured assent buzzed among the listeners. Side-long glances were exchanged.

David said, "No insult to the task force, but in-vestigators don't come any better than our own Mar-lin Andrik, Josh Phelps and Cletus Orr. With them in charge, I saw no reason to bring in anyone from the outside."

Technically, he was an outsider himself, being born and raised in a different county, but the name of this vapid version of a pissing contest was spin.

Terry Wilkie, a delivery driver for the local indus-trial laundry service, said, "No sense in it 'atall. I don't pay taxes so a bunch a foreigners can come in here at the first sign of trouble and tell us how to run things.''

''Keeping it local spares you from sportin' egg on your face, too.'' Knox's recessive chin cocked to one side. ''Don't it, Dave?''

Damn it to hell and gone. He should have made an excuse and walked away when his nemesis asked about the investigation. Should have known he was laying bear traps, the way he did whenever more than a handful of rubberneckers were in the vicinity.

Knox grasped his jacket lapels, statesman-fashion. ''Call in the cavalry and you'd have to explain how that old codger got the drop on you. How he managed to draw and fire at the lunatic that murdered his wife and Jasmine Chau before your gun ever cleared the holster.''

''Fact is,'' David said, his tone icy and clipped, ''the man you called an old codger is a retired federal agent. And the incident didn't occur quite as you described.''

''Oh, it didn't, huh?'' Knox rocked on his heels. ''How many shots did Mr. Thomlinson fire at that Bogart fella?''

''Three.''

''How about you, Dave? How many rounds did you get off at him?''

A deep breath, exhaled slowly, didn't ease the knot behind David's belt buckle. With his eyes locked on Knox's and burning for want of a blink, he answered, ''None.''

The Elvis poseur huffed out a laugh and spread his

hands. "Then what part of the *incident* didn't occur quite the way I said it did?"

"Mr. Thomlinson was seated approximately eighteen feet nearer the intruder than I was. There were no obstructions—human or structural—between him and the shooter. Mr. Thomlinson became an obstruction to my line of fire when he jumped up from his chair in front of me."

"I get it. It was *his* fault you clutched."

Terry Wilkie warned, "Back off, Jessup. You weren't there that night. All you know about what happened is what you've heard."

David would have taken heart in the delivery driver's defense if skepticism wasn't reflected in the faces peering up.

"I'm a taxpayin' citizen of this county and I've got a right to express my opinion," Knox blustered. "I'm not the only one wondering why it is the sheriff could draw his weapon fast enough to kill Stuart Quince and walk away without a scratch, but didn't fire a single shot at a homicidal maniac standing dead-bang in front of him."

A shrill voice from the back of the group said, "Jasmine and that poor man's wife might be alive today if he had."

Knox pointed in the woman's direction. "See? I told y'all I wasn't the only one. Bet there's plenty more of you too shy to speak up."

David said, "Or too respectful of the Chau family and their daughter's memory to have a shouting match on the sidewalk in front of their church."

To a person, the crowd lowered their heads and fidgeted in place. David quietly excused himself and stepped off the sidewalk.

The woman who'd condemned him sounded like Muriel Oates, Jessup Knox's baby sister's best friend. Whether it was, or not, didn't matter a damn. Not when he'd go to his grave wondering if Jasmine and Eulilly would have survived if he'd reacted a few seconds faster.

Just as he reached his patrol unit, his pager vibrated in his coat pocket. The last four digits of Andrik's office number and 10–47 appeared on the readout. The two combined translated as *Call me, pronto*.

Hannah paused to collect herself before entering the Critical Care Unit's cubicle. An hour removed from Tripp Irving's office hadn't lessened her resentment at being manipulated and the uncertainty of whom or how many were pulling the strings.

Cathy Nash at the First National Bank of Sanity had confirmed that the Valhalla Springs accounts were as flush as Mrs. Pyrtlbarszczak said they were. Late-night wire transfers from Metropolitan Bank in Saint Louis had compensated for the tardy, quarterly deposits.

All was supposedly well. Nothing to worry about.

Yeah, right.

Hannah looked down at the library book in the crook of her arm. Reversing it, her fingers grazed its protective plastic sheath. Manipulation seemed to be the order of the day, although she preferred to think of her scheme as interpersonal engineering. At least her intentions were honorable.

Sophonia still appeared weak and ancient. Her complexion rivaled the bed linens for whiteness, but her eyes were bright and there was nothing frail about the hand gripping Hannah's.

She asked the obligatory "How are you feeling?"

"How d'ya think I'm feeling? I'm making water in a sack 'neath the bed. Got bedsores festering on my behind. Haven't had a drop of bourbon whiskey for days and all they give me to eat is bouillon and Jell-O."

Hannah laughed. "I'd say a lot closer to your old self than you were the last time I visited."

Sophonia's gaze strayed to the door. "Is Delbert parking the car? He promised he'd be here for *Judge Judy* and *Court TV*. There's a lulu of a murder trial on. Already missed out on most of it."

"No, he's..." Hannah's voice trailed away. She hadn't seen or heard from Delbert since the welcome-home potluck at IdaClare's Wednesday night. If he'd called, he hadn't left any messages. If he were sick, she'd have heard about it.

She thought back to Marge's flush-faced, beer-breathy return to IdaClare's cottage last night. Talking faster than a country auctioneer, Marge admitted that IdaClare was being a trouper, but the "little vacation" from her and the Furwads had worked wonders.

Could Casanova Bisbee have had something to do with Marge's giddiness? Romance *had* been in the air, starting with Leo and Rosemary's kootchycooing, David's proposal and IdaClare's strange and sudden chairpersonship of the Chet Thomlinson Fan Club.

"I'm sure Delbert will be here soon," she told Sophonia, then looked around the cubicle. Medical machinery's blinking buttons and LEDs were the sole entertainment provided to Critical Care patients. "Is he bringing you a TV?"

"Naw. That boy nurse said he'd fetch me one." Her mouth puckered at a corner. "Gotta pay for it myself. Medicare'll fork over twenty bucks for a water jug. Not a nickel for something to do 'sides stare at the wall."

She squinted at the book Hannah carried. *"Romeo and Juliet?"* A groan converted to a cough. "You didn't bring that to read to me, did you?"

"You don't care for Shakespeare?"

Her gesture implied she could take him or leave him. "He spun some good yarns. 'Specially for a fop that wore tights and slung the tutu 'round his neck.

"Got no love for all that *thee*s and *thou*s stuff. Sounds too much like preachin'." Sophonia glanced at the door again. "Get enough of that nonsense from the hospital's sky pilot."

Seating herself in the visitor's chair, Hannah opened the book at random. *"Romeo and Juliet* has always been my favorite."

"Bunch of mush. The two of them run around like chickens, then come to a bad end. Worse'n a soap opera."

Their eyes held a full minute. Comprehension and

anger sparked in Sophonia's. "You were here when Jedo came to call." It was an accusation, not a statement. She turned her head toward the window. "Delbert said you were too smart for your own good. What'd you do, chase down Jedo after he left?"

Hannah didn't answer. Didn't move.

"Whatever that devil-dog son of the South told you, he doesn't know the whole story. Never even knew the *half* of it."

"Jedo says he found a note in the meeting tree," Hannah said, "but it was you, wasn't it?"

Sophonia picked at the sheet, then nodded.

If she'd said no, Hannah would have changed the subject. If intuition proved correct, neither Sophonia nor Jedo were aware of what had actually transpired.

"Had he written you any notes before then?"

"No. One was plenty. Vilest thing I ever read, before or since. Jedo never loved me. Not the least little bit. Courted, lay with me, asked me to elope, all to hurt me for who I was."

By her voice and expression, she was once again a young girl of fifteen, besotted with a handsome boy and the belief that, against all odds, dreams can come true.

"I was sick with hurt. Thought I'd die and prayed I would. I knew I'd healed some when my prayers were for Jedo dying from something slow and painful."

Her whisper of a smile turned bitter. "Then I truly was sick. It wasn't long before Mother guessed the cause."

Hannah remembered David warning her during the Osborn murder investigation that the thrill of the hunt is intoxicating, but the harder you concentrate on the puzzle, the easier it is to forget the person being torn apart and put together again in the process.

She reached out and laid her hand over Sophonia's. "I'm sorry. I shouldn't have—"

"Cozened me into talking with that book?" Her hand turned palm up and squeezed Hannah's. "You didn't. Made up my mind last night to tell someone, after I heard the doctors talking. They thought I was asleep. Playing possum's the only way to find out what's what 'round here."

Lips pursed, she took several breaths of oxygen. "My arm may mend, but it'll be of no use to me. My ticker isn't working to suit them, either. I swore the truth'd be buried with me. Maybe that sky pilot brainwashed me with his repent and forgive hoorah."

Hannah said, "Why don't you rest for now. I can come back tomorrow."

Sophonia jerked her hand away. "I shoulda known. Who wants to listen to an old fool ramble?" Her fingers waved at the corridor. "Go see what's keeping that boy nurse. I want my TV."

"You aren't an old fool, Sophonia. Far from it. I'll listen to whatever you care to talk about, after you get your strength back."

"Save your pity for someone that needs it. Strong is being sent in shame to live with church people you don't know from Adam. Bearing a child when you're a child yourself. Giving your son away to strangers, sight unseen."

"Oglethorpe ran out on you because you were pregnant?"

"Didn't—" She wheezed and batted at the water glass on the bedside table. Hannah guided the straw to her lips and held it until she motioned *enough*.

"Thas' better. Mouth's drier'n a popcorn fart." Nostrils flared, she inhaled oxygen like a scuba diver staving off the bends. A pinkish hue washed her cheekbones, but faded again when she spoke. "Mother made me swear on the Bible I wouldn't tell Jedo, or anyone else.

"Said if a single soul found out, Jedo's papa would hear of it. The baby was an Oglethorpe. The old man'd move heaven and earth to find it. Buy him back, or steal him outright."

Hannah shook her head. "And then what? Pass the child off as his own? The Oglethorpes had a lot of clout, but no one would have believed that for a second."

Disgust tightened Sophonia's features. "No, the baby would have been Jedo's. He loved music and books, like his mother. The old man feared his only son and heir was— Back then, folks called 'em Nancy-boys."

The vernacular had changed but not the attitude. The ignorant, idiotic terror that sons who demonstrated more interest in the arts than the manly variety were homosexual.

When Hannah had first met Jefferson Davis Oglethorpe, it was clear he'd worshiped his father. His family tree dripped military heroes, captains of industry and manor lords like skeins of Spanish moss. Failure to conform with his father's criteria for manhood must have been devastating.

"After old man Oglethorpe got my son in his clutches, he'd have sent Jedo to stay with kin in Tennessee for a year or two. Spread tales about the sweet young bride he'd taken. Turn up later a widower with a baby boy to raise."

Hannah wasn't a Shakespearean scholar, but if the bard didn't use that for a plot, he should have.

Bitterness and resignation infused Sophonia's voice. "Watching my son grow up without ever touching him, talking to him…" Her chin buckled. "That, I wasn't strong enough to do. Keeping him secret deprived me of my child, but deprived Jedo of him, too. Fair is fair."

It wasn't though, and she knew it. Not to the baby, to her or to Jedo.

"When I came home, my father didn't speak to me ever again," Sophonia said. "A Pugh fornicating with an Oglethorpe was a blacker sin against nature than murder.

"I commenced to go as wild as a March hare. Being doomed and all, I caroused around like the sinner I was."

Her quiet chuckle was as wicked as her grin. "Lemme tell you, sinnin's a passel more fun than God-fearing, particularly in those days. Beaus I had aplenty. Wouldn't chain myself to any one.

"Law how it pleased my soul that, as many ladies as Jedo squired about town, he never took a bride. Had no earthly idea he had a son and heir out yonder, somewhere in the world."

Hannah couldn't fathom how such a secret had been kept for so long, especially in a town the size of Sanity. King Hiram and Amaryllis Pugh's silence must have been as complete as their daughter's.

"What about your brothers and sisters?" she asked. "They didn't know, didn't wonder why you'd been sent away?"

"Two didn't live a year. The others passed on as youngsters. That's why my father hated me so. The only child that survived had turned on him."

More likely, Sophonia was a constant reminder of his betrayal of her. What was it Great-uncle Mort always said? Deal with the devil and you'll forever dance to his tune?

"Now that you know," Sophonia said, "it's up to you to tell Jedo the truth after I'm gone."

"Me? Oh no. You can't ask me to—"

"Every secret has its price. That's yours to pay for knowing mine."

Her eyes closed and she sighed. "There's a book at my house. The middle's hollow. Papers inside. Name of the hospital…our son's birth date. The day the nurse said the couple adoptin' him took him home. Give 'em to Jedo. Please."

Arguing would sap her flagging strength. Hannah promised she'd deliver the papers to Oglethorpe, but, "Can you tell me where the book is? Which room?"

She thought Sophonia had fallen asleep when she answered, "The parlor." An elfin smile appeared and an eyelid slitted open. Gazing downward at the collection of Shakespeare's plays Hannah held, she said, "You'll know it when you see it."

David swung his legs off the desk when Andrik strolled into the Outhouse. "What's with sending me a get-your-ass-over-here-pronto page, then disappearing for damn near an hour?"

"Women." Motioning for David to keep the chair, the detective hiked a hip onto the corner of the desk. "Two seconds after I paged you, the wife called. Couldn't get her car started. I said, 'What do I look like, Triple-A, for Christ's sake?'"

David grinned. "And Beth proceeded to tell you how you'd look when she got through with you if you didn't come arunnin' with the jumper cables."

Marlin lit a cigarette. "She had the sweetest disposition you ever saw when I married her. Never yelled. Never singed my shorts with the evil eye." Smoke streamed like a flue from a corner of his mouth. "Can't imagine what's come over her the last five, ten years."

"Want a couple of hints?"

He pulled a UPS mailer from under his arm. "Then when I went to pick this up at the courthouse, the Guppy couldn't find it. It hadn't been a half hour since she signed for it and called me, but abrafuckincadabra, it was gone."

David felt for Heather Gray—sort of. Marlin's fury

had no doubt curled her hair but the girl did set new lows for inefficiency.

The mailer's return address piqued David's interest. "The pay phone records?"

"That, or the department racked up one helluva long-distance bill last month."

David hung his suit coat on the back of the chair and rolled up his sleeves. Marlin cleared everything off the desk except the computer, phone and ashtray.

The call detail printouts—and there was a fat stack of them—looked like a standard long-distance billing statement: forty calls per page, dates and times, terminating numbers, duration and charges.

David divided his half of the paperwork by the originating pay phones' numbers. No collect or incoming calls would appear in the records because the phone company derived no income from their placement. The same was true of outgoing pay phone calls billed to calling or credit cards. The cardholder's next statement would itemize the charges but not the CDR.

Marlin wrote out a crib sheet listing numbers to watch for, though each received scrutiny, particularly if in multiple. Those in need of cross-referencing later were highlighted.

The work was as tedious and time-consuming as searching for the proverbial needle in a haystack. Marlin lit one cigarette off another; a gray cyclone roiled and swirled overhead. Numerals transposed side by side, or above and below. Fives blurred into sixes. Ink dots disfigured ones into sevens and vice versa.

David washed down three aspirin with lukewarm diet soda. The pot of crude oil Marlin had brewed was gone. Neither had dulled the pickaxes bludgeoning David's temples.

Marlin picked up the crib sheet, pushed up his reading glasses to rub his eyes, rechecked the record, then triple-checked both. "Stupid, stupid, stupid."

"What is?"

"Me." The detective stomped across the room for the case's accordion file. Muttering to himself, he snatched out a folder and slapped it down in front of David. A finger jabbed the social security number D. K. Bogart had written on his job application. "See that?"

"Uh-huh."

Marlin grabbed a sheet of telephone records. Midway down, he pointed at a number. "How about that?"

David's eyes shifted from one to the other. "I'll be damned."

"I oughtta be fired. Being blind and stupid cost us two days' time."

Waving away the smoke cloud buffeted by Andrik's temper tantrum, David said, "Bullshit. Beat yourself up if you want to, but you didn't cost us anything."

"No, I just dicked around tracing Bogart's sosh to a kid in Alexandria, Virginia."

"Two-two-four is a Virginia prefix. Nobody would have guessed it's an area code."

Marlin thumbed his chest. "*I* should have. Drones

don't yank bogus social security numbers out of their asses. The only thing most of them are smart enough to know is that they'd blow a cob trying to memorize nine random numbers in sequence.

"A fake sosh is nearly always something their pin-head brains can remember. Birth date, plus a house number. A high-school locker combination and their girlfriend's bra size. A friggin' damn *phone number*."

While Marlin's rant wound down, David pushed away from the desk. A collection of dog-eared, out-dated phone books were piled on top of the corner filing cabinet.

"Don't bother," Marlin said. "I already know what area 224 is the code for. Which is another reason a bell should've gone off."

David turned, his expression begging the obvious question.

"Chicago." The snarl in Marlin's voice put a profane twist on the word.

After pondering a moment, David said, "Which pay phone were those calls logged from?"

"Right down the street. The closest one to Bogart's apartment."

"There's no way to prove Bogart made any of them."

Marlin took his cell phone from his jacket pocket. Its automatic blocker would come up *Unavailable* if the recipient subscribed to caller ID. "The hell there isn't."

# 14

From the banked azaleas fronting the portico to the bronze statue of a mounted soldier on the lawn, the antebellum house on the bluff overlooking Sanity's city park was a graceful, genteel embassy of the defunct Confederate States of America.

Hannah's knock was answered by a woman of about sixty who was drying her hands on a kitchen towel. "May I help you?" she inquired, as though certain she could not but etiquette demanded she ask.

Hannah supplied her name and identified herself as a friend of Mr. Oglethorpe's. "I realize I should have called for an appointment, but might I speak with him a moment?"

The woman looked Hannah up and down. "Mr. O has mentioned you a time or two." She stepped back, pulling the door wider. "Follow me."

The musty smell of old house, heirloom furnishings and carpets and their fossilizing steward clung to the entry's grand hall. The mellow tang of leather bookbindings, acid decomposing the pages within and the dankness of a room shuttered against sun damage even on cloudy days was added as the woman opened the library's double pocket doors.

Hannah paused to allow the maid, housekeeper, cook—whatever her title—to tell Jefferson Davis Oglethorpe of his unexpected guest.

"He'll see you," she said, adding in a low, Mrs. Danvers whisper when she met Hannah midway across the room, "Do be brief. Mr. O hasn't been well all week."

A gravelly voice from the bowels of a high-back chair snapped, "I am neither ill nor deaf, Odessa. Bring Ms. Garvey the refreshment of her choice and me a glass of brandy."

Hannah motioned "No, thank you," then moved to the conversation area angled near a burled-mahogany fireplace. Light funneling from a linen-shaded lamp yellowed Oglethorpe's features, which time had already carved like antique scrimshaw. His smile was welcoming as he urged her to take a seat, but Hannah thought he was the saddest-looking man she'd ever seen.

"Please, don't keep me in suspense, my dear. You've come to tell me the obituary of my dreams is being composed as we speak, haven't you?" He wrung his gnarled, liver-spotted hands. "If only the marksman had aimed for her head, I'd have been spared days of fearing she'd recover."

Hannah sat back, crossed her legs and twined her fingers in her lap. Lips twitching a ghost of a smile, she gazed into his rheumy blue eyes and said, "Bullshit."

The gleeful posturing ceased. His expression blanked and he turned a bewhiskered ear toward her.

"Forgive me the infirmities of age. For a moment I thought you—"

"She did." Odessa thrust out a small silver tray bearing a half-full snifter of amber liqueur. "She said, 'Bullshit' to your crazy talk. It's high time somebody hushed your hateful old mouth."

Oglethorpe snatched the snifter from the tray. He knocked back the brandy and banged the glass down again. "Fetch me another, then gather your things and get out. You're fired."

Odessa clucked her tongue. "If I fetch you anything, it'll be water, and you've already fired me twice today." She looked at Hannah. "Will you be staying to supper?"

"She will not," Oglethorpe barked. "Show this infidel the door and bar it behind her."

Head tilted back and wagging as though beseeching the Lord to give her strength, or sharing an inside joke, Odessa exited the library like a cat in crepe-soled shoes.

Hannah and Oglethorpe commenced a staring contest, his blue eyes shooting fireballs at her bemused brown ones. He was outgunned and knew it, but she gave the old gentleman credit for valor in the midst of a losing battle.

"You are impertinent and crude," he said.

"And you are a fake, Mr. Oglethorpe. A lonely, torch-bearing old fool who counts his regrets in secret like a miser counts coins." Her voice gentled. "As does someone else I could mention."

He roared, "I've never struck a woman in my life,

but I'll take my cane to you if you speak that woman's name aloud.''

The man was a few feathers short of a whole duck, but Hannah was raised to respect her elders and their house rules, silly and despotic as they might be. ''I won't. I will speak *of* her, though…Jedo.''

He flinched at the nickname and lowered his eyes. ''I would expect no less from the daughter of a trailer-trash whore. Go on. Spew your filth. I shan't listen to a word of it.''

The insult barely nicked its target. Oglethorpe had a cur dog's nose for buried bones. He hoarded skeletons in his own closet to rattle whenever it suited his mood, or his purposes.

Besides, she'd been called worse.

''If you or she had listened to your instincts at the meeting tree that day, neither of you would have wasted your lives trying to hate each other.''

Overlong, brittle nails pecked and clawed at the armchair's upholstery.

''Just answer one question for me,'' Hannah said. ''Before you found that note, had you ever seen any-thing—a paragraph, a sentence, even her signature—written in her own hand?''

Ticks from the grandfather clock in the entry hall echoed loud in the silence. Had Oglethorpe issued a gruff ''No'' a second later, it would have been lost in the clock tolling the hour.

Hannah said, ''Until then, you used stones and moss and flowers to leave messages for each other. Love notes were too risky. Someone else might find them and tell your parents you were meeting on the sly.''

The upholstery continued to suffer his wrath, but a flush appeared above his shirt collar's starched rim and spread to his wattled neck.

''For the same reason, she had never seen your handwriting, either. Had no reason to question whether the note saying you'd never loved her, that you'd courted her to hurt her in the cruelest way possible and to spite her family, had actually come from you.''

His chin jerked up. His face contorted with anger, confusion, shock, then horror, and his eyes narrowed, squinting into the middle distance at a time and place sixty years removed from the present.

''Yes, Jedo. She found a note in the meeting tree, too. I'm not sure whether it was the day, or day after you'd planned to elope, but its wording was identical.''

Fist raised and shaking, he bellowed, ''Lies. *Lies.* How dare you defile my house with that harlot's damnable lies.''

''It isn't a lie and you know it, Mr. Oglethorpe.'' Hannah leaned forward, her elbows resting on her thighs. ''The two notes were historic documents. Evidence of the first time in a century the patriarchs of the Oglethorpe clan and the Pughs met and declared a temporary truce to their feud.

''Someone must have suspected you were meeting in secret and followed you, or her. Whomever it was probably thought family loyalty would eventually win out, but as a wise man reminded me just yesterday, forbidden fruit is the sweetest, the most intoxicating.

"It wouldn't take long for the spy to learn your routine, arrive ahead of you and eavesdrop. When he or she heard your plans to elope and your shrewd idea to set a date and an alternate one in advance, the spy was forced to intervene."

"No…no! You're mad, a raving *lunatic*. Get out. *Out,* or I swear on my father's grave, I'll ruin you and that whoreson sheriff of yours."

Hannah went on, "Several generations of hate-mongering must have come in handy when those notes were composed. All your parents and hers had to do was repeat on paper the most despicable, vicious things they had said to each other when they heard about your love affair.

"Hurting their children—devastating them—was a tiny price to pay to keep the feud alive. The four of them returned to their homes, arrogantly and heartlessly secure in the knowledge that they'd saved you and her from yourselves."

Tears meandered down his cheeks, silvering the creases and gullies in his skin. Hannah moved from the chair and knelt in front of him, her hand caressing his knee. "They'd have never succeeded if you and Sophonia had listened to your instincts. You knew she loved you. She knew you loved her. Maybe if you'd both been a little older, a little more willing to believe what your hearts told you was true…"

"What's done is done."

"No, it isn't, Jedo." She rose to her feet. "The rest

of the story is Sophonia's to tell. Go to her, like you should have sixty years ago, before it truly is too late.''

With that, Hannah strode from the room and let herself out the front door. Before she reached the portico steps, the confidence she'd felt when she arrived had sprouted self-righteous barbs.

The truth was a flimsy barrier against a legacy of hate, inordinate pride and a bitter, egotistical old man's vengeful nature. David's warning chorused by Eli Cree's droned in her ears as First Street's traffic thinned and accelerated at the city limits.

Jefferson Davis Oglethorpe didn't hold the patent on arrogance. She'd gambled with David's future by revising a homegrown, virtually forgotten Shakespearean tragedy. If Oglethorpe's support and cash trove took a one-hundred-and-eighty-degree swing to the Jessup Knox camp, David's term as county sheriff would end in a matter of weeks.

Oh yes. Life was good. Freakin' *splendid.* If David's unemployment coincided with Jack Clancy's declaring bankruptcy, she and the sheriff renowned for losing a primary election to a dipshit Elvis wannabe could ride off into the sunset together and live happily ever after in a cardboard box.

The thought wasn't funny then, or now, as she sat at her desk nibbling soda crackers and sipping a second cup of chamomile tea. Control was a state of mind. The swampy sensation of losing every vestige of hers, of being transformed into a cosmic dartboard with a bull's-eye as big as the moon, unsettled more than her stomach.

So had the note she'd found taped inside the screen door. David was sorry he'd missed her. He and Andrik would be in the neighborhood a while. If he was lucky, he'd dump the detective before he stopped by again.

Pretty tame for a portent of doom, but at present, leaves whirling a dervish on the lawn would have signified the deep dark bottom of the bad juju barrel.

Malcolm groaned to his feet, shook himself, then trotted to the kitchen, either for a drink or to escape her negative-ion emissions. They'd hardly spoken since she'd gotten home. Dogs, even dumbs ones, were said to be sensitive to their owner's moods. If she didn't shake hers, they'd both be raiding Itsy and Bitsy's Prozac stash by sunset.

The gasoline-powered engine rumbling outside the windows didn't belong to a police-packaged Crown Victoria. Delbert's souped-up, metal-bodied vintage Cushman golf cart sounded like an off-balance washing machine on spin cycle. Its blue-black exhaust repelled all mosquitoes within a fifty-yard radius.

Hannah saw no need to get up. The old fart never bothered to knock before breaking and entering. It was reasonable to assume he wouldn't when she was home and the front door was wide open.

The screen door slapped shut behind him. "What's up, ladybug? I saw the sheriff and Detective Andrik snooping around Jack's condo."

"Cops don't snoop. They investigate."

"Hmmph." Delbert plopped down in the chair beside the desk. His navy golf cap, green and yellow striped shirt, plaid walking shorts and calf-high, smiley-face crew socks almost matched. "Speaking of investigations, anything new in the Thomlinson case?"

"Not that I know of. I'm not even sure there *is* a Thomlinson case. A better question is, where have you been hiding the past couple of days?"

He scowled. "You got a problem with me keeping Sophonia company? IdaClare's got a flock of old biddies seeing to her. Sophonia's all alone in the world. Has been, most of her life."

Ouch. Crotchety had risen to new heights. On closer inspection, his eyes were puffy and he looked thoroughly exhausted. He slumped rather than sat in the chair, yet his sandaled feet jitterbugged on the hardwood floor.

Hannah's voice was soft when she asked, "She isn't going to make it, is she?"

As though the space separating them caused an audio time lapse, Delbert stared, started, then stammered, "D-did you say something?"

"Sophonia isn't going to make it, is she? That's why you're upset."

A palm smacked the corner of the desk. "Jehosaphat and criminitlies. She was sleeping like a baby when I left her a while ago, and who the hell says I'm upset?"

What patience and Christian charity Hannah possessed she'd left in Jefferson Davis Oglethorpe's library. "You're grumpier than usual, the bags under your eyes exceed airline regulations for carry-on luggage and you can't sit still."

The hairy-kneed mambo ceased. He tugged down the brim of his cap and crossed his arms at his chest. His lower lip flapped over the upper one.

God, he was adorable when he pouted.

"Well, you're a ding-danged ray of sunshine yourself, missy. I'll have you know, my prostate kept me up half the night, my golf game got rained out this morning and the sheriff's girlfriend is playing deaf, dumb and blind about a multiple-homicide investigation going on in my own backyard."

Delbert's hugger-mugger body language and pupils drilling a hole above her eyebrows were dead giveaways. Statements two and three were true. The first was akin to a high-school girl pleading menstrual cramps to get out of gym.

Nor had a flaming boinkarama with Marge last night put the fidgets in his boxers, or cost him any sleep. Hannah wasn't an expert on senior sex, but even a snuggle without any fireworks leaves a couple relaxed, not anxious and crabby.

Malcolm's entrance and ritual crotch sniff distracted Delbert long enough for Hannah to manufacture a repentant expression and an equally true-false comeback. "I didn't mean to pry. We're all stressed out, and hanging in limbo isn't helping. Realizing I hadn't seen you for days didn't either. The way things are going, I was afraid something had happened to you, too."

"No sense in that, ladybug." A facsimile of a smile appeared. "I've just been busier than a cranberry merchant."

"Doing what?" she blurted. "I mean, besides keeping the road hot between here and the hospital."

"This and that." He shrugged. "You know me."

Yes, she did. Too well. Murder, mayhem and Mike Hammer Bisbee went together like bologna, mustard and crushed potato chips on white bread. IdaClare being on the gumshoes' injured reserve list wouldn't hinder the cloak-and-daggering much.

Hannah's finger batted the tea bag's tag. Sneaking suspicions galloped from the back of her mind to the fore. She said, "I'm a little worried about Marge, too."

"Oh?" Right on cue, his knees dandled a duet. "Dunno why you would be. She's fine as frog's hair, other than IdaClare getting on her nerves now and then. You giving her a break last night helped a lot. Marge is pretty independent, you know. Once you're accustomed to living alone, it's a booger adjusting to having a roomie. Especially when it's at their house instead of yours."

Ye gods. Silence is golden. In a pinch, K.I.S.S. will suffice. Like David once told her, if suspects stuck with yes, no and just-the-facts answers, he could rent jail cells as efficiency apartments.

Hannah sighed. "I guess I'll have to take your word for it. I'd hoped staying with IdaClare for a few hours would give Marge a chance to relax, except she looked anything but when she came back."

A string of muttered expletives ended in, "You women are all alike. If you don't have something to worry about, you sit around worrying about not having anything to worry about."

Another truism, although Hannah didn't appreciate hearing it.

Delbert rocked forward in the chair. Malcolm took it as a signal for an ear scratch. Malcolm was wrong.

"You could use some R&R yourself, ladybug. Quit worrying about Marge and me. Hell, forget I was here. Just because I think of you as the daughter I never had, I shouldn't have asked you to betray the sheriff's confidence."

"Arrrgh." Hannah dropped her head in her hands. "Damn you, Delbert. I don't have any confidences *to* betray."

"That-a-girl. Stick to your guns."

"Will you listen to me?" She glared at him through a cage of fingers. "David and I have been playing phone tag for a day and a half."

The old fart graced her with a "hot-diggety, now you're cookin'" grin.

"Oh, all right already." Her arms fell to her lap. "But most of what little I know didn't come from David, Marlin or any official sources. Got that?"

Claudina Burkholtz was a civilian employee. Running into her after leaving Eli's barbershop and having lunch had been fun, but an informational bust. On a diet or off, it took more than a drive-thru Aunt Chilada's lite taco plate for the chief dispatcher to turn stool pigeon.

Delbert flipped back the cover of a mini spiral note-book identical to the ones David and Marlin carried. He licked the tip of his golf pencil and looked at Hannah expectantly.

"The shooter used the alias D. K. 'Deke' Bogart," she said. "Real name unknown. He's a drifter, maybe from Saint Louis or Chicago—another unknown—but they're pretty sure he was a member of the Black Gangster Disciples.

"The majority of the evidence points to a work-place massacre with revenge as the motive. Bogart was fired the day before, for assaulting Jasmine Chau. Eulilly was in the wrong place at the wrong time. Ditto Sophonia and IdaClare."

The tenor of Delbert's "Uh-huh" was synonymous with "My ass."

Hannah said, "Besides the eyewitnesses, Marlin in-terviewed me, Chet and Jack Clancy, among others, to tie up loose ends. So far, there are some holes and pieces that don't fit, but there always are.

"The prosecuting attorney is satisfied it's a work-place massacre, so the book on it will likely be closed today or tomorrow. Deke Bogart may never be iden-tified unless it's through a missing person's report."

Delbert's pencil remained poised, his notebook blank. "That's it?"

"I tried to tell you I didn't know much. I don't even *want* to know much."

"Hmmph." The notebook slapped shut. "Got your wish, didn't you?"

A car door slammed outside. Expecting David,

Hannah rolled back her chair to meet him and nearly upended it when Chet Thomlinson stormed into the cottage.

"What kind of operations are you managing here?" he yelled. "I'm gone one day—twenty-eight hours to be exact—to attend my wife's funeral, for Christ's sake, and what do I find when I get back? That my house was broken into while I was gone."

"Broken into?" Hannah repeated. "When? Was anything stolen?"

Malcolm's neck telescoped until his muzzle hovered half the width of the deck. Teeth bared, he growled a warning, as he had yesterday to Henry Don Tucker.

Chet reared back. "If that mutt bites me, I'll sue Clancy for every dime he has."

Hannah's grip on Malcolm's collar was window dressing. He was too big and heavy to hold if he lunged.

Delbert said, "Quit hollering and he'll simmer down."

"Butt out, Bisbee. This is none of your business." Chet's arm swung toward the door. "Why don't you take yourself and the dog for a walk, eh?"

To Hannah's surprise, Delbert stood, hands aloft as though he were a bystander at an armed robbery. "I'm going, but I guarantee, the dog won't."

From nose to tail, Malcolm stood as stiff as a lawn ornament.

"Later, Hannah," Delbert said. "Take it easy, Thomlinson."

She fought down panic, the lung-constricted, muscle-twanging fear and rage at feeling threatened in the place she felt most safe.

Hands on his hips and legs spraddled, Chet looked as tall and burly as David. She considered standing, equalizing their positions as much as she could. Malcolm's bristled ruff and back countermanded the idea.

Shoulders squared, she said, "I don't blame you for being angry, Chet. Coming home to—"

"Where were you last night around eight-thirty, nine o'clock?"

Hannah recoiled. "Excuse me?"

"That's when the neighbors across the street saw lights inside my house."

"You're accusing me of…" Laughter bubbled in her throat. She stanched it, but not an openmouthed half grimace, half smile. "Why in the world would I break into your house?"

"Just answer the question, Ms. Garvey."

She started to refuse on principle, but what the hell. She'd never had an ironclad alibi before. It would be a shame to waste it. "I was with IdaClare Clancy at her home, from about seven-thirty until almost midnight."

The instant she said it, she knew where Marge had been between those hours, along with Delbert and very likely—correction, absolutely positively—Leo and Rosemary. And that IdaClare was as ignorant of the Burglars' Night Out as she was.

The screen door's hinges yipped. "I can vouch for her." David strode in, his cop-face as cold as his voice. Steel-blue gaze locked on Chet, he tapped his thigh with his palm. "C'mere, Malcolm."

The giant Airedale-wildebeest bounded from the office nook railing toward the door David held open for him. "Now, don't you go to peeing on that fancy new Lexus's tires. Ya hear?"

Chet spoke for Hannah when he said, "Thank God you're here, Sheriff. I was just telling Ms. Garvey—"

"Oh, I heard what you were telling Ms. Garvey." Ten feet tall, bulletproof and malevolent summed up David's stance. "I didn't care much for the way you were telling it, either."

Chet wilted like an untied balloon. Leaning on the nook's railed divider, he bowed his head and murmured an apology. "Can't say as I blame you, Sheriff. What I said was way out of line."

A crooked finger dashed a trickle of sweat from his temple. "It's no excuse, I know, but when I saw that someone had been in my house while I was away… On top of Eulilly's death, the funeral—well, it was too much. Something inside me just snapped."

Hannah frowned as David took a notebook from his shirt pocket. By golly, next trip to Sanity, she'd buy a gross of them.

"I'm aware of the prowler complaint made to dispatch last night," David said. "According to the deputy's activity log, the house was secure. No sign of a forced entry, front or back. Nothing visibly disturbed."

"Not from the outside looking in, no."

"Was anything stolen? Vandalized?"

"Packing cartons were unsealed and retaped. Cabinets and drawers were searched. My computer was moved from the desk to the floor and a number of file dates indicated they were opened yesterday."

Chet looked at Hannah and chuckled. "Okay, it's crazy. I've *been* a little crazy since Tuesday night, but that's why I thought you had something to with it. I know you have a master key to every cottage and business in the development."

"Yes, I do, but that doesn't explain why you thought I'd used it to break into your house."

To David, Chet said, "Hey, I did some rule-bending with the Service I wouldn't want to answer for. The spouse is always the prime suspect in an unnatural death and civilians don't need search warrants. I thought Hannah might be lending an assist."

"That's pretty damn crazy, all right," David said. "With or without my knowledge, anything she'd found would have been inadmissible as evidence."

"We both know there are ways of making it admissible, Sheriff."

The planes of David's face could have scored brick. Chet staggered. A feral groan escaped his lips. Raking back his hair, his fingers balled into fists. "How's that for proof of insanity? God, if you needed more, you just got it."

David angled the visitor's chair away from Hannah's desk. "Why don't you have a seat, Chet. Take a minute to catch your breath."

Hannah had heard that buttery drawl before. He'd used it on her the morning Kathleen Osborne's body was discovered. In the spirit of better to give than receive, she chimed in, "Can I get you a cup of—"

"That's okay. I'm already up," David said. The set of his jaw added, "Hush and stay hushed, or you'll be helping Malcolm baptize the tires."

Neither she nor Chet spoke while cabinet doors thumped and glass tinkled in the kitchen. Over the sound of water running in the sink, Hannah thought she heard David talking on his cell phone.

He returned holding a highball glass between a thumb and forefinger. Tap water, no ice. Gee, the consummate host.

Chet thanked him, popped a pill in his mouth, drained the glass and put it on the desk. Rather than offer a refill, or a crust of moldy bread, David said, "If you don't mind my asking, where'd you get the notion that we suspect you, or anyone else, of having something to do with your wife's death?"

"Standard operating procedure. You'd be derelict if you didn't."

David sat sideward on the railing, arms folded on his thigh. A minute must have elapsed before Chet said, "As I told Detective Andrik, Eulilly and I didn't have a perfect marriage."

Hannah felt David's gaze shift to her. He said, "Is there such a thing?"

"Maybe not. Eulilly and I loved each other very much, but we came from different backgrounds— didn't have as much in common as we first thought. As time went on, that became more and more obvious."

Hannah slanted her eyes at David. "Love isn't enough to base a lifetime commitment on."

"No, it wasn't, I'm afraid," Chet said. "We separated a few times, never for more than a few days. The move to Mississippi was our biggest bone of contention. On the way to the party, I told her I wasn't sure my things would be on the truck when it left. She said the choice was mine."

Pain leavened his ragged sigh. "For all our problems, if I had another chance, I'd rather be in Mississippi with her than in Valhalla Springs without her."

David asked, "Did your wife object to you traveling alone? You attended coin shows, conventions and investment seminars pretty regularly, didn't you?"

"Five or six times a year, I guess. Eulilly went with me to some seminars, but coins didn't interest her. She said money you can't spend or put in the bank wasn't worth having."

"I understand you were attached to the agency office in Chicago in what, the late eighties? Early nineties?"

Chet smiled. "You *have* done your homework, haven't you, Sheriff."

"The department isn't quite as jerkwater as some would like to believe."

"Then you already know I was in Chicago from 1991 to 1994. Transferred to Jacksonville and retired from there."

"Except you didn't, entirely."

"What do you mean?"

David waved a dismissal. "Cops hang up their shields, maybe go fishin' more often than they once did, but they don't retire like other folks. Especially feds. Why, I bet a month doesn't go by without somebody calling about a cold case, or some psych patient that had it in for the president when you were making the rounds."

Chet's expression relaxed. "It's been known to happen. You can't teach an old dog new tricks, but you can pick what's left of his brain."

"Anybody ever contact you for info on a fella by the name of Antoine Klein? Or his son, Antoine Jr.?"

"Antoine Klein." Chet shook his head. "Sorry. No bells are ringing."

"Antoine Sr. was one of the original Black Gangster Disciples and a mean son of a bitch. He got the death penalty in prison the old-fashioned way—with a shiv between the ribs. Junior took up where the old man left off before he was out of elementary school."

Chet shook his head again. "Wish I could help, but my squad in Chicago didn't interact much with gangs."

"That's pretty much what I expected you'd say."

"Why the interest, Sheriff? Do you have reason to believe this Alphonse Klein is in the area?"

"Antoine," David corrected. "Oh, yeah. Klein was in the area, all right. Smack in the middle of town, until a couple of days ago. I reckon you could call his departure a mite unexpected, but he didn't get far."

He stood and offered his hand. "I appreciate your time, Chet. Detective Andrik is up at your cottage. Why don't the two of you do a walk-through just to make sure nothing's missing? I'll join you there shortly."

"That really isn't necessary, Sheriff."

"Maybe not, but I'll sleep better knowing we did a thorough job on the follow-up."

Chet hadn't reached the porch steps when Hannah said, "Care to clue me in on what that was all about?"

"Nope." David took a rubber-banded roll of brown paper lunch bags from his trouser pocket.

"Care to explain *why* you won't clue me in on what that was all about?"

"Patience, woman. You'll see soon enough." Using a pencil to nudge the bottom of the glass Chet drank from over the edge of the desk, he picked it up between his thumb and forefinger and dropped it in the bag.

A smooth glass surface. Tap water. No ice, ergo, no condensation to smudge Chet's fingerprints. "Jeez, and to think I thought you were just a crummy host. Instead, you're a freakin' genius."

"I have my moments." He motioned for her to meet him at the door.

Arms sliding around his neck, her tongue followed the curve of his lips with the tip of her tongue, then drew back. "Darling, there's more...*so* much more, awaiting you...after you talk."

He grinned. "No can do, Mata Hari."

"You don't trust me?" Her voice began at alto, surpassed soprano and ascended to shrill. "Have I ever repeated anything you've told me in confidence?"

"Yes."

Hannah slumped against him. "Oh."

His kiss pulled her upright, her body melding with his like a cat stretching after a nice long nap. She savored the feel of him, the taste of him, the radiant heat rushing the length of her, as rain tattooed the roof, its earthy redolence breezing through the screen.

"God, I've missed you, sugar," he said. "Sometimes, I wi—"

"Don't." Hannah felt a bit foolish, but knew he was about to say he wished he weren't sheriff. What he wanted was more uninterrupted time together, but a few days ago she had learned that wishes weren't necessarily words jettisoned on air, that watching what you wish for might be advice worth considering.

"Don't mess with success," she said. "Maybe the reason we get along so well is because we're seldom together long enough to argue."

"We've argued lots of times," he argued. "Fact is, the first time I kissed you was after an argument."

"No, it wasn't. It was—" She blew out a raspberry. "Will you answer a question before you ride off into the sunset again?"

An eyebrow bent at center. "Depends."

"Is Jack still a suspect?"

He hesitated, then nodded.

"Himself, or as a cocon—"

David silenced her with a finger pressed to her mouth. He whispered, "Both," then more loudly, "That's two questions, and that's one too many."

She glared up at him. "Actually it's three, counting the one I asked you earlier."

"Which I'll answer, if you'll give me half a chance." He thrust out the paper-wrapped highball glass. "Hold this."

She had no time to react before he stepped back, reached around the edge of the front door and pulled Delbert from behind it like a carnival booth's grand prize.

"How long have you been hiding back there?" A reflexive, albeit stupid, question. Directing a revision to David, she asked, "How long have you known he was hiding back there?"

"Since I saw him when I came out of the kitchen."

"And you just let him *stay there?*"

Delbert, his shirt clenched in David's fist, waggled his fingers for attention. He inquired in a voice amazingly similar to Donald Duck's, "Can I say something?"

"No," his captors answered in unison.

"By the time I spotted him," David said, "he'd already heard about the break-in, Chet accusing you of doing it accusing me of sponsoring it, and other details I don't want spread to hell and gone."

"Won't tell a soul," Delbert quacked. "Gimme a Bible. I'll swear on it."

Hannah hurled a flame-thrower look at the bug-eyed burglar, spy and all-around pain in the ass. Oh, it was tempting to rat him out.

The phone let her off the hook, so to speak. Leaving David to threaten Delbert with tortures of which neither the ACLU or AARP would approve, she answered with the standard greeting.

Static and a throbbing, low drone filtered through the earpiece. "Hello?"

Through the audio clutter, a tinny voice said, "Sweetpea, it's Jack. If anyone's there, don't say my name out loud."

A trapdoor opened beneath Hannah's feet. Her eyes closed against the sensory vertigo of a freefall plunge.

"I've gotta talk to you," he said. "Tonight. Alone."

"I'm not sure that's possible." She identified the noise in the background as an airplane's engine. A small plane, not his Lear.

"Make it possible," he said. "Meet me at Sanity Municipal at seven. Don't tell anyone where you're going, or why. I'll explain when you get there."

# 15

A deluge transformed the road into a suds-free car wash. Oncoming vehicles and Hannah's Blazer fired rooster-tailed salvos at each other as they passed. Miniature tsunamis burst white on their windshields and pinned wiper blades for a blind three-count.

The defroster cleared ragged portholes on the glass. An inch separated Hannah's chin from the steering wheel. Malcolm, riding shotgun, sat as stoic as a mother-in-law awaiting the proper, pre-impact moment to snipe, "I told you we should have waited until the storm let up."

A small blue sign with a biplane pictograph and left-pointing arrow was posted a helpful ten feet from the turnoff. Leaving the two-lane's asphalt for the access road's slurry chip-and-seal surface, the Blazer's rear end fishtailed across a flooded, low-water bridge. Loose gypsum pelted the undercarriage and fender wells before the tires found purchase.

Malcolm panted a *Wow, let's do it again, can we, huh?* while Hannah recovered from a mild cardiac infarction and pondered which area of Jack's anatomy she'd cream first with a tire tool.

She wasn't aware that Sanity had an airport until

she looked up its location in a chamber of commerce brochure. Despite the Municipal in its name, the barbed wire–fenced airstrip bisected by a concrete runway was privately owned.

Corrugated metal Quonset huts of World War II vintage served as hangars. A guy-wired radio tower shot skyward behind a row of cinder-block outbuildings. No vehicles were parked nearby, but a man was lugging a fuel hose toward a twin-engine Piper Cub.

Another man wearing the type of hooded slicker favored by school crossing guards waved from a hut's side door. Mr. Clancy, she presumed.

Hannah tightened the belt to her trench coat and exited the warm, dry truck. Malcolm dove out behind her, went splat and belly-surfed on the soggy grass. For giant Airedale-wildebeests, monsoons were a thrill a minute.

The space subwalled from the hangar's girded rib cage stank of dry rot, stale cigarette smoke, avgas, grimy coveralls and dust thick enough to plow. Malcolm's wet-dog stink was pleasant by comparison.

"I knew you wouldn't let me down," Jack said, helping her out of her coat. He hung his slicker on a peg beside it.

The haggard wretch she'd expected was nowhere in evidence. The hems of Jack's jeans were damp and rain glistened on the shoulders of his camel hair sport jacket, but his grin was as cocky as ever and not a strand of silver hair was mussed.

"I thought the same of you," she said, "until this week."

Jack stiffened. "I didn't have to rent a plane and fly down here to talk to you in person."

"Then why did you?"

"Because the runway isn't long enough for the jet and you deserve a face-to-face explanation."

Hannah gave him the benefit of the doubt that the order of his answer coincided with his first statement not his priorities.

"The silent treatment, eh?" He shuffled in place. "God forbid you should make this any easier, sweetpea."

"Up yours, Clancy."

"Okay, okay. You're mad as hell. You have every right to be."

"I was mad when you called Monday morning. I won't waste your time, or my breath, giving you an emotional laundry list of the crap you've put me through since then."

Nodding, he leaned against the edge of the desk and rested his palms on his thighs. "I know you don't believe in coincidence, so I guess you could call this week a comedy of errors, if there'd been a damn thing funny about it."

Hannah reached for her coat. "Let's go, Malcolm. I feel spin and excuses coming on, not an explanation."

"Oh, yeah? How's AIDS for an excuse? Or would it fall into the spin category?"

Hannah whirled, his every word a scalpel, eviscerating her in a few smooth, easy strokes. She staggered, darkness rushing up, closing in around her.

Clawing the air for an anchor before her knees buckled, she heard him say, as if from miles distant, "...thought I was a dead man walking until this morning, when I found out the tests were all HIV-negative." She knew, in that split second, she'd never loved him more.

His voice a calm monotone, he said, "What you're feeling is exactly how I felt when I read the obituaries in last Sunday's *Post-Dispatch*."

The residual terror in his eyes was as arresting as their cornflower-blue color. "Several months after you and I tried and failed to make love, and several months before I met Stephen, I was so lonely and miserable, I did what I swore I'd never do—make the gay bar scene."

"Oh, Jack..."

"I had a weekend fling with a baseball player the Cardinals had called up from the minors. He was just a kid—didn't know anyone in town, was as lonely and miserable as I was and had a helluva lot more to lose by not being discreet.

"I heard he'd taken a job in the Cards' front office when he didn't make the team. I never saw him again until Sunday, when his photo stared back at me from the obits.

"There was no euphemistic 'died after a long illness.' The copy read, 'died of complications from AIDS' in screaming black-on-white."

Hannah said, "You didn't—"

"Protect myself?" He shrugged. "If you'd asked me then, I'd have said yes. Except nothing's foolproof. Between my state of mind at the time of our two-night stand, and hindsight being a long way from twenty-twenty, I panicked. That's when a nerves-of-steel, million-dollar wheeler-dealer like John Patrick Clancy breaks down and bawls at his breakfast table.''

The haggard wretch Hannah had expected to see on arrival now swam before her eyes. Jack looked away and cleared his throat, directing his remarks at a crack in the concrete floor. ''I didn't want to know if I was infected, but I had to. My pilot's wife was in labor, so Stephen booked me on the first available flight to San Diego.''

''Why there?'' Hannah asked. ''Saint Louis has some of the best medical facilities in the country.''

''True, but Stephen said the University of California–San Diego's AIDS Research Institute was the cutting edge in diagnosis and treatment. If I tested positive, I couldn't afford to lose another day—another *hour*—or settle for anything less than the best treatment available. I stayed at the UC-Medical Center overnight. The techs ran every test they could think of, then ran some more.''

Hannah slipped her hands from his to push the damp hair from her face. Maybe she was the heartless, vicious one. Maybe her emotions had been pulled in so many directions the last few days, all she could muster was a cold, clinical rationality.

The hell Jack had been through explained a lot—his moodiness and hair-trigger temper, his refusal to answer Marlin Andrik's questions or hers, the sudden departure from Valhalla Springs and neither taking, nor returning, her phone calls. It didn't, however, explain everything.

The door to the hangar rattled open. A disembodied voice said, "I signed your name to the chit for the fuel, Mr. Clancy. The rain's let up, but we're losing the light fast."

"Okay. Be with you in two."

The pilot muttered, "That's seconds, I hope."

Jack stood and chafed Hannah's upper arms. "You heard the man." He chuckled. "Now that I know I'm not dying, I'm not keen on getting killed in a plane crash."

"So that's it, huh?" She pulled from his embrace. "Bombs aweigh, mission accomplished, let's turn for home, boys."

"I'm doing the best I can, Hannah. My best by you. I can't—"

"Did you have anything to do with the shooting at the Royal Dragon? With Eulilly Thomlinson's death?"

"*What?* I can't believe you'd even ask me that."

"Did you, Jack?"

"Are you nuts? No! Of course I didn't."

She tossed her head. "How about the quarterly departmental funds? Why weren't they deposited until today? Where'd the money come from to do it?"

"I didn't come here to—"

"Answer me, damn it. I've covered for you. Lied outright, or by omission, for you to David, Marlin

Andrik, your mother and the department supervisors. You said I deserved an explanation. Give me one."

"I already told you," he said, "it was a comedy of errors, but it's over, thank God. No prisoners taken, no more dead man walking."

"Not good enough. Not even close."

Features taut with anger, he spread his hands in supplication. "Clancy Construction and Development had cash-flow problems this spring, thanks to two outstanding lawsuits for nonpayment. Tripp Irving said the Valhalla Springs accounts were flush enough to delay the regular quarterly transfer.

"One suit was settled last Friday. I was to authorize the accounts transfer Monday, but gee-whiz, sweetpea, something came up and stupid me forgot to do it. Then Eulilly Bethune Thomlinson got killed. Mother got shot. A rolling blackout shut down the AIDS Research Institute's lab—no power, no test results.

"I couldn't work, couldn't sleep, couldn't function, for Christ's sake. Stephen gave me a hypo that knocked me on my ass and kept me there until the lab called this morning."

Hannah wanted to believe him, but, "Why didn't you just tell me that when I asked?"

He laughed up at the ceiling. It was a hollow, empty sound, yet it echoed off the cavernous, bowed metal above. "Well, for one thing, I thought you trusted me. For another, I thought you'd fill in the blanks yourself if I told you where I'd been and why."

Suzann Ledbetter

His smile was thin-lipped, his eyes narrow and dull. "It never occurred to me that you'd accuse me of two murders and attempted matricide. Or of siphoning money from Valhalla Springs to pay someone to do it for me."

Ignoring the stabbing sensation at her solar plexus, Hannah said, "Is that why Tripp went to Saint Louis yesterday afternoon? To transfer the money for you?"

"I haven't seen him since...hell, I don't know— last month sometime. Maybe longer than that. Now, if you'll excuse me, I have a plane to catch."

Jack started for the door, cursed, then turned. "Where'd you get the idea that Tripp was even in Saint Louis, yesterday?"

"The appointment calendar at his office. A notation said 'J/C—St. L—counsel.'"

Jack looked perplexed, then burst out laughing— this time the genuine, shoulder-shaking variety. "Lord Almighty damn, Hannah. Either his secretary wrote it backward, or you read it backward. It wasn't J/C, it's C/J, for Camp Jurassic. Tripp's son is a dinosaur freak, so his ex-wife signed the kid up *and* volunteered to be a parent-counselor to make sure she wasn't leaving her baby in the hands of a bunch of raving pedophiles.

"I can't swear to it," he went on, "but I'll bet fifty bucks Tripp's ex-wife had a hot date, told Tripp at the last minute that she was sick and begged him into taking her place."

Few thought faster on their feet than Jack Clancy,

but could he conjure that logical an explanation in nanoseconds?

He cradled her face. "Look at me. I know I left you hanging, but it wasn't intentional. I'm also aware that my name is on Hendrickson's suspect list and going to ground hasn't helped much."

"A masterful understatement."

"Okay, but can't you understand why this meeting is strictly between you and me? Why I can't—won't—tell anyone else the truth about San Diego?"

Her head shook as much as his hands allowed. "No. I don't. All I'm sure of is you're asking me to continue lying to David and everyone else by keeping my mouth shut."

"In that case—" Jack lifted her trench coat and his slicker from the wall pegs. "Walk me to the plane. If I don't get a move on, Sky King will take off without me."

Minutes later, Hannah gazed out the Blazer's side window into the foggy gloom at the Piper Cub taxiing down the runway. The plane's running lights blurred. She couldn't help thinking she'd just costarred in a role-reversed, below B-grade remake of *Casablanca*.

# 16

The cottage's resident Queen of Clean rested an elbow on the dust mop's handle and surveyed her domain.

Every piece of furniture—legs, spindles and stretchers included—plus the kitchen, both baths, even the switch plates glowed like the gold stars teachers awarded students for a job well done.

Centered on the trunk's lid, her heirloom S. S. Kresge's candy dish sparkled like genuine crystal. To one side, magazines were fanned with geometric precision. On the other, the Pulitzer Prize–winning novel she wasn't reading lay spraddled facedown, as though her literary pursuits had been interrupted.

Her desk was as orderly as a figurehead CEO's. Emollient cloths had conditioned the seating group's leather upholstery. The hardwood floors were dusted, lemon-polished and buffed with socked feet.

Hannah grabbed the bucket crammed with rags, spray cleaners and aerosol cans, dragging the mop behind her like a prehensile tail. If only someone would invent a cleanser that purged dirty little secrets as effectively as ~~ammonia~~ dissolved waxy yellow buildup.

A muddy-pawed Malcolm stared through the French doors from his exile on the deck. His woebegone expression didn't register a blip on her maxed-out Guilt-O-Meter. The weatherman had tempered today's more-of-the-same forecast with a promise that Sunday would be sunny and mild. Until time and Mother Nature proved him correct, Malcolm was persona non grata.

The clock, not her stomach, suggested lunch. Perusing the refrigerator confirmed her suspicions. Lots of food and nothing to eat. The doorbell confirmed another: it was impossible to retreat from the world if the world wouldn't freakin' leave you alone.

Socks skating soundlessly on the great room's floor, she angled toward the fireplace wall to peek out the window. A continental kit, twin hockey-stick taillights and acre of turquoise trunk were presumably attached to the unseen half of a '58 Edsel.

David and IdaClare headed a list entitled "If I Can't Talk to You Without Lying, I Won't Talk to You At All." It sounded like a bad country-western song, but Hannah's life of late *felt* like a bad country-western song, except the trains and prisons were metaphorical. James Bond Bisbee hadn't made the list, but she wasn't sure she wanted to talk to him, either.

"Aw c'mon, ladybug. I know you're in there," he wheedled through the cracks in the door.

Well, hell.

Delbert stood with golf cap in hands, wringing the

bejesus out of it. Malcolm slumped against him, undying love and hope radiating from his eyes.

"Wipe your feet on the mat," Hannah said, "and don't let the dog in."

Shutting the door on Malcolm's whimpering, Delbert whistled and said, "Spiffed up the place, did you? I haven't seen it this clean since the orderlies hauled Owen McCutcheon away in the loony wagon."

"How kind of you to notice."

"Pretty posies, too." He indicated the bush-size floral arrangement on the conference table. "I s'pose the sheriff sent 'em for...well, you know."

Jeez-us Louise-us and Thelma, too. The man could dig himself in deeper with a couple of sentences than most men could with a crane.

"No," she said, "he didn't." She refrained from mentioning she'd almost round-filed them when they were delivered. An inner voice of reason said trashing them was killing the message, not the messenger, ergo, a childish and sincerely dumb thing to do.

The same might be said of rearranging them in her own glazed pottery vase and chucking the faux porcelain, florist's model in the garbage.

Patience exhausted, Delbert said, "Okay, I'll bite. If David didn't send them, who did?"

"Chet Thomlinson. To apologize for his behavior yesterday."

She didn't quite catch what Delbert snarled, but it sounded like "sumbitch sucks up more than a goddamn vacuum cleaner."

He scowled at the flowers, his upper and lower plate at odds with each other. "Since I didn't bring you a ten-pound crate of chocolates, I guess I'm still in the doghouse."

"It would have been a nice touch," she allowed, "but you can't help being a pain in the butt and I don't have the energy to stay mad at you."

"Hmmph. No reason to be mad at me, anyhow. I didn't hare behind the door yesterday to snoop. My modus operandi was a classic D and P."

"Uh-huh."

He rocked on the balls of his sneakers. "Yep. Good ol' diffuse and protect. Works like a charm."

"Uh-huh."

"Out of sight, out of mind, but one false move and *whammo*." Legs spraddled in a martial arts stance, he did a slice 'n dice maneuver, then kicked his imaginary foe in the ankle. "I'd have had him before he knew which end was up."

Ye gods. Willard Johnson's beginning tae kwon do classes were an alternate form of exercise not a training camp for geriatric ninjas. A switch to tai chi or yoga might be in order.

"Of course," she said, "it's merely a coincidence that my very own crouching tiger, hidden dragon got himself an earful while he was D-ing and P-ing."

"Not much of one. I've got my sources, you know. Why, I could tell you and your sheriff some stuff that'd—"

"Get your skinny self hustled out the door in a New York second," she warned. "As for David, if you're withholding information from a multiple-homicide investigation..."

Like I am, she thought. If there was one thing she couldn't stand, it was a hypocrite.

Delbert's chin buckled. Determination brightened his milky blue eyes. There was a Barney Fife meets the Hardy Boys aspect to his amateur detecting, but to him, the possibility of a murderer going unpunished was as despicable as the crime itself.

"All I've got now are dribs and drabs of this and that," he said. "The *i*'s will be dotted and *t*'s crossed by tomorrow morning." Arching his snowy woolly-worm eyebrows, he added, "If not before."

"What are you going to do between now and then," slipped out before Hannah could clamp her mouth shut.

"For one thing, preside over a full-scale, Code Name: Delta meeting here tonight. That is, if you don't already have plans."

Hannah's bullshit detector howled like an air raid siren. Advance notice of a gumshoe gathering was a first. In the past, IdaClare and Company had just barged in—with or without the help of keys or Delbert's lock-pick gun—brewed a pot of decaf, served whatever horrendously fattening dessert they'd brought for refreshments and convened around Hannah's breakfast table.

"You, Marge, Leo and Rosemary have met in secret up until now," she said. "What's with this gang's-all-here routine tonight?"

Delbert flinched. "None of us wanted to leave you and IdaClare out, but the vote was unanimous."

"IdaClare and I didn't get a vote."

"Well, maybe not in person," he hedged, "but Marge put you girls down as no's in the minutes. The majority still ruled."

The gumshoes' brand of democracy was akin to wolves and sheep casting ballots to decide on a dinner menu.

"So why are you letting us in on tonight's meeting?" she asked."

"Hell's bells, ladybug. Do the math. Six heads are better than four, even if four of them are women and the other one's Leo."

It was a typical Bisbee comeback, yet something didn't jibe besides his chevron-print shirt and houndstooth slacks.

In light of being blackballed in absentia, a boycott of the meeting would be justified. It would also mitigate being charged as an accessory after the fact.

Except not knowing what the Mod Squad had up their collective sleeves was dangerous and snubs were notoriously difficult to pull off when the snub-ees had commandeered half your house.

Closing her eyes, she exhaled a martyr's sigh, then asked the tie-breaker question.

"Last I heard," Delbert said, "Leo's making homemade vanilla ice cream and Rosemary's baking a blackberry cobbler to go under it."

Hannah moaned and clutched at the office railing. The last time she said "Oh God" like that, she'd been naked.

"Nothing yet?" Tendons bulged like conduit at the back of David's neck. It was past two, but frustration had stolen his appetite. "What the hell's taking so long?"

Marlin hacked out a chuckle. "To err is human. To screw things up takes a computer. To screw them up, down and sideways takes a government computer."

David, Josh Phelps and Cletus Orr picketed the VDT on Marlin's desk as though visual harassment in multiple would induce faster results from the Automated Fingerprint Identification System.

AFIS provided law enforcement agencies access to a database composed of more than thirty million latents. Computerized analysis searched, read and rated prints numerically by points of similarity. The closest matches—usually fewer than ten—would be transmitted on a dual screen for manual comparison.

That morning, Marlin had lifted Chet Thomlinson's thumbprints, palmar zones and fingerprints from the water glass David had carefully handled and bagged at Hannah's cottage. Each latent was then digitized, and known parameters, including Thomlinson's gender, race, age and birth date, were programmed to speed the elimination process.

If it had, there was no tangible indication of it. The watchers all had work backlogged on their desks, but hope that a break in a complicated investigation might occur at any second had a hypnotic effect. Whatever the outcome, it would feel like progress.

Josh Phelps, the rookie and most computer proficient of the four, cracked the knuckles of his right hand, then his left. "The Secret Service's Forensic Division maintains and operates AFIS."

"So?" Marlin said around the cigarette he was lighting. "Tell us something we don't know, Ace."

"Thomlinson being an insider makes me wonder if he could have hacked into the system. Or into ours."

David and Marlin exchanged glances.

Phelps must have misread their expressions. "Hey, it's not as crazy as you think. Middle-school kids have corrupted Web browsers, airlines, banks—even the Pentagon."

David's computer literacy rivaled the average fourth-grader's. He knew which keys to punch to perform specific functions, but the machine was a tool not a toy. Much less a weapon.

"Thomlinson must have been proficient with the agency's system," Phelps went on. "The more familiar, the easier it is to hack in and scavenge security codes, passwords and breach firewalls."

Cletus Orr waved a get-outta-here. "Hack, schmack. Y'all are spoiled rotten. Used to be, we sat on our rumps for days flipping through ident cards. Now if it takes longer than five minutes for that thing to do our work for us, ever'body's shorts get in a twist."

The other three men stared in astonishment. Cletus

seldom strung two sentences together without a meal in between.

"We've been waiting a little longer than that." Marlin checked his watch. "About six hours and forty-seven minutes longer."

The paunchy veteran shrugged and lumbered to the door. "Let's saddle up, rookie."

"Hang on a sec," David said. "What's the realm of possibility here, Josh?"

He deliberated a moment. "It's late spring, it's a Saturday... Hypothetically, it's ninety-five, ninety-eight percent certain the demand has AFIS's hard drives in overdrive."

"Shee-it," Andrik said. "About the same odds that my wife'll be in the mood tonight. If I ever make it home."

Directing his remarks to David, the rookie said, "It all depends on whether this guy is slick or he's clean."

David nodded. "He didn't bat an eyelash when I thumb-and-fingered that glass. That says clean, since any cop would know I held it that way so his prints would be the only set on it."

"Or he's slick enough to play it clean with another cop." Phelps counted off his reasons as he articulated them. "He couldn't take the glass from you, tong-style. How obvious can you get? Refuse the hand-off—same thing. Dropping it was out, too. Whole, or in pieces, his latents were on the glass."

The plant saucer on Marlin's desk ratatatted like rim shots. He tamped out the Marlboro with the zeal of an arachnaphobic pulverizing a spider. "Corporal Phelps—and I use that rank loosely—I seem to recall saying, 'Tell us something we don't know' about a week ago, last Wednesday. Damned if I've heard anything yet that qualifies."

The rookie blushed to the roots of his sandy hair. "If Sheriff Hendrickson gave Thomlinson no choice but to play it slick, and there's a warrant out on him, or a conviction he doesn't want to surface, he might have the expertise to corrupt the files, overload the system, throw all kinds of monkey wrenches at it or at our end."

"Uh-uh." Andrik shook his head in the manner of a father patronizing a naive son. "The drone was a fed for twenty years. For elimination purposes alone, his prints must have been run through AFIS ninety jillion times. Anything incriminating would have shown up before now."

"Unless a crime was committed after he left the Service," Phelps said.

David glanced back at the VDT's screen. "Yeah, but what good would it do to gum up the works? Slowing us down won't stop us."

"If he didn't tamper with the records to prevent a match, stalling the results would give him time to bail."

No eye contact, no verbalization was needed to assure David that he and Marlin shared the same mental bandwidth. If Phelps was right and Thomlinson hadn't skipped yet, he could be charged for carrying concealed and held until AFIS responded, or an inquiry was launched.

If Phelps was wrong, if heavy traffic had slowed the system and Thomlinson was clean, David would be crucified for arresting the hero who couldn't save his wife but spared the lives of countless others.

"He's a material witness to a capital crime," Marlin said. "We could bring him in for questioning."

"Then what? AFIS coughing up a bucketful of outstanding warrants and convictions doesn't make him a conspirator or coconspirator in three homicides."

Marlin's quiet "No way, no how" revealed what he'd meant by his earlier "Tell us something we don't know" remarks. The downcast rookie and his silent partner left the Outhouse, but Phelps caught the door before it closed. "Give us a shout if you hear something."

"Sure thing, Ace" was the essence of Marlin's reply.

David turned the back of the visitor's lawn chair to the wall and folded himself into it. Ankles crossed and head resting against the warped paneling, he wished Phelps had kept his mouth shut. Hadn't reminded him of the dark side of desperation being the mother of invention.

Four days of intense investigation. Untold manhours he hoped he never had to justify. Yesterday's euphoric Joe Cool cockiness when Thomlinson's entire hand wrapped around that water glass. The adrenaline hit when Phelps gave him a final, cyberspacey straw to grasp.

Admit it, Hendrickson. Claudina nailed it from the get-go. You've turned this case every which way but loose and it's as circumstantial as when she said you didn't have a tree to bark up. Christ, you don't even have probable cause for a search warrant yet.

Chet Thomlinson smelled fishy. Jack Clancy smelled fishy. Separate or together, the inferences stank something fierce. The appearance of a meeting of the minds before Eulilly was killed and perhaps as recently as Clancy's logged refueling stop at the airport last night reeked like roadkill. Add the bank's tip about Clancy's money bunny-hopping from one account to another and what do you have?

A workplace massacre perpetrated by a Black Gangster Disciple named Antoine Klein Jr.

A Chicago gang unit task force member called it street justice shakes hands with CNN Headline News. He speculated that Klein was one of a wave of Disciple frontmen assigned to establish rural beachheads for expanding the drug trade.

A martian in Manhattan wouldn't have been more isolated than Klein was in Sanity, Missouri. The increasing frequency of pay phone calls to his mother in Chicago established that. Jasmine Chau's rejection and, very likely, his coworkers' "disrespect" were met with a hard-core gangsta's version of death before dishonor.

The officer even had an answer for the shooting's low death toll. "He'd never fired an assault rifle before. Scared the shit out of himself when he did. Reflex and recoil pulled it upward. It could as easily have pulled it down.''

A toilet flushed, then the rest room's door banged shut. Marlin rounded the short hallway, a file folder in his hand. "Have a nice nap, boss?"

"I wasn't asleep. Just thinking."

"So was I." He waved the folder. "Except this makes it multi-tasking, according to Beth. Efficient woman, my wife. She even grades papers in the can."

David groaned. "Did I really need to know that?"

Marlin halted. His mouth stretched into a leer. "Pizza. Thick crust. Everything on it. A giant iced tea, lemon, sugar and two packs of cigs."

"What in Sam Hill are you—"

"You want me to compare the latents AFIS is sending for my viewing pleasure? Then that's what it'll cost you, my man."

Delbert followed the angry physical fitness instructor into the community center's men's locker room. "Will you stand still a minute and just hear me out?"

Willard stuffed his tae kwon do gee and black belt into a nylon gym bag. "I've heard plenty enough already, Mr. Bisbee." He looked up. Betrayal clouded his eyes. "Here." He thrust out the folded twenty-dollar bill Delbert had given him. "The private lessons are canceled, as of now."

Delbert felt sick. His five-stage plan unraveling at stage three was the least of it. What he'd said to Willard had sounded fine when he rehearsed it, but had

come out all wrong. Worse than that, it had been hurt-
ful enough to cost him a friend.

He sat down on a bench, head shaking with remorse. "I'm sorry. I swear to God, I am. All I can
say is, if this Klein fellow was German, I wouldn't
have thought twice about asking Leo to make the call
for me."

Willard straddled the end of another bench and
yanked on his socks. For a church's youth minister,
the rasp of a tennis shoe's Velcro fasteners sufficed
as expletives. "Telling me you watched rappers on
MTV to try and learn how to talk black." A shod
foot stamped the indoor-outdoor carpet. "That's like
me telling you I watch *Friends* to learn how to talk
white."

"I know," Delbert allowed, "but I didn't mean it
that way."

The other foot hit the floor. Willard scrubbed his
face with this hands, then planted them on his thighs.
"Oh yes, you did. The difference between you and a
genuine racist is, a racist would have sense enough
not to say something that offensive to an African-
American."

"Hell yes, he...would." Delbert frowned, almost
certain he'd hit another clinker but not sure where.

"Well, my mother's catering a private party tonight," Willard said. "As usual, I got drafted into
helping." He chuckled as he picked up his gym bag.
"Hey, cheer up, Delbert. No hard feelings. I'll see
you Monday morning."

"Yeah." Delbert stood and held out his hand. His

whole body sagged as a second wave of despair pushed aside his relief at salvaging a friendship. "Tell your mom hello for me."

Willard nodded and started from the room.

Delbert glowered at the corkboard hanging on the far wall. Acid boiled in his gut at the memory of pacing his living room for hours after the caper with Leo, Rosemary and Marge—the physical struggle to stay awake until the coast cleared and he could sneak back to Thomlinson's cottage alone.

There was no satisfaction in the mental image of his pigeon's face when the pouch with five thousand dollars in cash was missing from its hidey-hole under the hall bath's cabinet.

During the debriefing after the first B and E, Leo had confirmed that there were no abnormally large withdrawals from Chet's bank accounts in the past sixty days, but several rare American coins valued at just under ten thousand dollars had vanished from his computerized inventory.

Delbert knew dealers and collectors were exempt from reporting cash transactions to the government unless they exceeded ten thousand dollars. He'd almost choked when Marge said, "Not to speak ill of the dead, but if Eulilly had known Chet came home from that convention in Chicago last month with that much money, she'd have been on the phone with her plastic surgeon in two shakes."

Rubbing his belly as though it could tamp the furnace blasting under his ribs, Delbert pondered reversing his strategy. Hubert Montague, who was dumber

than a stump, could place the supposed prank call to
Jack Clancy now as easily as later.

Flushing out Suspect B before Suspect A didn't
matter, did it? Especially if they were in cahoots.
Clancy was too far away to be blackmailed in person
tonight. He'd have to call Chet and send him to make
the payoff. Between the infrared photos Delbert
would snap at the site and telephone records of
Clancy's call, the sheriff would have all the proof he
needed to nab a pair of cold-blooded killers.

Unless Chet didn't show up. Or Clancy called David instead, reported the extortion attempt and the
woods were crawling with deputies when Delbert got
there.

His sneakers parted company with the floor when
Willard said, "Are you coming? I have to lock up
before I can leave."

Delbert whirled. "Please, son. You've gotta help
me. There's just no other way to do it."

## 17

The day's second, orgasmic "Oh God" without benefit of being naked escaped Hannah's lips. A scoop of hand-cranked vanilla ice cream melting over a slab of flaky crust and into a pool of oven-warm, sweet-tart fresh blackberries was almost better than sex.

Actually, she thought, her tongue swooping syrup and tiny seeds from her teeth, it was better than all the sex she'd ever had, combined. Well, except for David.

A bigger, ice-creamier spoonful rolled her eyes back in their sockets. "Anybody know which comes first on the list of seven deadly sins—lust or gluttony?"

"Gluttony," Marge said, a dribble of purple juice on her chin. "But lust is next."

"Lust before gluttony makes more sense." Ida-Clare's spoon wobbled en route to her mouth, but she was coping quite well left-handed. She also winked quite well at Hannah.

"Ah, my Rosemary's cobbler, it is both," Leo said. "Just like she is."

"What?" The birds in Rosemary's gilded-cage earrings swayed on their perches. "Are you calling me a glutton?"

Leo's frantic waves either signaled a time-out until he swallowed, or for someone to initiate the Heimlich maneuver.

"The glutton, it is me. For your cooking, for *you*, my darling. And the lust, I've got it, too." He nuzzled his bride's neck. "But already you knew that, eh?"

IdaClare sniffed. "If you don't mind, some of us don't care to taste this cobbler twice."

Hannah leaned back in her bar stool, smiling between bouts of stuffing her face. She'd missed the gumshoes, their meetings, their bickering, their refreshments, except— "I can't imagine what's keeping Delbert. It isn't like him to be a half hour late."

"He's probably visiting Sophonia and lost track of the time," IdaClare said.

Rosemary shook her head. "He wasn't there when we stopped by the hospital after dinner." She and Leo exchanged the kind of visual nudges couples do when neither wants to be spokesperson.

"We thought Sophonia was getting better," Rosemary said. "Not by leaps and bounds, mind you, but steadily improving. After seeing her this evening, we're not so sure."

Hannah looked down at her dessert, then laid the bowl on the counter. That morning, she'd planned a trip to the hospital, then she started cleaning, then Delbert dropped by, then... Excuses, excuses. The truth was, she'd gotten so ensnared in her own little world and worries, she'd put off till tomorrow what she should have done today.

"So weak she is," Leo said. "Her voice so soft, I could not hear her sometimes."

"She isn't in any pain, though," Rosemary added. "The nurse assured us of that."

"That poor woman. I feel just terrible about not being able to—" Pink blotches appeared on Marge's cheeks.

"I'm the one to blame, not you," IdaClare said. "You've been too busy taking such wonderful care of me to have a minute to yourself for days, let alone to visit Sophonia."

Marge's features retreated behind a veil of guilt. Her eyes slid to Leo and Rosemary, then she pushed her bowl away with the flat of her hand.

IdaClare, the only one present who was ignorant of Thursday night's escapade, continued, "Which is why first thing tomorrow morning, I'm driving us to the hospital. Lord knows how I came through with a broken arm and Sophonia was hurt so badly, but maybe if she sees me out and about it'll boost her spirits."

"Great idea, bad execution," Hannah said. "I'll take you and Marge to town tomorrow. It's too dangerous for you to drive with one arm in a cast."

In truth, IdaClare wouldn't win any blue ribbons with both hands on the wheel. Not unless bonus points were awarded for rocketing a Lincoln Continental from zero to seventy in the fewest, bloodcurdling seconds.

"I'll swan," IdaClare said, laughing, "you're too young to be such a worrywart. I drove tractors and stick-shift farm trucks one-handed before I was ten years old." She swung her coffee mug at Marge. "I got you here in one piece, didn't I?"

Her passenger's expression indicated a renewed belief in God and the power of prayer.

Hannah warned, "If Jack finds out you're driving, he'll take away your keys *and* your car."

"Well, he'll have to come here to do it, so let him try." The mug rapped the table like a gavel. "After I give that boy a piece of my mind for the way he's treated you, me and everybody else in creation, he'll be blistered from head to heinie."

Like applying gauze and adhesive tape to outward wounds, anger was a bandage for inner hurts, many of which were inflicted by good intentions. According to the law of "I know what's best for you," it's kinder to nick a loved one's heart than to trust them and bare your own.

Damn you, Jack Clancy, Hannah fumed. Damn everyone who's ordained me the keeper of the free world's freakin' secrets. Okay, all right, I prized out a couple myself, but this rat-in-a-bell-jar crap has to stop.

The phone rang, sharp and loud as the shrew in her head had been. Malcolm *bur-rurfed* and scratched at the deck doors. Had he been inside and the doorbell was ringing, he'd have barked at the phone.

"Delbert," the Schnurs said in unison.

IdaClare gave the kitchen's wall unit a scathing look. "Well, it's about time."

"This meeting was his idea," Marge said. "Tell him to hurry up."

*His* idea? zipped through Hannah's mind a second before she unhooked the receiver.

"Walt Wagonner, here," said the voice at the other end of the line.

She paused, expecting the usual "One *g*, two *n*'s" suffix.

"Hannah?"

"Huh? Oh! I mean, hello, Walt." Delbert had predicted Walt would delete the spell-check shtick eventually. Such as now, apparently.

Marge swiveled in her chair. "Is that Walt Wagonner?"

Hannah nodded.

IdaClare said, "Walt hates telephones. I wonder why he's calling Hannah at this hour."

"I'm glad I finally got through," Walt said. "Your phone was busy the other two dozen times I tried."

Rosemary chuckled. "Maybe he's asking her for a date."

Hannah scowled and finger-tapped her lips. "There was trouble on the line," she said into the receiver, then apologized for the inconvenience, also known as Malcolm the Wonder Dog.

He'd chowed down on the outside wires, either from boredom or in retaliation for his banishment. A Maintenance Department repairman had restored service just before the gumshoes arrived.

"A date?" IdaClare said, her voice loud enough to trigger a sonic boom. "Walt doesn't date, and besides, everyone knows Hannah is boinking the sheriff."

The sheriff's homicidal boinkee mouthed, *Shut up.*

Walt said, "Pardon me for taking my frustrations out on you. I'm trying to locate Delbert Bisbee. I don't suppose he's there, is he?"

Hannah surveyed the breakfast room as if James Bond Bisbee might have slunk by unnoticed. "Well, he should have been by now, but no, he isn't."

"Told you," IdaClare sneered to Rosemary.

"Why would Walt call here looking for Delbert?" Marge inquired of the cheering section. To Hannah, she stage-whispered, "Ask Walt why he's looking for him."

Through clenched teeth, Hannah said, "Shall I have him call you back when he shows up?"

Heads wagged and hands flapped to protest the adlib.

"I'd rather you told him to bring back my car," Walt said.

"Delbert borrowed your car?" Hannah's gaze slanted toward the table but not at it. "When? Why?"

Rosemary said, "Delbert borrowed Walt's Cadillac? And Walt let him? He's pickier about it than Delbert is the Edsel."

"I'm surprised it even runs," IdaClare said. "It's been in the garage since Walt flunked the eye test last summer."

Into Hannah's other ear, Walt said, "Delbert came

by in a panic late this afternoon sometime—four-thirty, perhaps a quarter of five. He said the Edsel was on the blink. If he didn't get to the auto parts store in Sanity before they closed at six, he'd be afoot until Monday.''

"That's odd," she said. "His car was running fine when he was here earlier."

Leo said, "Ah, the cars, they are like the people. The older they get, the more things break."

Acting on that suggestion, Hannah said, "Maybe it's just taking Delbert longer to find the part he needed than he thought it would."

"Possibly," Walt allowed. "Now that you mention it, he has resorted to scouring junkyards to find replacement parts no one makes anymore."

Except junkyards usually aren't open after dark. Hannah knew this, having been an accomplice to a moonlight shopping spree in her youth. No disrespect to the late Jim Croce, but when hauling ass through a vehicular graveyard, it's difficult to imagine anything meaner than a junkyard dog.

Then again, a flesh-eating Doberman standing between Delbert and a transplant for the Edsel wouldn't have a chance.

"Surely he'll turn up here or there pretty soon," she told Walt, as well as herself. "Let's leave it at, whoever sees or hears from him first calls the other."

Walt said he'd add her name to the "Where's Delbert?" telephone tree and bid her a good evening.

Marge, the unofficial coffee-refill dispenser, headed for the kitchen. "Car trouble doesn't explain why

Delbert borrowed Walt's Caddy instead of one of our cars."

"I agree," Rosemary said. "Delbert and Leo are best friends. Delbert and Walt aren't much more than acquaintances."

Leo shrugged. "My Thing, Delbert doesn't like. It is too small, he says."

"Well, I love your Thing," Rosemary said. "It's cuter than a bug's ear and just the right size." She glanced over her shoulder. "Isn't it, Hannah?"

Saying yes would have the same effect as a harpoon on a hot-air balloon. As the saying goes, thank God and Goodyear, the phone rang again. Fist jammed in her mouth to muffle her laughter, Hannah sprinted for the extension on her desk.

Background music blared from the receiver. A garbled voice surfaced between drumbeats. Thumbing her other ear, Hannah said, "Whoever you are, you'll have to speak up. I can't hear you for all the noise."

"It's Willard. Willard Johnson." An extended pause, then scuffling sounds, then the music abated several decibels. "Is that better?"

"Much, but where the heck are you, Willard? Out honky-tonking?"

"Try hunkered in a broom closet at some rich dude's house. Mom's catering a party for his daughter's eighteenth birthday."

Hannah's eyes raised to the hand-crocheted afghan draped on the rocking chair in the corner of the great room. It was her eighteenth and last birthday present from Caroline.

"The reason I'm calling is," Willard said, "have you seen or talked to Delbert tonight? I've tried his house and Mr. Thomlinson's a few times and no one answers."

Hannah sat down hard on the railing; a reflex, not a conscious action. "What's wrong? Why were you calling Chet?"

A hesitation, then, "Look, I'm probably overreacting. After all, Delbert's a great old guy and I like him a lot, but he's...well, you can't take everything he says seriously."

You should, Hannah thought, because beneath that eccentric veneer lies an agile, sagacious, logical mind.

"Tell me what he said, Willard." She beckoned to the gumshoes crowded in the breakfast room's doorway. "Let me decide whether you're overreacting."

Three sentences into his narration, she crooked a finger at Leo, then grabbed a notepad and pencil. *Make an excuse to leave,* she wrote. *I need Rosemary's gun.* Underlined twice was *Hurry.*

Marlin shoved his reading glasses up on his forehead, cocked back the desk chair and rubbed his eyes with the heels of his hands. "Remind me to give you a Ph.D. in latent comparisons before I have to buy a cane and a dog."

David's expertise ranked well below Marlin's, but he said, "I've already told you sixty-nine times that I'd give it my best shot."

"No offense, boss, but these mothers are almost

like clones. Your best shot wouldn't be good enough.''

David agreed, although sitting around watching pizza rinds fossilize in the delivery box while his chief of detectives squinted and cussed at the VDT was a mite shy of fascinating.

No candidate prints transmitted by AFIS bore the name Chester Arthur Thomlinson. David had been unable to reach Phil Webber to confirm whether an automatic block was built into the system to safeguard agents' identities. He and Andrik had bet twenty bucks against.

''Seven down, two to go.'' Marlin's jaw-cracking yawn sounded like the trademark MGM lion's snarl. ''Why don't you try to call Toots again. Surely to God she's off the phone by now.''

David hesitated. If he reached her, it would be natural to ask who she'd been talking to for hours. If he was right, if it was the elusive Jack Clancy doing his best song-and-dance number on her, she'd lie to David and he'd know it—and she'd know he knew it.

Damn it to hell and gone. Like they needed another brick laid in the wall between them. Like Hannah needed another no-win Hobson's choice to make, then live with.

Yeah, but if he'd learned anything from their relationship, it was that trust and honesty weren't necessarily conjoined. Trust was believing that a lover's detours from the truth the whole truth, and nothing but were judgment calls not betrayals.

David grabbed his cell phone off the desktop, then

cursed. The battery charge indicator was a couple of ticks from fuhgeddaboutit. The LED showed about enough range to ring Cletus Orr's desk phone, twelve feet behind him.

Andrik's phone receiver smelled like Marlboros and pepperoni grease. David chuckled to himself as he punched numbers on the keypad assigned to speed-dial one on all his phones.

An electronic bleat insulted his eardrum. David glanced at his watch, then the wall clock. The receiver clattered into its cradle.

"You gotta be kidding me," Marlin said, his eyes glued to the computer monitor. "Beth could bullshit with her mother till I had to take a second mortgage to pay the phone bill, but Toots? No way."

"Maybe it's off the hook and she doesn't know it," David said. "Or out of order. We've had plenty enough rain to swamp a transformer box."

Marlin grunted. "There was a lot of static on the line when I called Beth a while ago. She asked me how big a cubit was." His fingers spidered over the keyboard. "Another hour and you can go play phone man with Toots."

The estimated time of departure forecast a final dead end realized. Let the evidence stand as read; case closed. The light at the end of that tunnel was a smart, smart-ass, sexy antidote to depression.

"Phone man, hell," he said, anticipation rippling like gooseflesh. "Playing doctor is more fun."

"Huh-uh, compadre. A woman'll take customer

service over a general practitioner any night of…the week.''

Marlin nosed closer to the screen. An index finger tapped the page-down key once…twice. On the third, a rare grin began to spread across his craggy face. With a tone akin to reverence, he murmured, ''Fuck. A. Duck.''

His arms shot up as though signaling a point-after. ''Make that, our duck is fucked. Screwed, blued and tattooed.''

David rounded the desk in two strides, his eyes focused on the monitor. Harold Charles Metz's rap sheet and outstanding wants and warrants had more lines than a telephone book. Among them, multiple counts of mail theft, extortion, fraud, identity theft and one count of impersonating a federal officer.

Marlin scrolled to another screen. David didn't quite smite his forehead but damn near it.

Metz's list of aliases *read* like a telephone book. As well it should. Peter Drummond, M.D., Sergeant James Wheat, DEA, Byron St. Cloud, stockbroker, Frank Rizzo, civil engineer, Captain Bartholomew Warren, commercial pilot, and Matthew Patton, literary agent, were as real as Sheriff David M. Hendrickson.

Harold Charles Metz, also known as Chester A. Thomlinson, Secret Service, retired, had divined a new twist on identity theft. Instead of stealing a victim's name, social security number and other particulars to max out credit cards and drain bank accounts, Metz borrowed his victims' identities.

Obtaining a duplicate of an existing person's birth
certificate, driver's license and social security card
could be as easy as filling out forms and plunking
down the fees. Metz used the information to establish
new credit card and bank accounts in his victim's
name, but with Metz's phone number and mailing address.

In time, an unwitting mark might notice the additional accounts on a credit report. The IRS, or a state
department of revenue, could detect a discrepancy in
the mark's reported income and that ascribed to his
social security number. If not, as long as Metz paid
his share of the bills, kept the bank happy and his
nose clean, the odds of discovery were slim.

That is, until the wealthy women he'd romanced
and ripped off under various assumed names
screamed, "I've been robbed" after he vanished
without a trace.

"I figured Thomlinson for a lot of things," Marlin
said, "but a serial sweetheart scammer wasn't one of
them."

"Nope." David reread the complaint summaries.
"It answers some questions, though. Thomlinson's
SIG-Sauer was part of the costume, but he couldn't
apply for a permit to carry."

"His prints would have blown his cover."

"True," David said, "but he tripped himself up
yesterday. If he were a fed, he'd have known the
drinking-glass trick was a trick. No doubt, he studied
everything he could find on the Service, coin collect-
ing, Lord knows what else, but like Hannah, being a

civilian, he didn't have a clue that I was setting him up.''

"Score one for the good guys.'' Marlin lit a cigarette and exhaled with a gusty satisfaction not derived from shredded Virginia tobacco. "Phelps will be crushed when I tell him his computer theory crashed.''

"Electronic tampering isn't that far-fetched. If it hasn't already happened, it's bound to, one of these days.''

"Cletus will be thrilled. He's a prime field investigator, but if it were up to him, we'd still wear snap-brim fedoras and talk like Joe Friday on *Dragnet*.''

David grinned. Often as not, Andrik already talked like an R-rated Joe Friday.

As if proving the point, he said, "Shit,'' then looked up at David. "Metz's bogus G-man scam also means the real Chester A. Thomlinson lost a fiancée to a serial killer, his first wife and son in a car accident and his second wife to a postoperative infection.''

"Jesus, that's right.'' David sucked at his teeth. "For all he's been through, I'd say there were times when he'd have gladly traded identities with anyone.''

"Personally, I hope the poor bastard's shacked up on a beach somewhere with a couple of babes, hot and cold running beer, a fishing rod and a satellite dish.''

"Amen to that,'' David said. He thought a moment, then added, "Ironic that Metz aka Thomlinson left all his pigeons at the altar, save one. I wonder why he took the plunge with Eulilly.''

Marlin made a ''who gives a damn'' gesture. ''Could be she was the fattest bird in the flock. Why beat the bushes when he had an heiress in hand? Or maybe she wouldn't ante up the cash without an 'I do.'''

David's head tipped to one side. ''They were married almost six years, and he did sign a prenup. Maybe he loved her.''

Marlin make retching noises. ''Uh-huh. Jes' flat out crazy about her, until he hired Antoine Klein Jr. to blow her away.'' He keyed the computer's print command. ''Better call Ryder and rent us a truck, boss. We'll need one to haul all the wants and warrants on Thomlinson, aka everybody else, out to Valhalla Springs.''

David chuffed. ''Don't I wish.''

''What do you mean? If the dirtbag hasn't bailed, we've got his nuts in a cracker, man.''

A foul nastiness coated David's tongue. ''Everybody from the feds to the Dallas Police Department have him by the balls. All we get are front-row seats for an extradition battle.''

The detective reddened as though on the brink of exploding, or a heart attack. The first sheet of paper ejected from the printer crumpled in his grip. ''Are you saying we're gonna ignore this? Hell no, it doesn't prove he conspired to murder his wife, but it's enough to leverage a confession.''

With a weary sigh, David said, ''No, it isn't, and

you know it. Metz is a sociopath—almost has to be to have gotten away with scamming a busload of Ms. Lonely Hearts for this long.

"He'd also have to be pure-de-stupid to confess to homicide, conspiracy to commit, attempted homicide and a dozen other attending charges, when we have zip for hard evidence against him and most of the outstanding wants and warrants can be plea-bargained down to nothing much or dropped altogether."

Marlin demonstrated his unique grasp of the language by using the f word as a noun, verb, adjective, gerund, compound word, pronoun, and maybe a past participle in a single sentence. "So he walks. Again."

"Not walks. He skates, while we throw everything we've got into finding the glue to make those homicide charges stick."

Marlin smashed his cigarette in the ashtray, then parked the computer. "Sometimes I hate this job."

"If you didn't, you wouldn't be any good at it."

"Thanks, Sheriff. I can always count on you to shovel up the incentive."

Marlin caught the phone on the first ring. "Yo. Andrik." He glanced at David. "Yeah, he's here." He palmed the receiver. "IdaClare Clancy. Says it's urgent."

A hard chill racked David to the bone. His voice was blunt, harsh, when he identified himself.

"Hannah tried your cell phone, but it wouldn't work, so I called 911. Delbert's blackmailing Chet, and Hannah made Leo get Rosemary's gun and went after him—"

"Slow down, Miz Clancy. You're talking so fast you're not making any sense."

"Then shut up and listen faster. We've got a 10–35 in progress out here. Delbert made Willard Johnson call Chet and pretend he was what's-his-name Klein's brother. Willard told Chet if he didn't meet him at the old Sandusky place tonight with the rest of the hit-man money, he'd tip the police.

"Willard got nervous, called Hannah and told her Delbert planned to take infrared pictures of Chet at the payoff place to prove he hired Klein. Nobody's seen Delbert since he borrowed Walt's car this afternoon. Hannah sent Leo after Rosemary's .357 Magnum. When she couldn't reach you, she tore out of here by herself to find Delbert."

Black specks flitted in David's eyes. If he was breathing, his chest was too tight for his lungs to fill. "We're rollin', Miz Clancy. Stay put at Hannah's and stay off the phone."

# 18

"What did he say?" Marge asked.

"What could he have said?" Rosemary shot back. "IdaClare didn't hush long enough for him to say much of anything."

"The 10–35 report, she was making to the sheriff," Leo said. "Not the social call."

"Thank you, Leo." IdaClare shifted her cast from the top of Hannah's desk to the arm of her chair. The adjustment lessened the strain on her shoulder. It didn't relieve the dull throb, like an impacted tooth, that vined from the base of her skull and coiled in her stomach.

Her medication was hours overdue, but she daren't take anything. A half dosage knocked her out colder than a mackerel and she needed her wits about her.

The Greek chorus was perched on the breakfast room's chairs on the far side of the office nook's railing. They looked as worried, tense and—shame on us all—exhilarated as she felt.

"The sheriff said all he needed to. He and Detective Andrik are en route to the scene. We're to stay here and not use the phone."

Marge flapped a hand. "Hannah told us that before she dashed out of here."

IdaClare attempted a chuckle. "Those two do think alike, don't they."

Murmured agreements dissolved into ponderous silence. Rosemary nibbled her fresh manicure. Marge stared at the window as if it were a movie screen and *The Matrix* had just ended. Leo's chair chirped a fidgety tune.

"Anyone want more coffee?"

Marge's voice had the effect of a door slam. IdaClare winced, then shook her head. The Schnurs also declined, then Rosemary said, "But I suppose we ought to clean up the mess we made of Hannah's kitchen."

"The present, it is always a good time."

"Those bowls'll have to be soaked," Marge said. "Blackberry goop is too, uh...goopy for the dishwasher."

"Umm-hmm." Rosemary mangled a pinky nail.

"The ice cream, we will dump," Leo said. "Is melted—"

"We never should have let Hannah go after Delbert alone." That admission was easy, IdaClare thought. It spoke for all of them. The other thoughts, the private fears tumbling behind it, hurt.

Her mother had told her denial was a river where sorrows drown but never drift out to sea. She was right, of course, as she'd been about many things. If wisdom were infallible, experience would have had nothing to teach.

Rosemary clutched at her chest. "If anything happens to Hannah…"

"She has the gun," Leo said as though convincing himself it might afford a measure of protection. "And the .357 Magnum, it is a very *big* gun."

"If she knows how to use one." Marge's gaze flicked to IdaClare. It conveyed a silent *We know Chet does, and he won't hesitate to do so.*

Rosemary clasped Leo's wrist and turned his watch toward her. "How long has it been since you talked to the sheriff? Fifteen? Twenty minutes?"

"Three."

"No, no. That can't be right." Rosemary looked to Leo, who arched an eyebrow. "Are you sure?"

Marge leapt from her chair. "I don't care how long it's been. I can't stand this. Sheriff Hendrickson has a gun and Detective Andrik to back him up. We don't know whether Hannah's ever held one, much less fired one, and she's alone."

"You stay with IdaClare." Rosemary stood and tugged on Leo's shirt. "We'll be Hannah's backup."

Mouth agape, Marge cocked a hip and planted a hand on it. "Who the heck put you in charge? Why can't *I* go with Leo, and *you* stay with IdaClare?"

"Wel-l-l." Rosemary's eyes narrowed. "In case you've forgotten, he happens to be my husband."

"But I—" Marge gestured defeat. "Oh, go on, then. Arguing won't help Hannah a bit."

"Don't get in a swivet, Marge." IdaClare pushed herself to her feet. "We'll all go, as soon as one of you fetches my pocketbook."

"But my Thing, it is too small," Leo said.

"No, it isn't," Rosemary insisted. "But someone has to be here to answer the phone."

"Heavens to Betsy, Leo. Will you hush up about your silly ol' Thing?" IdaClare took her purse from Marge and fished out her keys. "My Lincoln has oodles of room, and if we, Hannah, Delbert, David and that detective are all in the same place, who's left to call?"

Rosemary acceded the second point, then said, "We're not letting you drive any—"

"It isn't a matter of let. It isn't even a matter of me driving, since I'm damn well going to, whether anyone rides with me or not."

Chin high, IdaClare marched to the door, hoping they didn't notice every step exacted a painful toll. "Y'all think I'm so gullible, I can't tell a money-hungry wolf from a sweet-talking lamb. Y'all think my heart would never entertain the notion of my son being in league with a murderer."

The brass doorknob felt as warm as a hearthstone to her touch. "Most especially, y'all think I don't know you love me enough to try and protect me from the truth. Well, I do know. That's why I need you with me when I find out what it is."

The Blazer skidded to a stop in a muddy lane. Hannah jacked the gearshift into Reverse, then relaxed her stranglehold on the lever. She sucked in a deep breath, held it, then let it whoosh from her lungs. It tasted like rancid almonds.

All right. You're going north again. The road will be on your *left*. No mailbox. A round xxx-wire fence full of rocks for a corner post. *Find it.*

Backing onto the highway, she cut the front tires and gunned the engine. Twice she'd missed the turn-off Leo had described. For God's sake, *find it.*

The abandoned Sandusky farmstead was Kinder-hook County's answer to a sunken Spanish galleon. The Panic of 1893 destroyed the family elders' faith in banks. They and succeeding generations allegedly buried their rainy-day savings in Mason jars cached all over the property.

Delbert, Leo and the cadre of Treasure Hunters Club members had tramped the hardscrabble hills and hollers armed with metal detectors, hoping to reap what the Sanduskys had sown.

Chet had tagged along a few times, in the event a stash of old coins had surfaced. Using it as a meeting place was the potentially fatal flaw in Delbert's scheme.

Until Willard sounded the S.O.S., Hannah had never heard of the Sanduskys, their farm or their re-puted cash crop. The odds were nil that Parnell Klein, a Chicago Black Gangster Disciple and mythical older brother of hired assassin Antoine Jr., as played by Willard, would have chosen it to collect the bal-ance of Antoine's kill fee.

Her eyes ticktocked from the roadway to the op-posite shoulder. Driving thirty miles under the speed limit and forty under the consensual norm on a curvy, hilly county highway was a vehicular death wish, not exclusive to her. The Blazer's emergency flashers telegraphed "I'm sorry, I'm sorry," but the apology was mostly declined.

Impatient motorists rode her bumper. Flicked on their high beams. Ignored the pavement's double-yellow lines and rocketed around her.

She thought she'd failed again when the headlamps of a passing dualie hauling a horse trailer glanced off a column of field rocks. The car behind her squalled its tires at the in-your-face blast of brake lights. Hannah agreed with every foul name the driver must have bellowed and aimed for the ragged gap in the under-brush.

Weeds not flattened by an earlier trespasser were slowly ascending, as if uncertain the effort was worth their while. From their trajectory, one or more vehicles had entered the Sandusky property. Whether they'd left again wasn't clear.

The Blazer's headlights seared the darkness, the twin beams visible far beyond their reach. Hannah switched them off. Drove a few yards. Doused the parking lamps' amber glow.

Night closed in, black and blinding. Hannah reached for Rosemary's gun, lying on the passenger seat. Rosemary's deceased husband had given it to her for their fortieth anniversary. Why, Hannah hadn't asked, but was relieved to learn Ilario Marchetti had died of natural causes.

The .357 was loaded but had never been fired. It was heavy, but well balanced. She clicked off the safety, praying that firearms expertise was like bicycle riding.

Shortly after moving to Chicago, three auburn-haired women in her neighborhood were abducted, beaten and raped by an assailant the newspapers dubbed the Titian Terrorist. Handguns became as common to many a Chicago businesswoman's purse as lipstick.

Owning a .38 and hours of target practice at an indoor range hadn't cured Hannah's fear of guns. But that fear ranked second to the fear of a psychopath who enjoyed dominating and brutalizing women.

The Magnum's long, cold barrel cuddled her thigh, the bore drawing a bead on the armrest. If the Blazer's door swung open, the attacker was in for a deadly surprise.

The truck rolled forward at its own speed. Striplings raked the undercarriage like talons. Her eyelids quivered and burned, straining to see through the murk and shadow-walls cast by thickset trees.

Branches thumped and screeched along the fenders when she strayed off the invisible track. Her mind projected images of Chet holding a gun on Delbert. Both turn at the rumble of her engine. Delbert executes a tae kwon do sidekick. Chet's gun flies from his hand. The passenger door opens. Delbert clambers to safety. The Blazer hurtles backward. Wheels a one-eighty. The rescuer and rescued haul ass for the highway. The end. Roll credits.

"Oh, sweet Jesus." Hannah fumbled for then yanked a dashboard knob. Light exploded from the dual high beams. Delbert had arrived *before* the appointed time to set up his cameras. Blundering through the dark, she could have hit him. Run over him. Run over his...

Don't even think it.

She romped the accelerator. Her left foot hovered above the brake pedal. The truck bucked and jounced over humps, into ruts and eroded gullies. The shoulder harness sawed at her neck, punished her collarbone.

The lane dipped. Rose. Opened onto a weed-choked clearing. Jettisoned large appliances, tires, furniture, mattresses and bedsprings represented a fortune saved in landfill fees. Battalions of bearded iris ringed the skeletal remains of a farmhouse. Scorched boulders edged a sizable campfire where a different kind of treasure hunter must use beer cans and condom boxes for tinder.

The grill of Chet's Lexus gleamed bright and golden, shaming the rusty scuppernong arbor beside it. No dark blue Cadillacs. No Delbert. No Chet.

Not in sight, anyway.

She lowered the window. If tranquillity had an aroma, it would be as fragrant as the air seeping in. Crickets conducted their nightly concert. Rustles in the underbrush were too light and quick to be human. Traffic noise whispered from the highway a thousand miles away. No cries for help. No sirens. No raspy voice called, "Is that you, ladybug?"

Common sense advised, in a familiar low baritone, "Lock the doors and sit tight."

"No," she murmured. "Not this time."

Headlights off. Interior light switched off. Motor running. Gun at ready. Check the rearview mirror. Side mirrors. *Go—go—go.*

She hit the ground running. Circled the back of the Blazer. Status quo. Not a sound other than her pounding heart. She started toward the Lexus, head swiveling. The spongy earth absorbed her footfalls…just as it would anyone else's.

Big as he was, David had been trained to move like a cat. Chet was retired Secret Service. He was out there. Watching…waiting.

*Cr-rack.* Glass tinkled. *Thud.* Hannah whirled.

A gunshot split the air. Its echo doubled, redoubled on itself.

David stomped the Crown Vic's gas pedal. Rocks and mud pelted the unmarked Chevy behind him. Andrik's voice boomed from the radio, *Baker 2–03 to dispatch. Shots fired. Repeat, shots fired, this –20. Where the fuck's our backup, Tony?*

The cruiser's front tires slammed into a gully, spun, then caught. With the steering wheel clenched in one hand, David swung the spotlight with the other. The beam pierced a break in the trees, swept a black Blazer's tailgate. The driver's-side door was open. Skeins of white smoke were dispersing to threads between it and a pearl-white Lexus.

Almighty God. Please, no. *No.*

David fishtailed to a stop beside the Blazer. Andrik

flanked its opposite side. They rolled from their vehicles, guns drawn, car doors acting as shields.

Yelling Hannah's name flouted procedure, like
Marlin screaming obscenities into the radio. Tough
shit.

A shadow crept across the Lexus's rear windshield.
"Don't shoot, David. It's me. Hannah."

Thank you, Lord. Asking if she was alone wasted
breath if Thomlinson-Metz had a gun on her. "Hands
in the air, Hannah. Walk toward the light."

"Are you—"

"Humor me."

The woman he loved more than life itself emerged
from behind the car. His mind itemized the particulars. Auburn-brown. Five-seven. A hundred and...
perfect. Jeans. Dark sweater. Hiking boots. Long-
barreled cannon in her upraised right hand.

"Did you fire the shot I heard?"

She nodded.

"Are you alone?"

"Yes."

David holstered his service revolver. "Then put
that hogleg down and get yourself over here."

She halted. "No."

"What d'ya mean, no?"

"Rosemary's first husband gave her this gun for
their wedding anniversary. I refuse to throw it down
in the wet grass and mud."

Well, of course. How insensitive of him.

Marlin snickered. "Want me to shoot her, boss?"

"Not yet."

David strode toward her, palm outstretched. "Give it up, Marshal Dillon."

His hand sank with the .357 Magnum's weight. For a woman afraid of guns, she sure as hell had borrowed a big one. "If you're alone, what did you shoot at, and why?"

"I heard a noise." She pointed at a junk pile. "Over there. Something jumped out—an animal. No sooner than I fired, I saw lights, heard a car coming fast. It could have been Delbert, could have been Chet driving Delbert's loaner. I ran and crouched behind the Lexus."

She looked up at him. "I had you in my sights until it registered that Cadillacs aren't equipped with spotlights."

Her smug expression tightened to a scowl. "Why wasn't your siren on? A little forewarning would have spared me from having the crap scared out of me twice in five seconds."

"Beg pardon for not being psychic." David opened the revolver's cylinder and tipped the barrel skyward. Five cartridges dropped into his hand. "Not forewarning Chet was my intention."

"He isn't here. Neither is Delbert."

"Lucky shot, Toots." A raccoon's tail was pinched between Marlin's thumb and forefinger. "Before you atomized the rest of ol' Rory, he'd have made a nice coat, all by himself."

"A good shot, not a lucky one," Hannah corrected. "It's been several years, but I was a certified expert with a .38."

David's "Say what?" didn't push past his tonsils. Light haloed in the distance. A patrol unit responding to a shots-fired would have the siren and lightbar cranking full blast. "Company's comin'."

Marlin scrambled behind a discarded refrigerator. David grabbed Hannah's wrist and ran for the cruiser. "Back seat. Floorboard. Facedown, arms over your head. Don't move."

The rear window's roof pillar afforded the best available cover. With his Smith & Wesson in a two-handed grip, he surveyed the area. Jungle on the right. Junk and a tumbledown house up the middle. A rocky wash to the left. Lovely place for a foot pursuit.

By the incoming headlights' width, the approaching vehicle was a full-size sedan. Glimpses through the brush made it out to be dark in color. A Cadillac, David hoped, with a skinny old coot behind the wheel and alone.

Yeah, well, if wishes were horses, he'd be afoot for life. The car was a black Lincoln. The driver, a pink-haired matron. Marge Rosenbaum rode passenger, with Leo and Rosemary Schnur occupying the back.

David stowed his pistol and opened the cruiser's door. "False alarm."

"Who's here?"

"The Mod Squad, minus Delbert."

"Shit."

"We do think alike, sugar."

When everyone started talking at once, Hannah loosed an ear-splitting whistle that would stop a taxi on a dime.

"Forget the I told you so's. Delbert isn't here. Walt's car isn't here. Chet's car is, but he isn't."

She glanced from David to Marlin. "I don't know about you, but I think Chet overpowered Delbert and loaded him in Walt's car, which is about to be involved in a fatal accident. Fatal for Delbert, I mean."

Rosemary said, "If Chet wanted rid of Delbert, why go to all that trouble?"

"It'd be stupid to kill him outright," Marlin said. "Willard Johnson knows the two of them met, where and why."

David added, "Thomlinson—real name Harold Charles Metz—may not know who placed the call, but he knows that a third party is involved. If Delbert disappears, or becomes a homicide victim, Metz is the automatic prime suspect."

A siren chirped on the highway. Better late than never. Marlin's expression reflected David's thoughts. Metz couldn't shoot, garrote or inflict any wounds a medical examiner would question during an autopsy.

It followed that Metz probably forced Delbert at gunpoint to drive to the crash site. It was easier to control and intimidate a hostage from the passenger seat. Delbert being Delbert, he was probably driving three miles an hour, if that fast. The wily detective wannabe was smart enough to realize Metz couldn't make good on threats to shoot him, for the aforementioned reason.

Marlin said, "If Metz is staging an accidental death, the car has to be totaled. Preferably burned to cinders to destroy forensic evidence."

IdaClare blanched and staggered backward. "Oh, dear Lord in heaven."

Leo caught her good arm to steady her.

Hannah said, "Then wherever Chet, er, Metz, took Delbert can't be too far away." She waved at the Lexus. "He'll have to walk back here."

"Is to the north, too, I think," Leo said. "Delbert, he came here early. To be believed, the accident, it would have to look like he was on his way home."

In unison, David and Marlin said, "Indian Point."

Marlin turned and sprinted for the patrol unit pulling into the yard. The deputy would be ordered to hide his vehicle and guard Metz's.

"Hannah," David said, "and the rest of you, get yourselves to Valhalla Springs and stay there."

"But—"

David wrenched open the cruiser's door. "Don't argue with me, Hannah. For once, just do as you're damn well told."

# 19

The cruiser's speedometer needle pegged ninety as if glued there. Shit-for-brains teenagers who thought the Devil's Backbone was a poor boy's LeMans, seldom pushed it past seventy.

Thoughts skittered through David's mind in cadence with the lightbar's revolutions.

If they'd guessed wrong about Indian Point, Delbert Bisbee was a dead man.

If they were right, but had delayed too long at the Sandusky place, Delbert was a dead man. It seemed like an hour, but from the time David heard the gunshot, to alerting dispatch of the situation and change in location had eaten only seven minutes.

If you're right about the place, but get there too damn late, do mention that time frame to Hannah, IdaClare and everyone for the comfort they'll derive from it.

Cold sweat vied with adrenaline's hot drizzle. Focus, fool. Head in the game not on the sidelines.

A second lightbar, strobing like a patriotic borealis, crested the hill behind him. The unit was closing in fast. Good. He needed all the backup he could get, including Andrik—wherever the hell he'd disappeared to.

On David's order, Marlin had pawed through the unmarked Chevy's trashed back seat for the Kevlar vest detectives keep handy but don't wear as a matter of routine. Body armor didn't take ten seconds to climb into, but neither flashing grill lamps, nor a dash-mounted red gumball, had been reflected in the Crown Vic's mirrors.

The patrol unit behind him clicked its lights like a trucker signaling a radar trap or road hazard. Well, speak of the devil, who declined speaking for himself on the radio. Andrik must have swapped cars with the deputy. Smart thinking. Two units converging on Metz should convince him he was outmanned, outgunned and flat outta luck.

The pumping sensation of antilock brakes reverberated through David's foot. He blew past the blood-brown highway department sign that read Scenic Overlook, ¼ mile. The No Rest Room Facilities in smaller white lettering was a warning and an invitation.

The modest were alerted to the dearth of latrines resembling upturned crates with warped doors. Those who marked territory like dogs interpreted it as Mother Nature's outhouse, with a view just up the road.

An oncoming highway patrol unit levitated around a curve as David barreled into the broad, asphalt apron leading to the overlook locals called Indian Point. Its panoramic view of smoky blue hills, shadowed hollers and limestone parapets stretching from horizon to horizon was as breathtaking as the ledge rock culminating in a sheer, sixty-foot drop to the creek bed below.

The access road's pavement narrowed to a lane and a half. Century oaks and pines on both sides were scarred by the fallacy that tight butt cheeks reduced a vehicle's width.

As though exiting a tunnel, the point's expansive verge exploded in David's headlights. A man—Metz—was running for the tree line. A car—a dark Cadillac—was rolling straight toward the precipice—and picking up speed on the decline. Tufts of white hair were visible above the driver seat's headrest.

David's eyes darted to the rickety post-and-cable guardrail. Matchsticks and wire. Wouldn't snag a go-cart. The Caddy would snap it like a bowstring.

He slapped the gearshift lever from drive to low. "Not if I can stop it, it won't."

He cranked the wheel hard right. The cruiser swerved into a wide arc. Cut left—sharp. Brake. Brake. *Gun it.*

The Crown Vic rammed the runaway car square behind the front bumper. *Bull's-eye.* Metal shrieked, groaned, crumpled. The cruiser's hood buckled. Impact rebound peeled the vehicles apart. The Caddy rocked, rolled on at an angle.

"Shit." David floored the accelerator. Wrenched the steering wheel. Tromped the brake. The Crown Vic sideswiped the runaway. Its rear deck swung like a door slamming shut.

For a split second, the cars spooned to a dead stop, then the Caddy's momentum and weight, and physics shoved the cruiser into a slow, sideward skid. The guardrail's cable grated the passenger side like a whetstone on steel. Inches from David's shoulder, the Cadillac ground the other side, the vibration humming in his chest.

*"Whoa, now...easy...'atta—"*

Posts cracked as loud as gunshots. The rear tire slumped off the edge. The cruiser swayed. Teetered. Silt chattered then free-fell into the void. The banshee howl of ledge rock raking the undercarriage ceased when the front wheel departed solid ground.

Expecting a sickening slide into oblivion, it took David a moment to grasp the intermission fate had bestowed. He willed himself to breathe, to think, before the inevitable plunge into the black velvet space between the here and the hereafter.

The Crown Vic was welded to the Caddy like a sidecar. Both engines were running. The stench of burning rubber and grayish smoke curled from David's spinning front tires; the same from the Cadillac's rear ones. The vehicular lockjaw and the cruiser's precarious position was their salvation—for however long it lasted.

David started to switch off the ignition. Second thoughts stayed his hand. No sense trifling with the miracle keeping the cruiser and the Cadillac in a dead heat to nowhere.

Delbert lay sprawled on his back in the front seat. Blood matted his hair. His face was a welted, bloody mess—every wound a badge of courage. Metz was younger, bigger, stronger and undoubtedly armed, but Delbert had put up one hell of a fight.

David knocked on the window glass, then tapped the horn. "Delbert. *Delbert.* C'mon, wake up. You get outta that death trap while you still can."

The patrol unit Andrik had borrowed and two highway patrol cars were visible through the Cadillac's windshield. Lightbars swept their huddled occupants in washes of red, white and blue. An ambulance and a fire-and-rescue truck arrived just as Marlin separated from the other officers.

Jogging toward the Caddy, he spoke into his handset. A casual, *Hey, boss,* wended from the cruiser's radio. *Don't respond. Reaching for the mike might upset the applecart. So to speak.*

"Funny. Real goddamn funny."

*We've got Metz cuffed and stuffed.*

"Good."

Marlin peered into the Cadillac's driver's-side window. *Jesus.* Static, then *Bisbee's in bad shape but he's breathing.*

He leveled his gaze at David. *Hope you're in the mood to save your own ass, 'cause I'm tired of breaking in new sheriffs.*

With that, he tossed the handheld to the highway patrolman behind him. Palm flattened against the window glass, he plied the Cadillac's door handle. The interior light blinked on. Teeth bared and clenched, he eased the door wider.

The cruiser shifted, its belly growling over rock.

Above the briny stink of his own sweat, David smelled gasoline. At any second, friction from the spinning tires would blow him, Delbert, Marlin and everyone else in the vicinity to kingdom come.

As if by magic, the Caddy's passenger window powered down. Reflex guided David's thumb to the armrest's toggle switch. Fume-laden fresh air gusted in as the glass lowered into its pocket.

"Your tank's ruptured," Andrik yelled, reaching around the Caddy's steering wheel. "On the count of three, kill your ignition. One...two..."

Both engines died at the same instant. The whine of spinning tires and transmissions began to fade as though a volume knob were turning. "Steady," David told the dashboard. "I'll sit tight if you will."

The incoming breeze's lethal perfume hadn't diminished, but the air felt cool and sweet on his cheek. After days of rain, the sky was clearing. The Little Dipper's handle was wrapped in a cloud, but the Big Dipper was silvery bright.

Hannah wasn't exactly superstitious, but she did have a thing about omens. Sure as churns make butter, she'd say the storms passing and stars in the night sky for the first time since I asked her to marry me was one.

David squinted out the windshield, then into the rearview mirror. "Tow trucks." Hope fluttered then took wing. "Three, maybe four tow trucks." He grinned. "If they can pull a car out of a ravine, they ought to be able to keep mine from—"

The cruiser shuddered. A metallic skirr sent bile

scalding up his throat. The world tilted several degrees on its axis. *This is it. End of the line.*

Panting, heart pounding, David coiled his fingers into fists on the steering wheel. He heard himself yelling, "Don't argue with me. Just this once, do as you're damn well told." The anger in Hannah's expression and hurt in her eyes swam behind his blurred ones.

"That was the sheriff talking, not me. Oh, sugar, I hope to God you know that."

The Crown Vic's window ledge ratcheted above the Cadillac's. "It wasn't me. I'm the guy who's loved you all his life but didn't know who you were until the day you walked out of my dreams and—"

*Hendrickson. Snap out of it!*

David did, with a full-body jerk, his head pivoting. "Now that I've got your attention," Marlin shouted, ditching the handset. It bounced off the collapsed gurney he straddled.

"You're coming in when I pull him out." Marlin grasped Delbert's ankles. Three EMTs crouched ready to help him hoist the gurney up and away from the car. Ten yards behind them, Hannah stood alone, ghost-white and trembling.

Not now, not ever will that woman do as she's damn well told, David thought. There'd be hell to pay, if he lived long enough to collect. Helluva incentive, that.

The last time David had crawled through a car window was twenty years and a hundred pounds ago.

And that was into a vehicle, not out of one and into another.

Belly-crawling wouldn't work. He was too tall, too long-legged and there wasn't enough space to maneuver. A cross between a race-car driver climbing from his vehicle and a back dive into a swimming pool was the best bet. The only bet.

The steering wheel cocked up with a soft thump. He unbuckled the seat belt, then his utility belt. Unholstering the Smith & Wesson, he checked the safety, then handed it butt first to Marlin. If anything survived the wreckage, it'd be his gun, and a slimy son of a bitch like Metz would find it.

Every move shimmied the cruiser a fraction nearer the edge. Intermission was almost over. No time to wrestle off a Kevlar vest.

He looked at Marlin. "Ready whenever you are."

In a voice as solemn as his face, he said, "I'll meet you on the other side, boss."

"Yep, you will." David swallowed to clear his throat. "One way or the other."

"One…two…"

David twisted at the waist. The window's rain gutter cut into his palms as he chinned himself. His head craned back and through the Cadillac's window. Knees bent, boots planted against the console, he pushed, wriggled, forced his upper torso out the opening.

With a grinding screech, the Crown Vic heaved upward, away from the Cadillac. The window ledge caught David at the belt line. His feet hammered the cruiser's roof. His face slammed into the Caddy's. Upholstery and trim strips raked his skin as the Crown Vic tipped higher, higher. If he hadn't turned his head a second before the cruiser pulled him out of the other car, he'd have been decapitated.

He grabbed the Cadillac's roof pillars to haul himself in again. His boot heels hung on the lip of the cruiser's window. Stretched diagonally between the two vehicles, struggling to free his feet, he heard a *crack*, then a thunderous roar.

Hands shackled his wrists, yanked, then pulled like an ox team. The next thing he knew, he was lying spread-eagle on the asphalt parking lot and an EMT was checking his vital signs.

The ground rumbled. David raised his head just as the Cadillac somersaulted sideways off the ledge. "Why— How did—" His eyes lowered, then narrowed. Wiggling his toes confirmed that the socked feet he saw belonged to him. "Hey! Who stole my boots?"

Marlin moved into view, a Marlboro dangling from his mouth and another forked between his fingers. Hannah sidled in beside him. Both were a bit fuzzy, but David was pretty sure she was grinning.

"You look like something the cat dragged out," she said.

"Me?" Marlin said. "Or him?"

"Both, actually."

"Have a little respect for my lifesaving technique, Toots."

He puffed on cigarette one and flicked the ashes

off cigarette two. "As for you, Sheriff, next time you want to be the rope in a tug-of-war with a Crown Vic and a Cadillac, give me an hour to set up a video-camera. We could have made a fortune off that stunt."

David waved the paramedic away and leveraged himself into a sitting position. Oopsy-daisy. If this were a cartoon, chirping birds would be circling his head. Getting vertical might take a while.

"Just for the record, would one of you mind filling in the gaps between the tug-of-war part and oh, say, thirty seconds ago?"

Marlin squatted on one knee. "You mean, the how-I-saved-your-life-again part."

"Uh-huh."

After a double hit of nicotine, he said, "Well, when those big damn canoes of yours got caught on the Vic, we knew it was going to do a human-catapult number on you."

He jerked a thumb at a highway patrolman leaning on the hood of his car. "Corporal Nesselrode latched onto one arm, I grabbed the other and we pulled for all we were worth."

David rotated his arm and winced. "That part I remember."

"Yanked you right outta your boots," Marlin said.

"That, I don't."

"Plan A was to haul you into the Caddy. Cushy place as any to clean the crap out of your drawers. Plan B went into effect when the Crown Vic's swan dive took a chunk of Indian Point with it—the chunk that happened to be holding up the Cadillac.''

Marlin glanced over his shoulder at the jagged lip of ledge rock shaped like an enormous bite mark. ''I gotta tell you, the highway department is going to be pissed as hell when they see what you did to their scenic overlook.''

''It's still scenic.'' David cocked his jaw to push the ocean out of his ears. ''The parking lot's just a tad smaller than it used to be.''

The hand he offered Marlin was scraped and crusted with blood. ''Saying thank you for saving my life sounds as lame now as it did a couple of weeks ago.''

''Like I told you, I'm tired of breaking in new sheriffs.'' He shrugged. ''Kind of tired of working overtime to keep one, too, but you're all that's standing between me and four years of Jessup the Dickhead Knox.''

David threw back his head and laughed. Never had it felt so good and hurt so bad at the same time. ''I'm touched, Andrik. Truly I am.''

''Thought you would be.'' Andrik stood. ''And by the by, I haven't forgotten that you owe me a kegger and a steak dinner from the last time I saved your bacon.''

''Neither have I.'' David's eyes slanted up at Hannah. ''Might could make a real celebration out of it.''

An eyebrow arched. ''Might could.''

Yes sirree, the woman was a walking, talking bundle of incentive.

Homo erectus hadn't taken as long to evolve from all fours to standing upright than David did. His head went into orbit again and sweat popped on the back of his neck.

Fighting the cold clammies, he said, "Good thing there's an extra pair of boots in my car. 'Preciate it...somebody get 'em for me."

"David?"

He frowned, though his face felt as if it was melting. Hannah was right there...a second ago. How'd she get...so far...away...?

# 20

Hospital waiting rooms don't change much in five days. Same magazines. Same meat-locker chilliness. Same CNN anchorperson mouthing what appeared to be the same news. Same sense of isolation.

No, it's worse, Hannah thought. Delbert was holding my hand the last time. Now he's the one raising hell about being admitted for observation. No wonder nurses are called angels of mercy. They'd have to be to dispense tender loving care to a patient howling about friends in high places at the ACLU, AARP, United Postal Workers Union, the Red Cross and Amnesty International.

He couldn't be sedated into submission, either. Head wounds and barbiturates didn't mix. Delbert had "fought that bastard tooth and toenail," until Metz pistol-whipped him unconscious and shoved him into the front seat of Walt Wagonner's Cadillac.

The Emergency Room doctor said Delbert wouldn't be released for several days. The gash in his head had been stitched, but three broken ribs and a wealth of defense wounds and contusions would keep him "illegally detained" a while longer than he anticipated.

Hero or not, if he didn't behave, Hannah would threaten to tattle to the hospital's administrator. She didn't know why Delbert impersonated a physician, but the blond nurse's aide who'd addressed him as "Doctor" and expressed dismay about his injuries was definite witness material.

The aide confided that she'd met the bogus Dr. Bisbee in the staff elevator and that he was an out-of-town forensics expert consulting with the sheriff on the Royal Dragon case. Very hush-hush, she warned. Don't tell a soul.

The old fart could sell ice to Siberia, but thank heaven his skull was as thick on the outside as inside.

The waiting room's door opened to an exhausted-looking Rosemary, Leo and Marge. "Any news?"

"Not yet. How's IdaClare?"

"Sound asleep, with an IV in her good arm." Rosemary sat down beside Hannah, followed by Leo and Marge. "The broken one is mending fine. The rest of her will be, too, with a day or two of complete bed rest."

"I tried to tell her she was overdoing it," Marge said. "She wouldn't listen."

Leo nodded. "Her lesson, I think, she has learned, though."

Hannah agreed. "I'm just glad she didn't put up a fuss when you took her keys and said you were driving her to the hospital, rather than her driving you to Indian Point."

"Oh, she fussed all right," Marge said. "But poor

thing, her heart wasn't in it. She was in too much pain and too nauseous to argue.''

Hannah had left the Sandusky place minutes behind the patrol car Andrik had commandeered. When IdaClare and Company didn't make an appearance at Indian Point, Hannah presumed the majority had voted in favor of a beeline to Valhalla Springs.

Rosemary sighed. A fingertip massaged a spot at the bridge of her nose.

''Why don't the three of you go on home,'' Hannah said. ''Better yet, as tired as you are, get motel rooms in town for what's left of the night. I'm sure Jack will be happy to pick up the tab.''

She'd do the honors, but that would be her secret. Peace of mind was worth every penny.

Rosemary said, ''I called him from IdaClare's room to tell him she'd been readmitted and why. I don't know how he could, but I'd swear Jack already knew.''

Hannah suppressed a smile. ''He's a pretty good guesser.''

''He's also a pawn in Chet, er, What's-his-name's murder-for-hire scheme.'' Outbursts were not Marge's forte, but her expression dared an argument to the contrary.

''For IdaClare's sake, I hope you're right,'' Rosemary said. ''Being worried sick about her son is partly why she's here instead of home.''

She couldn't know he'd been tested for HIV, could she? Her maternal radar was as sensitive as a Doppler system, but Jack had covered his tracks too well for even Marlin Andrik to follow.

"What do you mean, worried sick?" Hannah said. "About what?"

"Well…" Rosemary fidgeted. "Before we left your cottage, IdaClare told us she knew Chet—Metz—was flimflamming her, that we were working on Code Name: Delta and that Jack was our number two suspect. She also said she wasn't a hundred percent sure herself that he wasn't involved. That's why she insisted on going after you. She wants to know the truth, no matter what."

As if Hannah needed it, the explanation proved that IdaClare was smarter, shrewder and tougher than she was given credit for. Particularly by her son, who was too much like his mother to be fooled by or to conspire with a man as evil as Harold Charles Metz.

"Metz is a career con artist," she warned. "He'll do his dirtiest to implicate Jack and save his own neck. We'll just have to make sure he doesn't get away with it."

Rosemary gasped and clapped a hand to her chest. "I'm so relieved to hear you say that. Given that even IdaClare had doubts, I was afraid you didn't believe Jack was innocent, either."

"Well, to be honest, I didn't. I ignored my instincts about him as much as I did about Metz. Can't say when, but I changed my mind—about both of them."

A yawn as irrepressible as the Jaws of Life pried Hannah's mouth apart. With a dopey smile, she excused herself, then added, ''In fact, I've changed my mind about several things in the last day or so.''

''Ah, the prerogative, it is, for a woman's mind to do that,'' Leo said. ''Back, then the forth it goes—''

''And where it stops nobody knows?'' his bride finished for him. ''You got a problem with that?''

He gestured as if stopping oncoming traffic. Which he was, in a manner of speaking.

''Oh, now, don't get upset.'' Rosemary kissed his jowl. ''I was only teasing.'' To Hannah, she said, ''Jack and I talked quite a while, and not just about IdaClare.''

A familiar, where - there's - a - will - there's - a - way gleam sparkled in her eyes. Hannah guessed why, but this wasn't the time, place or person to discuss it with.

She pushed up from the chair, stretched and yawned again. Okay, faked a yawn, hoping for an epidemic so Rosemary, Leo and Marge would totter off to the Super 8 for some much-needed sleep. ''Gol-lee. What do you do when your eyelids weigh ten pounds apiece?''

''Splash cold water in your face,'' Marge said.

''Are you kidding? The girl has more mascara under her eyes than on her lashes, as it is,'' Rosemary said. ''A walk is better for sweeping cobwebs from the corners, anyhow.''

Leo caressed his pate like a fortune-teller firing up a crystal ball. Presently, he said, ''Chew the gum, maybe?''

''Great idea.'' Rosemary chuckled. ''If she nods off, choking on it'll rouse her in a hurry.''

So much for the power of suggestion. "I wasn't referring to me. I'm fine, but you're about to slide out of your chairs. Won't you please check into a motel so I have don't have to worry about you, too?"

The advisory committee went into a huddle. Whispering and nodding commenced. Democracy in action. When they separated, they were smiling the kind of smiles that struck terror in the hearts of retirement-community operations' managers. Or should.

Rosemary said, "How about a compromise."

Hah. God forbid that one of Hannah's motions would ever receive a unanimous vote. "Such as?"

"It takes half an hour or so to drive to Valhalla Springs, right?"

A trick question. Had to be. Frowning, Hannah gave a noncommittal nod.

"If we promise to stay in town tonight, what if we spend the drive time we don't need to hold down the fort here, so you go fix your face, take a walk—whatever."

Hmm. Not a bad idea. Make that an excellent idea.

"Deal. Except it won't take that long for me to check on Delbert and IdaClare, peek in on Sophonia and grab a cup of coffee from the canteen."

Marge waved a dismissal. "Don't rush on our account."

"The change for the machines." Leo squirmed sideways to access his trouser pocket. "If you need it, I have plenty."

Tears sprang to Hannah's eyes. Another random act

of kindness and the dam would burst. "Thanks, Leo. I have some in my purse."

Just as Hannah started out, Rosemary called, "Don't forget to do something about your face while you're at it."

Laughing softly through clenched teeth, Hannah swiped the tears away and headed for the elevators. No sooner had she slumped against the car's back wall than she bounced upright. Relax the body, relax the guard. Keep the riffs coming. Laugh and the world laughs with you. Cry, and you lose it, alone.

She'd held herself and her emotions together for hours by sheer strength of will. She'd concentrated on mental memories of David grinning, laughing, his mood-ring eyes—anything, everything, but him collapsing at Indian Point, his head lolling on the gurney, the oxygen mask strapped over his bloody, battered face.

Rage at the paramedics who said nonrelatives couldn't be transported in the ambulance with patients had held fear at bay, until she reached the hospital.

A second wave crashed over her at the emergency room. "Sorry, Ms. Garvey, but you know the rules. Family members only in the treatment rooms. Please take a seat in the waiting room. We'll keep you informed, as best we can."

Meaning, when we get damn good and ready. Assuming we don't forget about you, but so what if we do? After all, you aren't a relative or a family member.

That's hitting below the belt, Hannah admitted. The

staff didn't deserve it, despite their freakin' stupid, arbitrary, condescending rules.

Earlier, a chatty waiting-room nobody whose neighbor had dropped a skilletful of hot grease on herself shared similar frustrations, in the manner of misery loving company, whether company cared to hear it or not.

Hannah didn't, but committed the egregious error of saying hello when the woman flopped down beside her. Her second mistake was answering when Chatty Cathy inquired after Hannah's reason for occupying the waiting room.

"My, uh—a friend of mine fainted, that's all. Nothing serious, but it's better to be safe than sorry."

"Syncope. That's what doctors call fainting spells," Chatty said. "You were smart to let the docs take a look at her."

The woman had as much medical expertise as Malcolm, but Hannah kept hearing her prattle on about brain tumors, hemorrhages, heart failure, internal bleeding, embolisms...

Hannah jumped when the elevator doors slid wide. A middle-aged man in a lab coat paused to allow Hannah to exit, then said, "I'm sorry, but visiting hours are over. Long over. I'm afraid you'll have to leave the building immediately."

Hannah's eyes flicked to his ID badge, then down at her mud-freckled jeans and hiking boots. Her smile exceeded five-hundred watts. "I'm not surprised that you don't recognize me, Dr. McLoughlin. I'm not only dressed for fieldwork, I'm wearing quite a bit of it."

Gentleman that he was, he shook the hand she extended. "Dr. Helen Grafft. We met in the corridor—briefly—the day I arrived."

"Forgive me, but—"

"Helen Grafft? From Sheboygan?" Two-beat pause, fade the smile, do a quick eye roll. "The forensic specialist investigating the Royal Dragon shooting."

"Oh." The struggle was visible, but professional courtesy won out over skepticism. "Oh, yes. Well, of course, Dr. Grafft. From Sheboygan was it? I have a—"

"I'd love to stay and chat, but..." Hannah strode from the car. "Duty calls. Nice seeing you again, Doctor."

She didn't breathe until she'd darted into Delbert's room. "Dr. Bisbee, I presume?" she whispered, tiptoeing to his bedside.

A gauze skullcap hid his head wound. IVs and monitors nourished, medicated and guarded him. His cheek was scraped and puffy-purple, but he looked as peaceful as his snores sounded.

Emotion welled again. She blew him a kiss, told him she loved him and padded out the door.

A floor down and at the opposite end of the corridor, IdaClare was snoring, too. Other than the cast on her arm, the pain Harold Charles Metz had inflicted on her didn't show on the outside.

Hannah kissed IdaClare's temple, whispered she

loved her and made a promise to do everything in her power to help those inner wounds heal.

The Critical Care ward was busier than the floors above. Three staff members were jockeying a new patient's bed around a corner and into the adjacent cubicle. Telephones and a computer printer sang a discordant duet. A nurse pulling a machine attached to a wheeled stand looked askance at Hannah but hastened on down the hall.

Hannah marched into Sophonia's cubicle as though she belonged there, then stopped short. Hand rising to her mouth, she closed her eyes and sagged against the frame.

Tears streamed down her face, warm and unstoppable. Cupping her chin, her teeth nipped the fleshy fold of her index finger to stifle her sobs.

The railing was down on Sophonia's bed. Rather than hip-high, the mattress had been lowered to its minimum setting. Pushed against it was a visitor's chair with a cane hooked to the armrest. Seated, but positioned so he could share her pillow, was Jefferson Davis Oglethorpe.

Their foreheads were touching, their hands clasped atop the sheet. Those unaware of their history would think their love and devotion to each other had spanned a lifetime. That nothing short of death would ever part them.

In a way, Hannah supposed, they'd be right.

Turning from the room, she mopped her eyes and nose with her sleeve, smiling through her tears at the mascara smudges on the cuff. Rosemary wouldn't approve.

A man was hobbling along the corridor wincing with every step. Tall, broad-shouldered, strong. A knee brace extending from his thigh to his calf hampered his stride. Both hands were gloved in gauze. He had a split lip, two black eyes, a swollen nose girdled in paper tape and was a limping advertisement for the versatility of butterfly bandages.

"Yeah, I know," he drawled. "I look like something the cat dragged out."

Run into his arms. Throw yours around him. Kiss him. Scream hallelujah at the top of your lungs. Impulses fired like pistons, commanding, demanding, impossible to act on. Hands rearranged the air, eager to touch, fearful of hurting. They curled into fists and she blurted, "Thank God you don't have a brain tumor."

David's laugh contorted to a groan. "Please, sugar. If you love me the least little bit, don't make me laugh."

"Oh, Lord, I'm sorry. I just—"

"Can't help being you," he said, "and don't you ever stop."

Stretching on the balls of her feet, her lips brushed a not-yet-purple patch on his chin. "I love you more than anything in the world, and I thought I'd lost you forever tonight—twice. And speaking of forever, you'd better not *ever* do that again, because once I can handle, but twice is just too damn much."

Grinning obviously hurt, but he risked it. "I thought you didn't believe in forever."

"I didn't, until I met a couple of people who believed in it less than I do."

David recoiled. "I hope you don't mean the Thomlinsons."

"Not hardly."

"Well, it can't be Leo and Rosemary."

"Huh-uh."

He pondered a moment. "My head hurts."

She laughed, then crooked a finger. "C'mere. I'd rather show than tell, anyway."

Perplexed and a shade leery, he moved into the doorway of the cubicle. Comprehension dawned in a lengthy silence, then he murmured. "Well, I'll be. After all these years..."

Hannah smiled up at him, profiled in the doorway. He turned toward her, his eyes a soft, clear blue. "If those two can work out their differences, don't you think there's a chance that we can, too?"

Time slid backward in her mind. A tuxedo replaced his tattered clothing. The bandages and battle scars faded and the aroma of flowers scented the air. The band was playing "Could I Have This Dance," and they were waltzing as if they'd danced together...forever.

Laying her palm gently on his chest, her eyes met his and she whispered, "Yes."